SCATTERED

Aamna Mohdin

SCATTERED

The making and unmaking of a refugee

BLOOMSBURY CIRCUS
LONDON · OXFORD · NEW YORK · NEW DELHI · SYDNEY

BLOOMSBURY CIRCUS
Bloomsbury Publishing Plc
50 Bedford Square, London, WC1B 3DP, UK
29 Earlsfort Terrace, Dublin 2, Ireland

BLOOMSBURY, BLOOMSBURY CIRCUS and the Circus logo are
trademarks of Bloomsbury Publishing Plc

First published in Great Britain 2024

Copyright © Aamna Mohdin, 2024

Aamna Mohdin has asserted her right under the Copyright, Designs and
Patents Act, 1988, to be identified as Author of this work

All rights reserved. No part of this publication may be reproduced or
transmitted in any form or by any means, electronic or mechanical, including
photocopying, recording, or any information storage or retrieval system,
without prior permission in writing from the publishers

A catalogue record for this book is available from the British Library

ISBN: HB: 978-1-5266-5256-0; TPB: 978-1-5266-5257-7;
EBOOK: 978-1-5266-5259-1; EPDF: 978-1-5266-5261-4

2 4 6 8 10 9 7 5 3 1

Typeset by Newgen KnowledgeWorks Pvt. Ltd., Chennai, India
Printed and bound in Great Britain by CPI Group (UK) Ltd, Croydon CR0 4YY

MIX
Paper | Supporting
responsible forestry
FSC
www.fsc.org   FSC® C171272

To find out more about our authors and books visit www.bloomsbury.com
and sign up for our newsletters

For my Mama and Baba

CONTENTS

	Author's Note	ix
	PART ONE	
1	A Fine Line	3
2	When Faatma Met Mohamed	25
3	The Great Escape	57
4	The Making of a Refugee	87
5	The Separation	101
6	Finally in Europe	123
	PART TWO	
7	A Journey Back in Time	137
8	You Were Once Amina	149
9	Lunch with the Youth of Mogadishu	163
10	The Permanence of Exile	181
11	The Past Isn't Dead	195
12	Welcome Back to K-Town	203

CONTENTS

PART THREE

13	Girlhood on Two Fronts	227
14	Black and British	241
15	The Trauma that Binds Us	255
16	We Were Girls Together	269

Glossary 283
Notes 285
Bibliography 297
Acknowledgements 305

AUTHOR'S NOTE

I was a child who lived through the refugee crisis in East Africa in the 1990s and a journalist who reported on one in Europe twenty years later. It was only after going to Calais in 2015 that I started to look back, and learned my parents' full story.

The story they told me threw the options that had been open to them into stark relief. If my parents hadn't made the decisions that they did, the three of us would likely not have survived.

This is a personal book – it's about me and my parents, and it's about the very limited set of choices that they were handed by circumstance, and how those choices shaped our family and their lives. But it's also universal.

It's not hard to see which things have stayed the same between 1992 and now: governments and how they treat refugees; the media and how it reports on refugees. Former British home secretary Suella Braverman warned of a refugee 'invasion on our southern coast', an unprecedented comment from a government minister,[1] while media commentator Katy Hopkins likened refugees to 'cockroaches' and 'feral humans' in *The Sun*, one of Britain's most widely circulated newspapers.[2]

When twenty-seven people drowned in the English Channel in November 2021, the deadliest disaster in the Channel for more than forty years, former prime

AUTHOR'S NOTE

minister Boris Johnson said he was saddened by the tragedy, then announced a plan six months later to send all asylum seekers who enter the country 'irregularly' to Rwanda. When people drown in the Channel trying to reach the UK, they are often called 'migrants', their deaths reported passively.

The choices my parents made – leaving their home in Somalia to escape a deadly civil war, undertaking risky crossings, and putting themselves in the hands of other people who exploited their desperation – are still being faced in the present by displaced people from old and new conflicts. There are nearly 27.1 million refugees across the world, a staggering 41 per cent of whom are under the age of eighteen, according to the UN refugee agency.[3]

The truth stays the same, and so does the failure to accept it. There are currently no legal and safe routes for refugees to come to the UK unless they are from Ukraine or those from Afghanistan who can prove they are in danger as a result of working with the British government, according to Amnesty International.[4] The human rights charity believes the government is forcing people wishing to seek asylum in the UK to rely on dangerous journeys. This needs to change.

It is my hope that in telling my story this truth is recognised.

PART ONE

1
A FINE LINE

Faatma and her husband Mohamed are arguing about who suffered more from the Somali civil war. This back and forth is familiar terrain for their children. The couple shout over one another at their kitchen table, teasing each other as they debate their compelling cases.

'Who had more damage from the civil war?' Faatma asks. 'I have seen more suffering than you. No question.'

'But did someone with a gun put you against a wall and try to kill you?' Mohamed quips back. They both laugh as the sparring reaches a crescendo.

Faatma shakes her head. 'No, that's nothing. I was pregnant! Can you imagine? I was alone and in pain. I didn't speak the language. Anything could have happened.' She is now breathless with laughter and indignation.

Mohamed does not have a retort to that. Faatma, sensing victory, says: 'Exactly, chill out!'

Faatma returns to the story she was telling before the argument broke out. An undocumented refugee, she had been stranded on the Belgian-French border in 1999. Faatma had been trying to reunite with her eldest child, while pregnant with her second.

Her six-year-old daughter had already been safely smuggled into London months earlier. She was living with Faatma's sisters. Her daughter sounded happy on the phone, but Faatma was still worried. She hated being so far away from her daughter.

The plan was simple enough. Faatma, Mohamed and their daughter had been in Germany before they arrived in The Hague, and before then had lived in a refugee camp called Kakuma in Kenya. Faatma's daughter had made the journey from the Netherlands to the UK first – and now Faatma was attempting the same.

Faatma's daughter had left the house excited, too young to understand the magnitude of what was going on, and all that could go wrong. Faatma was meant to join her weeks later, but she kept failing in her attempts to leave The Hague and reach the UK.

During her first attempt, Faatma embarked with her husband's aunt on a ferry that was due to leave Rotterdam for Harwich in the UK. They were caught on the ferry before it departed, arrested and briefly detained. To their surprise, the two women were let go, but they were no closer to their goal.

Faatma's second attempt took place a little while later. She paid someone $500 to get her from The Hague to France, through the Channel crossing and to the UK. They had driven from the Netherlands to Belgium. When they arrived at the French border, Faatma was told she would be in London soon enough. She just needed to reach the French port, either Dunkirk or Calais, and then travel across the Channel.

But the car was stopped by border officials. Faatma and the driver were taken out of the car and questioned. They were told to show their papers. Faatma remained silent. The driver said he was just helping a family friend who didn't have a car and that he didn't know Faatma's documents were fraudulent. She went along with what the driver said, knowing that if she outed him for what he was they would both be in trouble.

The driver was allowed to return to his car. Before he left, he told Faatma she was on her own. 'The man said, "That's it, I can't do anything else for you. I have to go. If you manage to find a phone, call your husband or family to help you."

Then he left me there,' she recalls. 'I sat down for a moment and felt unwell because I was pregnant.'

Faatma didn't know where she was. She didn't have any money or food. She tried to push back the tears blurring her vision and ignore the thoughts that she had made a terrible mistake and that she would never see her daughter again. The years that led up to and followed the Somali civil war had been terrible, but she had always been able to find her way back to her child.

She was detained and taken to a nearby reception centre. She had managed, with the little English she knew, to tell the police officers that she was pregnant and in pain. They brought a doctor who checked on her and her baby with a scan.

'The doctor kept trying to make me smile. I didn't need to speak the language to understand human kindness. He was talking to me in a nice way,' Faatma says. His manner was a stark contrast to the staff she first met at the receptionist centre, who she said were cold. She was detained but she wasn't sure for how long. It was difficult to keep track of time. She remembers being given a cheese sandwich, but only managing to eat half of it.

She was then put on a coach, but she didn't know where it went. It was there that she met a young Indian man. 'I spoke to him in Hindi and told him what happened. I said I was caught by border guards and needed to return to my family in Holland. I told him I didn't have any money or food on me,' she says.

The man, who looked about twenty-four years old, told her to get off the bus and took her to a nearby cafe. He bought her food and drink, which she wolfed down. He then scolded her. "He said, "When you're pregnant, you shouldn't travel long distances without any food for yourself and your baby."' He gave her money to use a payphone and call her family.

The Indian man paid for a ticket to get her on a train that would take her to the Netherlands. He took her to the train station. When her train came, she said goodbye and got on it. She couldn't remember how long she was on the train before the police got on and asked people for their passports.

'When they asked me for my paperwork, I just said no passport. They told me to get off the train and I got off. They were two male police officers and one woman,' Faatma says.

She was in pain again when they asked her where she had come from. She grabbed onto her stomach. 'One of the men said "baby" and I said yes. Then he put me on the next train to The Hague,' she said.

While on the train, she sat beside a young African man. She tried to speak to him in English, but realised he only spoke French. Somehow, through their broken English, he understood she was trying to get to The Hague and return to her family. He told her he would help.

'I was so young, I didn't know anything,' she says, sounding astonished at what she had gone through. 'When we got off the train, he saw I was in pain and held my hand and carried the small bag I had on me.' She almost blushes when she says this, as if admitting to some significant impropriety. 'I was very young and I didn't know what to do, but he was a good man. He called my family using a payphone and waited at the station with me.'

Faatma's husband Mohamed and his family arrived in a car shortly afterwards. Mohamed looked stricken, 'like he was looking at a ghost', Faatma says between giggles. Her blush deepens. Faatma had been missing for over twenty-four hours when she and Mohamed were finally reunited.

Whatever joy Faatma felt when she was returned to her husband was shortlived. Her daughter was still waiting for her in London. Faatma feared what her daughter would have thought of her and her husband. Did her daughter feel like she had been abandoned? Would her daughter reject Faatma when she finally came to the UK?

'I was so scared I would never see you again,' she tells me. I smile at her: my Mama. She looks different to me, she always does at the end of one of my interviews. Sometimes she looks incredibly vulnerable, other times she has an almost superhuman strength.

I've been interviewing my parents since 2020. There have been a lot of difficulties in writing our story, but I always love this part; I never get bored of sitting them down, getting my notebook out, and listening to them tell me about the past. I am hungry for every new detail.

I am a correspondent for a national British newspaper and writing the word 'I' still makes me cringe. It doesn't come naturally to me. I can't tell people I'm writing a memoir without making fun of myself for doing this.

But every interview with them reminds me of why I am writing this book. I want to understand who my parents are and who they were. I want to understand the country we fled, Somalia: what it was and what it is now. I want to understand how and why we are now British, looking at the refugee crisis I was a part of as a child in the 1990s, and the European one I reported on as an adult from 2015. I want to understand what we had left behind once we gained and grew into our new identities in the UK.

I write because it is always the way I have made sense of the world. I do it now to make sense of us.

My mum made it into the UK just in time for my seventh birthday. We celebrated in a McDonald's in East London. Her fears never materialised. We bounced back easily into our loving relationship once we were reunited. My father joined us a few months later, just before my brother Aamir was born.

She turns her sharp eyes at Mohamed, my dad, my Baba. 'He never expected me to find my way back to Holland,' she says.

On that, my father agrees. 'You're right, I didn't expect you of all people to manage as well as you did. You who grew up in a bush part of Somalia.' This sparks another riotous argument and I watch them, trying not to laugh.

Two decades had passed since my mother's ordeal. The three of us sit in my parents' council house in East London. It is in this house where the past is returning to us, bit by bit. We are sat together on the couch in the open-plan kitchen and living room. My mum gets up to start cooking lunch. My brother Aamir walks in and we're eventually joined by my other brothers who live with my parents, Ibrahim, Hamid and Hussein.

I want to reach for my mum and dad, but I don't know how to close the distance between us. I had reported extensively on Europe's refugee crisis, written dispatches from refugee camps in Calais and Dunkirk in France, and explored why people were risking their lives trying to reach the UK. I did this while largely ignorant of my family's own desperate journey in the late 1990s.

I get up and join my mum in the kitchen. I ask if she needs help and she shakes her head and tells me to sit down. I see my mum smirking as I walk back towards my dad.

'You think you suffered more. You're dreaming!' Mama yells.

I first visited the refugee camp in Calais, a depressing port city in Northern France, in October 2015. It was a day of many firsts: the first time I'd crossed the Channel on a ferry, the first time I'd been to that part of France, and my first major assignment as a news reporter.

I was twenty-three years old and completely out of my depth. I had trained to become a science journalist and had graduated with a Masters degree in science communication a year before. I worked for different science publications, often writing viral stories. My favourite was about male *Caerostris darwini*, a species of spider that dramatically reduces its likelihood of being eaten by orally lubricating the females' genitals.

But as we entered summer in 2015, I couldn't ignore the extraordinary number of desperate refugees, largely Syrian, ending up on European shores. By then, like most people in the world, I had seen pictures and videos of desperate refugees reaching Europe, their boats crashing onto our shores. I had seen reports of refugees dying in their hundreds, the totality of their lives reduced to a single sentence in an evening news bulletin: 'More than 750 migrants are thought to have died when the boat capsized...'

I wanted to report on the refugee crisis, despite not having any experience in non-science writing. I was able to land a job at *Quartz*, an online news site, in September 2015. To my surprise, I was sent to Calais a month into my new job.

I started the day trying desperately to avoid making eye contact with a woman peeing in front of her car. The peeing woman, a tall and animated volunteer for a British aid group that provided vital supplies to the camp, had agreed to let me join them on their latest trip. I sat in the back of the car, while another volunteer, Rachel, a human rights lawyer and close friend of mine, was in the front passenger seat.

I was shuddering all over. We had left the UK just before midnight and arrived in Calais long before dawn. It was freezing and almost pitch black, the streets desolate as everything was closed. I was told we would have to wait several hours before the rest of the volunteering group arrived. I closed my eyes in an attempt to sleep, but couldn't. I tried to steady my heartbeat with deep breaths, but it beat on erratically.

We were parked less than a mile away from the refugee camp infamously called 'the Jungle', which at its peak housed nearly 10,000 asylum seekers from all over the world.[1] The volunteers arrived with donated food and clothes, which we packed into plastic bags once the sun rose over us. I came with my pen, notepad and phone, keen to talk to people, to ask them what or who they were fleeing, let them tell me about their hopes and dreams. I wanted to humanise the people being referred to as 'Europe's refugee crisis'.

I look back at my notes now and can't help but smile at how ferociously determined I was to make a difference.

On a clear day, the British coastline can be seen from Calais. For those of us with the right paperwork, the journey across the twenty-mile-wide Channel takes around an hour and a half by train or ferry. It is far more dangerous for refugees. Children had died trying to get into vans and lorries. Others were killed by high-speed trains while walking along the tracks.

When we arrived at the camp, I was taken aback by the media circus that was already there. Photographers and volunteers swarmed over a young boy who was wearing slippers that were far too big for him. He looked at me, confused. I walked around the entrance of the camp on edge, already regretting wearing all black as the sun beat down.

Two young Eritrean women who looked around my age watched me as I walked awkwardly in a circle. I smiled at them and was buoyed by their warmth when they waved back. They agreed to show me around the camp and said I could interview them so long as I didn't use their names or publish any pictures. I agreed and we walked in. They asked me as many questions as I asked them while they showed me the school, church, restaurants, library (called 'Jungle Books'), cafe and theatre that made the camp resemble a small multicultural town. Just about everything was covered in bright blue tarps that shone against the dull mud of the ground. They took me to the unofficial section for women and families. I saw a young mother washing her baby in a tub, a father hanging up clothes.

The young women invited me into their tent, where I heard of their harrowing journey to France. One of the women was called Yohanna. She told me she had joined the huge number of young people fleeing from Eritrea, searching for a better life. She had decided at a young age that she would resettle in the UK.

Yohanna had been captured by rebels in Libya, in the midst of a devastating civil war, and put in jail, where there was little to eat or drink. She endured almost daily beatings in her eighteen-month-long confinement. She escaped and made it onto a boat heading to Italy. She knew the risks of the boat sinking, and her drowning, but she insisted she had no other choice. She would describe the next few days on the boat as some of the worst in her life, jammed close to other refugees, as a rancid smell hung over them. Other women who joined us in the tent told a similar tale. So did men who agreed to talk to me.

But the interview that has stayed with me the most was the young Somali man I spoke to just before leaving the camp. I got lost and walked towards a British volunteer handing out food to a line of men, but he barked at me to get to the back of the line before I could ask for directions. I would be mistaken for a refugee in the camp twice more.

When I walked away, the Somali boy with a bike, who looked around eighteen, ran after me and offered to walk me to the entrance. I accepted and we walked together, him dragging his bike along the dirt road. He wore an easy smile.

'Were you born in Somalia?' I asked him.

'Yeah.'

'When did you move out of Somalia?' I heard how stupid the questions sounded as soon as I asked it.

'You're Somali, you understand,' he responded, almost incredulously.

'The civil war in the 1990s,' I quickly filled in, 'That's when you left?'

'Yeah,' he said, again. I nodded my head.

I didn't know it then, but these were my first steps in truly understanding the impact the Somali civil war had on me. My discomfort during this one encounter stands out to me as I go through my reporting notes and interviews.

I felt guilty. We had escaped the same war, but I was allowed to go in and out of the camp as a British citizen while the undocumented Somali asylum seeker walking beside me was trapped there.

I wrote that I felt weighed down by the British passport in my pocket, and this was true. But I felt a lot more than survivors' guilt then. I felt like a bubble; one that was floating away from who I thought I was, growing larger and painfully engorged.

When I got home, I struggled to sleep for many months, but I had an overwhelming urge to write. There was a pressure in my chest and melody in my mind that wanted to explode out of me, a bubble about to burst.

I wasn't exactly sure what yet, but I had a story to tell. I was just too scared to do anything about it.

I went to see my mum for lunch a few days after I returned from Calais. Since moving out a few years ago, I have usually seen her once every couple of weeks. She smiled when she opened the door, and kissed me on both cheeks. It was just us in the house; my brothers were in school and my dad was away.

She gave me a baati (a loose-fitted Somali dress often worn at home) to change into and I stood beside her, watching as she cooked an entire feast for me. The kitchen was small then, barely enough room for the both of us. She always cooked enough for me to eat with her then and to feed my housemates and me for the rest of the week.

When I told her how often I was mistaken for a resident in the refugee camp in Calais, she laughed, asked if I wanted a salad with the meal. I said no. My mum told me she wasn't surprised because I dressed like an impoverished refugee. 'You look like you bought your clothes from Poundland,' she said and shook her head.

I looked down at my ill-fitting jeans. 'I got them from Primark actually.'

She rolled her eyes. 'You have a job now, and money, please dress like it.'

I pushed on and told her what I had seen in the camp. I told her about the lack of running water, the mud that clung onto everything and the rats that scuttled past.

'Why did you go? Isn't it bad enough that we suffered through Kakuma?' she asked. She said it in the most casual tone, as if she was recounting a holiday we'd been on.

I said the word. Kakuma. It felt both foreign and all too familiar in my mouth. 'You would never believe how we lived in Kakuma. How we suffered!'

I tried to get her to slow down, but my mum went on. She seemed like she was in her own world as she told me of the unbearable heat, and reminisced about the friends we had. 'Do you remember Fatima?' she asked. 'Your friend Fatima?'

I tried to remember her then, but I couldn't. 'Oh, how inseparable you and Fatima used to be. You really loved each other.'

I tried wading through the memories of my childhood and was surprised at the internal resistance I met. I hadn't put much thought into my childhood before I arrived in the UK in a very long time.

We took the meal to the living room. 'Have you really forgotten?' Mama asked me. Her eyes were wide as she stared, incredulous. Had I? I didn't know how to answer her question. I didn't know how or why I had forgotten the refugee camp.

A year before that meal, while I was a Master's student, my parents had told me snippets of their extraordinary story of fleeing Somalia. Until then, I only knew that we claimed asylum in the UK when I was seven because of the Somali civil war. I had known we were refugees and I grew up disliking that fact. I knew my mum and I had lived in Kenya and then in Saudi Arabia, but the details were blurry.

They faded as I grew up in this country and I felt no need to hold onto them.

I didn't know that I had lived in a refugee camp similar to the one in Calais. Or I had known, and simply forgot. How does someone do that?

'I didn't know,' I kept saying throughout lunch. 'No, I can't remember.'

I wrote what I had learnt about myself into the piece I wrote for *Quartz*.[2] My dispatch from Calais was a smash hit and I became *Quartz*'s leading reporter on Europe's refugee crisis. It was the only story I wrote about the crisis from my own perspective.

I had assumed the camp my mum told me about was long gone. She didn't remember how its name was spelt and I soon moved on from that conversation we had.

If you are wondering why I didn't pursue what my mum had told me, I wish I had a more satisfying answer than I just simply wasn't ready to. I wanted to focus on my new job.

I reported on the record number of refugees that sought asylum in Europe in 2015 and the backlash they faced from politicians and the far right in 2016. I reported on Britain's decision to leave the European Union and the election of Donald Trump in 2016, and the new reality they posed for migrant communities. I reported on the rising efforts to keep migrants out of Europe and rising draconian policies, like Hungary's 2017 policy of detaining all asylum seekers.

There were plenty of positive stories too. In 2016, the International Olympic Committee allowed athletes from several refugee camps to compete as the first-ever refugee team in Brazil. I found out many of the long-distance runners in the refugee Olympic team had originated from a refugee camp in Kenya. It had been nearly a year since that conversation with my mum in the kitchen.

I called up the trainer and aid worker based in Kakuma who handpicked the long-distance runners for the Olympic games and interviewed him.[3] We spoke about the importance of sport for the camp residents.

I conducted the interview not realising that I had been one of these residents. I had by then completely forgotten the name of the camp my mum had told me about.

After the interview, I came across some pictures of the camp by the organisation FilmAid, which had set up a makeshift cinema that allowed residents of the Kakuma Refugee Camp in Kenya to see the Rio games from start to finish. There were so many children in the crowds. I was startled. I went to the toilet to try and take deep breaths. I was trying to get my heart rate to go down.

I sometimes had dreams of a girl watching Bollywood films in an outdoor cinema, the evening heat sticking to her skin. It was those images that came to me in the bathroom. I realised then that they were memories. I was that girl. I went back to my desk and looked at the pictures from FilmAid again.

I got home that day in a daze. I felt like I was having an out-of-body experience. I called my mum.

'Did you know that Kakuma still exists?' I asked.

'Really?' she shouted, excited. 'No, I didn't. Wow!'

'They are playing in the refugee team. The runners from Kakuma—'

'Who's playing? What team? What are you talking about?' Mama interrupted.

'The Olympics has a refugee team this year. They have refugees competing in swimming, running, and other sports. The runners are all from the Kakuma refugee camp,' I explained.

'Ahh, mashallah!' I knew she was smiling. 'Mashallah, mashallah. We will support them. They are our people! Okay Coco, I have to go, the boys will be back from school soon.' And then she hung up.

I looked around my flat and stared for a moment at my desk in my living room. It was quiet and I was alone. My reporting notebook was in my bag. I felt that urge to write again. I could hear that melody in my mind and body. It felt trapped within me; it was almost painful. I ignored it. I sat down and watched some TV.

I was told by my editors to expand my reporting subjects as interest in the refugee crisis waned. I reported more on culture, sports and politics, often covering elections in Europe. I found myself quite lost in 2017 and 2018, struggling to write much of substance. I left *Quartz* in the summer of 2018 and joined the *Guardian* as a news reporter in September. It was a thrilling new role for a national newspaper that I had dreamed of working at.

I returned to Calais in September 2019,[4] this time with a photographer. It had been four years since I first went there. The refugee camp had been dismantled by then, but asylum seekers still came. They were undeterred by the fact that the French government, like much of Europe, had grown more hostile to them.

The UK and French governments were adamant they didn't want to see a camp as large as the Jungle ever again. Refugees now faced near-daily police raids in which they were beaten and arrested, their tents and sleeping bags confiscated and destroyed. One humanitarian worker told me the police raids were a form of 'psychological torture'.

The photographer and I were told that the new camp in Dunkirk, where 700 refugees lived in an encampment in a gymnasium and the surrounding field, including many families and children, would be cleared out. We headed down at 3 a.m., hours before the authorities arrived, to interview the refugees there. It was freezing and almost pitch black.

The police arrived as the sun rose. They formed a human cordon around the camp and kicked out the press and humanitarian workers. They left me in the camp, assuming I was a refugee. I continued interviewing those who would speak to me.

As refugees were taken onto a bus, their destination unclear, I was told to get out of the camp by my editor. When I bumped into a guy as I walked through the camp, I suddenly became aware that I was one of the few women in the enclosed camp. The female asylum seekers were waiting in the nearby gymnasium, and many of the other women were not refugees and had therefore been removed.

When I tried to leave, the riot police pointed their guns at me and told me to get back. I showed them my press card and passport, but they refused to let me go and called their supervisor.

I couldn't help but think about the precarity of my citizenship as I waited. A scared teenage boy gave me a letter stating he was an unaccompanied minor and asked for help.

'I'm sorry, I don't know what to do,' I told him. 'I'm sorry,' I said again.

He shook his head and smiled. He looked even younger. 'No problem,' he said and walked off.

I was eventually let out. I found the photographer I was with and watched the rest of the refugees, many of them children, being forcibly boarded onto a bus and taken away. I thought of the line that separated us: the line that kept them on the bus and me off it.

I wrestled with this personal struggle in the years that followed. The past I had pushed to the back of my mind had moved to centre stage. It went from something I had stopped thinking about once I came to the UK to something that tore at the identity I had woven for myself over the past two decades. I felt myself awaken from a deep haze.

A refugee rights campaigner, who was a child refugee herself and arrived in the UK via the Kindertransport rescue effort, once succinctly summed up what had been stopping me from interrogating my past.

She told me, 'I find my refugee start still drives my life today. It's not just something that happened in the past. I'm still struggling to lead a life that was worth saving.'

My survivor's guilt had silenced me for years. I was scared I was not worthy of writing such a story because sometimes, often in the dead of night, I wonder why I survived and so many other refugee children died. And so many continue to die. I wonder why I got to resettle while so many refugees live entire lifetimes in camps that are meant to be temporary. Why do I have a passport in my pocket, while a young man escaping the same war does not? Why do I remain off the bus while so many others like me are forced onto it?

I can't answer these questions. I don't think I'll ever be able to find an answer for them. I can, however, not let that guilt prevent me from responding to one of mankind's most basic urge: the need to tell stories.

Faarax M.J. Cawl's first book, *Aqoondarro Waa U Nacab Jacayl* (*Ignorance is the Enemy of Love*), is widely considered the first novel to be published in the Somali language following the creation of a Somali script in 1972. It recounts an ill-fated romance, a tragedy of Shakespearean proportion.

I open the English translation of the book, published in 1982 by the Polish writer and academic B. W. Andrzejewski.[5] Cawl dedicates the book to the 'young people of the coming generations' who will be 'studying their mother-tongue'. I pause and think about him writing those words. I wonder where he was sitting when he wrote the dedication, what hopes he had for the future of Somalia. I sit with the fact that I am reading that dedication in English because I'm unable to read or write Somali.

Cawl published two more books. His second novel, *Garbaduubkii gumeysiga* (*The Shackles of Colonialism*), which includes a sweeping history of foreign influence in Somalia, was published in 1978. I can't find an English translation of the book, but do find a synopsis in a review by Andrzejewski.[6] There are two main protagonists in *The Shackles of Colonialism*: Goobdoon, a young man who has been educated in England and now works as a civil servant in Hargeisa, and his father, Samakaab, who resides in the Haud, a historic region that includes both Ethiopia and Somalia (now Somaliland). The novel is set in 1969, weeks before Siad Barre seized power on 21 October.

Goobdoon visits his father after several years away and finds he is displeased. Samakaab is notably disappointed that his son is besotted with British culture, but is painfully ignorant of his own country's history. Samakaab resolves to fill the glaring gaps in his son's education. He spends the next two days and nights, under moonlight, dictating to his son what he knows about Somali history. He instructs his son to write down what he says. There are no breaks in his continuous recitation.

Samakaab is interrupted when armed vehicles arrive at the village and begin shooting indiscriminately. He is shot, while his wife, Goobdoon's mother, is killed. Samakaab resumes his story once the attackers leave. At one point, Goobdoon's ink runs out and his father tells him to use his own blood instead. The son obeys.

I first came across Cawl (his name is also often spelt as Farah Awl) while reading about the Somali war in the *Guardian* archives during the spring of 2020. At the time, I was reporting intensively on the Black Lives Matter movement that had spontaneously erupted across the world, including in the UK. I was taken aback by the number of protests taking place across the UK, which had been under lockdown as a result of the Coronavirus. One weekend, I looked at each local authority in the UK (there are over 300) to see if there were Black Lives Matter protests hosted in each of their specific councils. I found more than 260 towns and cities that had organised demonstrations in June and July 2020. Many held multiple protests.[7] I showed the data to leading historians who described the Black Lives Matter movement as the largest anti-racist protest seen in modern Britain.

I still struggle to put into words how exciting it was to be in the midst of these protests, watching, interacting with and interviewing the young Black Britons who were leading this movement for racial equality. What struck me the most was their demand for everyone to know more about Black stories and Black history.

The protests had a profound impact on me. I watched as these young Black Britons spoke confidently about their place in this country: about their place in history. I could no longer live in ignorance about Somalis' past, that of my parents, and my own. I needed to know where I belonged. I wanted to confidently assert myself in history too. My interview subjects propelled me to learn as much as I could. And to write.

When I got access to the *Guardian* archive, Cawl fell into my lap. He was an engineer, a police force colonel and then a director at the National Transport Agency of Somalia when he wrote his first novel.

Prior to the 1950s, Somali writers had largely used the Arabic script to write down their works, or had used one of the colonial languages: English or Italian. While there was a total absence of Somali written literature, Somali literature has, for hundreds of years, been 'orally composed, memorised, and recited'.[8]

I didn't know that Somalia was once known as the land of poets until my early twenties. I am embarrassed to admit this, as I have always been drawn to poetry. As a teenager, I would stop by my English teacher's office and get recommendations of eighteenth- and nineteenth-century English poets similar to the ones we were studying. I'd eagerly return to tell my teacher about the poets I liked and those I didn't. I showed them the poetry I wrote that was a poor imitation of the poets I was being introduced to.

I read these poets in my room at home while my dad sat in another. It never occurred to me to ask about what poetry from the country we hailed from was like.

It is, thankfully, never too late to start. Somali poets were widely esteemed during the nineteenth and twentieth century and a vital source of communication.[9] They played an important role in traditional courts as well as political affairs. Classical verse poetry was the most respected as it was the poetry of the public forum.

There was a binding agreement between poets that they respected a sort of copyright law: any poet who memorised someone's poem and wanted to recite it afterwards was under strict obligation to do so accurately. It was considered dishonest to improvise or purposefully change words. The reciter had to also state the name of the poet at the beginning of each poem, as failure to do so was considered deeply unethical.[10]

During turbulent times, poets became journalists, spokespeople for clans and territory groups, and politicians. There is great power in poetry and Somali poets knew this, using it to call people to arms or to counsel for peace.

As a teenager, I would go to poetry readings and find myself shuddering at powerful recitations. I couldn't help but smile when I realised I am descended from many Somalis who were gripped by the same joys and aches. I liked that I too could slot myself into history.

Cawl published his first novel amid this rich oral culture. The novel, which was written in four months, was the result of a challenge by his friends at a party. There was great excitement over the development of the Somali script at the time and an urgency to cultivate Somali written culture. The government launched a literacy campaign, sending out hundreds of school students and their teachers all over the country to teach villagers and nomads how to read and write. The students and teachers were also instructed to write down folk stories from the various regions they were dispatched to in order to preserve them.

In an interview with the *Guardian* in 1982, Cawl is proud that his first novel sold out in six months.[11] It became an instant classic. He next appears in the *Guardian* archive in October 1991 – his obituary. As soon as I learnt of his existence, I learnt he was killed in the Somali civil war.

The obituary is written by Andrzejewski, who describes Cawl as 'a genial and most entertaining conversationalist' who was 'Somali through and through', true to himself and the traditions of his nation.[12] It was the only obituary I could find of a Somali in the *Guardian* and the rest of the British national press during the war in 1991.

The fifty-three-year-old Cawl was killed while fleeing Mogadishu. A group of armed militia stopped the truck he was in. In an interview published by the *Guardian* in October 1992, Cawl's wife, Halima Jama Nuh, recalls the horror that followed: her husband and son, Abdi Rahman, were rounded up with five other men. Halima ran towards them as they shot at her family. She fainted and when she awoke, she had a bullet in her leg and saw the gunmen taking the dead's personal belongings.

I had loved reading since I was little, but it was only just dawning on me how painfully Western-centric my understanding of and curiosity about literature had been. I had read all of Jane Austen's novels during a single summer while I was twelve years old – now I was twenty-eight, and only just learning about Faarax's work, his life and death. Without even realising it, I had brutally excised my Somali identity from my life.

I took out any books I could find on Somalia from my local library. I felt frustrated that of the non-fiction books they had about Somalia, I could only find ones about piracy and terrorism. Their authors were all white. Though the books' subjects were Somalis, they weren't written for us to read.

I wanted to write something to change that.

When the author and former *Guardian* journalist Gary Younge, a writer I respect very much, asks what I hope to achieve with this book, I stammer while trying to answer the question.

'I want to write a definitive account of the Somali civil war. I want people to know what happened and why it happened and who was hurt and who is still hurting,' I say, as we eat lunch in a Turkish restaurant in Hackney.

Gary nods his head as more words tumble out of me. 'So many people just don't know anything about the Somali civil war and I hate that. They think of Somalis and think of barbarism, of terrorists and of pirates. I want future Somalis to be given a nuanced picture of what happened.'

I think of Goobdoon diligently noting down what his father had told him about Somalia in Faarax's novel and want to do the same. I want the generations of Somalis that follow me to understand the soul of their ancestors' nation.

He gives me a thoughtful look and for a second I am scared he will tell me I don't have it in me to write a book. 'I'm not sure that's the book you're writing,' he says. I feel my heart drop. 'Do you plan on writing the ins and outs of different political groups, tribes and clans of the war?'

I shake my head. I don't know where the book will lead me or what it will look like, but I don't want to focus on clans.

'Are you planning on writing an extensive social and political history of Somalia? On how the nation state was formed and what led to its collapse?'

'I want to touch on this, but no, it wouldn't be the main focus,' I reply.

'So what would be the main focus?' Gary asks me. It is a simple question, but I don't have an answer to it, though it is obvious. It has always been obvious.

My first instinct when learning about what happened to my parents was to treat their story like any other journalistic endeavour. I researched what I didn't know and read until my eyes hurt. I wanted to simplify the academic papers and history books so they were accessible to a wider audience.

I realise during that lunch that the way to tell Somalia's story is not by authoring a comprehensive or definitive history book, but to write something much more personal.

I think about how I light up while listening to my parents' stories, which are so funny and moving. I like when bits of my past become less blurry, like something I can reach again. It is true that I want to understand the country that I came from, but, if I'm being honest, I want, mostly, to understand myself. I want to know where I fit in the world.

'A book about the Somali civil war is a noble aspiration, but from what you've talked about, it's not the book you want to write. The story you need to tell, the one you are best to tell, is your own. Don't shy away from that,' Gary says.

I give myself permission to do just that.

2
WHEN FAATMA MET MOHAMED

My mum is a great storyteller. Whether it is a story about who she bumped into while out shopping, or what she was like as a schoolgirl, she is good at keeping me hooked from beginning to end. She also has an impulse to embellish the truth. This can be a problem while writing a memoir of our lives. But, if I'm honest, I love this about her – her eyes darkening, hand expressions wilder, her voice raised louder with every retelling of a story.

The first time I sat my parents down to interview them for this book, I did so on a video call. They sat in their living room wearing matching pink fluffy dressing gowns, while I was at my desk in my house. Though we lived just five miles away from each other, I hadn't seen them in months. Coronavirus was raging through the UK and we were under strict instructions to remain indoors.

Baba is a short, slim man with tight black and grey curls. He shops once a year, during Boxing Day sales, and takes great pride in his style. 'I want them to know I am a man of fashion,' he tells me.

He is a pious and immensely curious man. He often calls me to ask for my take on whatever insanity has consumed British politics that week. He is also stubborn and closes in on himself when angry.

Mama is loud, excitable woman, who spends much of her day laughing. It's not hard to make her laugh, and when she does, it's accompanied by tears. She is quick to anger, but doesn't like to hold grudges. She is also short, warm and fiercely loyal.

I first asked them if they remembered when they fell in love. They rolled their eyes at me. They told me they had known each other for a while. Their respective families were close friends. I laughed and rephrased the question. I asked my father why he married my mother. He told me he was first drawn to her religious knowledge. My mum had memorised the Quran as a child and could speak Arabic.

When I asked mum the same, she paused. She told me she did so for her 'freedom'. Her father, my jiddo, was incredibly strict. She wanted to get out of his household and the grip he had on her social life, or lack thereof. We both laughed.

When I pressed her and asked if she had any romantic feelings for my dad, that surely she must have chosen him for a reason, Baba interrupted:

'Before I met Mama—'

'Can I finish my point?' Mama shouted.

'I had three or four women interested in me.'

'Everyone wanted you, Baba?' I asked, laughing.

'... Yes,' he replied.

And on it went. They filled in the gaps of the people they were before they became war survivors and my parents. These two identities, I would learn, are synonymous with each other. My parents are my parents because they survived the civil war, and war survivors because they are parents. My impending birth had driven them to live.

I didn't do a great job in that first interview. I had tried to be a journalist, but acted more like their daughter who would go to important appointments to translate for them. I interrupted often to fill in gaps while they paused to find the right words.

I had sent them an email with the twenty-six questions I was planning to ask a week before the interview. These questions – 'What was life like during the Siad Barre regime?' – were far too large to be answered in one sitting. I would learn that if I stayed quiet and let them take control of the interview, they would show me what I was looking for. They would show me who they were.

In our interviews, my parents speak to each other in Somali. My dad speaks to me in English, while my mum speaks to me in Arabic.

In this first interview, I made them talk about their lives before the war, their courtship and when the war began in clearly delineated segments. They used the same words to describe the time before: 'good', 'peaceful' and 'free'. I tried to challenge them on this when I first started interviewing them. I tried to tell them what I had read of Siad Barre, president of Somalia in the 1970s and '80s: his brutal repression of political dissidents and the lengths he went to in order secure power.

I stopped pushing as hard as I did when we spoke about tribalism under Barre. 'I read that Barre utilised tribalism to his advantage,' I told my father one afternoon.

Baba shook his head and said: 'No, he was against tribalism. He stamped it out when he came to power.' He clamped his hands together for emphasis.

I wanted to tell him that I had read that while Barre had publicly spoken out against tribalism, he used the tribal system for his own gains. I didn't say any of this in the end. I thought of my dad as a teenager listening to Barre's speeches against tribalism. I didn't want to take away the happy memories he had of Somalia.

After that first interview, I turned to newspaper archives to fill in the gaps. I searched for article clippings about Somalia in the British press from the 1970s to 1992. The image of prewar life my parents painted was divorced from the reality on the ground. I wondered if they were completely isolated from the events that preceded the war, or whether they had chosen to forget.

I had pictured my parents happy in their home and that suddenly being ripped away from them. I pictured Mogadishu as a beautiful, thriving city one day and a bombed-out one the next. But the archives show me that the good times and bad times bled into each other. The 1980s, when my parents had met, was a beautiful time for them, but it was also a time of soaring food costs and rising unemployment. The government had been veering from crisis to crisis.

The archives drove home another truth. My parents had played down the worst aspects of the war. They had turned their entire experience of the war into a dark joke – one that I loved laughing along to.

After that first interview with my parents, I come across an article published by the Associated Press in 1992 on Somali refugees fleeing on boats. It is the route my parents had been talking to me about; a route thousands of Somalis took in the winter of 1991 and spring of 1992.[1]

The Kenyan authorities, overwhelmed by the spiralling crisis in the neighbouring country, initially refused to allow a boat to land, the article noted. The Somali refugees waited onboard as negotiations continued between the UN refugee agency and the Kenyan government. Pregnant women were among the refugees that were left stranded for a week. Two gave birth on the ship and were taken to hospital once the boat was finally allowed to dock, alongside three other ailing people.

I wonder if the refugees in the article felt relief or dread once they landed. What did my parents feel? It was a straightforward news story, but I reread the article until the words began blurring into each other.

My mum, my favourite storyteller, had embellished to protect me. She paints a rosy picture of human endurance and unexpected kindness, but she, like thousands of others, had suffered immensely.

I think about my mum and my dad, both younger than I am now and faced with the daunting challenge of leaving all they knew behind. How scared they both must have been. Were they hungry, thirsty, tired? I try to see them when I close my eyes. I want to reach back, I want to save them.

My dad was born in 1963, three years after Somalia became independent. It was one of seventeen African nations to do so in 1960. In the ten years prior to independence, the north and south were under Italian trusteeship, assigned by the UN General Assembly.

The country had been split in two during its colonial period, with Britain ruling the north from 1884,[2] and Italy ruling the southern part, known as Italian Somaliland, from 1889 until 1941, when it was captured by Britain in the Second World War. It was a brutal colonisation that became more vicious when Italy fell under the Fascist rule of Benito Mussolini in 1922.[3]

Stories of what Somalis endured during the Fascist colonisation have been passed on from generation to generation. Once, my mum told me of Italian colonisers who would demand Somalis lie in puddles to be walked over so that the Italians didn't get wet. In some areas, Somalis were prevented from entering offices with their shoes on. In others, they were tortured and whipped to death. In the Janale region, Somalis were dispossessed from their land and forced to work on white plantations.[4]

I want to learn more about the post-war period and go to the British Library. In their Africa and Asia reading room, where visitors are not allowed to enter with a pen, I find a remarkable memoir, published in 1992, by Mohamed Osman Omar.[5] He was a former diplomat who worked for the democratic government as well as the Siad Barre regime.

After the Second World War, when Italy was defeated by Britain in East Africa, there was a debate about what should happen to southern Somalia. In the immediate aftermath, the south of the country was ruled by a British military administration while the north continued to be ruled by the UK. The return to Italian rule was discussed by various international actors.

At the heart of the resistance to colonial rule, meanwhile, was the Somali Youth League, which was founded on 15 May 1943 in the south of the country. It later became the country's first ruling political party.

I call my dad to tell him what I had learnt about Somalia's anti-colonial history soon after leaving the British Library, and he tells me that one member of the league, Dhere Haji Dhere, who organised the party when he was just seventeen years old, is a distant relative.

'His son lives here in London,' Baba says.

'Really?'

The Youth League played a crucial role in mobilising the demonstrations towards the end of the 1940s across the country, including two crucial uprisings: Dhagaxtuur ('stone throwing') and Somalia Hanoolaato ('Long live Somalia'),[6] also known as the Mogadishu riot of 1948. I learn of Hawa Tako (Xaawo Taako), a Somali female freedom fighter who was killed in January 1948 at the latter protest, where people demonstrated against the imminent return of Italian rule. Her image and name lived on in banknotes, street names and other political imagery, taking on a mythic status in the post-Independence era.[7]

The international community took notice of these demonstrations. In 1948, the United Nations Four-Power Commission, made up of the US, the Soviet Union, the United Kingdom and France, came to Somalia. The commission's mission was to discern the people's will and meet with the leaders of the different political parties.

The Somali Youth League was in support of a landmark proposal that called for the creation of a nation based on the borders of Greater Somalia. The proposal was initially backed by Britain. Known as the Bevin Plan, named after then Foreign Secretary Ernest Bevin, it called for the former Italian Somaliland, British Somaliland, the Ogaden and the

Northern Frontier District (areas that were then, and are now, within Ethiopia and Kenya respectively, but which have strong cultural and historical links to Somalia) to be brought together as a single country under a UN trusteeship led by Britain.

The proposal didn't get far, due to significant opposition from the US and the Soviet Union. The two opposing foreign powers accused Britain of 'seeking its own aggrandisement at the expense of Ethiopia and Italy'. Britain withdrew its proposal.

The commission decided instead that Somalia would be made a UN protectorate. The UN General Assembly assigned a trusteeship over Somalia to Italy from 1950 to 1960. Italy was tasked with preparing Somalia for independence over the course of the decade: only then would the country become independent. Somali nationalists were dismayed.[8]

I turn back to Mohamed Osman Omar's memoir and am fascinated by the chapter where he details these preparations for independence.[9] The Italians established the Amministrazione Fiduciaria Italiana della Somalia (AFIS, called the 'Trust Territory of Somaliland under Italian Administration' in English), which created a range of different schools that would help produce teachers, doctors, nurses and bankers, as well as developing a police force, army and other skilled professions.

I speak to my dad again and tell him I think it is interesting that although there were protests and people agitating for independence, there doesn't appear to have been a mass movement. There were no national strikes, no armed struggles to be won.

'It wasn't easy though, Somalis had to fight for it and people died,' Baba says.

'Of course, and I'm not saying freedom was just handed to Somalis. I'm just surprised that it has been fought almost entirely on the political sphere,' I try to explain. 'It all seems so bureaucratic and technical. It's so different to what happened in Algeria or Cuba.'

Baba laughs and says: 'At the time, it's what made us appear civilised and far more advanced than others. It's not a bad thing!'

'I didn't say it was!' I insist. 'It's just interesting.'

I use that word a lot – 'interesting' – when I don't know exactly how I feel about something. I can't find other books about the Somali independence movement, either nonfiction or fiction. It isn't for lack of trying. Ali Jimale Ahmed, chair of Comparative Literature at Queens College in New York, writes of a 'paucity' of written materials about the liberation struggles in Somalia.[10] Ahmed offers an interesting theory as to why: he writes that because Somalis had largely negotiated their independence from their colonisers, without major violence, there was perhaps an 'absence among Somalis of ... a "shared code of reference" forged in the heat of a common liberation war experience'.

One of the biggest obstacles facing the government was the lack of a written language. Somalia had long been an oral society until Cawl wrote his novel.

When written communication was used, it was done in a foreign language. The problem, as Omar noted in his memoir, is the array of languages people were taught across the country. In the north, Somalis learnt English as a foreign language. In the south, they had largely learnt Italian. Some Somalis in both the north and south also knew Arabic, as was traditional for a Muslim country.

Over the 1950s, Omar saw the country transform rapidly and become in effect a small province of Italy, with things being done 'the Italian way'.[11] Each government department was led by an Italian expert who taught his Somali counterpart, who would take over that strand of the civil service when independence came.

Omar was critical of this system of training, known as 'Somalizzazione',[12] and he wasn't the only one. In 1994, Basil

Davidson, a historian and journalist, blamed the collapse of the Somali state on the inadequacy of the institutions that were put in place during the 1950s. Omar described it as a system of training where someone learns to drive 'without knowing the functioning of the engine, or like sitting beside the driving instructor and merely being shown how to hold the steering wheel'.

In 1956, Somalis took to the polls in the country's first significant national election. In May, the first elected Legislative Assembly convened. The Somali Youth League won by a landslide and its leader, Abdullahi Issa Mohamud, was appointed prime minister. He led an all-Somali cabinet of ministers during the last four years of Italy's trusteeship.

The country also had little to no economic prospects and there seemed to be no plan for what would drive the country's economic engine. Somalia didn't have any large-scale economic assets to manage, while most of the small-scale economy was controlled by non-Somalis. So, as Omar asked, 'What then did political independence mean if the country had to depend economically on foreign powers?'[13]

Still, Omar and the rest of the country eagerly awaited independence. Omar wrote of people gathering in Parliament Square in Mogadishu on the afternoon of 30 June 1960. While the crowd waited for 'the hour of freedom at midnight', they talked, danced and chanted. Coloured lights had been strung up across the parliament building where Omar worked, and throughout the streets of Mogadishu.

The Somali national flag is a five-pointed white star on a blue background. Each point of the star signifies a territory that, all together, would make up Greater Somalia. While two of the regions, Italian Somaliland and British Somaliland, were being brought together geographically, the flag served as a reminder that three territories beyond the country's borders where Somalis made up the overwhelming majority – the French Somali Coast (now Djibouti), the

Northern Frontier District, which was given to Kenya, and the Ogaden, which is part of Ethiopia – were yet to join the new republic.

There were loudspeakers installed at the four corners of the square. An announcer told the crowd to be silent. The band stood to attention and waited for the signal to go. Once it did, the national anthem, called 'Soomaaliya Hanoolaato' ('Long Live Somalia'), blared. The flag went up and a twenty-one-gun salute punctuated the air. The Somali territories in the north and south combined, bringing together a total population of around three million under one banner. The new republic was born.

'We hugged each other. We laughed. We wept tears of happiness. We prayed for the country saying, "May Allah make it great." We danced. Women ululated. We congratulated each other. And this went on throughout the night, till the next morning,' Omar wrote.[14]

Omar's words move me in that quiet room in the British Library. I think of the people in the crowd and their perseverance for that moment. I think of their hope for the future. What started off with so much joy would end terribly in a few decades.

I call my dad again to tell him what I have learnt today. He listens patiently on the other end of the phone. He is always excited when I call, and we speak for a long time. I can almost see his smile as he listens to me finally showing an interest in Somalia's history.

It is a bittersweet moment. My dad and I largely speak to each other in English since I've forgotten much of my Somali. Though my dad is fluent in English, it's not his first language, or the one he prefers to speak in. We have found a way to communicate with each other, but I have only begun to understand the way we are limited by it.

I struggle to find the right words to tell him exactly how I am feeling. I wish I could still speak Somali so I could tell him how I was at first moved, then sad that it had taken me this long to have this conversation with him.

Instead, I tell him how much I enjoy delving into Somali history. 'It's good, good, good,' he responds, somewhat distracted. He tells me he has to go, not saying where. 'Bye, Baba,' he says to me, but the line doesn't go immediately dead.

I stay on and listen to the background for a few seconds. I haven't up till that moment thought much about the fact that he calls me Baba too. Was it a sign of respect for the eldest child in our culture, or something special between us?

In the library, I read on as Omar writes of his experiences working in parliament in the secretariat office. He saw the early, hopeful years of this extraordinary democratic period. The first National Assembly was made up of 123 members, of whom 90 were elected from the south and 33 from the north.[15]

Often when people talk about Somalia, they point to the remarkable homogeneity within the region. People speak the same language – Somali; follow the same religion – Islam; and share a similar culture throughout the territories. But the early years of parliament show that this alone isn't enough to build a cohesive national identity.

Parliament met twice daily whenever it was in session, once in the morning and again in the afternoon. Before each sitting, one of the secretariat staff would read out the attendance register and each MP would respond to his name being called. As Omar wrote: 'One would say "Presente", another would say "Present", yet others would say "Haadir", or "Waajooga" – Italian, English, Arabic, Somali – it was like the Tower of Babel.' Omar described how the 'whole business of the nation was being conducted through the medium of a foreign language.' While the president and the prime minister were fluent in Italian, other senior members in the assembly only spoke English or Arabic as a foreign language.

The style of dress was just as bewildering to behold, and for Omar, amusing. Some MPs had never left their villages before and were in the capital for the first time. They were visibly uncomfortable in the trousers they wore. Among the representatives, Omar saw people wearing three-piece suits, Egyptian-style khamis (a long robe worn often by Muslim men), a shirt and macawis (a traditional Somali sarong-like garment) and other combinations of these, such as khamis and macawis, or macawis with a suit jacket.

There was a free and open press during this decade. The Somali National News Agency drew information from Reuters, the Arab News Agency, the Italian News Agency and other foreign news organisations. Radio broadcasting had rapidly expanded, with daily broadcasts in Somali, Arabic, Italian and English. While the government used these broadcasts to push propaganda, they did not ban broadcasts from outside the country.

This freedom of speech was part of an extensive bill of rights that was written into the constitution. It also protected the freedom of association, assembly and private ownership. There was an independent judiciary and Supreme Court. The number of political parties increased from just eight in 1950 to over 100 by 1968.

More than one million Somalis voted in the 1964 general election.[16] A *New York Times* write-up of the election described women queueing in the crushing heat to vote alongside men at one of the country's 1,400 polling stations. I smile when I read, 'Politics is the national sport in Somalia, which has a tradition of democracy and a stable parliamentary system of government.' By the time I was born, Somalia would never be described as such again.

The Somali Youth League won half those votes and had a majority in the national assembly. Abdirashid Shermarke had been re-elected as prime minister. The rest of the seats went to eleven other parties. The Somali National Congress became the main opposition, with twenty-two seats, while the Somali Democratic Union had won fifteen seats.

Among one of the many parties competing for votes was SANU (Somali African National Union), which had roots in the Banadir region,[17] which roughly encompasses the coastal area between Mogadishu and Kismayo. My dad told me my grandad was a leading party member during this decade. I had only met my grandad as a baby and don't have any memories of him. He owned several properties across Mogadishu, including shops and a hotel. I was told he was a fair, progressive man. He encouraged the women in his family to go to school and work. Though he was often quiet, he was known for his honesty when asked his opinion.

I can't find much information about SANU in my research and wish I had asked my grandad about it before he passed away. He died in 2003 in the US, months after my brother Ibrahim was born. He had managed to resettle in the country with my grandma and many of my aunts and uncles. I remember it was autumn. I was eleven years old and had just started secondary school. When he became unwell and was hospitalised, my dad was desperate to see him, but he couldn't. He only had a refugee travel document and was unlikely to get a visa from the US in time.

When they spoke on the phone for the last time, my grandad was on his deathbed in a hospital.

'I considered flying to Mexico and going through the border,' Baba tells me.

'The US-Mexico border?' I ask, stupidly. What other border could he have meant?

'Yes, the one in the news now. I was ready to travel through it and smuggle myself into the country to go and see him. I wanted to say goodbye, but my dad said no. He said stay, I have your brothers and your mum with me. He said, "Don't put yourself at risk." He said "I am okay."' I nod and think of the lengths I would go to to say goodbye to my parents.

During the 1969 elections, SANU was able to win six seats in the national assembly, out of a total of 123 seats.[18] It was a small yet formidable political force at the time. Clan and familial loyalties were pervasive during Somalia's democratic period, with many political parties drawing on clan networks for support. My grandad and my father are against these dividing lines among our people, so much so that they didn't tell me what clan we originate from until I asked as an adult, when I learned that my mother is Ashraf while my father is Moorshe and Iskashito, a sub-clan of the Reer Hamar. I am incredibly ignorant about the clan system in Somalia. I have since done my research, but made the decision to not write about clans in this book. This is not just to honour the way I was raised, but to point to the ultimate uncomfortable truth: the civil war and state collapse was caused by Somalis hurting other Somalis.

Veteran Saudi journalist Khaled Al-Maeena put it best when, in 1996, he wrote in one of his dispatches from the country: 'Somalia's blood-bath is one of the most senseless conflicts in history. It is a battle between a people of the same clan, a people sharing the same history, the same culture and the same religion. It is not a war, but a suicide pact.'[19]

While the country was seen as democratic by the rest of the world, Omar wrote despairingly of how personal interest took precedence over what was best for the nation. He was particularly critical of the Somali Youth League, who by the end of the decade were syphoning aid money to themselves, family and friends. The people who needed it the most never saw it, leaving some to dub Somalia as 'the graveyard of foreign aid'. A thirty-one-year-old politician at the time was rumoured to have amassed a personal wealth of $5 million, Omar noted.

On 15 October 1969, Prime Minister Sharmarke was assassinated, shot dead by one of his bodyguards. His successor would be decided by the national assembly, in which the Somali Youth League had a comfortable majority.

Omar wrote that the person elected would reap financial rewards for himself and his own family and tribesmen.

The elections were scheduled to go ahead on 21 October. At 3 a.m., however, army officers took over. The elected officials were taken to an undisclosed location. The government had been overthrown in what would be described as a 'bloodless revolution'.

This revolution was led by Mohamed Siad Barre, known simply as Barre. Born in 1910, he had come of age during colonial rule. Barre had worked as a police officer; first for the Italian Fascist government, then the British from 1941 to 1950, and then later the Italian administration between 1950 until 1960. In 1952, Barre was among eight police inspectors taken to Italy for training.[20]

After Somalia reunified and declared independence, Barre had left the police force to become an officer in the army. He rose through the ranks quickly and within just five years became the commander of the army.

Radio Mogadishu played strange martial music on the morning of the coup. Those who left their houses found national monuments across the city surrounded by tanks and soldiers. My grandad was devastated.

'Why was your father upset?' I ask my dad.

'He was a democrat, Coco!' Baba shouts, using my nickname. I laugh and explain to him that sometimes I have to ask quite obvious questions to tease out people's ideals and motivations for the reader.

'Oh, okay, yes: Jiddo was very sad. Yes, the democratic government was rife with corruption, he felt the country wasn't given a chance to sort it out,' Baba says.

My grandad was in the minority. Crowds took to the street to welcome the revolution. Barre had been able to sweep into power against this backdrop with a tantalising message of hope. In the declaration released by the new Revolutionary Council soon after the coup, Barre vowed to restore justice and equality before the law; to defend the right to work; to fairly distribute the nation's wealth; to eradicate hunger, disease and ignorance; and, perhaps most importantly, to eliminate the tribalism that pervaded politics.

Somali researcher Mohamed Haji Ingiriis noted a particularly startling story that is often told of this time.[21] A Somali student was on his way to school in Mogadishu when Barre took over the government. The student, upon hearing the news, joined demonstrations in favour of the coup. I thought I had misread that and immediately paused and re-read the line again. Why had they celebrated? I thought back to Omar's writing – the 'corruption, nepotism and total disregard for the common man' had driven the people to such despair that they would have welcomed any change at that point.[22]

When, as the anecdote goes, the student was asked by his teacher why he hadn't come into school, the young man proudly declared he went to the demonstrations to welcome the country's changing political winds. The teacher responded: 'If you endorsed a military coup d'état in that way, it'll take you years to resist them in a different way.'

The teacher's warning would indeed come to pass. The once jubilant student would take up arms to fight to topple Barre's military regime.

The initial symbol of the revolution, which appeared in the first charter, was a gun, a hand and a Quran in the background. The declaration was in Italian. In 1970, a year after the coup, Barre issued a second charter which declared Somalia a socialist state, driven by the principle of scientific socialism. This time, the Quran, hand and gun were gone. There were no symbols on the second charter, which was also written in Italian.

The irony of my ignorance about Somalia's socialist history made me laugh. I went to university during the height of the student movement in the UK in 2010, where thousands protested against increases in fees, the removal of vital grants and other austerity policies that were being viciously imposed on the poorest in the country. I was swept up by the radical fervour, reading and debating anti-capitalist and feminist thinkers and trying to relate their ideas to my own life. I had read the work of Russian revolutionaries such as Lenin and Leon Trotsky – but I had been utterly unaware in this time of my country's own experiment with Marxism. I called my friends comrades, without knowing that Somalis were once told to call each other 'jalle' – the Somali equivalent.

The second charter declared: 'as from October 21, 1970, the Somali Democratic Republic will adopt Scientific Socialism.'[23] 'The people were told that socialism was a transitional phase towards communism,' Omar wrote. The president declared: 'we have chosen [this] ... because it is the only way for the rapid transformation of the country into a developed and economically advanced nation.'[24]

After first rejecting aid by the Americans, which came with the condition that the country embark on 'reasonable policies', Barre announced his eagerness to develop relations with the Soviets. The Eastern bloc was initially hesitant, with Soviet leaders unsure of the character of the Somali revolution, but Barre successfully seduced them and Soviet presence was more widespread by 1972. The Soviets were Somalia's primary provider of military equipment, training and advice. The size of the Somali army had increased from 4,000 soldiers in 1964 to 17,000 by 1974.

In 1972, Omar, who was by then a diplomat in China, was called back home to undergo a three-month training course in a military camp. A new edict forced every civil servant to undergo this training. The government claimed that the purpose of these camps was to reassert the primacy of Somali culture and eliminate foreign influences. For Omar, it was an obvious ploy to brainwash people.

Omar questions whether Barre, who spoke often about scientific socialism and communism, had ever read a book on these subjects. 'He certainly had not been to a school where it was taught,' he wrote. 'But he wanted to teach it to the people of Somalia.'[25]

The Supreme Revolutionary Council created a new department called Xafiiska Xiriirka Dadweynaha, which later became Xafiiska Siyaadda (the Political Office). This department was tasked with promoting socialist policies. The office established centres for orientation across the country, where representatives spoke every week on a range of topics.

People were not able to speak freely in these meetings, which they were soon obliged to attend by the Political Office, Omar wrote. Those who didn't were seen as anti-revolutionary – a dangerous charge.

The government also introduced a national self-help programme called Iskaa Wax u Qabso ('volunteering'). The programme involved the construction of essential infrastructure, such as schools, hospitals and roads. As part of this national programme, Mogadishu residents were tasked with cleaning the city's streets. But instead of inspiring a collective sense of community and self-improvement, the initiative embittered residents, Omar noted. He wrote that while every civil servant was expected to take part, soldiers and militia did not participate.

The regime discouraged Somalis from hanging around non-Somalis. Omar didn't realise how far this fear extended until he had coffee with an old acquaintance, a non-Somali. After they had paid for their drinks in the cafe and tried to find somewhere to sit, they found the entire shop, except the two workers, had emptied. People only returned to the cafe once his friend had left.

Omar likened the conditions in Somalia in this period to George Orwell's *Animal Farm* – a telling comparison, since the government banned circulation of the novel and it was a crime to own it. The book had been translated into Somali by an unknown translator and was secretly distributed – although Omar remarks that he never saw an actual copy.[26]

At the end of each meeting in the reorientation centres, participants had to sing a revolutionary song dedicated to the president. The song described him as 'the victorious Siad' and the 'Father of Knowledge'. He demanded to be referred to as the 'father of the nation', 'the untiring' and the 'light of Africa'. His photo was always displayed in meetings, alongside posters of Karl Marx, Friedrich Engels and Vladimir Lenin.[27]

Somalis responded to this totalitarian regime in a very Somali way: by telling jokes. A favourite concerned a native of Mogadishu who had a dream that the government had collapsed. In the morning he told his dream to someone and was arrested and tortured for days. After he was released, he met the security guard who had imprisoned him. The security man asked him if he had been having any more dreams, to which the man responded: 'Don't I first need to sleep?'

Barre was, in every sense of the word, a dictator. But that doesn't stop many from looking back at the first years of the revolution fondly: these are commonly known as the 'golden years' of Barre's regime. My parents included.

It was during these years that Somalia saw the development of its own written language and established an impressive literacy campaign. During the democratic period, the government always faced significant opposition whenever it tried to adopt a written script. Some wanted to adopt a Latin script, while others wanted Arabic. When rumours spread that the elected government was considering the Latin script, for example, pressure groups that opposed the move protested and claimed it was un-Islamic.

When the regime announced its decision to adopt the Latin script on 21 October 1972, it was not met with protests or complaints. People were far too scared to go against the revolutionary government. A month after the announcement, the Somali language was introduced in government and quickly replaced the two foreign languages, Italian and English, in which the civil service had been operating.

My dad was nine years old, but still remembers the campaign that was launched to spread awareness and increase literacy rates. The slogan was 'Haddaad taqaanno bar, haddaadan aqoonna baro': 'if you know it, teach it; if you do not know, learn it.'[28]

My dad tells me that the students in the years above him and teachers were sent to remote villages to teach the written language as part of the campaign. Schools began exclusively teaching in Somali.

'This was a big mistake,' Baba says. I am surprised he feels this way.

'Don't you think it was important for Somali students to learn in their own language?' I ask.

'Yes, but we shouldn't have abandoned other foreign languages,' Baba explains. 'To do so prevented Somali students from competing in the world.'

'You think the policy isolated you?'

'Pride and culture is important, but so are key skills like foreign languages,' Baba says. I'm not sure I agree. I wish I could tell him why in Somali.

Under Barre, Somalia joined the Arab League and ushered in significant improvements in healthcare and education, alongside the development of public infrastructure programmes. The government was also widely praised for its impressive response to the 1975 drought.

Omar, who is extremely critical of Barre, described him as a talented orator. 'When he addressed the people he had the knack of making his words stick in the minds of his audience. He could address and hold the attention of a mass rally for hours – a three-hour speech was not unusual – though he never took a written speech or notes with him to such gatherings.'[29]

I find a pamphlet of the speeches Barre had made across the years and see that he often spoke out against tribalism. In a 1975 speech, in which he congratulated the students who took part in the literacy campaign, he described tribalism as the country's archenemy. 'Of course we should also battle with capitalism. But where is it located in our society, considering the fact that there are no classes here? It is to be found in tribalism. This is where the capitalist, the bourgeois class is to be found. And through which door does the enemy come, where does colonialism, its agents and lackeys make their penetration? They all penetrate through tribalism.'[30]

I wonder whether my dad was in these crowds as a child and what he must have felt. What dreams and hopes did he have for himself and for his country? My dad was one of eight siblings in an upper-middle-class family in Mogadishu. When I ask him to describe what life was like then, he comes back to the same word: 'safe'. It's all he can remember feeling before the war.

But that sense of safety slowly began to crack.

In the British Library, I come across a report from Africa Watch, a human rights organisation established in 1988 under Human Rights Watch's umbrella,[31] that noted the arrest and imprisonment of General Jama Ali Korshel, the first vice president of the Supreme Revolutionary Council, on 20 April 1970. Korshel was charged with attempting to launch a coup with the help of a foreign power. Other senior members of the council, including General Mohamed Ainashe, General Salaad Gavere and Major Abdulkadir Dhel, were executed by firing squad on 23 July 1972.

As a warning to the rest of the country, Radio Mogadishu would play the following song whenever people were executed in the police compound:

Same diidow
Dabin baa kuu dhigan
Laguugu dili doonee
Daneestow duulkaagu
Waa daldalaad
Aan dacwo lahayn

Those [of you] who
Reject
The goodwill [of the Revolution]
A trap awaits you;
You will be executed
Opportunists like you
Face death by hanging
Without appeal[32]

The song was also played on loudspeakers installed on vans that drove around the city.

In 1974, Emperor Haile Selassie of neighbouring Ethiopia was overthrown in a military coup. Barre sensed an opportunity to claim the Ogaden region in Ethiopia, which many Somalis see as a rightful part of the so-called Greater Somalia. Though Ethiopia had a larger army (44,500 to Somalia's 23,000), Barre believed he had an advantage because of how well the Soviets had equipped the Somali army.[33]

But Barre overestimated Somalia's importance to the Soviet Union. By 1976, Ethiopia had deepened its own relationship with the Soviet Union, and took on a stronger anti-American stance. In December, Colonel Mengistu travelled to Moscow where he agreed a £385 million arms deal with the Soviets.

For themselves, the Soviets hoped that Ethiopia and Somalia would move past their past enmity and form new relationships based on their common Marxist ideology. They were wrong.

In 1977, the Soviets organised a regional summit between Somalia, Ethiopia and Soviet ally the People's Democratic Republic of Yemen (PDRY). The Soviets had hoped the meeting, which took place in Aden, would inspire solidarity and fraternity between the different countries and consolidate a strategic partnership in the region. The meeting was attended by senior figures of those countries, as well as by Cuban leader Fidel Castro.

The deadlock in these meetings was the Ogaden region. The Somali government rejected the proposal of a federation with Ethiopia until the Ogaden issue was resolved, pressing for the right for self-determination for its people in the region (many of whom wanted to join the Somali republic) – while the Ethiopian government defended the integrity of its national borders.

Castro went to Mogadishu to discuss a peace settlement with Barre, but found him unwilling to listen to counsel. In later years, Castro would reflect on the Barre he knew as 'above all a chauvinist'.[34]

Ultimately, Barre invaded the Ogaden region on 12 July 1977, in the face of Soviet and Cuban disapproval. The Soviets first publicly criticised the Somali military action, then intervened in the conflict, providing Ethiopia with military support. Somalia was furious and expelled Soviet and Cuban advisers from the country. The Soviets responded by upping their arms shipments to Ethiopia.

The tide turned against Somalia in January 1978, after the Soviet Union provided Ethiopia with huge military support and Cuba sent combat troops and other military personnel. In March 1978, the Somali army retreated.[35] Somalia was defeated.

After the disastrous Ogaden war and the collapse of the relationship with the Soviet Union, Barre began courting the support of the United States and was rewarded with American money and military weapons.

'This is when the downfall of Somalia began,' Baba tells me.

Bribery and corruption had become the norm a decade into the so-called socialist revolution, with authorities taking little to no notice. The embezzlement and misuse of public funds had made some young men in politics millionaires, Omar wrote. It was a particularly difficult time for ordinary people, as the country faced crippling food shortages and prices soared.

And while Barre spoke out against tribalism, he was adept at pitting different groups against each other. Omar describes the 'childish act' of the propaganda office commissioning an effigy that was meant to represent tribalism, which would be buried in a ceremony.[36] But of course the gesture was hollow – Barre used tribalism to achieve his own ends constantly.

Omar writes that in the past tribalism in Somalia had actually played a unifying role. Each tribe had its own leaders who worked together to resolve differences, and the collective created a system of mutual assistance. This tribalism had become harmful once it stopped being used as a means to work and communicate with other groups, and people instead used those connections for personal gain.

Politicians used tribalism to get elected during Somalia's democratic period, but Barre's use of tribalism was 'unprecedented' following the Ogaden war.[37] The national army underwent a radical reorganisation. It went from being a professional army to a clan militia, where an army captain from one clan was more powerful than an army general from another. Barre also relied heavily on his wider family, and their promotions collapsed what little morale existed in the army.

My father spoke often of the strength of the Somali army and the outsized role the military played on the continent. I had thought he was exaggerating until I read about it myself. The Soviets had equipped Somali air forces with MIG 15s, 17s and 21s, Ilyushin 28s, Antonov 24s and eight helicopters by 1976.[38]

In 1974, the Organisation of Africa Unity held a heads of state meeting in Mogadishu. When some of the African leaders were shown military exercises, they were stunned to learn that pilots flying the planes in the air manoeuvres were Somalis, Omar wrote. To convince them, Barre took them to the airfields. Upon seeing the pilots were Somali, one visiting president remarked: 'Brother, you could single-handedly liberate South Africa.'

Somalia had supported South Africa in its fight against apartheid, inviting anti-apartheid leaders to the meeting and joining the economic boycott of the apartheid regime. Somalia was sending this kind of support across the continent. Barre's government dispatched military experts, as well as healthcare professionals, to Equatorial Guinea to aid its fight for independence; trained pilots from Burundi; and sent military reinforcements to Mozambique to assist in their fight against Rhodesian and Portuguese forces.

My dad graduated from high school in 1982 and was forced, like every other student, to go to a military training camp as a conscript. 'We were there for three months. Everyone had to do it, both girls and boys. I remember learning to use American guns,' Baba says. Somalia had broken ties with the Soviet Union by then and courted the US for weapons and aid, which the Americans were all too happy to provide.

I ask whether he had fun and he shook his head. 'It was really difficult. It was so hard, I really didn't like it. It was very regimented. Everyone had to go to sleep at the same time, eat at the same time, and do their chores and exercises at the same time. It was very tough.'

He then said he got into 'a dilemma' and after some coaxing he tells us what happened.

'If you made a mistake, you would be punished. I remember one time I did something wrong. On Thursdays, we were allowed to leave and see our families. I returned late and got into big trouble. I was told as punishment that

I had to run sprints around the track in the afternoon. I was forced to do other exercises like push ups. The sun was so hot and I felt so dizzy. I couldn't go on after doing it for an hour and vomited.'

It's terrible, but my mum and I can't help but laugh. He isn't helping his case that he is the more resilient of the pair.

My dad continues, unperturbed. 'I decided I had had enough and jumped over the fence and escaped to my parents' house.' I am crying with laughter at this point in his story. I can see him, young and from a wealthy family, unused to such physical demands on his body and unwilling to bend to such authority.

'I stayed for some time, but I was encouraged to return. My aunt's husband was a military general and he intervened on my behalf and I was able to come back without any problems,' Baba says. After he graduated, he worked as a physics teacher for a few months before he went to India.

As a child, my mum always dreamt of being a writer. She told me this after she saw my published byline. She beamed at me when she said it. 'I wanted to be a journalist. I loved to write things down in my notebook and ask questions,' she explained. 'All I have is my children now. I dream through you guys. Your achievements are my achievements. I am so proud.'

I thought of how similar we were, and yet how different. I thought of another lifetime, a life lived, where she might have been able to continue writing.

As I was wasting another morning scrolling through the internet, I came across Audre Lorde's poem 'A Litany for Survival'.[39] In the poem, Lorde writes of parents seeking new futures for their children, 'so their dreams will not reflect the death of ours'. I thought, again, of my parents' sacrifice; of the realisation of my dreams, and the death of theirs.

At first, the poem left me feeling dejected. But as I kept rereading it, a new meaning emerged from Lorde's poem: a call to arms to push past the discomfort, the fear, which silences voices that exist on the most marginalised planes of society. It was a call, as Lorde wrote in her poem, 'to speak/ remembering /we were never meant to survive'.

I set up follow-up interviews with my parents, but decide to do them separately. While there is something electric whenever they are in a room together – when they are laughing, arguing and teasing each other – I want to push them out of their comfort zones. As a family, we always turned to jokes to cope with difficult memories, but I worry this is preventing them from being vulnerable with me.

I ask my mum if she is ready. I have read about Somali history in books, reports, newspaper archives and research papers since we last spoke. I have taken in and digested the words of historians and writers about the country in the run up to the war. It is time for her to enter the narrative. She says yes, and I turn on my recorder.

My mum was born in 1975 in Somalia. Her mother was Yemeni and her father of Somali and Yemeni heritage. She is one of five sisters, the second youngest, and two brothers, one older and one younger. The household spoke Somali and Arabic fluently.

She was born in the midst of great upheaval for women in the country. On 11 January 1975, the revolutionary government introduced a family law that proved to be controversial. The law, which was announced on the thirtieth anniversary of Hawa Tako's death, required divorces to be settled formally in court, no longer made dowry a requirement for marriage, allowed for equal inheritance for men and women, and put restrictions on the practice of polygyny. It was a huge leap for women's rights in the country, with Barre declaring, 'As from this day Somali men and women are equal.' But it came at a significant cost.

Researcher Iman Abdulkadir Mohamed, from Georgetown University, writes in a 2015 paper that the government's support for women's rights was 'more structurally detrimental to women than liberating' as it tied women's emancipation to an oppressive and rapidly deteriorating regime.[40] She argued that the law appeared to have 'more to do with disempowering traditional religious authority than with advancing women's rights'.

Barre soon got the showdown he wanted. Following Friday prayers at the Mosque of Cabdulqaadir in Mogadishu, Sheikh Axmad Maxamad, a notable religious leader in the city, stood up and criticised the law. He decried it as 'arrogant' and a serious 'transgression of the borders of the Law of Allah that is unacceptable to the Somali Muslims'. Other sheikhs also got up to speak out against the law.

Barre ordered security forces to surround the mosque and cut off the electricity in a bid to silence the sheikhs. The forces swarmed in, arresting hundreds of people. Following a sham trial, ten sheikhs were sentenced to death and twenty-one others to lengthy prison sentences.

Prominent activist Maryan Cilmi was one of many to plead with Barre to pardon the sheikhs, but the president refused. Mohamed argues that activists like Cilmi knew that the death of the sheikhs would forever stain their cause for gender equality.

Omar described the public executions of the sheikhs as a 'sad and sorrowful day for all Somalis'.[41] The sheikhs condemned to death were lined up at the stake, their hands and legs tied, and their eyes blindfolded. They were executed by firing squad, sending shockwaves across the whole country. Opposition groups, operating underground and covertly, seized on growing disapproval to agitate for the government's removal.

The first wave of the country's brain drain followed these executions. My mum's family was one of them.

Her life was marked with grief at a young age. She had lost her own mother when she was just six years old. She can still remember collapsing when she heard the news. My grandfather, who worked at an oil company, took my mum and her sisters to Jeddah, Saudi Arabia, soon after.

My mum describes her childhood and teen years in Jeddah as idyllic. She remembers cooking food with neighbours and being 'incredibly popular' in school. While her older sister Amina excelled, often coming out on top of every exam, my mum and her other sister Sacidiya were relieved whenever they managed to scrape a pass. 'People would say, how is it possible that Amina is your sister and you're like this?'

My mum and Sacidiya were close but could not be more different in looks and personalities. While Sacidiya was tall, light-skinned and timid, my mum was petite, dark-skinned and loud. 'Whenever anyone said anything horrible to her, she would tell me and I'd go and beat them up,' Mama says. 'But Sacidiya would then run away.'

My parents' families knew each other. After he graduated, my dad studied accounting at a small college in Bhuna, India. He was actually late to apply for the college he wanted; he thought of taking a gap year when a friend told him of a better college in Bhuna which would take him in if he played for their football team.

'I went there and I started practising with them. I played in this final game they had. I was the only Black player, the rest all Indian. And when we won, they gave me admission,' Baba says, proudly.

My dad was there in 1984 when Indira Gandhi, the prime minister of India, was assassinated. 'All the shops were closed. We couldn't even find a place to get food.'

'You have a knack for being at the wrong place at the wrong time,' I say, and we both laugh.

While returning to Bhuna for his second year, he stopped in Jeddah, Saudi Arabia. He stayed at my mum's family home. My mum's sister would tease her and make jokes that she fancied my dad. My mum often made him spaghetti. At the time, she dressed like a boy, my Dad told me: she particularly loved Michael Jackson then and tried to copy his hairstyle.

Both their lives remained difficult, however, and chances for them to meet were rare. My mum and Sacidiya's lives were upended again while they were in secondary school. Their father lost his residency and was told he would be deported to Mogadishu. Though my mum had begged to be allowed stay with Amina, who was married by then, and to finish school, she and Sacidiya were forced to go with their father. My mum was devastated to be leaving school and her friends to go to a country she knew very little about.

The trio flew to Mogadishu and spent their first night in my dad's house. They went to watch the annual military parade soon after she arrived. My mum's face lit up and she laughed when my dad told me about the parade. She hadn't thought of that memory in decades.

There were a few videos online of military parades during the 1980s. I watched all that I could find, which gave me a glimpse of the life my parents once had. The comments underneath the videos were always the same: a mixture of joy and sadness.

My parents speak of Siad Barre in the same way. They ache to go back to the time of his reign simply because of what followed: the unravelling of the basic fabric of society, the terrible trauma, the near-permanent state of destruction.

It's no wonder then that they, and many Somalis living in exile, romanticise a past that gave them a sense of value and pride. For them, Barre's rule is the last time they were truly themselves, before they were forced to shed their skins and become refugees.

Mogadishu was a huge culture shock for my mum when she first arrived. When she lived in Saudi Arabia, she had to cover her face and wasn't allowed to speak loudly in public. In Mogadishu, standing next to my dad at the military parade, she saw women in colourful clothes, wearing the bright blue of the Somali flag.

As their families were close, it was easy for my parents to stay in touch in Mogadishu. A romance soon developed between them. When I ask my parents when they got married, I am astonished to learn they had initially eloped. My mum was convinced her father wouldn't let her marry. After the ceremony, my parents returned to their respective homes. 'We never stayed together. I stayed in my house and he stayed in his. He would come over and say hello,' Mama says. My grandad ended up giving his blessing to the match. Once he did, they had a huge wedding.

'It was the social event of the year. We had dancers and a very famous singer at the time. I was so happy and excited when I was getting my henna done. Baba's mum made sure we had everything and that everyone would be very jealous,' Mama says.

'It was the perfect wedding,' she adds. 'Baba's mum even got up and danced. I wish I could show you the video, but we lost it. I don't even know where it would be.'

The celebration was followed by loss. My mother's first child, a boy they called Mohdin, was delivered stillborn. My mum gave birth to the baby in the house, with my dad waiting in a different room.

'When they brought the baby out of the room, he thought he was alive and he asked to hold it. They told him he had died and Baba started to cry. I went into a deep depression when I lost my first child. Baba cried, but he didn't want to show me he was crying. He wanted to make me happy so he would take me out,' Mama says.

My mum went on to have three more miscarriages. 'I remember how scared I always was. I would always run to the toilet to see if there was blood,' Mama says. A doctor diagnosed her with toxoplasmosis. While on a business trip to Italy, my dad bought the medicine she was prescribed. The treatment worked.

Later, when my dad left the room and my mum and I were on our own, I ask her again about their marriage. My mum remembers going to Mecca as a teen and asking God that she marry a man with 'a clean heart'. She didn't care about money or looks, she just wanted someone who would be there for her. 'Your Dad annoys me, yes, but when I need him he never lets me down.'

3
THE GREAT ESCAPE

There aren't many videos documenting the beginning of Somalia's civil war. I realised this as I watched clips of bombed-out and bullet-ridden buildings in Mogadishu one evening. Soon after I first started interviewing my parents, this became a morbid routine that I performed once or twice a month. I would wait until I was home alone and watch and rewatch any clips I could find on YouTube of the Somali civil war. I would pause the grainy images every now and then to focus on an individual man or woman, or even a couple.

I would hold my breath. I couldn't move. There was that pressure in my chest. I wasn't exactly sure what I was looking for. Perhaps I hoped to spot my parents in the archive footage. A younger version of the ones I knew.

When I close my eyes, I see my parents sitting in a living room in a low-rise flat in East London, with its overbearing velvet curtains and plush patterned carpets. I see us watching *American Idol* and having our weekly argument over pizza toppings. I see them fighting over who should be eliminated and making me laugh so hard I almost choke on a pizza crust. I didn't know the life they had lived before I was born. I couldn't picture them in the violence that consumed Somalia.

But they were there.

My parents became newlyweds as things were spiralling out of control in the country. As Mohamed Osman Omar, the former diplomat, wrote in his memoir, 'the struggle for survival had become acute' for ordinary Somalis. The majority of government workers were forced to turn elsewhere for money as their monthly salaries no longer covered the most basic of provisions. The civil service was 'on the verge of collapse', Omar wrote, with work grinding to a halt. There was no stationery and typewriters were put aside because of a lack of paper.

While the people suffered, the wealthy roamed the city in Land Cruisers at a time when water and diesel were scarce commodities. The poem 'Land Cruiser', which became a famous song, best captured the absurdity of the situation, where the ruling elite drove around in luxury cars while begging the international community for aid:[1]

Waa maan
gurracan iyo garasho jaan
laankuruusar gado
soobari Galley

It's absurd
and ghoulish reasoning
to purchase a Land Cruiser
while begging for maize donations

The country's unravelling started in the north, in the region now known as Somaliland. In 1988, the government was accused of violently crushing the Somali National Movement (SNM), an organised guerrilla group formed in opposition to Barre's regime in 1981.

One of cities in the north was Hargeisa, which was seized by the SNM along with a few smaller towns in May 1988. The government responded by sending South African mercenaries to bomb the city into oblivion, according to Omar. One French aid worker, who was evacuated from Hargeisa, told journalists at Nairobi airport that he had seen 150 dead bodies at the hospital he worked at, and over a thousand dead bodies littering the streets. Hargeisa had been so severely pummelled, with 90 per cent of the city destroyed, that it was now being referred to as 'the Dresden of Africa'.

Refugees from the north, many of them women and children, soon filtered into Mogadishu. It was then that my dad heard of the atrocities that were occurring. I asked my dad if he was scared, if he saw the war coming. He told me he expected Barre to remain in power. He couldn't imagine a Somalia where he wasn't.

More refugees fled to Mogadishu. A popular joke at the time hinted at what was to come. Barre was getting his haircut when his barber asked him a question:

Barber: What's all the excitement in the countryside?
Barre: It's just the regional games. What else did you think?
Barber: Oh, very interesting. Then aren't the finals going to be in the capital?[2]

The violence did indeed eventually arrive in Mogadishu. *Africa Watch* reported that in July 1989 government soldiers arrested hundreds of people from a southern suburb in Mogadishu. The soldiers took around 45 men to Jasiira beach, which is west of Mogadishu, and executed them.[3]

Leading politicians, including Somalia's first president, Aden Abdulle Osman, along with businessmen, religious leaders and intellectuals, decided to respond to the spiralling situation. They published what would be known as the Mogadishu Manifesto on 15 May 1990. It called for Barre to step down, for the country to hold free elections, and for the restoration of human and civil rights.

The manifesto eviscerated Barre's legacy. It condemned the indiscriminate killing of civilians, including women and children, the destruction of public facilities such as wells and schools, the lack of respect for law and human rights, widespread corruption and the economic disaster brought about by his regime. It demanded a caretaker government to pave the way for a political settlement.

The manifesto asked daring questions: 'After all, once European colonialism has left for good, is there any Somali who has any right to rule, colonise, or worse still enslave other Somalis by force?'[4]

Omar was in Mogadishu when the manifesto was published. He had returned on a brief break from his posting in India. He pointed out the symbolic significance of how the manifesto was presented: it was signed by 114 people on 15 May 1990. It proposed a transitional government made up of thirteen individuals.

'There are 114 suras in the Koran; 15 May was the foundation date of the Somali Youth Club which later became the Somali Youth League – the main party of the independence movement; there were thirteen founding members of the SYC,' he wrote.[5]

In July 1990, Barre appeared on TV to address the nation on Eid al-Adha. The country waited to see how he would respond to the open letter. Omar noted that the government generally used such occasions, such as Independence Day or Eid, to announce amnesties for political prisoners. There was a general expectation that Barre would announce some form of reprieve for the signatories.

He didn't. He instead called for the arrest of the men who signed the letter. A trial was ordered, with the signatories facing the death penalty. All were ultimately acquitted and released – but the police reportedly shot and killed people who were protesting outside the court during their trial.

Six months after the manifesto was published, war came to Mogadishu, and to my parents. On Sunday 30 December 1990, the opposition forces launched a major assault on the capital. Barre attempted to defend himself and his rule, with little success.

Routes out of the country were dwindling: citizens were leaving the city either in cars or on ships because the airport was no longer operating. When the fighting got uncomfortably close to their home in Hodan, my family discussed leaving. My mum was the fiercest advocate for leaving the country, but most of the family wanted to stay. They decided on a compromise and agreed to temporarily leave the city and stay with my mum's brother in the nearby town of Merca.

I am sitting beside my dad when I look up the distance between Mogadishu and Merca on Google Maps. 'Yes, it was around 90 kilometres,' Baba says to me. It would now take two hours by car. They had taken a bus. They don't have many memories of the journey. When I prod, Mama rolls her eyes and exclaims: 'It was thirty years ago, Coco!'

They waited in Merca as the fighting intensified in Mogadishu. Many of Barre's former allies abandoned him at the end. On the evening of 27 January 1991, Barre finally fled – hidden in a military tank. My dad, still in Merca, was shocked. He heard about Barre's departure on a news bulletin on the radio on BBC Somalia. The whole family sat around the radio. There was a moment of silence, before conversation and questions exploded.

'Let me give you an example of how much I didn't see this coming,' Baba says. 'I went on a business trip to Italy in September 1990.' He wouldn't have gone on such a trip if he thought the country was on the brink of war. While on the trip, he had heard of rumours of people mobilising against Barre, but didn't believe it would amount to anything. 'No one believed at the time that he would be defeated. We thought he was too powerful,' he explains.

He returned from his trip two months later in November 1990. 'Had I known what was to come, I would have stayed and got your mum and my family on the next plane out of the country,' he tells me. I wonder how often he thought about that moment and how different our lives would have been if we had left on one of the last planes out of the country. How heavily do these 'what ifs' weigh on him? I didn't ask him at that moment. It felt too cruel.

The family had another discussion of what to do next after Barre was deposed. 'We waited. We thought when Siad Barre left, things would go back to normal,' Baba says.

They agreed to return to Mogadishu. 'Initially we were happy because we thought we would get something much better than Barre, but we ended up with something a hundred times worse,' Baba says.

In Mogadishu, there was a sense of relief and joy. My parents thought the worst was over once Barre left the city. The United Somali Congress (USC) formed an interim government. The group promised free and fair elections. The port was reopened and essential workers in electricity, water and health were urged to return to work. The Italian government said its ambassador would be returning to Mogadishu to resume work.[6]

The country had to rebuild a functioning and stable political structure after two decades of a brutal dictatorship. But it was in desperate need of the most basic supplies: water, food, fuel and medication.

In May 1991, the north declared itself the independent republic of Somaliland. The Somali National Movement's red, white and green flag fluttered from the roof of government buildings. Unlike in the south, stability was quickly restored in Somaliland. The government began the work of disarming civilians and started reconstructing Hargeisa and the other cities destroyed by Barre's regime.

In the rest of Somalia, a mass of refugees were fleeing to Kenya. In May, there were at least 100,000 refugees crossing the land border of Somalia and Kenya; others were boarding boats leaving from Kismayo.[7]

My parents went the other way, returning to their home in Mogadishu, but were divided on what they should do next.

We begin eating lunch. I move my notebook to the side away from the food so it doesn't get dirty. My mum is particularly excited to serve her new recipe of chapitas. 'Taste it, I watched a woman show me how to do it on YouTube. It is how the Moroccans make it.'

My dad and I bite into it and tell her it's tasty. I turn to my dad, with his mouth stuffed with food, and ask how he was feeling at the time.

He swallows. 'We lived on hope during that time. Always we hoped. We loved our country, we had everything we wanted and our living standards were good. We didn't want to leave and become refugees elsewhere. So we lived on hope,' Baba says.

My mum remembers things differently. She had wanted to leave Somalia for close to a year at that point. The country was largely alien to her, as she had grown up in the Middle East. She struggled with cultural differences and wanted to start anew elsewhere.

'Mentally, I was not okay. I felt like an outsider. Even the Somali I spoke was slightly different to the one that your dad's family spoke. I felt like I was always one step behind and playing catch up,' she tells me. The political crisis and the outbreak of fighting had only deepened her desire to leave, but my dad was always able to convince her to stay.

I see that Africa Watch was the leading human rights organisation responding to and analysing the crisis at the time. The executive director of this fledgling new organisation was a Somali woman – Rakiya Omaar.

From December 1990,[8] Omaar wrote a series of dispatches for the *Guardian* on the rapidly deteriorating situation in Mogadishu. Nearly everything she warned would come to pass did. I reached out to her and we spoke in 2020 over a video call. She is in her home in Nairobi; I am in London. I find her to be warm and generous with her knowledge.

Much of her early writing feels painfully prophetic. Rakiya warned that it would be dangerous to depose Barre without a concrete political project to fill the power vacuum he would leave behind.

'There was so much unanimity, for the most part, and so much desire and consensus that nothing could be discussed or decided until Siad Barre had left. I think people, movements, and politicians just papered over any other potential source of dissension or conflict or competition,' Rakiya told me on our call.

She added that while people were worried by what would follow him, 'I don't think anyone expected the massive, prolonged, endless and hideously dangerous power vacuum that came.' My dad nods in agreement as I recount this.

'I don't really understand the power struggle that followed, can you explain it, Baba?' I ask.

While eating, Baba says: 'So Ali Mahdi [a prominent businessman and politician] declared himself the temporary leader after Barre, but they didn't talk to anyone about that decision.'

'So it just happened?'

'Yes! And then the problem started when Mohamed Farrah Aidid, or General Aidid [a notable army general and diplomat], wanted power.'

The USC had hastily declared Ali Mahdi interim president. A report by Africa Watch noted that General Aidid, a major figure in the Somali army, objected to this and a rupture within the USC was formed. A reconciliation conference in Djibouti in June and July 1991 brought Ali Mahdi and General Aidid physically together in the same place along with other political groups, but there was no breakthrough in a peace settlement.[9] The mediations had failed.

'My father told me, if these two men start fighting and they refuse to compromise, there will be no peace in this country.' My grandad had been right.

Both men were claiming the title of interim president of Somalia. Baba's voice is still laced with frustration and anger when he speaks of them.

'Ali Mahdi used to be a businessman and Aidid's a military general,' he goes on. 'Both had different agendas, different people in their camps, and though they come from the Hawiye clan, they represented different subclans. They both lacked structure among their command chain.'

'When you try to lead an opposition, you need to have someone that's president, someone that's vice president, someone that's secretary and so on. There needs to be a general order. You need a mix of people with civil service knowledge and people from the military. And the soldiers must be well trained! Neither man had any of this,' Baba says.

A report from Africa Watch describes General Aidid's forces launching an all-out attack on President Mahdi's positions on 17 November 1991. The attack was partially successful, with Aidid's forces taking serious ground in the city, but he had failed to remove Mahdi's forces from their strongholds in the north of the city. The fighting continued unabated. Africa Watch described it as 'continuous but inconclusive.'[10]

Everyone had been so focused on removing Barre, 'but none of them had a plan for what happened after. We can never forgive these two men.'

Baba finishes his food, gets up, and takes both his and my mum's plates. I offer to wash the dishes. He sits back down and continues.

'Barre also caused big problems. The opposition asked him to leave peacefully. He was promised amnesty and allowed to leave the country if he wanted. In that scenario, the military would have remained intact. If that had happened and there was just a political change, then we would never have had the problem we did. But Barre refused,' Baba said.

When I ask my dad to describe the battle in the winter of 1991, he just shakes his head. 'There are no words, Coco, it was terrible, so terrible.' He says this as I finish washing the dishes. I look out to their garden and remember how often I would lie there as a teenager, reading my books, totally ignorant of the past.

I sit back with my parents and tell them that is enough for the day. But my mum adds that during that terrible, uncertain time, she was unbelievably happy. 'You were about to come into my life.'

In the autumn of 1991, my parents were living in a six-bedroom house in the Hodon neighbourhood of Mogadishu with my dad's parents, brothers and sisters. The war was in full swing. They rarely left the house: when they did, it was to get essentials and check on nearby family members. This was done by the women in the family, as men who left their homes were often captured by militants and forced to fight. Africa Watch wrote that nearly every street corner in Mogadishu was held 'hostage' to different groups of heavily armed young men and boys.

I return to my parents for another interview. We have developed an enjoyable routine: I come for lunch, we eat and talk, and I leave knowing them slightly better.

By then, it was impossible to leave the country by plane. Those who wanted to escape had to take their chances on the road or on boats. 'There was a big risk with both. A lot of people died on the road, and a lot of people died on the boats,' Baba says.

Once the truce collapsed, the battle was brutal. Human Rights Watch reported the use of field artillery, anti-aircraft guns, heavy machine guns, mortars, AK-47s and air-to-air missiles mounted on jeeps in the streets of Mogadishu. Many of these weapons were fired by teenagers who had been forced into the war. They became known for their wholly indiscriminate targeting.[11]

Civil authority had collapsed. There were no jobs and food was scarce. Desperate looters would maraud around the street, robbing and killing people that crossed their path.

According to Africa Watch and Physicians for Human Rights, an estimated 14,000 people were thought to have been killed and 27,000 injured in Mogadishu between November 1991 and the end of February 1992.

Mogadishu was divided between the north and south by General Aidid and Ali Mahdi. In General Aidid's area, in the south of the city where my parents were staying, there were four hospitals, staffed by Somali doctors and nurses who worked long hours under extreme circumstances with no pay.

In the northern part of the city, controlled by Mahdi, the lack of medical facilities forced a group of Somali doctors to form the Health Emergency Committee. They used a seafront villa to operate on patients and requisitioned nearby houses to use as post-operative wards. This became known as the Karaan Hospital, and for several months it was the only medical facility available. This changed when international humanitarian organisations began opening emergency hospitals.

I read this startling description of Mogadishu from Africa Watch to my dad: 'Mogadishu has become a place of unpredictable death, with no one in authority and no one capable of enforcing a social commitment to order. Everyone appears armed. Whoever draws first carries the day, since there is no civil authority to punish someone who robs or kills.'

'Would you say that was true?' I ask him.

My dad nods. 'It was chaos,' he says.

My parents learnt to ignore the sound of shelling and bullets as they told stories to pass the time. A tense new normality had settled in. 'There were a lot of problems, but we were happy. We were about to start a family and had big meals together,' Mama says.

My mother was the first to lose hope that things would return to normal. 'I remember walking to my dad's aunt's house when a bomb exploded – boom!' Mama says. 'I was on the floor. I was in shock, I thought I had died.'

She was uninjured but could barely move. The dust had slapped her across the face and her body ached.

'Baba's brother found me and shouted and ran over. He helped me and I looked at him with my eyes open,' she tells me, widening her eyes to show me. She laughs and I laugh too. 'I looked like a crazy person, like I was possessed.'

Their resources were dwindling and they needed money. My grandfather was ill, having suffered a terrible heart attack that had put him into a coma. Though he regained consciousness, he was not strong enough to travel.

'I didn't want to leave my mother and father,' Baba says. There is a soft pain in his voice. I stop the interview there.

I re-listen to the interview days later. It is markedly different to the rest of the conversations we've had so far, which were all peppered with laughter. I call my mum and tell her I feel a deep sadness and something else I can't put to words. I'm not sure I'm making much sense, but she tells me she understands. 'He had to leave a lot behind.'

I text my dad 'I love you', without any explanation. He texts back, 'I love you too.'

I read in the *Guardian* archives that Save the Children was one of a handful of charities still operating in Mogadishu in the early nineties.[12] Many left because they could no longer guarantee the safety of their staff. The early reporting often quoted Hussein Mursal, a Somali doctor who worked for Save the Children in Mogadishu during the most intense period of the war. He now lives in London: I reached out to him and he agreed to be interviewed.

Hussein was, like my father, part of the generation of Somalis raised during Barre's golden years. He got a scholarship to study all the way through to university and then did a Masters in international public health in Leeds in 1989. Soon after graduating, he accepted a job at Save the Children's Sierra Leone office.

Though Hussein was trained to work in a hostile environment, he was shocked as he watched the total collapse of civil society in his home country. He remembers the exact moment he realised the country had reached a point of no return. He was on an unusually empty Somali airlines flight from Rome in the winter of 1989, heading to Mogadishu for his Christmas break. When he landed, he met a government minister who looked at him in shock: 'Why are you coming back?'

When Hussein saw the scale of the growing humanitarian crisis in Somalia, he immediately quit his post in Sierra Leone. He wanted to be working in Somalia full time. 'It was madness. Nobody could walk, you know? But the world wasn't paying attention,' he tells me.

Hussein was given a contract by Save the Children to run their operation across the whole of Somalia. He had three large programmes, with an office in Hargeisa and two in Mogadishu. He assembled around twenty international staff members across the country, providing them with a huge group of armed men for protection. In the countryside, he was responsible for setting up some of the very first health clinics.

The key to his operation was winning acceptance from the local community, Hussein said. He resisted the temptation to lock himself and staff up in a building away from people or immediately leave at the first sign of danger. He believed the programme had to find a way to live within the violence.

'I was telling them people have to accept the risk,' he said. 'The day the community does not accept us, then we leave. Whether we have armed protection, it doesn't matter.'

Still, Hussein admits he often felt scared. His driver was shot and killed, one of many losses around him at the time He didn't realise how much the trauma had intertwined itself with every fibre of his being until he was re-stationed to Nepal in 1994. He was attacked by vicious nightmares.

'How could I have exposed myself to that?' he asks.

Many international aid organisations had pulled out in 1991, evacuating their staff, and refused to return. But Hussein was steadfast and remained. I asked Hussein why and he replied: 'I needed to be useful.'

By the spring of 1991, the children in Mogadishu were severely malnourished, and famine was looming over the city. Hussein used one of Save the Children's offices as a base for journalists keen to report on the unfolding crisis. He told the press that some of the children at the clinic had one or two weeks to live if food didn't arrive quickly. But the international community did not respond to Hussein's warning that a catastrophe was imminent. The aid that did manage to trickle in was inadequate.

The reluctance of the UN and other aid agencies to return and establish centres to provide food and aid was met with bewilderment by some, and with anger by many more. By then, Somalia was short of almost everything – except guns. Hussein remembers the 'miraculous' delivery of a pregnant woman who had been shot. The bullet, which had punctured the placenta, was pulled out from the baby's spine. The mother and baby had survived. She named the baby Xabad, meaning bullet.

The fighting intensified in Hodon and my entire family were forced to flee to a house in Hamar Weyne, the oldest district in Mogadishu, where the Italian architecture is particularly beautiful. I search for it on Google Maps and see it was beside the sea. I wonder if my parents could smell the ocean air from their window.

I decide to interview my parents separately to understand how they came to the decision to leave. I speak with my mum first.

'Your dad's father, Allah yerhamo [may Allah have mercy on him], always supported me. I told him I can't go on living in Somalia, especially now that I am pregnant. I told him I was scared something would happen to my child and that we would die there. You dad didn't want to leave his father and wanted to stay with him,' Mama says. 'But your grandad understood. He always understood.'

One evening, my grandad told my dad he wanted to speak to him alone. My dad knew what was coming. 'He ordered me to take mama and leave. He said she is very scared and she can't have her child here. It's not good for the baby,' Baba says when I interview him. 'He told me to focus on my wife and child. He said don't worry about me, and that inshallah [God willing] he would be fine. He told me to protect his grandchild.'

My dad wanted to say no. He wanted to say he would stay and that the fighting would ease soon, but they both knew the war would only get worse. The hopelessness that my mum first felt had infected the rest of the house. My dad went to his bedroom and told my mum that they would leave in the next few days. My mum was relieved, but the moment was bittersweet. They didn't say much to each other that night.

'Your mum and I were the first in my family to leave,' Baba tells me.

My mum couldn't see her sister, Sacidiya, because she lived in a neighbourhood run by different militants. She couldn't tell her that she would be leaving the country. My mum prayed that she would find a way out and for them to be with each other again.

My parents packed light and left the rest of their belongings behind. They were travelling with my dad's two aunts and their children as well. The goodbyes were brief, but weighed down with a longing that no one dared to address. They instead spoke of returns and reunions that would not take place.

They left behind their family and their friends. They left behind the shop my dad worked at and the restaurants my mum loved to eat in. My dad left behind the school where he discovered his love of maths, the mosque he prayed at, the beach he played football on.

Some things, like their easy laughs at a dinner table, would return. Much more would not.

My parents were nervous when they got onto the beaten-down truck that would take them out of Mogadishu. They struggle to describe how it looked to me, three decades later, so I show them the different images that came up from my Google image search. They both shout 'Yes!' when I find a picture of a truck that looks exactly like the one they got on. They lean over my laptop to focus on the picture as I stand in between them.

My father estimates that along with his group, there were more than twenty people on the truck, but he can't be sure. Among the passengers were armed men hired to escort and protect those fleeing.

The road ahead would be extremely dangerous. Different armed militants controlled different areas. Someone's clan meant they could pass through one without much trouble, but would be killed in another. So passengers would pay one group of militants from one clan to be allowed to pass through one area, and a separate group to safely pass through another.

When I get home after my interview with my parents, I try again to imagine them in Mogadishu. I can't see them in the destruction, but somehow I can see them on that truck.

As the truck moves, I see my parents looking out of the window at Mogadishu, their city, their home. The once gleaming buildings are pockmarked with bullet holes. The city's beauty is dimmed, but it hasn't disappeared. When the truck is out of the city, I can see my dad turning back to look again. My mum looks straight ahead.

There are 484 kilometres between Mogadishu and Kismayo. Google Maps tells me a journey by car between the two cities, along the coast, would take nine hours and thirty-five minutes. How long did it take in the middle of a war? My parents can't remember exactly. It could have been four or five days.

My mum recalls feeling cramped on the truck. She didn't look much at my dad, who radiated anxiety and something else. A loneliness she wasn't ready to confront yet.

On the journey to Kismayo, the truck was brought to a halt in a village called Bulo Marer, 124 kilometres out of Mogadishu.

'This is where your book will get very interesting,' Baba suddenly declares. When they arrived in the village, my dad got out of the truck and noticed an armed man watching them.

They would spend the night in the village, sleeping out in the open on the dirt floor, beside the road. I ask, perhaps stupidly, if this was the first time my dad had slept on the floor in his life. It was. He adds they were scared to sleep away from the road for fear of being attacked by animals. He remembers it being hot.

'That must have been very hard,' I say, looking down at my notebook. Baba nods and says: 'Yes, very hard.' He looks too lost in thought to say much else. His sudden excitement about telling me this story dims slightly.

When I listen back to the transcript, I see neither of us say anything for close to ten seconds. 'Bismillahi,' I say, desperate to fill the silence.

I ask again what he remembered feeling that night. He says that if he showed me a picture of the house they lived in Mogadishu, I'd see how standard it was, likening it to houses in London. They had left all that behind. 'We were normal people,' Baba says. That too had been left behind.

When they woke up, they looked for something to eat, but my father can't remember if they found anything. Baba went on. 'Then around 10 a.m., I saw a group of armed boys and men from an opposing tribe come to where they were sitting. They were offering to sell their goats to the passengers. People would normally have sold a goat for $25 to $30, but the men tried to sell it for $1.'

'Why was he selling it for so cheap?' I ask.

'I think they killed the farmer who once owned the animal,' Baba says.

My dad can't remember how long they stayed in Bulo Marer. It could have been one day or two, maybe three. The truck was full of helpless men, women and children. When it was time to board the truck again, the armed men refused to let my dad go. He was asked what clan he belonged to.

My mum was sitting at the front of the truck, beside the driver. She looked on as the men peeled my dad away from the rest of the group. She was frozen to the spot. I asked her what she did. 'What was I meant to do?' she exclaims. 'This isn't a movie, this is reality.'

The men put my dad up against a wall. 'I couldn't talk,' my mum says in English before switching to Arabic. 'It's like when you're overcome...' She then goes back to English: 'You're crying without making noise.' She still can't express the extent of her terror in just one language.

My dad walked away from the truck with the men, knowing they planned to kill him. He remembers talking, waffling desperately, but can't be sure what he said. He does, however, remember not feeling scared. To this day, he doesn't understand why he wasn't.

Two older boys, who were travelling with my parents and extended family members, insisted my dad was not part of any warring clan. They began fighting the armed men, despite having no guns themselves. It was a desperate bid to protect my father.

The driver who was also protecting the convoy suddenly appeared as well, and asked what was going on. 'He was armed like Rambo,' Baba tells me. There was a tense standoff, with all the men shouting at each other. The driver said that if my father was killed, then he would kill them all. The men let my father go and he walked back into the truck, dazed and in shock.

'It was the luckiest day of my life,' Baba tells me with a smile.

Later, my mum tells me, 'I was too strong in that place, honestly.' I wait for her to laugh or make a joke, but she doesn't. I don't know what to say. I think about reaching for her, but she gets up and starts cooking before I move my hand.

I ask my dad why people were so willing to kill each other, and he lays the blame on tribalism. People from one clan would kill people from another indiscriminately, and then that clan would retaliate and do the same. People were no longer seen as innocent individuals.

'The fighters on all sides didn't care about civilians, they didn't care about the children,' he says.

There was another long pause.

'Did you eat the goat?' I ask.

Things didn't get much better once they arrived in Kismayo. My parents stayed with relatives of my father's. The city was heaving with the dispossessed. My parents tried to get used to their new temporary home. They had dinners together in the living room and plotted where they would go next.

My parents had fled the violence in Mogadishu only for their next destination to become a war zone itself: they now found themselves in the middle of a crucial devastating battle in the civil war. General Aidid had patched together a force to fight Somali Patriotic Movement (SNM), another faction in the war, in the city. He eventually won and captured the southern port of Kismayo.

My parents had been in Kismayo for a few days. My mum was in the kitchen eating breakfast when a bomb exploded. The windows shattered and she was submerged in dust. The room quickly filled with smoke. 'We couldn't breathe,' Mama tells me. She heard more shelling and was scared by how close they were.

She heard screams to run. My mum went to her room and took her family's gold jewellery with her. She was barefoot, having forgotten to get her slippers when she ran out of the house. She was with my father's aunties and their children. A member of the extended family, in a car, saw my mum walking on the street and stopped, took her shoes off her feet and gave them to my mum. 'I'll never forget how she helped me,' Mama says.

It wasn't limited to where they were staying: fighting had broken out throughout the city. They walked aimlessly for a while. My mum was so thirsty she was forced to drink water that had petrol in it. Bombs kept going off behind them. They refused to turn back. She laughs as she tells me this. A group of boys had tried to rob them. My mum told them she was pregnant, and asked if they wanted her to open her stomach to prove it to them. They left her alone, and she breathed a sigh of relief that they hadn't got close enough to find the gold she was carrying.

'Alhamdulillah, I didn't have any bad thing [happen],' Mama says. She means that she wasn't sexually assaulted. But that she could say this, while telling me of her escape – starving, dehydrated and running away while being shelled – speaks to how dire the situation was.

They were then stopped by a vehicle which had five or six men sitting inside. One, whom my dad describes as a fighter, recognised my mum and the others in her group. He leapt out of the car to help them. He put himself at great risk, as he was an obvious target of attack because of his clan.

They all got taken in by a family friend and my mum couldn't stop crying. 'I thought Baba had died,' Mama says.

Where had my dad been? He was praying at the local mosque when the fighting began. It was a Friday and even in the middle of a war, he didn't want to miss jummah prayers. He was walking back to the house when he was shot at by armed men who were already outside the house. The armed men chased my dad. He ran with his family that had gone to pray with him. He was told to go with them, as people would assume he was from the warring tribe. He ran away, unsure what had happened to my mum.

'You left mum behind?' I ask.

'I was being shot at, Coco! It was the end of the world,' Baba says. I laugh and apologise. I didn't mean to suggest he was doing the wrong thing.

He reached the nearby town Goobweyn on foot. Google Maps said this journey would take close to three hours. I tell my parents that and we all laugh. When my dad got there, he didn't know what to do or where to go. He saw a mosque and went in. He sat and prayed; he can't remember how long he was there.

A man approached him and asked if he needed help. When my dad told him what had happened, the man took him in and let him stay at his home. 'I'll never forget his kindness,' Baba says. I notice he echoes word for word what my mum says about the people who helped her.

My dad has tried to find the man since then, but has never been able to, even though he can remember his face clearly almost three decades later. The man let my father sleep in his bed. It was surrounded by a mosquito tent. He fed my father and told him he would help in whatever way possible.

The next morning, after morning prayers, there were soldiers with a microphone blaring out a message that they would not kill civilians. Their fight, they said, was with armed militants. 'They said civilians, from whatever tribe, were welcome to return to Kismayo and would not be harmed now that they had captured the city,' Baba says.

My father decided to go with the soldiers back to the city. He was scared and didn't talk to anyone, but he was brought back to the city safely. He can't remember exactly how he tracked down where his family were staying, but he did.

My parents reunited. My mum looked at my dad like he was an apparition. They decided they wanted to immediately leave the city. Some of his family were going to travel to the camp in Kenya by car, but my father refused, insisting that the boat would be safer for him and my mum. 'I would rather take my chances in the sea with sharks,' Baba reasons, 'than risk being dragged out of a vehicle and shot.'

In the present, the three of us laugh hysterically. There are tears in my eyes. We're laughing at how close they came to losing each other, laughing at their stupid dumb luck, laughing because we still can.

The boat journey to Kenya was still dangerous. Most were small fishing boats cramped with dozens of people. They risked drowning before ever reaching the Kenyan coast, or being stranded at sea for weeks.

I return to Google Maps again to see how far my parents were from the Kenyan border. It was around 200 kilometres overland. This would take around three and a half hours in a car today. I looked at the ocean on the map and zoomed in. The expanse of blue forces me to close the tab and take a deep breath.

There was very little room to move on the boat my parents boarded. I ask my parents how big the boat was and they just say it was 'small'. I show them pictures of boats refugees have recently used to find sanctuary. The first picture, a large fishing boat with no cover, was close, but too big. There were more than fifty people on board in the photo. There isn't space for anyone to move. 'But it was like that, we sat like that,' my mum says. I show another picture and it's again too big. It's the fourth picture of a small Somali

THE GREAT ESCAPE

fishing boat, with a motor engine at the back, that is the best representation. It is about eight metres long and there are no covers. 'It looked just like that,' Mama says.

My mum can still remember the smell of fish. She was starving and thirsty. She sat beside some boys who tried to show her how to cook the catch. They cooked what they had on the boat. 'It was delicious.' She remembers feeling quite happy and entertained as the boat headed towards Kenya. 'I was taken care of by the others on the boat. They treated me like family.'

My dad, on the other hand, couldn't stop vomiting. 'Baba had fainted,' Mama says and laughs hard. He couldn't bring himself to eat anything. I feel his pain. My dad and I both get really bad travel sickness, particularly on long car journeys.

At the beginning of the journey, the boat had nearly capsized. They stopped somewhere one night to refuel and allow passengers to rest on the shore and gather more essentials.

When day broke, my mum woke up and started walking back towards the boat with the women. She saw the group of men walk towards the boat as she sat down in her spot, but couldn't spot my dad. She tried to ignore the sense of panic that started to grip her as the boys and men started boarding the boat. She asked the boys who were sitting beside her where her husband was and they shrugged. Someone answered, probably still sleeping. She began crying and begged them to not leave her husband.

The boys tried to calm her down and offered to go back for him. There were grumbles in the group, but before the boys got off the boat, they saw a man running towards them, shouting at them to wait. My dad got on the boat, looking dishevelled, and sat beside her.

'Can you imagine?' Mama says to me, outraged. My dad looks sheepish beside her.

The passengers talked about their lives. There were plenty of differences. But as the boat rocked its way down the coast and towards Kenya, they became bound by one commonality: they were shedding who they once were. They were becoming refugees.

The vast majority of the press today, including the BBC, refers to people fleeing similar violence as migrants.

In November 2021, around the time I am interviewing my parents about their time on the boat, a record number of people – twenty-seven, including pregnant women and children[13] – died after a dinghy capsized off the coast of Calais. A note went round to the editorial staff at the *Guardian*, reminding us to avoid using the term 'migrants' or 'migration crisis' and use the word 'refugees', or better yet, 'people'.

During my career as a journalist, I have written many stories about migrants and refugees dying at sea, always with the best intentions. But had I ever unconsciously stripped people of their humanity? I go back to the newspaper archives and read those pieces as my TV blares the news of the 'migrant Channel tragedy'.

I open another window on my desktop: a UN report from August 1992, which reports the deaths of half of 600 Somalis crowded into a medium-sized freighter as it docked into the port of Mombasa.

The journalist in me knows that I have to try and distance myself from the Calais tragedy, to report objectively, but I can't feel neutral. I feel overwhelmed, like the past and the present are happening all at once.

I'm in bed when I read in an update that one of the two survivors of the Calais boat is Somali. I stay in bed for the rest of the evening and feel a tightening in my chest, a weird separation of myself, like I'm not really here. At times, I find myself slightly scared that I won't be able to take my next breath and feel surprise when I do.

I read that a twenty-four-year-old Kurdish woman is the first victim of the Channel tragedy to be identified. Her name is Maryam Nuri Mohamed Amin. I share a picture of her smiling on Twitter. Details of the group's ordeal slowly emerges throughout the week.

Mohammed Shekha, one of two survivors, said their desperate calls to both British and French authorities were ignored. The boat lost most of its air and the currents pushed it back towards the French coast. The passengers held onto each other for hours, hoping that help would come. When they couldn't hold on anymore, people started letting go and went under water.

The end of the 1992 AP story reports that nearly 200 Somali refugees trying to reach Kenya drowned when their wooden sailing ships crashed on reefs.[14] It doesn't say when. Since 2014, around 27,845 people have died or gone missing while crossing the Mediterranean Sea.[15]

I look at the similarities between the refugee crisis I was born into and the one I report on several decades later. Their fear and desperation is the same. Their deaths are the same. The response from the neighbouring countries, the indifference and hostility – that too has remained the same.

Hundreds of thousands of Somali refugees reached Kenya in 1992. The vast majority of this exodus of people were children and women, travelling on foot or by boat. They arrived sick and starving. Many congregated in the makeshift camps set up near the coast or the border cities of Liboi, Ifo, Hagadera, Dagahaley, Wajir, Mandera and Marsabit.

My parents landed on a beach near the village of Ngomeni. Their small boat had slowly been filling with water and they were relieved when they saw the coast. As they neared it, they could see Kenyan police or border guards (they're not sure which), holding their guns and shouting. They guess it was the police. My parents couldn't hear them.

They waded through the water to get to shore. My mum doesn't remember if the water was cold or warm.

My parents didn't understand what was being said to them on that beach. Someone was able to translate that the Kenyan police were allowing the women and children to come on shore. My mum was helped onto the sandy beach. It was the first time she was in a country where she didn't understand the main language.

The police then allowed the men to come on shore as well. An argument broke out between the police and those who could speak Swahili; when my dad asked what was going on, he was told the police were trying to take them to a camp. The group of Somali refugees feared they would be killed there and refused to move. They moved further into the town and waited. A group of locals came to offer help, bringing food and water.

'The small town was overwhelmingly Muslim,' Baba says, 'and wanted to help their Muslim brothers.'

There was a fight for food and water. My mum sat on the ground and was unable to move. She was exhausted and felt sick. My dad looked at the people hitting each other for bread and, despite being starving and desperate for water, couldn't bring himself to join the fray. 'He looked at me broken,' Mama later tells me when we are alone together.

One of the boys who had kept her entertained with jokes on the boat demanded food and water be given to Mama. She was moved by their kindness, but also felt small and embarrassed. The people around her were also hungry. She whispered her thanks when food and water was eventually given to her. So did my dad.

They were taken to a makeshift camp, but don't remember the name. I look into whether there were any articles written about Somali refugees in Ngomeni, but can't find any. I instead came across an interview for an oral history project led by Haden Griggs, a Master's student on a graduate programme at Utah State University. The project's purpose was to help high-school students better understand the experiences of Somali men who came to Utah as refugees.

Aydrus Mohammed, who took the same route as my parents from Kismayo when he fled with his family aged three years old, said in the interview:

> It's Kenya's island, so, cause we're traveling by boat, we landed in Ngomeni, and most of the people in Ngomeni, majority, like 100%, they're Muslims, and we were Muslims, so they help us. That's when, like, a Muslim brother, and a Muslim brother, you know. So, they help us, they gave us like a little bit of food, and the Kenya police, they came in and they took us to like, we call it *rumande*, like a jail, but it's just, you stay there, but you're not being – like, your case is being processed.[16]

I wonder if Ayrdus Mohammed had been on the same boat as my parents. I wonder how many boats full of desperate Somali refugees had landed in 1991 and 1992.

Aid workers eventually came to the makeshift camp, which had already begun to swell with other refugees. The scenes before them and across the country in other camps were devastating. Children were dying daily.

The Kenyan government began to bus refugees off to other camps. There were fears about the conditions of these camps, and what was being done to Somalis there. My dad didn't know what to believe, but he feared that if they ended up in one, they'd never be able to leave.

One of the locals helping the refugees was a Somali doctor. When my dad introduced himself, the doctor recognised his name and asked if he was related to someone else he knew. He was. The doctor offered to take my parents to his house. He warned that while he could take my mum out of the makeshift encampment on the pretext of taking her to the hospital, my dad would need to jump over the fence that had been put up.

When they arrived in the house, they were given a room and slept in a bed. After their time travelling, unsure of what terrors they would be faced with next, they took a deep breath.

'We were finally safe,' Mama says. I reach out and squeeze her hand.

I don't know how to describe our bond, but I know it's not simply one of a mother and daughter. Our shared trauma made us something more. Something bloodier and all-encompassing. We reach for it whenever we need comforting and pull at it when we want to hurt each other. It has been the only constant in my life.

I was twelve years old when my grandad, my mum's father, died. I ran back from school and comforted her while she cried in her bed. I held her tightly and told her I couldn't imagine a world where she wasn't alive and with me. She told me that that day would come, but I shook my head and said I'd go first.

In my mind, that made more sense. She laughed and told me that, despite how sad she was, it's natural for a parent to die first. She held my face in her hand. I didn't say anything because I didn't know how to tell her that nothing about her not existing while I continued to breathe felt normal or natural. It still doesn't. That tear would cause a wound I'm not sure I'd ever recover from.

I would miss her embellishment the most. In the initial telling of this story, Mama says: 'The boat capsized and we all almost drowned. We had to swim to the shore.'

I go to find my dad in another room and tell him this. 'Your mum, wallahi,' he laughs and shakes his head. 'The boat sank as it neared shore. We all fell in the water, but we were next to the shore.'

I laugh so hard I have tears in my eyes. I walk back to the living room, where my mum is resting on the couch. I tell her I'm going home and we hug goodbye.

When I get home, I Google the Indian Ocean and see it is the warmest ocean in the world. It ranges between 19 and 30 degrees Celsius, averaging warmer temperatures closer to the coast. I think of the mum I left on the couch, watching her favourite Turkish drama and waiting for her children to return from school. She looked relaxed as I left her.

I think of the young woman she was in Ngomeni, desperate and dishevelled. I want to reach back and comfort her and tell her she will be okay.

4
THE MAKING OF A REFUGEE

Somalis are known for giving each other bizarre and at times rude nicknames. My mum is known as 'Faatma John' or simply 'John'. When I asked why, she told me that when she was a child, she had a crush on a Kenyan man called John, who often visited her neighbourhood. She would try and sneak out of her house to catch a glimpse of him.

Somalis are given these nicknames from a young age, and they form an important part of a person's identity. Writing for the BBC,[1] Justin Marrozzi notes that his nickname – 'white hair' – was written on his ID card. He writes of his encounters with other nicknames, including Faroole, or 'no fingers', for a man who lost two fingers in a terrorist attack; Farurey, or 'harelip', for, you guessed it, a man with a harelip; and Madaxweyne, or 'big head', for whoever is president.

Barre was reportedly never able to divest himself of the nickname from his youth, Afweyne ('big mouth') – despite the efforts of his allies.

My dad is known as Nakuja ('I'm coming'), a Swahili phrase for someone arriving at a destination. A childhood friend randomly called him that name when my dad was young. 'I don't know why he called me Nakuja, but that day when he called me Nakuja, then everyone called me Nakuja,' Baba tells me. It wasn't until he fled Somalia to Kenya, and was among people speaking Swahili, that he first learnt what it meant.

Mama's side of my family, as well as my parents and siblings, call me Coco. I get different explanations when I ask why – an aunt said it was because I giggled when she sang the word to me.

It is one of many names I have been known by. When I was born, I was named Amina. It is a common Muslim name. I think it's beautiful – it reminds me of me looking at my mum wearing her Somali dirac (a dress-like Somali garment worn to special events) and gold earrings. I am not sure I can still call it mine. When I hear it, which isn't very often now, I still answer, but I do so with some discomfort. It is like putting on a coat that I have outgrown, or perhaps abandoned.

I have had other names too: and now Aamna. They both represent distinct, transformative points of my life.

While my parents were far from Somalia and the war that raged on there, the fighting had cast a long shadow over Kenya. The refugees that escaped were grappling with new, difficult challenges that were borne from the conflict.

My parents and I spent some of the early months of my life living with an uncle in Mombasa, Kenya. The doctor who had given my parents shelter gave my dad money to take him and my mum to the city. This was where many refugees who didn't want to be in a camp were settling.

My parents were hoping to find someone from their family in Mombasa. When they arrived, they saw desperate Somali refugees wherever they turned. Some made their own unofficial encampments on the streets or lived in abandoned buildings. Other richer Somalis had taken over fancy tourist resorts in Mombasa's north coast.

My parents first went to a family member of my dad's who turned them away: there simply wasn't enough room. They used the money they were given to stay in a rundown hotel that was taking in Somali refugees.

'That was the worst place I ever stayed. It was worse than sleeping in the street,' Baba says. 'We were sleeping with the animals. There were rats in the room and we were itching and scratching all night.'

My parents eventually found my mum's brother, who took them into his home. They were able to wash themselves and eat. They made phone calls to family members dispersed across the world letting them know they had safely fled Somalia, while trying to get information about family members still stuck in the country.

It was a hectic time. At one point, my dad was told that his father had been killed in the fighting. 'My sister held a small prayer in his honour after we were told he was killed. Then another message came and said it was another man with the same name as my father who had been killed. I felt so happy, I cannot describe it properly,' Baba says.

My grandfather and the rest of his family were eventually able to join my parents in Mombasa. It was the first time my grandad had lived anywhere outside of Somalia.

'He never had any interest in living anywhere else,' Baba says. 'He loved his country, his home city.' My grandfather would live the rest of his life without returning to his country.

Mama describes that time in Mombasa as 'difficult'. They were regularly harassed by the Kenyan authorities, especially the police, who would check the possessions and paperwork of any Somali walking by. Refugees would be taken to refugee camps several miles away.

'I would always have to carry money when I left the house because the Kenyan police will catch you and take you away,' she says.

'Was the money to bribe them?' I ask.

'Yes, to get them to leave me alone,' Mama explains.

A report by the Immigration and Refugee Board of Canada noted a distressing incident on the weekend of

15 and 16 August.[2] Armed Kenyan police reportedly burst into the temporary shelters of around 2,000 Somali and Ethiopian refugees in Nairobi and Mombasa. The police rounded up the refugees at gunpoint and forced them to board lorries, which drove them to refugee camps. The raid separated families and many small children were left behind. In both cities, the police were apparently in search of any 'Somali-looking persons' staying together in large groups.

The hostility from the local population was also palpable to my parents. Their neighbours resented the refugees who had suddenly arrived in their thousands. The area had its own economic hardships, which were worsened by the unprecedented situation. This anger often exploded and fights broke out in the street.

A 1992 article published by the *Baltimore Sun* reports on this growing backlash in Mombasa.[3] It noted that desperate Somali women who were forced into sex work had running battles with the established Kenyan sex workers. These fights included black eyes, broken bones and knife wounds, and were wince-inducingly dubbed the 'whore wars' in the local press.

The piece also featured a striking anecdote: a simple interaction between Somali and Kenyan men in a courtyard in the old city of Mombasa.

'It took all of my money to get myself on the dhow,' a former Somali government worker from Mogadishu said. 'Now what am I to do? Sit here until Somalia is put back together? That may never happen.'

His friend, who stood beside him, said: 'In Mogadishu, I was a painter, but here there is no work, only surviving. And the Kenyans, the ordinary people, they treat us badly, as though we had a disease.'

The conversation was overheard by a Kenyan truck driver, who angrily snapped: 'You are allowed to come here and share in our food. We could have made you stay back in Somalia, where you slaughter each other.'

A Mombasa merchant joined in. 'These Somalians, they are not grateful,' he said. 'We give them a chance to survive and they complain all the time. Some of them rob us, and they crowd into our streets.'

These voices in this anecdotal fight would typify the interactions between these two neighbouring countries for the next thirty years.

My parents were wired money from family members and friends in Europe, Saudi Arabia and the US. This, though vital for their survival, wasn't a permanent solution. My dad didn't want to keep asking family members for money, but there was no work available for him in Mombasa. My mum was grateful to be allowed to stay with her brother, but knew she needed to find a place of her own.

Of course, I was unaware of all this. One of my favourite photos from the time sees the three of us sat beside a river in a park, with a high-rise block of flats behind. It is dated March 1993. I am just under one in the photo, bundled up in my dad's arms. My mum's sister had sent my parents money for them to buy new clothes, and my dad is wearing a black suit, while my mum is in a dirac.

I ask my mum to send me the photo. She first grumbles she can't remember what album it is in, but texts it to me soon after. Looking at the photo in the present, I smile at my dad's neat afro and my mum's styled hair. She looks beautiful.

One thing startles me. When I remembered the picture, I had always thought that my parents were smiling. But looking at it now, I realise I've remembered wrong.

They are not smiling in the photo. They are squinting, both their mouths stuck in a twisted grimace, as the sun shines directly into their eyes.

Death hung in the air in 1992. Children were dying in their hundreds daily in Somalia and in the encampments around Kenya.

My mum didn't want to leave me alone for a moment. Her eyes were almost always glued to me. Often, she would stop what she was doing to reach for me and check I was breathing. She was particularly scared when I slept and my eyes were shut. She would wake me up in the middle of the night to see if I was alive.

Human Rights Watch described 1992 as the most tragic year in Somalia's modern history.[4] Journalists and international aid workers admitted to the Bay, Gedo and Juba regions in Somalia after Barre's exit described the scene as 'apocalyptic', saying that the famine had already reached 'unparalleled proportions'.

The farming communities in those regions had already suffered under Barre's regime. They had few weapons to defend themselves against the brutal occupations of various warring factions. These factions engaged in the systematic looting of food, livestock and household possessions. They had even stolen the clothing from people's backs. Many farmers were too scared and too weak to leave their homes and starved to death.

This was exacerbated by the rival factions blocking any humanitarian aid, with warlords refusing to allow food to be delivered to areas that were not under their control. Hunger had become a weapon of war. Aid workers spoke of their protracted negotiations to deliver vital food to areas that needed it. Even when they were allowed access, there was still the risk of attack from undisciplined soldiers or bandits.

The towns of Baidoa, where some in my mother's family originated from, and Baardheere became the locations of 'the most appalling famine camps seen in Africa', according to Human Rights Watch.

THE MAKING OF A REFUGEE

To get a better understanding of what was happening in those areas, I speak to the veteran Irish aid worker Geoff Loane, who was based in Mogadishu at the time, but worked across the country. I had noticed his name crop up a lot in the archive news reports I read; the *Irish Times* had described him as the mastermind of the International Committee of the Red Cross relief operation in Somalia. Loane, who now lives in Ireland, agreed to talk to me over Zoom.

He struggles to describe what he saw. 'It's a period I don't tend to talk about very much. It's quite difficult, to be honest.'

Despite the unprecedented crisis facing the country, aid workers like Loane were struggling to get attention from the international community. Human Rights Watch noted that officials at the US State Department's bureaus of African Affairs and Humanitarian Assistance raised concerns about Somalia's unfolding famine and called for desperately needed aid, but were largely ignored. It was the year of the 1992 US election. President Bush's political advisors wanted to keep the focus on domestic issues.

To get the attention of the international community, Loane knew he needed to work with the press. The world needed to see the catastrophe unfolding. Loane and his team worked with many journalists, bringing them to Mogadishu and Baidoa. He remembers one particularly famous article, which made a significant difference, by *New York Times* journalist Jane Perlez.

'I simply can't tell you or describe to you what it was. But you'll find the article.' Perlez had somehow found the words to describe the horrors Loane was trying to get the world to see. 'I don't know how she wrote it but she did,' he says.

Perlez had been brought from Nairobi to Baidoa: she published an article on the front page of the *New York Times* on 19 July 1992 under the headline 'Deaths in Somalia outpace delivery of food'.[5]

I can locate Perlez's article easily in the archive. The accompanying picture is devastating: dozens of starving children are lined up against the wall, some looking into the camera. I focus on one child whose bones protrude. The children pictured used the last of their energy to reach the feeding centre in Baidoa, Perlez wrote. Hundreds died while they waited there.

The dead were buried in hastily made graves, while 'the body of a teenage boy who had just died was pushed under a bush until the feeding was over.' Perlez interviews a mother who was crying over the loss of her fifth child, whose death from hunger was one in 7,000 in the past month in Baidoa, according to the Red Cross. The town then had a population of about 40,000.

I read and reread Perlez's article, but the magnitude of suffering is still incomprehensible. Projections at the time showed that one third of Somalia's population, estimated to be up to six million people, would die in the next six months if food wasn't pumped into the country. Around 30,000 civilians had been killed when the fighting restarted in autumn 1991. More than 300,000 Somali refugees had fled to Northern Kenya in the last six months, my parents among them. Around 2.5 million Somalis had been displaced.

The article mentions some of the names of the children that had died on that day: ten-year-old girl Ruquia, four-month-old Mahoumoud Abdul, the first and only child of twenty-two-year-old Kuresh Mohamed, and ten-year-old Abdul Kadir Isak. Of the estimated 220,000 people who died during the famine, the overwhelming majority were children.

The story did what good journalism should do: it triggered a response. There were discussions in Washington and in New York, forcing the US government and UN to engage at a political level. Africa Watch accused the US of going to 'extraordinary lengths' to thwart diplomatic and humanitarian initiatives. Congress was supposedly worried about the financial cost of such an intervention, following recent peacekeeping operations in Yugoslavia, El Salvador, Western Sahara and Cambodia. African leaders had responded angrily, Africa Watch notes, accusing the US of double standards.[6]

Planes of food were sent, but for many they came too late.

In a subsequent piece published in December 1992 in the *New York Times*, Perlez would write that Somalia had lost a generation. By then, one in four children under five had died in the famine in Somalia. Some areas were hit much worse than others; as many as 70 percent of children under five had died in Baidoa.[7]

This term 'lost generation' comes up again and again as I trawl the newspaper archives and NGO reports. A *Washington Post* article published in September 1992 bears the headline 'Legacy of woe awaits "lost generation" of Somalia'. Its opening paragraph asks, 'What about the children who live through this crisis?'[8]

Sam Toussie, an epidemiologist with the International Medical Corps, describes how 'amazingly resilient' the surviving children are – but adds that 'Somalia has lost part of a generation, that's for sure.'

I had heard the term 'lost generation' used in relation to the First World War. But here on the pages of these articles and reports was a generation being lost in real time – and that generation was my generation, my cohort. By the time I went to Calais in 2015, the same warnings were being made about Syria's 'lost generation'. Now in 2024, the same title has been conferred by the international media on the children of Palestine.

History had repeated itself – because every war produces its own lost generation.

I came across reporting by Peter Biles, then a freelance East Africa correspondent for the *Guardian* and the BBC. Biles was one of the first foreign journalists to enter Mogadishu after Barre fled. His report on Somalia's 'lost children' opens with 300 young Somali orphans living in a run-down shelter just outside of Mogadishu, who had been effectively abandoned.[9]

Biles is now based in the UK, and I'm also able to convince him to speak to me. We speak over video call. He is wearing glasses and a T-shirt, and has an authoritative yet relaxed presence. He has a voice made for radio and speaks slowly but assuredly. We end up speaking for more than an hour.

Biles first flew to Mogadishu with a Médecins Sans Frontières (MSF) team – the visit lasted only about half an hour. The MSF team had set up at the airport because of the insecurity and were desperate to be evacuated. The team quickly offloaded supplies and the workers jumped on the plane. One American said he saw somebody shot at the perimeter of the airport.

When Biles returned to the city on a charter flight with another aid group for the second time, he was able to stay for several days.

'I never really worked in a country and witnessed the total collapse of the state in such a dramatic and short period of time,' Biles says.

During our chat, he goes through his notes and published articles. One article, published for the BBC *Focus on Africa* magazine, was titled: 'Somalia: What Will Happen to Siad's children?'[10]

'We went to Afgooye, and came across this orphanage where all the children had been abandoned. They were left lying on the ground in the orphanage. It was in 1991. Just two or three weeks after Siad had gone,' he tells me.

'What was the piece you wrote in the end?' I ask.

'It posed the question, what is the future for Somalia? Which at that stage was very uncertain. It was really just painting a picture of what it was like. It was a combination of euphoria and hopelessness,' he says.

I'm not sure anyone would have been able to answer that question, or predict that a member of this lost generation would get in contact with Biles, some three decades later, with her own questions.

I bring this up in our conversation. 'Was it slightly strange to get that message from me nearly three decades later?' I laugh as I ask the question.

'It was a bit, yes,' he replies.

Kenya had taken in more than 300,000 refugees by 1992.[11] My parents had managed to stay out of the refugee camps that had formed. The nearest one to them was Utange, located five kilometres west of the main port of Mombasa.

I find a video on YouTube from the Red Cross/Red Crescent's historic film collection of the camp in 1992. It's ten minutes long. The comments have been turned off.

I flinch when I see a woman lying on a stretcher, in pain, as someone cleans a wound on her arm. A Red Cross official explains to the camera that the camp was planned to hold 7,000 people, but there were 18,000 people officially in the camp by the time of filming, and another 4,000 just on the periphery.

People threw their excrement wherever they could. I pause when one Somali refugee who is a doctor says that he will refuse to resettle in Europe or the US. 'I'll wait here,' he says. I wonder how long he waited. Did he ever change his mind? Did he return to Somalia? If he did, what did he return to?

The aid workers interviewed say there is a desperate need for a larger child feeding centre. In the video, a young girl holds onto a baby, possibly a sibling, as the infant is fed by a nurse. The nurse asks to see her mother. It's not clear if the girl understands, or if her mother is even alive. Children are filmed vomiting when given food because their stomachs are simply not used to it.

The video unsettles me. I spend days thinking of how many of the children in that camp, and the others both in Kenya and across Somalia in 1992, survived. According to a

UNHCR official, in April 1992, the death rates in these camps were among the highest in the world.[12]

The refugee camps across Kenya were built as a temporary measure, intended to last until the end of the war, but many Somalis who inhabited these camps would never return home. In the years that followed, smaller camps like Utange were closed down and the refugees resettled in either Dadaab or Kakuma. Those two camps still remain today. They are some of the oldest and largest camps in the world. Kenya has done a huge service by continuing to house so many refugees on its soil for so many years. The debate on refugees in the UK almost always focuses on deterring them from coming to the country, and not on supporting neighbouring countries who take on a huge load.

I ask my mum whether she ever hoped she would return to Somalia while she lived in Mombasa. She says no: the connection she had to Somalia and to Mogadishu had been severed by the war. She was relieved to be out of the country. My dad, on the other hand, held onto hope, but it grew slimmer every day.

My parents dreamed of resettlement. Some family members and friends had managed to gain asylum in the US, Canada and some European countries and my dad was eager to join them, but we couldn't yet get access to the West. My parents decided my mum and I would go to Jeddah, Saudi Arabia, with her sister and that my dad would work undocumented overseas. He would send money back to us whenever he could. While he did that, my mum would apply for asylum.

I ask my parents if it was difficult to split up, and they said yes, but again, they had few options. Every day they stayed in Mombasa, they risked being rounded up and taken away.

My mum and I said goodbye to my dad and flew to Jeddah. I was around one year old by this point. We would see him intermittently in the years that followed. In fact, for the first seven years of my life, I didn't really know my dad at all. He was always someone I spoke to on the phone, who I imagined having adventures in different countries. The truth was different. My dad took any manual labour job he could find and slept wherever he could. He missed us dearly in that time apart, he tells me.

I wonder how different our relationship would be if we didn't have to spend so many years apart. I wouldn't say my dad is closer to my brothers than me, but I do envy my siblings. He has always been in their lives, from the day they were born in the UK. He was there when they learnt to walk, talk and learn the first few surahs of the Quran. I didn't have that.

Meanwhile we began our life in Jeddah. My mum worked at a funfair. I don't really have many memories from that time of my life. In the next three years, our applications for asylum in the US would be rejected. My mum would cry at night and wonder why she was being punished.

My entire world was that flat we lived in, with my two aunties and my cousins. We were crammed in together. We didn't have much, and were living undocumented in the country, but we were happy. We were safe.

Or, we thought we were.

5
THE SEPARATION

I am sitting in a Turkish restaurant with my family when I find out my mum and I were forcibly separated for a year.

We are in Ilford, East London, on a sunny day in August 2020 – having gone months without seeing each other because of the Coronavirus lockdown. The restaurant is dark indoors and I'm a bit frustrated that we can't enjoy the sunshine outside. It is a rare treat in London.

I can't remember now why we were gathered – quite possibly because I had told my parents I wanted to write a book about their lives. My four younger brothers are sitting with us, looking at their phones.

My mum is sitting next to me, perusing the menu. I show her a picture and ask, 'Do you remember this place?'

'Yes, our house in Western Road!' " Mama exclaims in the restaurant. A few other diners look our way, but I ignore them. She beams.

Just this morning, I went to the very first flat we lived in in the UK. It was a two-bedroom, upper-floor flat. We were a family of four at the time we lived there: my mum, my dad, my brother Aamir and I.

The flat is less than three miles from the place I now live, but getting there felt like I was travelling back decades. I haven't been there since I was a child. I don't know why, but something has been calling me towards the flat over the past few weeks. I have decided this summer that I want to write a book, but I haven't managed to write anything down.

I needed to see that home before I could get any words down. I had to go back to the place where I had begun the process of creating myself.

I had walked towards Western Road that morning feeling dread. I didn't initially recognise the houses on the street and was worried it meant that I wouldn't recognise other places from my past. Would I feel just as distant and detached if I returned to Kenya and Somalia?

When I saw it, I sighed with relief. The door stood there just as I remembered it.

For a second I'm a child again, walking to school, the trees on the left-hand side and shrubbery on the right. I smiled when I walked down the same road I did more than twenty years ago and see the sign for Southern Primary School. This was my second primary school, the one I transferred to after moving in with my mum. I recognise the school logo, the points of a compass, and remember how proudly I'd worn it embossed on my jumper.

I remember the start of the new millennium, how scared I was hearing the fireworks from my bedroom; I remember dial-up internet; I remember Pokémon cards; I remember my parents making each other laugh in that kitchen – they didn't know how to behave around each other after being separated for so long; I remember looking into my brother's crib and not feeling alone; I remember feeling at home.

Would it be the same if I went back to Somalia and Kenya? Would memories return? Would it take on a new tone or colour? Would that be a good thing or a bad thing?

I wanted to knock on the door, but felt too scared. Coronavirus was still raging and I didn't want to risk unknowingly harming someone vulnerable inside. I took pictures outside instead.

I stood there for a while. A woman across the road watched me, curiously, and I laughed. 'I know I probably look like a weirdo,' I said. She laughed back.

THE SEPARATION

I stood gazing at the house, only snapping out of the daze I was in when I got a text from my mum to say they were getting ready and would be heading out to the restaurant soon. I rushed to the restaurant to make it there before them.

'Yes, I went to the flat today. I wanted to see what it looked like. I wanted to go back to somewhere from my past,' I tell my mum. She shows the picture to my dad. 'It feels like the place where our life really began,' I say to them both.

My mum nods. She looks very far away while looking at the picture. 'We suffered a lot before we got there,' Mama says.

'Yes, in Somalia and Kenya,' I say.

'No, not just there,' Mama shakes her head and hands me back my phone. 'We suffered in Jeddah as well. When the police came to our house, they took me away!'

'Oh, is this when the police asked me if you were my mum and I said no?' I laugh, shifting as the bread and dips are placed on the table.

'Yes, and then I was in jail for several weeks and then sent to Djibouti,' Mama says calmly, as she cuts a piece of Turkish bread and smothers it in hot sauce.

I look at her confused. 'Wait, you were actually deported? When did this happen, for how long? I thought the police let you guys go after a brief detention.'

She laughs, a big belly laugh that makes her eyes glassy. 'No, I was deported and I didn't see you for a year, Coco! I told you I really suffered. And that jail, la illaha illa Allah [there is no god but Allah], I really, really suffered.'

'If you are done suffering, the man is here to take our orders,' Baba says, and laughs at his own joke. She rolls her eyes, but I can see she wants to laugh too.

Questions rise and then block my throat as everyone says what they want to eat. It's only when the food arrives that I can bring myself to ask questions. 'Where did they take you?'

'I was arrested with my sister,' she says.

'Sacidiya?' I ask, and she nods.

'We were in prison for...' Mama pauses as she tries to remember. 'Maybe two weeks? Then I got sent to Djibouti, and Sacidiya to Ethiopia.' She is laughing as she tells me, and despite my amazement I smile back at her.

What happens next surprises me, as a journalist. I have by now a ferocious appetite for everything that had happened to my parents. I press them for details and love to sit and listen to them tell me their stories. But at this moment, I don't feel curious. I feel deadened to what my mother is telling me and simply want to move on. I don't want to interrogate, I want to hide.

Sitting in the restaurant, a memory from my childhood surfaces, from when I was about nine years old. I'd woken up at the break of dawn and found an empty space where my cousin Loula, who was at mine for a sleepover, had been. I panicked. I spent the next few hours looking for her in our small flat while my parents slept. I searched the same places over and over – under the couch or bed, in the kitchen cupboards, out on the landing – in the desperate hope that she would magically reappear. My parents finally woke up and told me that my aunt had taken her home while I slept. I was devastated and felt my chest caving in. I felt painfully, consciously alone.

I feel that loneliness in the restaurant and it surprises me. Up to this point, every new piece of information I have learned about my parents has made me feel closer to them. I have felt myself standing stronger in who I am in these past few months. But hearing about my mother's deportation makes me feel exposed and vulnerable.

I won't ask any more questions about the deportation for another two years. I want to write that this is unlike me, but I have come to realise that it's something I have been doing my whole life. I have been running away from this moment since I was a child.

That week, I have a nightmare that I haven't had in years. I am always a child in the dream. I find myself in a room where I'm told my mum has been kidnapped by the devil. I search for my mum throughout London, growing ever more desperate to find her.

When I do find her, and regardless of the different routes I take every time I have this nightmare, it is too late. She is chained up, the life gone from her eyes. A horned, bestial devil is beside her. He is smirking. Sometimes her body is mutilated. I wake up once I touch her corpse. It is always warm.

The nightmare follows the same script, but sometimes the person being kidnapped changes. Often, it is one of my brothers. In my dreams, I'm able to find some of my brothers but wake up in a panic and drenched in my own sweat because I am too late to save the others.

My therapist asks me to close my eyes and go back to that moment. I cringe, and hope she doesn't notice. This therapist, who specialises in refugee and childhood trauma, is one of the best in her field. I have been getting better since I started to see her, but I still feel self-consciousness.

'I know you're sceptical, but just give it a go. I want you to close your eyes and do the following breathing exercises,' the therapist tells me.

I do as she says. I close my eyes and breathe in and out to a count of eight. The therapist tells me to make a sound as I breathe out, any sound that comes naturally, but I cringe again. I can't bring myself to.

We do the breathing exercise over and over again until I feel really relaxed, almost sleepy.

It has been a year since my family lunch in Ilford. A year of struggling to sleep, of an anxiety that feels both crippling and overwhelming. I feel embarrassed and I don't understand what's happening to me.

I tell the therapist of my mum's deportation from Jeddah, of what I know about it. We have been slowly going through the events in my life to get to this point. I was four years old at the time of the incident.

'I can't believe we are several sessions in and we haven't even got past my early childhood. I've lived several lifetimes before I've learnt to read,' I joke at the beginning of the session. She smiles, but doesn't laugh. I hate that I can't make her laugh.

I continue to take deep breaths and sink further into nothingness. At this moment, I am consumed by the simple miracle of breathing into my nose, feeling my chest rise, breathing out of my nose, and feeling my chest slowly come down.

'I want Coco to feel safe to come out,' the therapist says. The therapist established early on that my 'inner childhood self' would be called the name she responded to: Coco. I accepted it was a good way to distinguish the adult I am, Aamna, from the child I was, Coco, while working through difficult past experiences. I still felt awkward about it.

'Erm, I'm not sure,' I say and smile. My eyes are still closed and I wonder if she's annoyed.

'Coco needs to know it's safe to enter the room. Is it safe?' my therapist asks.

The question throws me for a moment. I am in my own room, in my own bed. This session is being done over video call on my laptop. This is the safest place in the world for me, but I can't say yes. Why can't I say yes?

'I want you to remember the room you would have been in on that day,' my therapist says.

'I don't think I can remember it,' I answer quickly. 'I'm seeing the living room of the flat my aunt lived in in Jeddah when we went to visit her after we settled in London. I was about ten years old. We went because my mum's father was dying. It's what I'm seeing, but I am not sure if it's the same flat from when I was four years old, from when it happened.'

I keep my eyes closed, but it's more of a strain to do so.

'That's okay, it doesn't matter if the image in your head now is real or not. It doesn't have to be an actual memory, it's just how your brain has stored it right now,' my therapist says.

I think this is odd, but I don't tell her. I always thought it was important that traumatic memories were remembered as accurately as possible so they can be dealt with most effectively. I didn't realise that whatever felt real to me was real enough in that session, real enough to let me ease into it.

'What's the room like?' my therapist asks.

'It isn't very big. There are those Arab floor sofas on three sides of the wall, the fourth has a dining table and some chairs.'

'How many people are there in the room?'

'I am not sure. I think it's me, and my mum, and her three sisters, as well as her aunt. I think my two cousins, a girl around my age, and her brother who is a teenager, are also there. It does not feel overwhelming. I am used to this crowd,' I reply.

'Talk me through what happens,' my therapist tells me.

'I don't know if it's real memories or—'

'It doesn't matter,' my therapist interrupts me. 'Let Coco talk us through what happens.'

I take a few deep breaths. I feel small and afraid. I tell her how it plays out in my mind.

There are bangs on the door and the room falls silent. There are whispers among the adults. I don't know if someone lets them in or they burst through the door: two armed police officers, in black and blue. The air in the room changes.

It all happens very quickly. They grab my mother and her sister, my aunt Sacidiya. My mum reaches for me, but I move out of reach. I am being held by someone and clinging to her: I think it is my great-aunt or one of my mum's sisters.

'Is this woman your mum?' The man in the terrifying uniform asks me. He is roughly holding my mum by the arm.

'No,' I answer.

My mum gets taken away.

'Do you know what happens next?' my therapist asks me. Her voice sounds muffled, like I'm listening to her underwater.

'I don't know what happened next. I don't know, I—'. I am breathing quite heavily.

'Stay in the room,' my therapist says. 'What do you think happens next?'

'I think I will go to one of the bedrooms,' I say. 'I go and sit on the bed.'

'Are you alone?' my therapist asks me.

'Yes.'

My therapist then asks a question that surprises me. 'What does Coco want right now?'

'I don't know,' I say. I feel very cold.

'Do you want one of the adults in the other room to comfort you?'

'No,' I answer. I feel angry.

'Who do you want right now?'

'I want my parents,' I say. My voice cracks and betrays me.

'Do you want your dad?' I think the question is odd, but I don't tell her that.

'He isn't in Saudi Arabia—'

'It doesn't matter,' my therapist says. 'Let's establish what Coco needs right now and try to give it to her.'

I want to tell her that I don't understand how that will help. What is the point of doing that now? It is too late for Coco – too late for me. I don't say that it feels pointless.

'Is it okay for dad to come into the room?' my therapist asks. She is being gentle with me. I want to tell her she doesn't have to be. I want to tell her that I am strong and that I won't break so easily.

I nod.

'Can dad give you a hug?'

'No,' I say, quite firmly. I don't want to be touched by anyone. I feel raw and exposed, like a layer of skin has been peeled off.

'This is your dad speaking, Coco. I want you to know that what happened is not your fault. It isn't any of our faults. Mum and I haven't left you because we wanted to, we have been forced to be away from you. We are trying to get back to you. We love you,' my therapist says.

I listen, frozen in time.

'This is only temporary and we will be together again soon,' my therapist says.

Tears run down my cheeks. I notice them curiously, as if they are coming out of someone else's eyes.

I nod again. I can't talk.

'Do you want mum to come into the room?'

I shake my head.

'Okay, mum won't come into the room. Do you want to say anything to dad?' the therapist.

I shake my head. There is so much I want to ask, so much I want to say. Why do some children get to live their lives never worrying about whether they'd see their parents again? Why am I always losing one of my parents? Why was this the life that was chosen for me? Why don't I just get to be a child?

My throat feels blocked with raw emotions. I am scared to hear what will come out if I open my mouth.

'Dad is leaving the room now. What do you want to happen next?' my therapist asks. She is still so gentle.

There is a long pause.

'I want to be alone,' I say.

'Okay,' my therapist says.

I am staring out of the window in that room. The sky is midnight blue.

The next breath I take is painful and I open my eyes. I feel like I've taken my head out from underwater and I can breathe. I take deep breaths. I feel shy. It is the first time I've cried in a session.

'You took yourself out of that quite quickly,' my therapist notes.

'I needed to get out,' I say.

'I understand, but next there's a more gentle way of coming out of that,' she explains. 'So it doesn't feel so sharp and sudden.'

I nod, but at that moment, I don't have any interest in going back into that room.

I leave the session surprised by the depth of pain I had felt. How could one child feel that much pain?

It is Ramadan in 2022 and my family and I are all fasting. Mama and I are in the kitchen. My dad is still on his business trip to Somalia and the boys are upstairs in their bedrooms. It is a grey, bleak day, not long after my therapy session.

I have come round to do another interview. After our conversation in the Turkish restaurant, my mum and I have only spoken briefly about the deportation. This is the first time I have set out to hear the details in full.

I first ask her about our life in Jeddah, Saudi Arabia. We lived with her sisters and dad while my dad was looking for work in other countries.

'I used to work because Baba didn't have any money to send us. My father used to help us, he paid the rent, but I worked to get you anything extra you needed,' Mama says as she cooks. 'I used to work in this funfair. I took your aunt Amina's card that allowed her to work because I didn't have any papers.'

I start putting the dishes in the dishwasher as she continues to cook. 'Did you like working at the funfair? I imagine it was a fun job.'

'I didn't like it, but I didn't want you to need anything that I couldn't give to you. I was a good mum, mashallah [God has willed it]. When my children need something, I won't let them down. I try to do it,' Mama says.

'Life was very difficult,' she adds, 'Baba, he feels very bad. He cries when I tell him I'm working, he thinks I'm working as a maid in a house. I say to him no, I'm working at the funfair. He get upset because—'

There is a pause.

'He didn't want a life like this?' I offer

'Yes, that I am working in a job I don't like and he is far away and he can't help us,' Mama says.

'And then we left Jeddah because of that?' I trail off. 'Actually, what do you remember when those people came?' The words fly, somewhat incoherently, out of my mouth.

'Who are the people who took us?' Mama asks.

'The border guards,' I answer.

'What border guards?' she says, and opens the microwave door.

'In Jeddah, when they took you,' I reply, and an errant laugh slips out.

'We entered the country with a visa,' Mama first explains. Amina's husband, my mother's brother-in-law, who was a Saudi national, had sent us the visa.

My mum seems calm as she continues to cook. She uses her handheld blender to turn the chickpeas she just washed into mush.

'Why did you go to that place they put you in?' I ask

'Where did they put me?' she asks, looking confused. I know I am being a terrible interviewer. I clarify my question.

'We didn't have the right paperwork, so that happened,' Mama says. I prod her to explain. 'Some people say they don't have the right papers and that's why they take us.' She suspects a neighbour reported them.

There is another pause. This is the most awkward interview we have done to date. We are dancing around each other.

'How old was I, like four?' I ask.

'Yes, four something.'

'Was I in the room when they took you?'

'Yes, you were in the room and they asked you if this is your mum, and you said no, and you're stuck with Aunty Halima because Aunty Halima—'. Mama turns on the blender again and I struggle to hear her. Aunty Halima is her father's sister, my great-aunt. She continues 'She told you to say that she was your mum or you'd get into big trouble. I wanted you to stay safe, I didn't want to take you where we were going.'

My mum and Sacidiya were arrested on the spot.

'You didn't know where you were going?' I ask.

'I thought they would send us back to our house, but they didn't do that,' Mama says, 'They took us to jail.'

We never got to say goodbye. Did I reach out to her? I can't bring myself to ask her the question. I know why I said she wasn't my mother. But still, how could I do such a thing?

'How long were you in jail?' I ask instead.

'Two weeks,' Mama answers.

'What was the jail like?' I ask.

'Like jail, Coco,' Mama says and laughs. 'How else would a jail look? That is a stupid question.' I giggle too, relieved she has found a way to break the tension.

'It was a dirty place. There were a lot of people there. We were sleeping on the floor. It's not a normal jail, it's the place they take refugee people,' Mama says.

There is another pause as she continues cooking. I stand beside her awkwardly. Dialogue from the show that's on the TV seeps in from the other side of the room.

'Can you cut these vegetables please into small strips?' Mama asks. She shows me where she now puts the cups in the kitchen. I wonder if she doesn't want to talk about this anymore. I am wrong.

Mama says, unprompted, 'Life in the jail was very difficult. The people, the toilet was very dirty, you're sleeping on the floor.'

Family members visited my mum and her sister in jail and said they were doing everything they could to get them out. I was kept away. They spent two weeks in that jail before they were separately deported. The Saudi officials asked them where they were from and ought to be returned to. While Sacidiya asked to be sent to Ethiopia, my mum asked to be sent to nearby Djibouti.

Mama was told of a family member who lived in Djibouti that could take her in. He was a government official who she hoped would be able to help her quickly get a visa to Ethiopia and then back to Saudi Arabia. It's a decision she regrets till this day.

'Did you want me to come with you?' I ask.

'No, why would I want you to come with me?' Mama says. 'Can you take out the bin please?'

I do as she says, joking that at least she saved me from the hell of the jail. 'Thank you very much,' I say and we both laugh.

We continue cooking and cleaning. 'Mum, you really went through a lot. Why aren't you a crazy person?' I ask.

'Why do you want me to be crazy?' Mama quips back.

'People who go through war lose their minds,' I say, as a joke. But my curiosity is real.

'I have faith in Allah. Everything is written from Allah,' Mama answers.

We move around each other in the kitchen. 'I don't remember this at all, you know?' I say to Mama. I am not sure that's true. I don't tell her about my therapy sessions and the fear I had tapped back into.

She arrived in Djibouti alone and miserable. It had been weeks since she had seen me and the mere mention of my name was enough to spark overwhelming feelings of despair and self-loathing. There were days when she was scared her sadness would drive her to madness.

'I left Sacidiya. I was alone. I don't know anybody. There was no one I knew there. They were the worst days of my life,' she tells me.

I wasn't doing any better in Saudi Arabia. I had become depressed. Her sister, Amina, called her often and let me speak to her on the phone. I didn't sound like myself.

I had stopped eating and looked constantly towards the door, waiting for my mum to return. I became more withdrawn with each passing day that she didn't. My refusal to eat had become so severe that I was taken to a hospital. The doctors became alarmed: I was malnourished and needed urgent care.

My mum lived with some so-called family friends in Djibouti for several months. She felt there was very little being done to help her get the documents she needed to go to Ethiopia and return to Saudi Arabia. Instead, she worked relentlessly: her days were filled up with cooking, cleaning and doing whatever chore was asked of her by the husband and wife.

'I hated that place. Why is it when a woman is in trouble there are others ready to exploit her thinking she won't say anything because she is a woman? That if she stays in your house, you can do whatever you want?' Mama asks this while looking away from me, as if she is directing her questions to the world.

My mother knew she needed to get out of that house. She had managed to befriend the neighbours, who would often hang out in their front gardens with each other. Eventually, she confided to one Arab family that she was being exploited by the family and they told her to leave the house and live with them. She was invited to stay with a woman in that family who lived nearby, who was the same age as my mum: it was this family that helped her go to Ethiopia.

THE SEPARATION

'I'll never forget how much that family helped me. They gave me money when the money your dad sent never reached me. We danced together and laughed together. They helped despite the huge difference in our languages. Everyone was kind to me, including the mum and dad. They took me to the airport, they did everything,' she tells me. 'I'll never forget them,' she repeats to herself.

My mom thinks of this family often, just as my dad thinks of the man who helped him in the mosque. I now think of them both often too. Do they think of my parents? Will they ever know of the impact they had on their lives, on mine?

My mum found Sacidiya quickly when she went to Ethiopia. When she told her what she went through, she responded as sisters often do: 'Why did you not listen to me and come straight to Ethiopia?' My mum and I laugh.

My mum called her father, who sent a man with money to them. They waited months but were finally able to get the documents they needed to apply for a visa. They dressed in traditional Ethiopian garments when they went to the Saudi Arabian embassy. During the interview, when my mum told the workers at the embassy that she was Muslim, she was asked to recite the Quran. They got the visa weeks later.

The year apart felt like decades to us both. When my mum returned, I carried the pain of the separation like a second skin. It hung off me.

'When I opened the door to the flat after Amina picked me up from the airport, you took one look at me, ran to the other room, and started crying. I kept crying and Amina cried too. You cried and I don't know why. For a week, every time you saw me, you would start crying. You hug me and you start crying. At night, you would sleep with me and hold onto my hand. We suffered, wallahi [I swear to God]. We suffered a lot,' Mama says.

Upon returning, my mum realised we couldn't continue living in Saudi Arabia as undocumented refugees. 'We didn't have papers to stay in Saudi Arabia, which meant you couldn't go to school or have any education,' Mama says. The threat of further deportations also loomed large over us because we would never get the documentation we needed.

My mum heard of other family members who were living in refugee camps in Kenya that were resettled in the West. She decided that was our best shot at starting a new life for the both of us. She was done waiting for that life to miraculously happen. She needed to fight for it.

We couldn't go directly from Saudi Arabia to Kenya, as we couldn't get the right visas and passports. First, we had to return to Mogadishu, a city she had vowed never to set foot in again. I was with her. The fighting was particularly brutal then and we went to sleep to the sound of shelling and gunshots.

'It was so awful and so scary,' Mama says.

I think of how often Muslim women like my mum are portrayed as passive victims, and how this could not be further from the truth.

We didn't stay in Mogadishu for long, perhaps a few weeks, before taking a bus to an airport. We flew to Nairobi and then got a bus to Mombasa. When we arrived in the city, we went to the nearby Barwe refugee camp and registered ourselves.

We arrived as the camps along the coast were all being shut down in 1996 or 1997: my parents don't remember exactly. I was around five years old. Refugees who were there were moved to either Dadaab refugee camp or Kakuma. We were taken to the latter.

I spend much of the so-called pandemic years, between 2020 and 2023, wondering which memories were real and which were created by my mind filling in the blanks. I wonder whether it matters when the feelings behind them are the same.

THE SEPARATION

I think a lot of Coco, of the child I was. While I am drawn to my parents' younger selves, I don't have the same sense of curiosity about myself. There is so much pain with Coco and I don't know what to do with it. I had wrapped up this pain and placed it somewhere deep within me, in a place where I couldn't easily find it again.

The pandemic years were therefore like plotting a map of the maze that my memories and emotions were dispersed across. I would go down one route and hit a dead end. In others, I found mutilated bits of myself that I had hidden away, parts of me that never healed. I go to those parts of me and truly see myself.

I walk through the maze to what I think are the earliest memories of my life. They are from the Kakuma refugee camp.

I remember walking through a marketplace, staying close to my mother's side. It is hot, the sun's rays so fierce I can't stop squinting. My mother is on my right in this memory, and at one point I turn to my left. I see a dejected and incredibly thin man sitting on the floor. I stop and stare at him until my mum tells me off and holds onto my hand. I'm too scared to look back at him as we walk further ahead, but I feel both drawn to him and terrified by his suffering.

I have another memory of asking my mum if we could get a drink, either a Fanta or a juice shake, during a warm evening. The heat doesn't feel unpleasant. There are others in the living room of our shanty accommodation. My mum is in a deep conversation, but it goes over my head. She agrees, but I am not sure if she took me herself or someone else did.

In the next memory, I have the drink in my hand and am looking up at warm washes of red, yellow and lights. They remind me now of fairy lights. I spend the rest of the evening watching a film on a TV that we all crowd around. I have no idea what we watched, but my mum tells me that Bollywood films, dubbed into Somali, were a regular feature in the camp.

I remember how scared I used to be of going to the toilet, which was just two imprints of feet and a hole in the ground. I was small enough to fall in. Kakuma is also the place where I contracted malaria and almost died. I remember lying in a bed in what could have either been a room or a tent. In this memory, my mum is sitting in a chair beside me. She looks anxious, her face stricken with fear. I remember wanting to put a smile on her face; I remember pretending to have a seizure, shaking my body and only stopping when I was wracked with laughter.

My therapist doesn't think this memory is very funny.

'What do you think you were trying to do in that moment,' she asked me when I first told her about it.

'I was trying to be a jokester,' I said. 'I guess I was trying to lighten the mood.'

'And what did you need in that room?'

I had shrugged, but she pushed me, so I closed my eyes and went back to that bed, to that moment.

'I needed my mum to tell me I would be okay,' I said. And I felt it again; the deep emotional pain that reverberated around my childhood self.

The type of stories from Kakuma I get from my mum are dependent on her mood. When she is feeling happy, she smiles as she recollects the community we were once part of. She loved the friends she made and the stories that different people told late into the night. She loved the comradeship in life's most basic tasks, from cooking to cleaning. She loved that I was surrounded by so many different children and adults who cared for me. We never felt alone.

I got my nickname Shayshay while in the camp. My mum doesn't know what it means, but she remembers the song a distant relative would sing. He would sing 'is it Shayshay?' whenever I walked into a room. He had a beautiful singing voice.

'You never just walked in,' Mum tells me. 'You always made an entrance. You would wiggle your hips like this when someone sang your song.'

One time we were invited to have dinner with a Somali family on the other side of the camp. It was too far to walk. We needed to get on a motorcycle taxi. My mother hired one for us, but when it was time to get on, I refused. I screamed and wailed that I didn't want to be on the motorcycle. My mum tried to calm me down, but I kept refusing. We walked for over an hour, my mother seething beside me.

I think back to the memory I had of my first day of school. I am holding onto the hand of a friend as we march through the dry bushland with great excitement. It is Fatima's hand.

A friend of my mum had told me to watch out for the lions on my way there. Fatima wasn't scared, but I was. I kept vigilant, stopping every now and then whenever I thought I saw something in the distance. I know now he was joking, but I can't help but smile that the idea of being eaten alive by lions wasn't enough to stop me from attending school.

But there is so much I don't remember about life in the camp. I don't have any real sense of how long I was there. I ask my mum and she too struggles. She has given me several answers: either a year, a year and a half or just under two years. She doesn't remember the exact month and year we entered, nor the month and year we left.

I don't remember my last night in the Kakuma refugee camp, or leaving it. Did I understand then the life-changing journey I was about to embark on? I don't remember the time we left the camp, whether it was in the middle of the night or the day. I ask my mum if we were free to go or if we had to sneak out and she says that no one stopped us from leaving, that we weren't prisoners in the camp.

I don't remember what we packed. Was I sad to be leaving the school, to be leaving the friends I had made? Was I sad to be leaving Fatima? Was she sad when she learnt I was leaving? What, if anything, had the adults told the children?

What, if anything, could we comprehend about what lay ahead of us?

I let my parents paint a picture of what was once hidden in the dark. I ask my mum what made her decide to leave the camp and take our destinies into her own hands, instead of waiting for a resettlement decision through UNHCR. She said, again, that she found herself unable to keep waiting for our lives to begin. I was growing up quickly and she didn't want me to be one of the young people who would spend their entire lives in the camp. I wonder if seeing me go to school for the first time spurred her into decisive action.

We couldn't afford to get a plane so we were driven all the way to Nairobi – a journey that can take between thirteen and sixteen hours depending on the route.

My dad was waiting for us in Nairobi in a hotel. I don't have any memories of this and didn't know this happened until Baba told me while I was interviewing him. He couldn't remember how many years it had been since we last saw each other. We are sitting together in the living room, my mum cooking in the kitchen, as he tells me of this reunion. He had smuggled himself through the Kenyan border from Ethiopia without a passport. I close my eyes and realise I don't have any memories of my dad before coming to Europe. This small fact doesn't startle me, it just fills me with a strange, muted feeling. An acceptance that borders on pain.

We left the hotel and rented out a house, Baba tells me. Our joy from the reunion was short-lived. My mother and I were set to embark on a dangerous but life-altering journey.

I don't remember my final night in Nairobi, in Kenya, in Africa, as a refugee. My mum tells me I was excited and wouldn't go to sleep. My cheerfulness only deepened her anxiety and she had to stop herself from being annoyed with me. I was eager to throw myself into the unknown in the way that only children are able to do. She was consumed by all the things that could end up going wrong.

THE SEPARATION

My dad was also nervous. We were travelling with one other woman, whom I don't remember. My parents, my dad's friend and this woman were driven to the airport. My dad said goodbye to us once we parked and waited, anxiously, outside the airport.

My parents had paid a hefty bribe to Kenyan officials to let us go through immigration. My dad's friend had stayed with us as we passed through the different checkpoints at the airport. The man left our side only once he saw us boarding the plane. He left the airport and found my dad, who was pacing outside. He told him that his wife and child were on the plane.

'I was very happy when the aeroplane left. It was the happiest day,' Baba tells me, with a wide smile on his face. He looks momentarily younger, and I wonder if he had the same smile outside the airport.

My dad told me that the story, ours, finished once that plane took off. I laughed in response because for me, the story had just begun. From this moment on, I can truly remember.

6
FINALLY IN EUROPE

We landed in Germany in 1998. The airport was busy with people, yet at the same time lifeless. I remember being struck by the grey and silver interior, by the escalators, and, most importantly, by all the white people. I felt out of place and clung to my mum.

We were taken into a room by two officials and told to wait. Once they left, my mum turned around to me and handed me some money to hide. She tucked it into my chest and told me to hold onto it. I nodded.

Two female guards returned. I stood back as they strip-searched my mum. I watched her undress. She did so calmly, even smiling back at them and at me. They kept their smiles on their faces, trying perhaps to reassure us. I was terrified that they would search me too. I wanted to scream, but I was incapable of making a sound. I wanted to cry, but I was unable to form any tears in my eyes. They patted my mum down. She looked cold. I stood frozen beside her.

I don't remember how long the strip search lasted, but I was relieved when they let my mum put her clothes back on. She looked so small without them. I was scared I would be next, but we were allowed to leave the room. We left the airport, but that room stayed with me. I did not know then how often I would come back to it, how it would go on to shape the way I understood Black bodies, including my own.

However much time passes, I still find myself walking back into that room in my memory, stepping into the shoes of that terrified child looking up at my mum as she undresses. I sometimes still flinch when I see a Black person fully undress, either in real life or on screen. I spent many years of my life struggling to change in front of other people.

We were provided temporary accommodation and moved to a one-bedroom flat. I remember that place clearly, its layout and how the entire place brightened when the curtains were open and the sun was allowed to look in. I fell in love with it almost instantly and would walk in and out of the rooms that were our own; from the small kitchen, to the bathroom, to the hallway, to the bedroom, and our living room. I couldn't believe we had the place to ourselves.

Our neighbours were an Arab family. We became instant friends. They were a mother, a daughter who was just a few years older than me, and a son, then a teenager, who had a severe learning disability. We spent most of our time together, me with the children, and my mum with their mum.

The days in Germany passed easily. I remember the first time I saw and felt snow. We went to a park beside a church. It looked so soft and inviting. Without a second thought, I ran straight ahead and dived into the snow, only to be left speechless at its brutal cold. I backed away and initially let the other children play with the snow. After some encouragement from my mum, I joined them and we made snowmen. We spent hours in that park.

My mum's two eldest sisters had resettled in London with their children. My parents had decided to make the UK our home while we were in Kakuma. My mum wanted to be with her family and they had been positive about the UK's treatment of refugees.

I registered at the local school, and I still have a vague memory of my first day. I walked into a classroom of children playing and didn't feel held back by the fact I didn't speak the language. I wanted to get involved. I was playing with two girls when a boy came towards us and pushed me away. He didn't want to play with me. I was left alone.

I don't know if it was the following evening, the next week or if months had passed, but that memory is interwoven with a disturbing incident. I am back in our flat, sitting down looking at my skin and feeling a powerful sense of revulsion. It was the first time I had ever felt this way. I had never really thought about having dark skin, had not thought of being Black until I was in a space where I was the only one. While sitting there in that flat, for the first time, I wanted to be white.

I scratched my legs and saw the white, ashy streaks the scratches left behind. I started scratching myself all over, with a desperate vigour. I wanted to cover myself in those white ashy streaks. I scratched as deep into the skin as I could, wanting to tear at the blackness. I didn't stop once I started bleeding: I kept scratching, growing more upset, until I was on the brink of tears. I only stopped once my mum walked into the room.

I had seen my dad a handful of times in the near six-year period that we were separated. I didn't have any memory of it so when he joined us in Germany, I met him like a stranger. But I was excited that he was there and that my family were together once again.

He had turned up to the flat. Funnily enough, it's not him returning that I remember, but my mum. I remember the smile on her face when he came into the flat. I ran to him and hugged him tight.

It took me a while to adjust to having a father figure in my life. When, for example, I was struggling in the shower and called for my mum to help, my dad came in and I screamed at him to get out. I felt embarrassed at the idea of him looking at my naked body. When I came out, I explained to him sternly that I was a grown girl now and needed my own space. My parents did their best not to laugh.

My life, in the months that followed, kicked into high gear. After years of waiting around as refugees, suddenly everything was happening all at once. My mum and I left Germany with my dad and went to the Netherlands. We stayed with members of his family who lived in The Hague.

We didn't stay in the Netherlands for long, but I loved the time we spent there. We lived with my great-aunt's children, who were beautiful teenage girls. I was desperate to emulate everything about them, from their sense of fashion to the way they laughed. They took me out to restaurants, to the local funfair and to hang with their friends.

As for my departure, I have no memory of leaving The Hague, nor of arriving in London. I don't even remember saying goodbye to my parents. Was I scared or excited? Of all the things I don't remember, this is what I am most frustrated by. Why don't I remember saying goodbye to my mum or where that goodbye took place?

I have vague, dark memories of waiting for my aunt Amina in a house in London that felt cold and uninviting. I was relieved when Amina walked through those doors and took me into her warm embrace. I kept smiling and giggling as I sat in the front passenger seat of the car, the joy feeling like small bubbles popping off across my skin.

By this point I was around six years old, months shy of being seven. It's from this moment that my memories go from a muted tone to a blazing Technicolor. The memories before are like watching a confusing film on an old TV, while those after feel like sitting in the front row of a 3D cinema. It's difficult to put into words but from that car ride onwards I feel like it's *me* experiencing those memories, it is *me* living in those moments. I recognise and see myself in that child in the car. I no longer have this divide between Amina and Aamna. Aamna takes over.

I watched the trees go by with giddy excitement, enjoying the warmth of the early spring sunshine on my face. When the car parked, my family, including half a dozen cousins, ran out of the house to meet me. Some I was meeting for the first time, others I hadn't seen in years. My aunt laughed at my desperation to jump into my cousin's arms and told me to let her take off the seatbelt first. I was off and out of the car the second she did.

I ate McDonald's for the first time and only liked the chips. I gave my burger to a teenage cousin who let me borrow his watch. I was fascinated by its ability to turn the volume up and down on the TV. I watched my first English-speaking film, *The Lion King*, and was saddened that Simba's father's death was permanent, that he didn't ever return. It was the only time I felt vaguely sad that day, but it didn't last long as I was encouraged to play with my cousin Loula. She was the only cousin my age and had been trying to get my attention all day. We played in the kitchen together.

My life went on as I waited for my parents to join me. They were still in the Netherlands, making attempts to cross over. I initially lived with my aunt Amina, her youngest daughter, Umal, and her sons, Ahmed and Mohamed. I slotted into the family easily: it was a loving house and each day was filled with some adventure. My aunt was particularly sensitive to my needs in those early days, showering me with presents so I never felt lacking.

One sunny day, she bought me a pink bike. I'd never had such a wonderful present before and hugged her as tight as I could when she showed it to me. Once she got training wheels put on, I learnt to ride around the neighbourhood in East London, with her encouraging me.

I was then moved, I'm not sure exactly when or how long after I arrived, to live with my other aunt, my mum's older sister, Umalquair, and her three daughters: Aaliyah and

Ilham, who were then in their late teens, and her youngest, Loula, the cousin closest to me in age. There was a place available at Loula's school and it was agreed it would be best if I attended the same one as her. My two aunts were practically neighbours, so it didn't feel like a big jump.

Loula and I were inseparable both at school and at home. Though I hadn't been in the country for long, Loula quickly followed my lead, often with embarrassing consequences. When I told her I knew how to cut hair, she let me cut her fringe. Her mum was furious with us both. 'I can't believe how many stupid things you convinced us to do,' Loula says when we talk about it in the present.

I still tease Loula about a time when the two of us were sitting in the back of her mum's car, and were asked who our best friend was.

'Loula!' I said, straight away.

'Polly,' said Loula. Polly was a girl we went to school with.

'You're never going to let this go,' a very annoyed adult Loula says. 'Don't tell me you're going to put that in the book.' But what's the point of writing a memoir if you don't get the last word?

It was while I was living with Loula that I went to my first English school. I was wary and quiet on my first day, choosing to stay with the boy in my class who offered to show me around. I quickly acclimated to the school day. I liked sitting in classrooms and the hours we spent learning, I liked the hot food we got to eat during lunch, I liked that we had two different periods of break, I liked the huge playgrounds we got to run around in.

I don't remember learning English. My memories jump from not knowing the language in my first few days in the country to suddenly speaking it fluently. Maybe it was just that easy. I wasn't an exceptional student, but I found myself doing well enough in those first few months.

We became friends with our neighbours' children and would often knock for them and ask if they were allowed to come out and play. Those days were filled with learning the new *NSYNC songs and our first embarrassing crushes on boys. Once, I was instructed to ask a boy who lived down the road from us if he wanted to be our friend's boyfriend. She was a sweet, short blonde girl who was too shy to ask herself. I walked down solemnly, taking the task slightly too seriously, and ran back, overjoyed, when relaying the news. He said yes and was brought into our group, watching films with us and riding our bikes together.

We had lavish parties for people's birthdays, inviting all the children in the neighbourhood. In one picture of these parties, I am smiling straight into the camera as we stand around a table ready to cut the cake. I look happy.

But while the months I settled in the UK without my mother were filled with a lot of love and joy, I had carried her absence with me. It was a dull ache I learnt to ignore because I didn't want people to think I was not grateful for everything they'd done for me. At times, however, the pain was too overwhelming.

One afternoon, my cousin Ilham was looking after me and her younger sister Loula. They were teasing each other in the way that sisters do. I watched on with a profound sense of loneliness. I tried to remember what my mum looked like and started to panic when I couldn't see her as clearly in my mind's eye as I had before. I closed my eyes and tried to remember her easy smile and her deep, dark eyes and couldn't. I felt a buzzing in my throat and a numbness in my feet.

I burst into tears – to the shock of both of my cousins – and became hysterical. The anguish I had held on a tight leash for so many weeks tore through me. I howled as I cried out.

I fell to the ground. Ilham, then just a teenager, rushed over to me and tried to hold me but I pushed her away. A voice, like a high-pitched drone, reverberated in my chest telling me the same thing over and over again: *everyone I love will eventually leave.* I kept crying until I passed out.

When I came to, Ilham was kneeling beside me, stroking my hair. I looked up and held onto her as I choked out the last remaining sobs. Loula was still standing over me, looking on. She seemed almost too terrified to come near me. Was she scared I'd gone crazy and would infect her?

I got up, we ate dinner, and we never spoke about that incident again. When, over twenty years later, I called Ilham to ask if she remembered, she went silent for a while and then simply said, 'I'll never forget, Coco.'

Most of all, I remember the day my mum and I reunited. I was told that she had finally made it through the border and would be with us before the end of the day. We waited for her arrival at Amina's house. I felt nervous, but didn't want to let anyone else know I was. I didn't want them to know that I was scared that when she came, she wouldn't love me anymore. What if she didn't recognise me as her own?

I was scared she would be angry with me and I thought of the new experiences, such as eating fast food, that I had happily embraced in her absence. Had I betrayed her by continuing on in my life? Would she think I had left her behind?

As an adult, I can't help but feel both happy and sad that at that moment in time my mum and I were sharing the same fears of our separation. I am happy that our love for each other is so deep and alike, but sad for how young she was, and how quickly I had to grow up.

On the day of my mother's return, I kept those thoughts to myself. When I was asked if I was happy that my mum was returning, I nodded and flashed a brilliant smile.

When my mum arrived, we all crowded around the door; I stood at the back. When the door opened, she walked through with my aunt. I remember that moment so clearly; she was wearing jeans and a jumper, and had her hair in two plaits. I don't think I had ever seen her in such clothes before. She didn't look like my mum, she looked like a teenager.

I ran towards her then and noticed something when I hugged her: a small bump. She was pregnant. I was confused, excited and, I realise now, decades later, a little bit sad. Before she arrived in the UK, she was only ever my mum. It had almost always just been us two. As I held tightly onto her, I knew the borders of the relationship we had had changed forever.

We didn't immediately live together once she arrived. My mum lived between her two sisters' houses as she waited for my dad to join us in the UK, while I continued living with Loula and her family. Once my mum had been able to find a house for us to live in, near my aunt in the East London borough of Newham, she sat me down and asked me a question.

'Do you want to live with me?' Mama asked, looking into my eyes. My life had been so disrupted, she didn't want to bring more unwanted change. I answered easily and immediately: 'I want to live with you. I always want to live with you.'

When we spoke about this moment, years later, we laughed about it. 'You always knew who your mum was,' she said.

We moved into the house on Western Road. I remember how pleased my mum was when we went to get my new school uniform for the primary school that was down the road from us.

On the day my father was supposed to arrive, I sat on the stairs that led up to our flat. I don't remember how long it took him to smuggle himself from the Netherlands into the UK too, but I imagine it was a few months after my mum arrived. I sat for hours, looking at the door. I kept telling myself that today would be the day that I got my family back, that we would finally be complete, that I would be whole.

My mum, then heavily pregnant, came to the landing with a solemn face. She said my father wouldn't be arriving, there had been another problem. I burst into tears and got up to walk to my room, but as I did so, the door opened and there he was, smiling from ear to ear. I didn't have time to be angry at my mum's joke. My dad ran up the stairs. I cried into him when he lifted me into his arms and held me there.

The days and weeks that followed were momentous ones for us. It was the first time in my life, and the first time since my parents became parents, that we lived together, permanently, in a house that was our own. We had nowhere to go; it wasn't a pitstop to the next destination. We could plant roots here and they could go as deep as we wanted.

Not long after, Aamir was born with much fanfare in Newham hospital. I went to visit my mum and my new brother with my dad. My mum smiled at me when I walked into the room. We hugged and I stared at my brother. I couldn't stop staring at him.

We arrived back at our house transformed: a family of four. I loved the normality of that moment and the many moments that followed in that house.

'Now, your book is finished,' Baba says. 'The story is done.'

I laugh at him as he claps his hands.

'I'm sorry Baba, but it's not finished,' I say, smiling at him.

'What! What else do you need to write? We have gone through the war,' Baba says.

'This isn't just a book about the war,' I try to explain to him. My mum shouts from the kitchen that lunch is almost ready.

'This is a book about finding where I belong in the world,' I tell Baba as we both get up to join my mum. 'I need to go to Kenya and Somalia.'

'You want to go to Somalia? To Mogadishu?' Baba asks, bewildered.

'Yes,' I say, laughing. 'I need to.'

FINALLY IN EUROPE

I don't know much about the country in the present day. I spent the majority of my childhood avoiding any association with Somalia. I didn't want anything to do with what I saw about Somalia on the news, from the terrorism to the economic insecurity and the constant threat of famine.

The realisation that I need to return to Somalia first came upon me when I found myself looking at the country's profile on the BBC website.[1] It told me that the country had been moving towards stability since the formation of a new internationally backed government was installed, following decades of violence and local power struggles. *There are 17 million people currently living in Somalia and the main languages spoken are Somali and Arabic.*

When I tell my dad this, he disagrees. 'Somalis speak Somali in Somalia,' Baba says, firmly.

'I'll let the BBC know that feedback,' I shoot back.

Life expectancy for men is 55 years for men and 59 years for women.

The British Foreign Office advises against all travel to Somalia, and only essential travel to three regions in Somaliland.

The main terrorist groups to fear are Al-Shabab, which over the Noughties controlled large swaths of Somalia. The other groups that have threatened Somalia's security are Al-Qaeda and more recently ISIS.

The Foreign Office also warns that there is a significant risk of terrorism, kidnapping, and maritime crime. It also notes the regular occurrence of natural disasters, such as drought and flooding.[2]

I read this and think: this cannot be the only way I allow myself to understand the country my family is from.

'Why are you going to Mogadishu?' Mama shouts, breaking me out of my trance. I don't know how to explain to my mum, especially after understanding what she did to get out.

'When I go back, I can take video recordings and send them to you,' Baba says. He is not as insistent as Mama that I shouldn't go, but I know he is worried.

I shake my head, 'No, Baba. That's not enough. I need to go there, I need to go back.'

PART TWO

7
A JOURNEY BACK IN TIME

The journey is an important motif in most Somali stories. Whether a story is recited orally or written down, the movement from one geographical place to another is vital for the narrative. It often forms a rite of passage for the hero.

In his analysis of Somali literature, published in 1997, Professor Ali Jimale Ahmed describes the journey motif as a 'prerequisite for truly knowing a person'.[1] He quotes a Somali proverb, 'nin aan dhul marin dhaayo maleh', which literally translates to 'a man who has not travelled does not have eyes.'

This is widespread in the Western canon too. I first learnt about the 'hero's journey' in fiction as a teenager in my English class. In this template, men receive a call to adventure in a faraway place, which challenges and changes them. Joseph Campbell, American writer and theorist, details the stages and steps the hero takes in this narrative trope.

As a teenager, I didn't see myself as a hero that would ever embark on this journey, but I am. My first trip to Calais and the conversation I had with my mum in her kitchen sparked my compulsion to learn about our past. I felt consumed by who my parents were, by the war and its aftermath. I have been on an inward personal journey, but there is a physical one calling me too.

It is for this that reason I am flying to Nairobi on 8 March 2022. After interviewing my parents over a two-year period,

I am ready to return to the countries that had shaped our story. I am ready to know my dad, my mum and what they left behind in a new way. I am ready to better understand my country of origin, my culture and, perhaps, myself.

I don't have much of a plan, which worries me. My dad is waiting for me in Mogadishu, but I've only booked my flights to and from Nairobi. I am unsure what I want to do in Somalia or in Kenya, or how to get from one to the other. UNHCR has thus far pushed back on my requests to visit the Kakuma refugee camp; I have been told that as a result of Covid, only essential personnel are going in and out of the camp.

I haven't booked any meetings or interviews with people. I only know that once I make it to Mogadishu I will be seeing the house my parents once called home, and my family's hotel.

My father first returned to Somalia in 2012, twenty years after I was born. When he went, he visited the hotel that his father used to own. It was in ruins. He committed himself there and then to rebuilding it back to what it used to be. I am fascinated by this need to rebuild. Mogadishu is hardly a tourist destination, so I know he isn't driven by money, yet he has spent the past decade trying to recreate what was lost to the past. I want to understand why he goes back.

It is International Women's Day. As I am leaving my house, I look at my poster of Somali women protesting for the release of American communist and civil rights activist Angela Davies. It hangs in the hallway beside the front door. The protest took place in 1972 in Mogadishu. I smile at the picture.

It didn't take me long to get ready. I had packed and showered the night before.

I haven't slept very well. I tell my family and friends that I am nervous, but that is just half the truth. I am terrified and keep thinking of all the things that could go wrong. I take a beta blocker and check my passport is in my bag for the

A JOURNEY BACK IN TIME

fourth time that early morning. I keep taking it out of the bag whenever the panic grips me that I don't have it with me.

I say goodbye to my husband and leave the house at 5 a.m., travelling to Heathrow Airport in the dark. London is alive, as the city always is, with people heading to work or on their way back home after a night out. I get on the Heathrow Express to Terminal 5.

I remember the opening chapter of one of my favourite memoirs, *The Return*, by Hisham Matar. He is standing at the airport terminal waiting to board his flight to Libya with his wife and his mother. Matar, who was returning after thirty-three years, fears what awaits him as he prepares to cross 'the chasm that divided the man from the eight-year-old boy'.

As I hurtle towards my terminal, I think of the chasm that I too am about to cross. Will this journey hurt? The question felt childish but I couldn't let go of it. Will Coco be waiting for me on the other side? Will I be able to bring our two selves together?

On that morning, I felt so distant from my British friends, but closely connected to strangers like Matar. Living in exile is both an isolating and unifying phenomenon. Many people in my life cannot relate to my experiences, but there are others in the world, forced to leave their homes, who know exactly what I went through. It is a unique tribe to be part of.

For such a momentous trip, the journey is thankfully uneventful. I get through security and sit down to have a scrambled egg and smoked salmon bagel for breakfast. I drink a cup of tea while I look at my emails. Once my gate is called, I make my way to my plane. I am relieved when I see I won't be sitting next to the large group of young American university students that board just before me.

While I hate being in airports, going through security and border checks, I love flying. I like how small the passing clouds make me feel as we jet past countries and continents. I read a book in one sitting, and start another. When my neck begins to hurt, I put on a film.

I think I'll get scared the closer I get to Kenya, but I don't. My heart rate stays the same as we fly over the Sahara desert around El Oued, a city in Algeria.

I keep my eyes glued to the window when the pilot says we will be landing in forty minutes. I see the city open itself up to me. It shines yellow, burnt orange and white in the night. It is just after 10 p.m. local time. When I squint, I can see cars moving. They look like ants.

Was I sitting in the window seat when I left Nairobi all those years ago?

I sail through immigration, armed with my folder of Covid documents, and meet my hotel taxi driver. After I check in at the hotel, I go to bed tired but happy.

The panic I was expecting to feel finally hits me the next morning. I'm scared about my journey onwards to Somalia. I also need to book another PCR test, but find myself unable to do that either. I sit in bed for several hours that morning scrolling on my phone. I listen to my favourite surah in the Quran, Surah Al-Baqarah, and after taking several deep breaths I am able to get out of bed and book both the PCR test and the flight to Mogadishu. I let my dad know I'll be arriving in two days' time.

Though there are direct flights from Nairobi to Kenya, I couldn't find a reputable airline offering one online. A friend who lives in the city tells me to go through Addis Ababa in Ethiopia instead: it is a longer journey and more expensive, but it is safer, I am told.

Later, I meet my cousin Hani for the first time for a late lunch at a busy chain restaurant, which serves everything from pizza, spaghetti, burgers, to a seafood platter and steak. The restaurant is over two floors and is filled with businessmen, families and students when I get there. I grab a table and wait for her. We embrace like long-lost friends when she comes in.

Hani is a few years older than me and grew up in Nairobi. We have very little in common, but get on instantly. She is an aspiring model and fashion designer with a really large following on both Instagram and Facebook. We both order chicken wraps and chips, and she convinces me to get a milkshake.

I ask her what she does. 'I sell clothes and accessories. My Instagram is a great platform to advertise these products. And I'm also a content creator.'

She is a lot shyer than I expect her to be, but also warm. She is taken back when I tell her it only took me 25 minutes to walk to the restaurant. 'We have Uber in Nairobi,' she tells me and I nod, but tell her I like to walk, which she laughs at.

Hani had mostly lived in Nairobi, but was born in Dubai. She lived in Mogadishu for a few years in her late twenties, returning to Nairobi just before the pandemic hit. I'd never heard someone so young speak so lovingly about Mogadishu. She yearns for it.

'Mogadishu is the only place that feels like home,' she says. 'If the security situation was better, I would live there all the time.'

When I ask why Kenya isn't home, especially as she went through schooling in the country, she shrugs. 'You feel really lonely in Kenya and like you don't belong.' At times she didn't feel welcome by Kenyans, she says: 'They feel like we took over their country.'

When I tell her I am writing about the Somali war, she congratulates me. 'Our family wasn't affected by the war,' she says, just as our food arrives. I look at her. Did she also grow up not knowing the truth of what our families went through?

'Both our grandad and my parents are survivors of the civil war,' I say.

She looks at me, surprised, but doesn't ask for any more information. She asks instead if I will take pictures of her and the food. I happily do. At one point, she gets up and asks me to take a video of her walking around the restaurant. I laugh at how confident she is.

I leave the restaurant feeling less guilty for taking as long as I did to look into my family's past: it is clear that in our family we have all made a habit of not speaking of what had happened. Perhaps this shadowy silence has helped us to move forward.

I return to my hotel and repack before catching some sleep. I will be flying to Mogadishu in a few hours. I feel scared and nervous. What am I hoping to get from Somalia? I wake up, realising I slept through my alarm. I am lucky to not miss my flight to Mogadishu.

I wear an abaya for the first time in my adult life and put my headscarf on. I do so because it's a requirement for women in Mogadishu. I look at myself in the mirror and like the person who looks back.

I drink a cup of tea once I check in at the airport and laugh at just how milky it is. I used to be teased for how much milk I put in my tea in London, and finally I understand where that taste came from.

It is a two-part trip. The first part is a two-hour plane journey to Addis Ababa, the capital of Ethiopia. The layover there is tiresome. I can't access any Wi-Fi on either of my phones and I suddenly feel cut off from the world. I sit among the group of Somalis waiting to board the Ethiopian Airlines plane to Mogadishu and start to feel like a fraud.

I listen to the conversations around me. Some speak of their long journeys and their exhaustion, others of their reasons for returning. Most have been to Somalia before. I hope no one talks to me: I don't want anyone to realise how poor my Somali has become.

I am feeling scared. I allow myself that small admission. The fear builds up as the time to board the plane inches closer. There is a small blue screen above the gate door that simply says 'Departing to: Mogadishu, Departing Time: 09.10'. We all stand when the status changes to 'Boarding'. It flashes in bright green. I shuffle onto the plane in a daze and though the sign on the gate says differently, I can't believe I will soon be in Mogadishu. It feels as improbable as being on Mars.

I stand in line beside a short white man who looks to be in his mid-thirties. He has large, wide eyes and tanned, textured skin. He is gripping his red European passport and I wonder if the fear on his face matches mine. I turn so he doesn't strike up a conversation with me. I don't want to stand out by talking to the only non-Somali in the group.

I end up talking instead to two Somali women who seem to be around my age as we board the shuttle bus that will take us to the plane. I do so after hearing their London accents. They are wearing black headscarves and abayas, like me. One is slightly shorter than me, the other towering over us. They both wear kind, easy smiles. Finally, I start to relax.

'Is this your first time returning to Xamar?' the shorter one asks me. I remember my dad telling me Xamar is the Somali word for the old part of Mogadishu, but it is now used to describe the whole city.

It's interesting that she asks about a return, assuming I have been to the city before. Or, by phrasing the question in that way, maybe she's suggesting that regardless of whether you have ever been to Somalia, any trip to the country for a Somali person is a return in some way.

I don't say this because I don't want to be weird. I also don't know how exactly to answer the question. I decide on the truth.

'I don't really know Mogadishu. I was last in the city when I was a small child, but it wasn't for very long. It's where my parents are from,' I say.

'Are you travelling alone?' the short one asks, impressed. She does most of the talking.

'I'm only alone for this journey,' I say, 'My dad is waiting for me in the city.'

'You're really brave to come back,' the taller one says.

I smile at her. 'So are you, I guess.'

We board the bus. 'How do you girls know each other?'

'We met on the flight from Turkey,' the shorter girl says, 'I didn't see you on that flight? Did you come from Turkey?'

'No, I came from Nairobi,' I say. 'I was in the city for a few days before coming here.'

'Everyone heading to Mogadishu does so by flying through Turkey, it's much easier, walaashay [sister],' the taller one says.

'I'll remember that next time,' I say. Am I really already speaking of a next time?

My exhaustion and fear ease once I am sitting on the plane. I am by the window again, beside an older Turkish man and a young Somali man. I manage to sleep for an hour, but wake up once we cross into Somali airspace.

I see the Mogadishu coastline below. It's beautiful.

I sit in a haze of sleeplessness, my ears largely blocked to the conversations around me. My surroundings roar to life once we land. I feel wide awake. I look around me, trying to drink it all in, but the sun is too bright and it beats down on us viciously. The buildings around me are white and they shine brightly in the daylight.

Once we disembark, I shuffle towards immigration. There are two queues: one for citizens and residents, and another for 'ajnabi' (foreigners). I stand in the foreigner queue, with the majority of people from the plane. There are a whole array of passports in our queue: South Africa, the US, the Netherlands. I can see clearly that though we are all Somali, the war truly has scattered us across the world.

As I move towards the top of the queue, one airport worker asks: 'Are you okay?'

'I'm fine,' I say in Somali, before immediately cutting back to English to admit, 'I don't speak Somali very well, I'm sorry.'

The worker looks at me in surprise and asks: 'Are you Somali?'

A JOURNEY BACK IN TIME

I nod and he laughs. 'Don't worry, you'll be okay,' he says in Somali. 'Learn Somali quickly though. It's not good to have a Somali person not speaking Somali.'

'I'll learn,' I say.

When I got to the border official, we have the same interaction about my Somali, or lack thereof. I promise again to learn Somali.

'You need to pay $60 for the visa,' the border officer says.

I put my card on the table and he looks at me incredulously. 'You can't use that here,' he says.

'Is there no cash machine nearby?' I ask and he laughs again and says, 'No machine in the whole area.'

I remember then the emergency cash in my wallet. It's £60 exactly. 'Can I pay with British pounds instead?'

'Yes, but I won't give you any change,' he says.

'I don't mind,' I say. He stamps my passport.

As I am walking past immigration, I hear a man shouting 'Amina'. I know a close family friend named Mohamed, who works as a manager in my family's hotel, will be picking me up from the airport. He got a special pass to be allowed into the airport, which has the strictest security of any airport I've ever seen.

He instantly knows who I am when I walk through security. He later tells me it's because he can see my father's face on my face. The thought warms me. Mohamed walks towards me and envelopes me in a hug.

'Welcome to Xamar!' he says, almost shouting. I look around to see if anyone notices us, but they're all absorbed by their own reunions with loved ones.

I hug Mohamed back, but don't know what to say. I feel like a deer caught in headlights. I keep asking myself, am I really here? Is this really happening?

Mohamed helps me with my bag and we hurry into his car. I first notice the heat and it isn't as unbearable as I thought it would be. I struggle to keep my eyes open, having left my sunglasses in my luggage.

There is a group of armed soldiers in the carpark we're in, staring at us. I must look odd, the way I keep looking at everything, like a child in a sweetshop. I wave at the soldiers and they look startled. I slowly put my hand back down.

I stick my head out of the car as we drive out of the airport, looking at the streets, the children, the markets, the buildings, the goats, and cows. The buildings are nearly all painted; they look sunken and relaxed against the sun. Most shop signs are decorated in blue. We stop at checkpoints, but the city is far from the warzone I had envisioned.

I almost don't recognise my dad when the car stops beside a hotel and a shopping mall. He stands on the pavement and waves at us. He has been in Mogadishu for a month now, returning, as he always does, for business, and for his soul.

He looks younger than I have seen him in decades. He wears a pink shirt, white linen trousers and sunglasses. He looks happy.

I jump out of the car. We stand and stare at each other for a moment. We don't hug, just smile at each other, laughing. We don't say a word as I walk towards him, and let what is left unsaid settle between us. I, Aamna, stand beside Mohamed: here he is with his eldest child, his only daughter, in the city he was born in and once called home.

In American-Vietnamese writer Viet Thanh Nguyen's debut novel *The Sympathiser*, the anonymous main character, who flees Vietnam following the fall of Saigon, talks of a refugee's ability to time travel – because it is time, not space, that defines a refugee.[2] 'While the distance to return to our lost country was far but finite, the number of years it would take to close that distance was potentially infinite.' Refugees everywhere ask themselves the same question: when can we return?

Seeing my father for the first time in Mogadishu made me realise that my dad, too, lives in two timelines: the man he was in Somalia in the early nineties and the father he is in London now. Like Nguyen's narrator, he occupies 'the here and the there, the present and the past'. He is, like refugees before him, like refugees to come, a 'reluctant time-traveller'.

This is where my thoughts turn as Baba and I stand facing each other on the same stretch of road he had once walked on as he made preparations for my birth and arrival to this city. As we walk side by side that morning, falling into step with each other, he says what he has been waiting three decades to tell me.

'Welcome to Somalia, welcome to Mogadishu, welcome, finally, home.'

8
YOU WERE ONCE AMINA

Initially, I am upset when I learn I won't be staying in my family's hotel in Mogadishu. I feel like that was the main point of my trip. My father explains, however, that the hotel I am staying in is right next to his and one of the best in the city. When I ask why he didn't want me to stay in his hotel, he says he wants my return to Mogadishu to be a 'five-star experience'. I can't help but laugh.

The three of us walk into Marhaba Hotel, located at Olow Tower in Makkah Al-Mukarramah Street, a busy road in Mogadishu. The building, which has six floors, towers over the others on the street. The windows are covered with what looks to be green film. It is surrounded by other smaller hotels, shops and fast food restaurants. The road is jammed with cars and tuk-tuks. I struggle to notice much else beside the consistent beeping of horns.

At check in, I am taken to a corner where a woman searches my suitcase and asks me to turn on all my electronic devices. I panic for a moment when she turns on my Kindle. I have a lot of romance novels on the devices, with some embarrassing covers. I wonder if anyone has been arrested in the city before for reading a book with a cover of shirtless man. It thankfully goes straight to the chapter I last read.

She pats me down and I do everything she asks in a daze. She smiles when she says she is done.

The room I am brought into is large. It follows the brown and green colour scheme of the hotel's logo: the desk, bedframe, wardrobe and one set of curtains are brown, while the bed covers, the other set of curtains and the chair are white. There are two double beds. 'You'll be moved to a room with one bed in a couple of days, they aren't available right now,' Baba tells me. I take a deep breath of cool air once the AC is turned on. When I see the beds, I realise how tired I really am. My dad and Mohamed leave me alone for a few hours to sleep.

I get up just before my dad calls to ask if I am hungry. 'You've been sleeping for ages!' he says.

Baba and Mohamed arrive in my room around twenty minutes later and we decide to eat in the hotel's rooftop restaurant. Before we go, Mohamed says that reception wants to make a copy of my passport. I give it to him and he opens it and looks curiously at it.

'Ah-mnah,' Mohamed says. 'Why is it spelt like that?'

'Her name is Aamna in London,' Baba says.

'Aamna,' Mohamed says, letting the name roll around his tongue. He shakes his head. 'You're Amina. You were once Amina.'

I don't know what to say in response so I smile.

We walk to the rooftop restaurant and I am stunned by the spectacular views of the city it offers. It is the late afternoon and the sun beats against the sky. High-rise buildings are nestled among thick trees, rectangular single-storey homes, sandy roads filled with people strolling. There are masses of cars and red tuk-tuk taxis beeping incessantly.

The late lunch I have, the chicken shawarma wrap with chips, is incredible. It reminds me of my mother's meals, and I love that. I feel her close to me. During lunch, I am encouraged to try a 'spondias shake', a fruit juice made of hog plum. It's delicious and refreshing.

Once the sun sets, I walk down the road to see my father's hotel. The streets are loud and intense. People are sitting on the roadside in plastic chairs, drinking tea and talking. We walk into my family's hotel without much fanfare. My dad proudly shows off the interior, from the wallpaper to the tiles. 'I chose each one,' he tells me of the decorative choices he points out. 'I wanted it to look like before.'

The hotel reminds me of him, or maybe he is showing me who he used to be. As he gives me a brief tour, I immediately understand why he came back. So much of the past had crumbled around him, but this hotel was one of the few things he could bring back to life.

We go into one of the rooms and have tea with my dad's cousin, Liban, and his wife, who are both staying at the hotel. Liban is a decade younger than my dad.

'Is this the first time you've returned to Xamar since the war?' I ask Liban and he says yes.

His wife, Faduma, who has a strong Minnesotan accent, tells me she has never been to Somalia at all. 'I was born in Kenya and there before being resettled to the US,' she tells me. 'Oh man, I was so scared when I first arrived in the country. Are you scared?'

I look at my dad and smile. 'No, I don't feel scared.'

My dad breaks into a story in Somali and I listen intently, trying to keep up. I haven't seen him speak so freely and continuously before. My mum is usually the talkative, outspoken one when they have people round. I enjoy just sitting there and letting the conversation sink in.

'Do you understand?' Faduma asks me and I nod. I am actually surprised by just how much I can understand. I feel like I am tuning into a radio frequency I haven't listened to since I was a child.

When we finish our teas, Baba, Mohamed and I walk back to the hotel I am staying in. The two men are a funny sight to behold, Mohamed tall and lanky, my dad plump and short.

My dad hugs me goodnight. It is the first time we have embraced since I arrived, and I don't want to immediately let go. We've never been particularly physically affectionate, but I want to convey to him how happy I am to be here.

I sleep soon after, and my night is a strange one. While I am half asleep, I hear what sounds like shelling, and cries for an ambulance. The sounds are distant and I can't tell where they are coming from.

I get out of bed in the middle of the night and walk to the window. There is no catastrophe, just people talking and cars driving by. Was it an old memory reaching out or something I was making up in my head?

After my first night's sleep in Mogadishu in over two decades, I get ready to head to the beach. I have breakfast at the rooftop restaurant: an omelette with toast, orange juice and a cup of tea. The cook nods and smiles at me every morning of my stay. It takes me a while to adjust to the heat outside of my air-conditioned room but once I do, I happily read my book and eat my food. I call my dad once I am back in my room.

I look outside my hotel room window and see a small herd of goats standing beside the main road. I am reminded of my mum. She once told me of her return to Mogadishu with Sacidiya, two young women who had not yet been brutalised by war. They giggled at the farm animals on the roads, so different to the streets in Jeddah. I could hear her laugh in my hotel room, both as a late teenager and as my mum.

It is her birthday and I miss her terribly. I call her, but she doesn't answer. I leave a message.

I go to Liido beach with Baba, Mohamed, Bilal and Faduma. I force myself not to laugh when I see the ridiculous flat cap my dad is wearing to the beach. I instead make a mental note to take a picture and send it to my brothers.

In the car, I try to see everything I can of the city. We pass through several checkpoints that don't seem to be that well monitored, the guards almost always waving us through.

To get onto the beach, though, security pats us down and checks our bags. The female security guard is perplexed by my disposable camera. I explain what it is and let her take a photo, but she refuses to give me the camera and insists on keeping it with her until I leave.

We first walk up and down the beach. I see young people playing football and swimming. No one is wearing swimsuits – people are just swimming in their ordinary clothes. There are small boats offering tours across the coast. My dad shakes his head when I ask if he wants to go on one of the tours. 'I don't want to ever go on a boat like that again,' he says, smiling. I laugh at him, remembering Mama making fun of him vomiting as they fled to Kenya by boat.

We have lunch at the Elite hotel, where I eat seafood spaghetti, listening to my dad insist that the 'remixed Italian food' in Mogadishu rivals what we get in Europe. My meal comes with a side of banana. Somalis eat bananas with almost everything. Lunch is lovely and I feel so happy when I return to my hotel. My mum calls me back and hearing her voice in Mogadishu makes me feel like my heart is going to burst with joy.

In the evening, I meet with my friend Abdi, a communication specialist I first crossed paths with in Colombia in 2017. We had both been attending the One Young World conference, a summit that brings together world leaders from across the world to discuss the global community's most pressing problems. I attended as a journalist, Abdi as a representative from Somalia. He immediately added me to the group of Somalis attending the conference. He was great at connecting Somalis with each other, and it is why I am particularly keen to meet him while I am in Mogadishu.

Our meeting is awkward at first, as my dad, Mohamed and his friend insist on meeting Abdi too. 'For your safety, we need to know who you are meeting with,' Baba says.

I understand that, but I worry that my friend has walked into some bizarre interrogation.

My dad warms instantly to Abdi, who speaks about his decision to split his time between Mogadishu and Stockholm, where he grew up. When my dad is satisfied I will be safe, Abdi and I head off on a tuk-tuk. We first stop at a hip coffee shop, where young Somalis hang out in small groups or sit alone, hunched over their laptops.

I tell Abdi about wanting to meet other young Somali creatives in the city. I want to know what draws them to Mogadishu and what keeps them there. I want to know how the city affects the work they want to create and whether they ever felt like leaving. I realise now how embarrassingly Western and narrow-minded these questions are.

I still can't understand why young talented people would want to live in a city that I can only associate with destruction – despite the fact that I am standing in a cafe being asked if I want oat or regular milk with my tea.

Abdi then takes me to the studios of Astaan TV, a popular TV station, to meet Rageh, a tall, good-natured twenty-nine-year-old who agrees to show me around the building. Rageh is a leading filmmaker and production manager of Astaan TV, which is fast becoming the country's premier digital TV station. The station, which has just moved into a new, state-of-the-art building, employs around three hundred people. It creates a range of content, from soaps and news segments to reality shows.

Rageh shows me and Abdi around the different studios. 'We film one of our most popular TV shows here, *Who Wants to Be a Millionaire?*,' Rageh says.

'Do a lot of people apply?' I ask.

'Oh yes, two thousand people have applied to be on the second season this year,' Rageh says.

'Wow, that's a lot of people to choose from,' I say.

Rageh nods and says, 'We will shortlist the contestant to a few by Ramadan, which is our busiest month of the year. We release a lot of shows during Ramadan.'

The building is largely staffed by men that night, but Rageh adds that the company is working proactively to hire more women, including holding women-only training in film editing and camera operating.

'Most of the staff are under thirty. We are all very eager to create our own image of Somalis and Somalia. We think it is important for Somalis to define themselves for themselves,' Rageh tells me.

Their most popular shows are the music ones, and I am shown where the country's leading musicians perform; intense dramas are also popular. Rageh is heavily involved with the dramas. He takes us to his office and shows us the latest script he is working on. The room is covered by boards breaking down episodes scene by scene.

'The vast majority of the actors are relative newcomers who responded to call-outs and auditions we regularly hold,' Rageh tells us.

He points towards one show's board, where a young woman falls in love with someone her family doesn't approve of. It is about to premier its second season following the huge success of the first one. I ask if the story will have a happy ending and Rageh laughs. 'It is unlikely. Though the script is not yet finished. Somalis don't like happy endings,' he replies.

Abdi agrees. 'When for example the BBC news bulletin is on and there isn't a segment on war or strife, the elders call for it to be turned off, saying there is nothing of value on the news today.' We all laugh.

Abdi hails a tuk-tuk for me and we say goodbye. I travel back to the hotel alone, awash with different emotions. I wonder what my story would have been had I stayed in Somalia. Who would have Amina been? Would I have wanted to be a storyteller? I think of what Rageh said about Somalis defining themselves for themselves. How would Amina have defined herself? How do I define myself now?

When I get back to my hotel, I call my dad and give him a play-by-play of how my evening went. He recognises the TV station and tells me it was the one that vox-popped him a few weeks ago as he was playing football with his friend. He sends me the link to the interview.

My dad is visibly awkward on camera. Like all Astaan TV content, the segment and interview is done in Somali. It starts with a group of men who look to be between fifty and sixty. The men, the narrator tells us, once played football together as children.

They had come together to bid farewell to Abdullahi, known to everyone as Morgan. I laugh at the nickname he has been given. He once played for the national team. They also came to welcome my father and celebrate his safe return to the city.

I gasp when I see a shot of a large mural of my dad's face painted on the wall of the football court. It reads, 'Welcome Coach Mohamed Nakuja'. I also don't understand why it calls my dad a coach. I ask him.

'Oh that's a mistake, it should say businessman,' Baba says.

The comments underneath the video praise Morgan and my dad as legends back in the day. It hits me that these strangers on the internet and those on the field probably know my dad in a way that I never will.

During the interview, my dad, sweating from the game he just played and wearing a lime green football shirt, says he is happy to be playing football with his friends and to have returned to his country. He speaks of his hopes and prayers that peace and prosperity will soon return to Somalia. He is asked by the interviewer how much the country has changed since his return.

'I first returned to the country in 2012, after being away for twenty years. I have been coming back ever since, alhamidduluh,' he says and tries to walk away, but the interviewer stops him to ask another question about Somalia.

'A lot has changed, alhamidduluh, the country is progressing and doing much better now,' he answers, and looks hopeful that the interview is coming to an end. It doesn't.

'How important is sport in Somalia?' the interviewer asks.

'Sport is very important and I hope more people play sports. I want it to become more prominent than it was before the war,' Baba answers. Finally, the interviewer leaves him to continue playing with his friends.

My dad starts sharing more of himself following that night. He is invited to speak at a university by a friend, who is a professor of agriculture, about his import and export business of natural oils and seeds. He sends me a picture of himself lecturing in a hall in front of students. He is wearing his ridiculous flat cap again. I decide not to pass this on to my brothers. I want to keep a piece of my dad to myself.

I go to sleep and wake up asking myself the same question: how do I as a Somali define myself for myself? I want to meet a Somali writer that does just that.

I ask around for a published author, but I can't find someone who has time to speak to me. I tell my dad, who tells me to leave it with him. He cancels the meetings he has scheduled and goes to a local bookstore. I wait in my hotel room.

Baba and Mohamed buy three books at the shop at random. 'We asked the shopkeeper to call the authors and tell them my daughter wants to meet them,' Baba says.

I squeal in embarrassment and confusion. I have so many questions: why would the shopkeeper have those numbers? Aren't we being too demanding by making such requests?

I don't have to ask in the end. 'He calls them, one says he is busy at work, another doesn't answer, but a third says we can visit him today at lunch,' Baba tells me.

'Today?'

'Yes, get ready, we're going to come get you,' Baba says.

Baba and Mohamed pick me up shortly and we first have lunch. It is while eating another delicious pasta dish that my dad realises he has forgotten the books he just bought. He has also forgotten the titles.

'You need to act like you're a big fan,' Baba tells me between bites.

I panic slightly; I will be interviewing this man with almost no information about his work.

'I don't have any information about the book, Baba!' I say.

'It is a sociology book on...' he pauses and has a think. 'On the impact of remittances on the Somali family. It is a short book, which was published a few years ago. It had some local success.'

How on earth is a sociology book on remittance payments going to help me answer my question about how I define myself as a Somali? I don't say this; I just eat my pasta.

After lunch, we get into a tuk-tuk and head to a bank: the author, it turns out, is also a bank manager, and we will be meeting him where he works. I note down questions on my phone. The bank manager, also called Mohamed, finally invites the three of us in.

I sit with the three Mohameds in an office in a bank: the family friend and hotel manager, the banker and my Baba. My father kickstarts the meeting by explaining the book I am working on.

'She forgot a lot of her Somali and she is working on it,' Baba says. It is the first time I feel pain to have him acknowledge my deficiency in speaking Somali in Mogadishu, like I've let him down. 'She is not too bad, but I will translate any words that are lost in between.'

The three Mohameds then look at me. I start the interview the way I normally do, by asking the subject if they have any questions while I get my bearings. The author asks why I have chosen him and what specification I had for the writers I interviewed. I thought: great, the two questions I don't have an answer for.

I have a think, before saying, 'Right now, it's much more open, I don't have those strict selection criteria. But I'd like to have someone very young, some of them middle aged and someone old, hopefully a range of people to represent different time periods.'

My dad translates what I say, but I think the banker already understood me as he laughs at my answer.

Baba looks at me and says, 'You can start your questions.'

'Could you tell me why you decided to write a book?' I ask the banker, and then look at my dad. 'What made him want to publish it?'

'He understands,' Baba says to me. 'You understand English well,' he says to the bank manager.

'I've seen a lot of social problems in Somalia, specifically family problems. I've been working in remittances for a long time and during that time I have seen a lot of family problems,' the bank manager says. 'At that time I was a bank manager in Kismayo, working in remittances. I have seen many fathers telling me not to tell their wives about remittance they had received—'

Baba's laugh echoes throughout the room. It is almost a cackle.

The interview is somewhat chaotic. Baba interrupts often:

Banker: Then another woman saying please don't tell my husband –
Baba: Husband!
Banker: Because the children are separately feeding each other. That's why I say how can you solve this issue?
Baba: The title of the book is *Family Solves*.

I give my dad a quizzical look. Later, my dad admits that he got someone back at the hotel to send him a picture of the front cover of the book, and had received it at that very moment.

> *Banker:* I leave Kismayo and came to Mogadishu in 2013. So I've got the chance, but that time I was—
> *Baba:* Very busy.
> *Banker:* I was too busy. Then I thought how I could contribute—
> *Baba:* Socially—
> *Banker:* Then I decide to write that book—
> *Baba:* Okay, that question you answer.

I don't know how to do journalism like this, but I'm weirdly enjoying it.

'Did you know anyone who has written a book before, or did you decide yourself that you're going to do this?' I ask.

'Really, at that time, I had only seen one book on family relations. It was emphasising sex issues,' the banker says.

The banker tells me the name of the book in Somali. 'It means sexual enjoyment,' Baba says, sounding matter of fact and unfazed. I try to keep my face cool and hide the fact I am dying of laughter on the inside.

I do not know how I am to define myself as Somali, but I am quickly learning I won't be getting those answers in this room.

'My job was to travel around regions of Somalia ... And that made it possible for me to interview people, including the eldest of the family. I designed the book and got lots of experiences in it,' the bank.

'How did you find a publisher for the book? Was it very difficult?' I ask and the banker looks confused, so Baba translates in Somali. There is a light of recognition on the banker's face.

'At the time, it was incredibly difficult to find a publisher in Mogadishu. As someone who has never written a book before, it is very difficult to publish because you don't have any networks,' the banker says. 'I went to a printing company and after I printed the book, I took it to the bookshop. It is called exposure marketing—'

'Promotional,' Baba adds.

'I printed something like two thousand books and they are almost all finished,' the banker says. 'There are twenty, thirty remaining.'

'Mashallah, it's very very good,' Baba says.

'Did you go to Mogadishu's first book fair?' I ask.

'Yes, to promote. I went in 2016 and that time I was living in Mogadishu,' the banker says.

'Are you seeing more people publish books now?'

'After the book fair happened, a lot of youth—' the banker starts to say.

'Trying to publish,' Baba fills in.

'But before that, it was very rare,' the banker says.

'Very rare,' Baba echoes. 'I think he was one of the first people trying to.'

'Do you want to write another book?' I ask, and the banker says yes.

He says he wants to carry out an online academic course on the topic. My dad says, 'Mashallah.'

'Do you want to translate into English?' I ask.

'Yes, it's better I think. I know Somali people who don't speak the language who need this book,' the banker says.

But it is very difficult to get books translated to English, the banker tells us, before Baba turns to me and blurts out: 'I think you could translate?'

Trying to move away from this question, I ask the banker to tell me of his favourite Somali authors. He said he loves a variety of authors, but his favourite is the beloved Somali novelist and one of Africa's most highly acclaimed writers Nuruddin Farah.

Throughout the interview, the banker kept emphasising the importance of relearning Somali – which has come up repeatedly since my first encounter at the airport. I tell him that I want to, that I want to be able to read Somali books in their original form.

The interview is perhaps the first time my dad has seen me in action as a journalist. I want to impress him. By the end, I realise my dad wants to impress me too.

When the banker declares he was one of just a handful of people who had managed to publish a book in Mogadishu in 2013, before the advent of the book fair, my dad claps. Later, when we bundle ourselves into a tuk-tuk, he looks at me and asks: 'Well, did I find the perfect subject for your book?' I smile and nod.

This city, which is my dad's home, should be my home too. I should know its streets intimately, I should be able to speak to my dad in Somali. This and so many other commonalities were taken from us. We were reaching for each other again, finding new ways to connect.

I leave that interview knowing I would have been a writer, and that the need to tell stories is one with a long and established history in Somalia. I wonder whether I would have written fiction or been a journalist here too.

It isn't easy to be a writer in Somali, especially a published one, but I now know I would have been able to do it here too.

9
LUNCH WITH THE YOUTH OF MOGADISHU

I find myself consumed by the same question in the days that follow: what would my story have been had I stayed in Somalia?

I think often of the girl I would have been, the woman I would have grown into, the life I would have led. What would my play, as well as my work, look like had we stayed in Mogadishu?

I know there aren't any real, meaningful answers to the questions of whether I would have been a writer or the adult I would have grown into. Yet I can't stop myself trying to find those answers. It is a thought experiment that is helping me feel less rootless. It ties me to my Somali identity.

I also want to understand the city and this country through the eyes of my peers. I set up meetings with young people, around my age, living and working in Mogadishu.

It's their words, ideas and hope that I find myself most drawn to. I won't ever be able to know this city like they do, but I don't want to leave without at least getting a glimpse of Mogadishu that isn't marked by my family's own tortuous relationship with it. There was and is so much more to the city than that.

I first meet my cousin Hani's friend, who is called Shaima. I didn't know anything about her other than what my cousin had told me: she is fun, around my age, and will be able to tell me what I want to know about Mogadishu. She is over an hour late, but I don't mind. By the second day in Mogadishu, I have come to factor these delays into my schedule.

Once we meet at the restaurant, we are soon laughing like old friends. Shaima had just quit working at Elite Hotel, the restaurant where I had lunch at the day before. The restaurant is owned by an MP and former finance minister, and is popular among government officials and members of the diaspora.

Heavy security often surrounds the restaurant. But still it has been attacked multiple times by terrorist organisations such as Al-Shabaab. At lunch, Shaima tells me she is a victim of one of those attacks.

I sit frozen in my seat as she recalls how she was almost killed. She tells me her tale in a characteristically Somali way: by making incredibly dark jokes about it. She tells stories like my mum does, like I do. We are the only two on the rooftop restaurant and she doesn't hold back. Her arms and eyes are wide and expressive.

'I was working in my office when I heard a loud bang. I thought it was an explosion in another building,' Shaima says. 'The first explosion was followed by a second bigger one. I realised then something was happening in our building, but I didn't know where.'

She tells me she looked up and saw the panes of the fractured window. 'I knew I was in trouble, but I couldn't believe it. My mind and body were in different places. I was just sitting there and couldn't move,' Shaima explains.

She adds: 'When I could feel my arms and legs again, I ran into the hallway and screamed at the workers to run upstairs for cover. There was a bulletproof door on the top floor that we all knew about. I was telling people, run, run, run! But I couldn't move again. Someone I worked with grabbed my arm and told me to go to the safe room with him. But I wouldn't move, I kept shaking my head.'

They could hear guns and the Al-Shabaab fighters then, but Shaima remained rooted to the spot. 'The guy then slapped me hard around the face and I came back to my senses. I took his hand and we ran up the stairs towards the safe door,' she tells me, mimicking herself sprinting. 'But the door was locked. We kept banging on it screaming to be let in, but no one was opening the door.'

'And where were the militants?' I ask her.

'I could hear them coming up the hallway and stairs!' She had taken out her phone from her pocket and called her manager. 'He didn't answer. So I just kept calling, calling and calling. I went crazy, shouting, throwing myself at the door.'

I could see the scenes unfolding in my mind like something out of a TV show. Shaima called her manager again and he finally answered the phone and opened the door to let them in. He asked her if there were any other employees who needed to be let in and she answered no. The door was closed behind them.

Shaima didn't have a moment to relax. The fighters were soon at the door and firing at it. By then, a cold sense of acceptance washed over her. 'The angel of death looms heavily over Mogadishu,' Shaima tells me. 'I had accepted that I would die.'

The story suddenly got less funny. She would not be the only young person I met on my trip with this attitude towards death. It's hardly surprising: the random, and at times devastating, occurrences of terrorist attacks in the city take their toll. But it is crushing to see so many young people, with so much to live for and so much to give, live in this state.

'I called my father and told him I was going to die. I said goodbye before he could say anything and hung up the phone,' Shaima says. 'I didn't want to talk, didn't want to explain or answer, so I just ignored the calls that came in.'

She then said the Shahada – 'I bear witness that there is no deity but God, and I bear witness that Muhammad is the messenger of God' – the most sacred statement in Islam.

When someone wants to convert to Islam, they do so by reciting the Shahada. It is the oath whispered in a newborn baby's ear, and what Muslims strive to have as their last words as they die.

Shaima didn't feel hopeful once the police arrived and continued praying in a corner. The people in the room spoke to the police through the window, but it only reinforced how trapped she felt. A rope had been thrown into the room. The police then attached guns to the rope, which they pulled up.

'They gave you guys guns?' I interrupt.

She laughs and says: 'Yes. We were told to fight for ourselves and shoot any fighters who got in. Some of the employees had used the rope to climb down the building.'

It wasn't until a number of people had escaped through the window that Shaima found her will to live. 'I grabbed the rope and tried to climb down, but ended up falling, sliding down and cutting my hand,' Shaima tells me as she stretches out her hands across the table and shows me the scars from the rope burn. They are jagged, livid. I hold her hands and squeeze them. I feel so glad, in that moment, that she is alive, laughing and sitting opposite me.

She breaks our reverie with more jokes. The attack had had an unexpected long-term effect: she had become a meme. 'There were pictures of me hanging from the building that had gone viral on Facebook. It was so embarrassing. It turned into a big joke,' she says. The Somali sense of humour had triumphed.

'I was then taken to a hospital and was going so crazy that they had to put me to sleep. I didn't know who I was or where I was. I was in so much shock. I was really, really unwell. I was in the hospital for several days,' she tells me and, again, I can see it. 'When I left the hospital, they told me of the employees who were killed. That was very hard. The deaths are difficult to grieve when they are so young.'

Shaima went back to working at the hotel for another two years before she quit. She had been unemployed for just two days when we met her but she already had exciting plans for her future. She tells me she wants to set up her own business, a frozen yoghurt shop. 'It is my favourite dessert and there are lots of these shops in Nairobi, but there aren't any places selling it in Mogadishu. So I want to be the first.'

Shaima tells me a bit about herself. She was born and raised in Nairobi, Kenya, but moved to Somalia in 2015, soon after finishing higher education. Her family had moved there by then and she couldn't afford to live in Nairobi alone. The first few months in the city were miserable.

'I couldn't speak Somali and didn't know anyone in the city besides my mother and brother. I felt so bored and alone. In Kenya, I would go to the gym and do stuff, but there wasn't anything like that here. I had put on so much weight when I first came,' Shaima says.

She loves football and was part of a women's team in Kenya, but initially hadn't been able to pursue that passion in Mogadishu. Many frowned on the idea of women playing football, while the extremists were willing to kill over it.

'One day I was complaining to my brother that there is nothing for me to do in Somalia. There are no gyms for women, there's nowhere to play football,' Shaima says. 'But then he tells me that he saw a group of Somali girls playing in the local stadium. I was so shocked and told him not to lie to me, but he took me to see them and I joined them. We trained together and got serious. We were good.'

The team had support from the sports minister and from the local FIFA organisation. The team were promised funding. They trained waiting for that money to come. It never did.

'The team entered into competitions to face other African countries, but we couldn't go because of a lack of money,' Shaima tells me. The lack of financial support has meant the team has floundered ever since.

For now, Shaima is happy to see girls and women playing football together on Liido beach. 'When I first came to

Mogadishu, it was only ever boys that played. It's nice that's now changing.'

It is a small, but important step forward in the country's slow march back to normalcy, peace and prosperity.

I thank Shaima for talking to me as our lunch ends. When she leaves, I think of my relationship with death. It isn't this all-consuming thing that hovers over me. I wonder at first whether that would have been different if I had remained in Mogadishu, but quickly dismiss the question. If I had stayed, it would have been in a country not ravaged by war. Would Al-Shabaab have ever existed? Would Shaima be burying her friends and colleagues?

I go back to my room to look up the attack and see reports by several leading news organisations on the siege, now several years ago.[1] Al-Shabaab militants detonated a car bomb outside the hotel before storming it. Witnesses told the press that the initial blast was heard across Mogadishu and people fled the area.

Around sixteen people had been killed, in addition to five militants, according to the police. Senior government officials from the information ministry and the defence ministry were reported to be among the dead. Dozens more people were reported to be wounded. Shaima had been among the more than two hundred people who were rescued from the hotel. Security forces had sealed off the hotel soon after arriving and engaged in a fierce battle with the attackers inside.

The siege came to an end after four hours. I could hear Shaima's laugh as I read those words. I find it remarkable that both can coexist so close to one another: laughter and death.

The following day I meet a photographer called Leyla. I was introduced to her through a contact at work. She is a sweet, small woman in her thirties. She had lived in Somalia as a child before fleeing the war when she was around seven years old; she returned and now works for an NGO in Mogadishu.

Again, we instantly warm to each other as soon as we sit down. Her accent is a reflection of the whirlwind childhood that I was growing to understand was the norm for our generation of Somalis; after fleeing Somalia, she had lived in Italy for a few years before resettling in the US.

Leyla first returned to Somalia to visit her grandmother, at a time when the Islamic courts were beginning to take control. The city has transformed since then, she tells me. 'It is now buzzing with life.'

Leyla returned to the US to go to university in 2011, but often visited Somalia. She travelled regularly between the two countries. 'I was living out of my suitcase then, travelling between Atlanta, Hargeisa and Mogadishu. I didn't have a place I called home then,' she tells me.

Leyla wanted to settle somewhere. Eventually, she would choose Mogadishu.

'Why did you choose Mogadishu?' I ask her.

'My mum and grandmother had relocated to the city and I wanted to be close to my family. There is also something about Mogadishu that draws you in. It is always calling you back,' Leyla says. She speaks of Mogadishu like it has its own gravity.

She was also done with the US: 'I felt an isolation and othering in Atlanta that didn't exist in Mogadishu.' Burnt by the racism she had experienced in the US, she felt she was faced with a choice: either stay and fight for her community in Atlanta, or move permanently to Mogadishu and help in the country's great rebuilding. 'I chose Mogadishu,' she says.

'Do you feel like the city and the country have changed since you permanently moved back here?' I ask.

Leyla nods. There is hope. 'It is infectious. People are returning in droves with this burgeoning hope. We are blessed with a beautiful country with plenty of opportunities and natural resources. We just need the strength to come together and utilise it,' she tells me.

I then asked her about her photography. She first took it up as a hobby, doing street photography. She was told to have a man accompanying her when in Mogadishu and to expect people's curiosity.

'I really love taking portraits of people. I particularly like pictures that focus on people's eyes so I ask my subjects to look directly into the camera,' Leyla tells me.

'Why do you want your subjects to look into the camera?'

'It gives them a sense of agency in the photo. I hate when people take photos of Somalis in the city where they look helpless,' Leyla explains. I could see she is particularly sensitive to being someone who has grown up in the West now wandering the streets of Mogadishu taking photographs of the locals. 'I didn't want to take dehumanising pictures of people,' she tells me.

'I doubt you do.'

I love listening to her talk about photography. She tells me she still struggles to balance her love of photography with her faith. It's a struggle I understand intimately.

'I have grown up believing that a person's eyes are the window to their soul,' Leyla says

'And it is haram [forbidden] to take a picture of them?' I ask. She nods. 'I know some Muslims believe it is haram to draw a picture of someone, and I guess photography can be seen as a natural extension of that. How have you tried to reconcile this struggle?'

'I decided to turn my internal battle into a project,' she says.

'Did you find an answer?' I ask, and she laughs

'No, I didn't, but I am at a much better place for asking the question,' she says. I know then that I'll come back to this answer often.

LUNCH WITH THE YOUTH OF MOGADISHU

As we speak more about people returning to the city, Leyla admits she is surprised at the number of Somalis who were either born abroad or grew up in another country who have since moved to Mogadishu. They don't have any memories of the city or the rest of the country, yet still they come – from Canada, the UK, Sweden and the US.

'Why do you think that is?'

'I think the country is starting anew. There are plenty of opportunities to make your mark here. The Somalis who have come back are young. They bring the optimism of youth with them,' Leyla says. 'I remember once at a recent dinner party in Nairobi, I was introduced to two young Somali women who had plans to move back to Mogadishu. These young women talked excitedly about their hopes and dreams once they're settled in the city, and what they were keen to achieve. I was at the party with my friend. We both tried to temper their excitement with a reality check, by being honest about the obstacles they were likely to face.'

The young women had listened, but remained undeterred. The hope still glittered in their eyes. When Leyla saw it, she backed down.

'I realised then that their hopefulness and eagerness was a good thing. It would drive change. And even if they made mistakes and hit walls, any step forward was ultimately a good thing,' she tells me.

We move on to talk about the differences between those who had lived their entire lives in the city and those raised abroad – between the locals and the diaspora.

'People in the city can often tell who was what before they even opened their mouth. Once, when I was out walking, a security guard asked me where I was from and how long I had been in the city,' Leyla says.

She had been shocked – she thought she had been blending in. 'I asked the guard how he could tell and he said it was in my walk. He told me that those from the diaspora walk like robots. They move very quickly, going from one place to another with a determined look on their face.' We both laugh.

The guard had said to Leyla that the diaspora have a different conception of time. 'As they are always rushing from one place to another,' Leyla adds. I think of how I thought I had been blending in too.

'What do you love most about Mogadishu?' I ask as we eat.

She tells me about her communal family life, the weather, the food and the beach. 'I feel deeply connected to the sea. It is the place I always go whenever I want to come back to myself.'

When she first arrived in Mogadishu in 2005, she asked to go to the beach. She was told she couldn't because it wasn't safe enough to do so. She grew more desperate to go until, eventually, her brother found a way to get her to the sea. They found a small patch of land not controlled by one of the warring factions. 'I fell in love with the city after that first swim.'

We finish up our lunch and order tea. We take a short break to look at the views of the city from the rooftop we are on. The city hums along, the sun blazing hot.

'Sometimes, I wish Somalia could temporarily cut itself off from the rest of the world and be an isolated island,' Leyla tells me as we gaze onto the city's squat skyline. 'I want us to be able to rebuild the country alone and find ourselves without outside influences.'

We sit back down at our table. 'What do you find most frustrating about living in Mogadishu?' I ask.

'I hate the clan system that still grips the country. I am really frustrated by the current political system, where MPs are elected not to represent certain regions based on political ideology, but chosen by each clan to represent their interests. It was meant to be temporary, but has instead solidified divisions. The government is rife with corruption, and is preventing transformative change the country needs,' she says.

We talk about the extreme trauma that so many people in the city suffer from. She believes many people suffer from post-traumatic stress disorder, but that it isn't talked about. 'You can see it through people's cold rage. It still shocks me how quickly situations can escalate and how violence can suddenly burst through.'

'What did you initially find to be strange, but have since got used to?'

She pauses before answering. 'People in Mogadishu are very calm about death. People walk around in the city knowing that they can suddenly find themselves in the wrong place at the wrong time and be suddenly killed. I have heard countless stories of close misses and near-death experiences.' I think of Shaima, of my mum.

Leyla continues: 'A friend who was walking down a street they walked down on a daily basis for years decided one morning, for reasons that are unclear, to take a different route. The friend later found out a bomb had gone off on that same street and people had died. You leave your house with the understanding that one day you could be one of the unlucky ones. I think this closeness to death can put you on edge.'

Before she stands up to leave, I ask if she feels hopeful about the future. I often ask this question in interviews for work.

'The answer to that question changes every day,' Leyla says. 'Overall, I have mixed emotions about Mogadishu's future. Sometimes I feel hope, sometimes I feel frustration, sometimes I feel despair.'

My conversation with Leyla has me thinking about how I will capture Somalis in my story, just as she captures them on camera; both for work and for this book. Do I fall into the same pitfalls that other Westerners have? Do I give Somalis enough agency? What does that even mean?

I meet many other young Somalis, but the person that ends up having the most profound impact on me is a poet, Falastine. It is strange that I feel this way, considering that she doesn't speak English, and I don't speak Somali very well.

Falastine bursts into giggles when she sees me and draws me into a tight hug. I feel like a family member that she hasn't seen in years. I smile at her as we walk to the hotel's rooftop restaurant, which is fast becoming my office in the city. It is only when we sit down that I realise Falastine doesn't speak English.

'I have been using an online translator when we were texting. I was so keen to meet you,' she tells me in Somali. My smile widens. I felt excited to put whatever Somali I remember to good use.

The excitement, however, melts into frustration. While I understand what she is saying, I struggle to speak back in Somali. I can't form the words I want in my mind, I can't get them out of my mouth.

There is a scientific term for what I am experiencing on that rooftop restaurant – first language attrition. It is a process where someone slowly loses their ability to speak their first language, their so-called mother tongue. Linguists started studying the phenomenon in the 1980s. The rate of that loss is specific to each individual: some forget the ability to speak or understand the language completely, others lose their proficiency, while some, like me, have a general understanding when spoken to, but struggle to speak it back.

I grew up with two first languages, Arabic and Somali. My mum told me I had an impressive command of both languages, even while living in Saudi Arabia, but that I was always stronger in Arabic. When I came to the UK on my own, I picked up English rapidly and immersed myself into my new country. That process came with a heavy cost.

When I was reunited with my parents, I could still speak Arabic, but English had become my dominant language. As I grew up, my ability to speak Arabic withered, but I could still understand it fluently and hold a decent conversation. To improve my reporting, I went to an Arabic language class when I was twenty-two and found myself picking up the pieces I had thrown away. I remember how comfortable I felt when I went on holiday in Lebanon and found myself able to hold my own. I started talking to my Arab friends in Arabic, and put myself in more classes to improve my literacy skills.

Things were different with my Somali. I don't have any memory of being able to speak Somali. I am told that as a child I did so like an old gossiping woman. When I lost the ability to speak it, I didn't feel any urge to rediscover it. It's terrible to admit, but I didn't at the time see it as much of a loss.

Research shows that age is the most significant influence in the process of first language attrition. The leading researcher in this field, Monika Schmid of the University of Essex, once told me that a child growing up speaking one language would have acquired the grammatical rules of that language by the age of six.[2] The knowledge of that language is then consolidated between the ages of six and twelve.

Schmid describes the phenomenon of first language attrition as a process where two languages are struggling to compete with each other for resources. In 2018, when I first researched first language attrition for an article, she told me that as I had learnt English as a child, I was using a lot of energy to not speak Arabic or remember Arabic sentence structure.

When, for example, I was learning to say 'bread' and 'milk' in English, I was building up a so-called mental barrier that blocked the Arabic version of the words. If, now, I want to remember how to say those words in Arabic, there is a slight pause. Schmid describes this as the energy needed to override that inhibitory mechanism. How powerful that mental barrier is depends on how young the speaker was when learning their second language and how deeply immersed they remained in their mother tongue.

Her explanation helped me understand why I found it more difficult to say sentences out loud, but struggled far less when trying to understand what someone was saying. It is why so many first-generation child immigrants go on to be able to understand a language, but struggle to speak it.

When I reread the article I wrote on first language attrition five years ago, I find it interesting that I only discuss recovering my Arabic skills. I don't mention anything about my Somali.

First language attrition doesn't just affect children. Schmid told me about the remarkable case of German tennis player Steffi Graf, who is married to a native English speaker and has been living in the US since 2000. She sparked astonished headlines in the German press when in 2007 she began her acceptance speech admitting that she now struggled to speak German. 'Sorry, I cannot speak German so much,' she said to the crowd.

In a paper published in 2021, researcher Lydia Palaiologou, who is based in Amsterdam, reviews the research done so far on first language attrition in first-generation immigrant children.[3] She notes in the paper that often for these children, the loss of one language occurs simultaneously with the acquisition of another. How much, if any, loss there is of the first language could be down to what some researchers describe as a 'critical threshold'.

Literacy too can play an important role. A child that knows how to read in their native language is less likely to experience significant attrition. Most children learn to read between the ages of six and seven; by then I had resettled in the UK and the first language I learnt to read was English.

Immigrant children who are well embedded in communities in which they speak regularly in their first language are also less likely to face significant attrition. According to a 2000 study that Palaiologou links to, German immigrants who maintained steady contact with native speakers through expat communities, religious groups and other community-based social contexts managed to avoid language loss in the following generation. By contrast, Dutch immigrants who didn't maintain the same level of contact with native speakers had second-generation children who were completely monolingual in English.

Researchers therefore recommend what they describe as 'dual-language acquisition' for immigrant children. This is where they are encouraged and supported to speak both their home and host language. But why is this important? Palaiologou pointed to research that showed how important the maintenance of a native language is to strengthening family cohesion, building intimacy and transmitting cultural practices and ideas from the parents to the children. In doing so, immigrant children are able to identify more strongly with their family and culture. Failure to do so can lead to the inability to effectively express oneself, which can trigger learning disorders, anger issues, anxiety and depression.

I might have been able to piece back together my ability to speak Arabic, but something more destructive had occurred with my Somali. Something I had feared was all too permanent.

It is that question – is it gone forever? – that stays with me when I try to interview the poet that afternoon. I had felt this bold new confidence since arriving in Mogadishu. I felt Somali in a way that I hadn't before and thought the words would finally return. I feel something tear at me on the inside when it doesn't.

Falastine takes out her phone and opens an online translator to talk to me. She slides her phone towards me and asks me to put in what I mean in English so she can read it in Somali. She does so with an encouraging smile. It helps ease with whatever turmoil is going on in my chest.

I ask her to recite her poetry to me. I don't understand much of what she is saying during her recitation, as her poetry utilises a more classical Somali, but I feel it somewhere within me. We are the only two people in that rooftop restaurant; the city around us seems to quieten as she recites poem after poem to me. It feels like we are the only ones in the world. I put her poem into an online translator and I tell her it is beautiful.

Falastine tells me she got into poetry because of the country's long love affair with it. She types into Google Translate: 'Did you know Somalia is known as the land of poets?'

I nod. I try to tell her to speak to me in Somali, that I can understand it, but I think it's easier for us both to use the translation service.

She types into the translator: 'Do you know of any Somali poets?'

'I do now,' I tell her. She laughs in delight.

She types: 'I want to become one of the country's greatest poets.'

I grab my phone and ask: 'Why do you write poetry?'

This time she speaks when she replies. 'It helps me express myself. I am inspired to write by so many things, from my mother to the sea. I dream of being a full-time writer, but right now I am studying public administration at the Somali National University. Inshallah, I hope to get a job as a civil servant to be able to support my family.'

She then adds: 'The evenings are for me, for writing. I write until I can't anymore.'

Falastine has never left the country and doesn't feel a need to go elsewhere. She returns to typing. 'Somalia is my country, and I don't think there is a better place to live.'

She looks at me curiously before asking if she can ask me some questions. I nod. 'Why did you return to Somalia?'

'I want to learn more about my country and its culture. By being here, I hope I can be myself when I go back to London,' I type. I am unsure whether the Somali translation truly gets at what I am trying to say.

I apologise that we are communicating through an online translator. 'I need to relearn my Somali,' I tell her.

She reaches out and squeezes my hand and says: 'I am so happy you want to learn the language. You should listen to stories and poems in the Somali language. You can do it, don't worry, and I will help you,' Falastine says.

I am taken aback by her warmth and generosity. 'Why did you come meet me?' I type.

'I love meeting Somali girls from the diaspora. I like meeting those who want to find out more about people like me in the country,' she tells me.

The war had created a rupture, where one generation grew up outside the country, and another in it. Perhaps meetings like these are crucial to closing the gap between us.

I told her how much I valued our meeting, and she told me it was important to her too. We hold on to each other for a long time when we say goodbye.

10
THE PERMANENCE OF EXILE

Baba speaks often of the beauty of Hamar Weyne, the oldest district of Mogadishu. He was born there and it's where his family originates. I get really excited when one day, after I finish an interview, he tells me he is going to take me there.

We travel in a tuk-tuk with Mohamed and another of my dad's friends. In his memoir, former diplomat Mohamed Osman Omar described Hamar Weyne – where he too had grown up – as a place where people did not talk to strangers. I wonder how true that still is. The roads become more unwieldy the closer we get, the sand taking over paved roads. We are edging closer to the sea.

Baba points out notable landmarks while in the cab and towards things that once were there, but had been lost since the war. My favourite is the former offices of SANU, the political party my grandad was associated with. It is a shopfront now. SANU and other political parties from the 1960s no longer exist.

We get out of the tuk-tuk once we reach Hamar Weyne and walk through the small town. I see the Italian architecture my dad told me about in London. We walk through a busy marketplace. The buildings still wear the brutal scars from the war, more so than the centre of Mogadishu, where I am staying. But although the area is dilapidated, I can see the beauty my father had reminisced about.

'Some of these buildings were built a hundred years ago. I hope that one day it goes back to what it used to be,' Baba says as we walk side by side.

We walk until we reach the old marina. There are children playing football up ahead. It isn't until we get there and I am looking out at the bullet-ridden homes that look right onto the sea that Baba tells me the other significance of the row of houses.

'This is the house Mama and I lived in with my family when the fighting during the war increased,' Baba says. I look at the last place my parents lived in before they embarked on their long journey of leaving Somalia and becoming refugees.

I remember my parents telling me about this place when I first started interviewing; I had wondered if they could smell the sea air from the city centre house they had lived in. I stand there transfixed by how close the sea is. The smell is comforting. Was it of comfort then?

Before we step into the house, my dad points to a spot just ahead. 'This is where the truck that took us parked to pick us up,' Baba says. I turn to him: 'You haven't forgotten where the truck was parked in all these years?' He shakes his head and says, 'I don't think I ever will.'

We walk into the house and I am met with a loud chorus of greeting by family members.

Family member 1: Amina!
Family member 2: Welcome, welcome!
Family member 3: Mohamed's daughter is here at least!
Family member 2: Amina, how long has it been?
Family member 1: Years!
Family member 5: Welcome! Welcome!
Family member 1: Do you remember me? I held you as a child in Mogadishu!

I don't know what to say. I just smile awkwardly in response.

The living room is dominated by men. They tease my dad for letting me forget my Somali, watching me to see how I respond. I laugh. The oldest woman in the room tells me to call her Ayeeyo, which means grandmother in Somali. She isn't my grandmother, she's my dad's aunt, but I happily agree to it.

She pulls me into a hug and explains my background to the room. 'Her mother is Arab, she is Ashraf. Amina lived in Saudi Arabia. Oh, the Arabs have stolen my daughter away from me for too long, but she is here now and she will remember her Somali now she is home,' Ayeeyo says.

I feel safe in her arms. I sink further into her embrace. She takes me to the next room. I realise it is her bedroom. She speaks to me in Somali and is patient at my jumbled attempts to reply in kind.

I tell her I am a writer and that I am working on a book. She hugs me tightly and tells me it will become a huge success. I tell her of my life in London, of my family. She tells me of her hope that they will visit Somalia too.

She gives me a baati to change into, saying it will be more comfortable in the heat. She makes me a cup of tea and gives me sweets to eat before lunch is served.

She gives me her phone, opens the TikTok app, and we watch videos together. Is there any corner of the world that this app has yet to penetrate? She also shows me videos of important events in recent years that I haven't been able to attend, like her daughter's wedding.

Other women, also older, join us in the room. They show me their phones and I piece together the fabric of their lives through photos and videos they show me, interspersed with their stories – a boy around my age studying in Nairobi, an older daughter in the UK.

They call their adult children to FaceTime me, and I am teased again, this time for my accent. The family I speak to over the phone, all young like me and speaking English, tell me repeatedly that I am brave for 'returning to Mogadishu', and that I have inspired them to do the same. I tell them to come. 'The city is beautiful and I was scared before but I feel safe here. It is important to come back for your sense of self,' I tell one male family member around my age in Nairobi. Where did I find the confidence to speak with such authority about Somalia?

A staggering amount of food arrives in Ayeeyo's room. I am asked by them all to take pictures and videos of the spread. The footage is sent to family WhatsApp group chats. The war has scattered our family members across the world, but we find a way to hold onto each other by sharing the most minute details of the day.

We eat to the sound of my extended family's notifications constantly going off: parallel conversations in overlapping time zones, showing what people are eating, what they saw on their walks, the weddings they are at. Apps like WhatsApp are helping to maintain a link between us, a new type of virtual intimacy in a family that has been ripped apart.

My mum is in many of these groups. She calls when she sees me in one of these posts and screeches with laughter. 'I can't believe you're in Hamar Weyne,' she keeps saying. I can't either.

I eat an alarming amount of food. When I say that I can't eat more, I am met with stern faces. During lunch, I want to ask the group of women I am sitting with why they are here. I want to ask why they hadn't left the city with the rest of their family members. But I don't: I know instinctively that, however curious I feel, these aren't the right questions to ask.

At one point, my dad calls to check I am okay. He has gone to the local mosque with the other men and asks if I feel lonely, but I don't. I let the chattering of the elders of my family around me sink in. I am so grateful to be in their presence.

When Baba returns and peeks into the room I am sitting in, he initially doesn't recognise me. By then, I am wearing the scarf and baati like all the other women in the room. I love the feel of the fabric on my skin and the bright colours. Baba shouts 'Oh my god!' when his gaze finds me and he finally sees his daughter. We all laugh.

'She is one of us now, a Hamar Weyne girl,' Ayeeyo says. My dad beams at me.

The dessert comes and somehow I have room to eat that too. When I look like I am stopping, Ayeeyo feeds me with her own hands. I am full to the point it hurts by then, but I am happy too. When my dad announces we are leaving, I am given bags of food to take with me. Ayeeyo asks if I like the baati and scarf and when I say yes, she tells me they will stitch more for me before my return to the UK. As we make our goodbyes, I linger in every embrace.

My dad and I return to the hotel in relative silence. He calls me soon after we part.

'Everyone loves you and has been telling me how great you are,' Baba says.

I smile into the phone. I can hear the pride in his voice.

'I love them too.'

'Rest for a bit and I'll come back for dinner,' Baba says.

'I can't think of food right now,' I moan.

'I said later! Not now,' he says. I wonder if I'll be rolled back on the plane to London.

'Okay, I'll see you for dinner,' I say and try not to laugh.

I read for a few hours and end up having dinner with my dad and Mohamed in the hotel rooftop restaurant. We all have a chicken shawarma wrap and a spondis milkshake.

'Do you like spondis milkshake, Amina?' Mohamed asks.

'Yes, I've been having it every day,' I tell him.

Mohamed tells the waiter that the glass he got me isn't enough and to get a jug for us all. I try to tell Mohamed that there is no need, but he waves me away. When the waiter returns with a huge jug of the drink, I think I'll need to be airlifted to London.

During dinner, I tell Baba and Mohamed how well my interviews with young people in Somalia are going.

'Good, good,' Baba says before pausing. 'Well, when are you going to interview me?'

I am startled by the question. I am not sure why. It is the only thing I had planned to do before leaving London, it is the main reason for this trip. Yet, for some reason, I don't have an answer for him. Have I been avoiding it? Perhaps. The more I learn about Mogadishu, the more I understand what my dad has given up for me.

'I'm ready to interview you whenever you are. Just let me know when,' I bluff. 'I need to do the interview at the house in Hodan. It's important we talk there.'

Baba nods and says, 'No problem. We will go after dinner.'

I panic and feel unprepared. Things then move very quickly.

The house is a five-minute walk from the hotel I am staying at. It is a warm evening, the sun yet to set. My dad walks in step beside me. There are constant beeps from the end-of-day traffic. I turn often to look at him. He glows beautifully as we walk through the golden hour. As we turn right from the hotel, the roads give way to sand.

We walk past a group of boys playing football right in front of a mosque. I ask my dad whether he ever feels emotional seeing young boys playing football in the same streets that he once did, knowing that his own children didn't have that experience. He tells me he does, every time. 'But, back then, the streets were a lot cleaner and it was safe,' Baba adds. He just can't help himself.

As we pass the boys, I see a beautiful but slightly rundown house that has a Mediterranean feel to it. 'That is our house,' Baba says. He calls out to someone to open the gates. As we stand in front of it, I try to take it all in, but I can't.

I move in a daze as we step through the door and enter the front courtyard. I can hear my dad explaining that his whole family lived in the house together as I turn round to look. We go in and walk upstairs to the living room. I remark that the wallpaper is beautiful before my dad's friend, Forna, who I last saw when I was a child in London, embraces me in a hug. 'Amina!' he shouts as he holds me tightly. 'You're meant to be tall,' he says, and I laugh. At 5'2, I probably haven't grown much since he last saw me.

My dad shows me what used to be his parents' room, the balcony that looks onto the mosque and the boys playing football below, the kitchen and the bathroom. He then takes me to the room that used to be his and my mum's.

'I can't imagine coming back to such an important room thirty years later,' I tell him. It's where my mum and dad spent the first few years of their marriage.

'Not much has changed,' Baba says of the room. The bed and the AC have stayed in the same place. The house and the surrounding area were totally destroyed by the war, but my dad has been slowly rebuilding it.

The house we are in was first built in 1967. My dad moved in then as a child. My mum moved in after they got married. He has spent the past twenty years meticulously restitching the past in this house: finding the same wallpaper, even trying to ensure the floor was the same.

'Do you see these tiles?' I look down at the floor. They are beautiful Italian tiles. 'They're from 1967. I never changed anything.'

We sit in the living room after my dad prays. I have a list of questions on my phone, but don't end up reaching for it. I want the conversation we are finally going to have to be as natural as possible.

Baba once told me that he wanted to rebuild this house and the hotel so that there was a place for our family and others to stay whenever we wanted to come to Somalia. He wanted there to be a place here that we could call home.

'How are you feeling?' I ask him.

Baba smiles and says, 'Fine,' and I start giggling. I don't know why but a sudden shyness comes over me. I have interviewed my dad countless times in the past two years, but this feels different, more important than any interview or conversation we've had before. He looks at my recorder and I tell him not to be nervous.

'When you came back in 2012, why did you come back? Who told you it was safe to come back?' I begin.

'Okay, Uncle Forna, he came back because someone told him it was a little bit safe and the war had stopped. The fighting had gone on outside of Mogadishu. So he came back to rebuild his family house. He renovated it. He came here and this road was very bad, there were a lot of dogs, lots of sand, and all the buildings were damaged, including ours.'

'And then Uncle Forna called me in the middle of night. He left me a message on the telephone. He said, "I'm in Mogadishu, and Mogadishu is okay. Please come and benefit from your strategic house and shops." He said rebuild and rent it. And then I came,' Baba says.

That voicemail propelled my father into action. He returned to the country. He began renovating the shops, hotel and house, after calling his brothers and sisters and pooling their finances together.

'You kept the character of the house,' I say.

'Yes, I kept the character,' Baba agrees.

Forna is sitting beside us and says: 'It was bad when we came here before.'

I try to remember exactly what I was doing in 2012. I was in my second year of university. When my dad told me he was going to Somalia then, I was scared and upset. I didn't understand why he was going, I didn't understand the magnitude of what he was doing.

'Next question,' Baba says, cutting through my reverie. His impatience makes me laugh.

'What did you feel when you came back in 2012?'

'I felt very happy to see my country and I felt very scared. It still wasn't that stable. When I came from the airport, I didn't recognise our house. I moved all the way down to Hamar Weyne, where it was a little bit stable,' Baba answers.

He stayed with his cousin in Hamar Weyne for around five days, and then in another district in Mogadishu with a sister who has since died. He finally met up with Forna and the two returned to his home together. Some of his childhood friends had teased him for being so scared to return home and told him to come, that there were no issues there.

My dad was the first in his family to return. Four of his siblings soon followed. He would return to the country at least once a year from then on. In 2015, my dad and his sister brought their mum with them. They took her back to Hamar Weyne. 'It was very emotional,' he says. My grandmother stayed for around six months in the country, but then started to feel unwell. She couldn't eat food properly and got severely anaemic. She flew back to Minneapolis, where she had been living, to get a blood transfusion.

I ask my dad to expand on what he meant when he described that initial return as emotional. 'The city is very damaged, very different. You can remember and you're happy that you're back in the city you lived in, happy to see people you haven't in a long time, but the city is broken.'

The city he is now showing me is exciting, but it isn't the one he grew up in. I will never be able to live in the Mogadishu of his past: it is long lost to us all. I think then of the permanence of a refugee's exile. I think of how he could return to a specific geographical place, but in the ways that matter, he is not really there. He is in exile even when he is back home.

'You'll never see it. That's gone,' Baba says. 'Our happiness, old friends, safety, freedom, no worries, it'll never come back. We'll never get that again.'

I ask if he has any hope that something better can come for the city and the country. 'Yes, yes, there's still hope that it could be better than before. But better for young people, not us.'

'Because you guys remember what it was like?'

'Yes,' he replies. 'We won't be as happy as we were before. When you're young, you're always very happy. You have the freedom to be happy. You're not thinking of your responsibilities. You can go to the cinema that used to be round the corner from here, come back and sit here, where we were always talking, we were happy.'

For my dad, and those like him, their home city will always be compared to the one from their past. They exist in both timelines. I think back to Viet Thanh Nguyen, and of my dad as a reluctant time traveller. Nguyen writes that science fiction books depict time travel as something characters use to go back and forth in time, but refugees 'were only going in circles'. I have thought before of my dad as frozen in two timelines, but he too is moving in circles. He is constantly reliving the past, marching towards destruction, while much of his present is spent trying to go back.

I ask him how it feels to show me this.

'I'm very happy to see...' he says before pausing. 'Memory, memory, it's a memory.' I see those memories dance across his eyes. 'When I sit here, I can remember your mum and I sitting here, sometimes fighting, sometimes laughing.'

I ask if my mum had a short temper then as well. 'Before, she would get very angry and cry quickly. That was the stress I was facing,' he says, and I start laughing. I could see them too then, young and newly married, completely different from one another but still trying to find a way to each other.

'What is your hope for this country?' I ask.

'I have a big hope for this country. In this country, we never use our resources. This country has big resources, including petrol, iron and oil. This country needs a well-established political system. This country still needs better security. All these things, when they finally happen, you can live in this country and live an unbelievable life because of the weather, fresh food and where we are located,' Baba says.

I tell him that the city agrees with him, as he somehow looks younger than he ever does in London. I ask if he is planning on retiring to Mogadishu.

'Yes, of course,' he says. 'Nearly every Somali person, around eighty to ninety per cent, needs to retire here. That's why I've been rebuilding. I'm now nearly sixty.'

I tell him I like the idea of him being happy and old in the country, and that I could perhaps send any children I go on to have to him.

'Yes,' he smiles at me. 'Every one of us needs to be connected here. It's why my second project is to get the children to be able to talk in the Somali language.'

I nod. It is the first time I have heard him say he wants to do something about not being able to talk to his children in Somali.

'The most important thing I can advise you is that Somali people have talent, Somali people have educated people, Somali people have people your age. Connect with Somali people, it's the only way you can help develop your country, religion and people. But if you only associate with other foreign people, you're away. How many impressive people have you met in the past few days with unbelievable talent? Keep talking to them. Even if you're speaking to Somali people in English, you're still part of the community.

'It's not necessary to learn Somali, just keep talking to them. Then, they'll move you back to Somalia,' Baba says.

I ask him, while laughing, if that is his ultimate goal. His siblings have started making preparations to be able to return permanently to Somalia. I'm unsure if the younger generation in our family will follow.

'When you're coming here, and when you're living in London, you're a different person,' Baba says.

'It's easier to be yourself here?'

'Yeah,' Baba says.

'Not all the pressures of living somewhere like London,' I say. 'Now I'm here I totally understand why you're coming back.'

'We're very proud of what our father did. We wouldn't have been able to come back without him. We wouldn't be able to enjoy ourselves like this,' Baba says. We sat feeling his absence, now more than ever before. 'I was the one chosen from my brothers and sisters to continue his legacy.'

I have wondered over the last couple of years, since I began my project, whether my not speaking Somali has weakened our bond. I see now that I have been wrong to worry. I finally see him in a way that he needs to be seen, and, in turn, he sees me too, sees me reaching out, sees us closing that gap.

When I get back to my hotel room, I send my mum the pictures I took of the house. She sends me a voice note immediately, exclaiming: 'This is our house! This is where I lived.'

'It's been a long time, wallahi,' Mama says.

My time in Mogadishu goes by quickly. The trip is a greater success than I could ever have dreamt it would be. I have my dad to thank for that. When I try to, he interrupts to simply say, 'It is my duty.'

I'm not sad to be leaving Mogadishu: I know now that I will come back.

I spend the last few hours in Somalia in my family's hotel with my dad. We watch TV together as he tells me about a funny incident that occurred the evening before. They had been sitting just outside the hotel in plastic chairs, drinking tea and coffee after praying maghrib. They heard what sounded like an explosion from the car beside them and all ducked to the ground. The car's front hood was on fire. It was while my dad was on the floor that he looked up and realised that it wasn't an explosion, but the engine overheating. We both laugh, my dad shaking his head. We then fall into a comfortable silence.

Baba and I say goodbye outside the hotel. Mohamed takes me to the airport. I don't look back as the car drives away.

Watching Mogadishu's skyline from my seat on the plane, I think of a passage from James Baldwin's *Giovanni's Room*.[1] The narrator, a gay American man, spots a sailor dressed all in white striding across a boulevard in Paris. He looks at him with a deep sense of longing. 'Perhaps home is not a place but simply an irrevocable condition.'

I had returned to the passage over the years ever since I first read it, even though I had stumbled over the concept of an 'irrevocable condition'. But as I leave Mogadishu, I notice that I am different – and that my idea of home has changed too. I am taking a bit of Mogadishu with me, and I am leaving a bit of myself behind: a small part of the pain I had been carrying with me. I have been shedding that pain bit by bit over the last few days: it eased off me with every conversation with my dad, with every chicken shawarma wrap I had on the rooftop, with every step I took on the beach, with every adhan that calls the city to prayer, with every taxi ride I took, with every handshake, hug and smile, with every question, with every night's sleep.

11
THE PAST ISN'T DEAD

I leave Mogadishu in the evening and fly to my first stop: Addis Ababa. My mum is on my mind as I wait in the airport before my onward flight to Nairobi.

I keep thinking of her deportation from Saudi Arabia, that violent separation between us, and her waiting in Addis Ababa to come back to me. I keep thinking of her fear, her anguish, her determination. She was younger than I am now when she flew out of this airport back to Saudi Arabia. Was she as exhausted as I am now? Did her muscles ache in the same places? Was she scared? Was she hopeful? I feel my chest tighten. She is braver than me, braver than most people I know.

When I arrive in Nairobi, it is close to midnight. I have arranged to stay with my cousin Hani for a night. When I finally get to hers, I fall asleep immediately, but it is a terrible sleep. I have strange dreams that I can't remember the next morning and a weird sinking feeling in my stomach that I can't name. I wake up disoriented and heavy.

I decide there and then to book a flight to the other side of Kenya, to see the beach my parents landed on when they escaped Somalia. I feel the sense of peace I left Mogadishu with ebb away. But I have to follow them, have to follow this through.

I land in the coastal town of Malindi the following day. I don't have a plan for how to get to Ngomeni from Malindi. I just know it is an hour north by car and that I have to go.

The taxi driver who picks me up is Muslim and tells me most people in the town are. He asks what I am doing in the city and I explain that I am trying, to the best of my ability, to retrace the steps my parents had taken while escaping the Somali civil war in 1992. He tells me that he remembers the terrible refugee crisis that had engulfed the town, pointing, as we took a bend, to a near-empty car park. 'That was where many refugees were put to be processed when they arrived,' he says. I look back for as long as I can.

I ask the taxi driver, who tells me his name is Abu Bakr, if he would be willing to drive me to Ngomeni beach and we agree to a fixed fee. We exchange numbers and I tell him I look forward to seeing him the next day.

The beachside hotel I am staying in is beautiful. I allow myself for the day to feel like I am on holiday. I change into my swimsuit, go for a swim and read by the pool. At dinner, one of the hotel staff tells me about a beach party that takes place every Monday. It is a few minutes away on a motorbike taxi. I want this trip to be an opportunity to learn more about my parents, my country and myself. I am succeeding on that front, but who says I can't have fun too?

I go on a motorbike taxi, a first for me, and laugh and screech along the road. The driver laughs along with me. When we get there I see that the beach party is completely empty. I sit at a table by myself, looking at the bright moon, and read my book. It is hardly the making of a wild night.

By midnight, though, the place is heaving with young Kenyans. I know I face something difficult tomorrow, but tonight I feel like a student on a gap year.

I introduce myself to a group of women who look to be around my age and they welcome me as one of their own. We dance the night away. I don't tell them why I am in Kenya, where I come from and where I am yet to go. Do my parents ever have these moments of escape too?

When I later tell my mum about the beach party, she laughs at how alike we are. 'A few months after you were born, I saw your dad's younger brothers were getting ready to go out to a beach party. I told them they had to take me with them. They initially said no, but I told them I'd tell the others where they had gone so they allowed me to go with them,' Mama says.

She got dressed up and went to the party, leaving me behind with her sister. 'I was dancing and having so much fun and then I was so shocked when I turned around and saw your dad and his friend coming towards us. I kept thinking "Am I dreaming? Is he really here?"' Mum tells me, her eyes wide. 'And then he comes up to me and dances with me. Can you believe it? He said we will party tonight, but he will not go out dancing again.'

Abu Bakr arrives promptly the next morning. I tell my husband where I will be at what time. I give him instructions on when to call me. If after an allotted time, he struggles to reach me, he should contact the hotel, who should contact the police and the British embassy. Though I felt carefree the night before, the weight of being a female journalist travelling alone slams into me as I close the car door and we head off.

The Foreign Office warns against all but essential travel to Ngomeni, as the town and surrounding area has been the site of terrorist attacks and kidnappings. Is going to Ngmoeni beach essential? I think of all the ways this trip could go horribly wrong. I dream of being kidnapped in startling vivid detail. I jump when Abu Bakr asks if I want to turn the radio on. I nod and it blares Afrobeats for the rest of the journey.

I relax as Abu Bakr tells me about his life. He has two children, a young boy and older daughter, and has lived in Malindi his whole life. He points out notable attractions as we drive out of the town, including the main mosque and the local bars. Malindi is an eccentrically coloured town. I love this about East Africa, how in many towns and cities shop owners don't just have a beautiful store sign, but paint the entire outside of the shop. Did the town look the same when my parents were here? What has changed in the time between our arrivals, and what has stayed the same?

It is a blistering hot day as we drive north. The black car we are in doesn't have any AC and I feel the heat in a way that I haven't since coming from the UK. It is sticky and oppressive. It beats down on my face as I tell Abu Bakr about last night's beach party.

When we stop at a checkpoint at a bridge, I clench my fist. 'The security has been increased because the bridge was often targeted by Al-Shabaab,' Abu Bakr says. 'The bridge is beside a lake that was a major source of water for the region. The road we are on was a famous one that led all the way to Somalia.'

As the minutes pass, the smooth roads give way to sand and gravel, and the surrounding area looks more rural. It is a bumpy ride.

We pass a sparsely populated village. The road gets narrower. I hold my breath as we approach two large trucks carrying workers. I feel my heart pounding and when I briefly close my eyes I can see my parents on the truck. I open them and focus on the young men ahead.

Abu Bakr announces, with a flourish, our arrival in Ngomeni. It looks like the villages we have just passed. The ground is reddish brown, as are the squat handful of buildings that stand erect across the town centre. My sense of unease deepens.

There are children and young people hanging around in the town square. We slowly drive past them in the car. Abu Bakr points out the Broglio Space Centre, a project funded and developed by the Italian government in the 1960s. He explains that it once served as the site for the launch of Italian satellites. I hadn't known about the huge Italian influence in the area. The vast majority of the restaurants in Malindi are Italian, and last night, at the beach party, the white people were all Italian.

THE PAST ISN'T DEAD

I am about to ask Abu Bakr a question when he cuts the engine and pauses the car at a fork road. He is unsure in what direction he needs to turn. He veers left and the question dies in my mouth as I see the sea.

We go up a hill. The unease I feel is still there, but it moves aside for something else. I'm not sure what yet, perhaps anticipation. We park on the top of the hill and get out without saying a word to each other. I look down at the beach. I worried, before I came, that I wouldn't be able to find the exact beach my parents landed on, but I know immediately that I am in the right place.

Just over a week ago, Baba had pointed out the exact spot where their journey began in Hamar Weyne, also looking onto the sea. Now I am standing in the place where it ended, where my parents stopped being citizens of Somalia and became refugees.

We walk down the hill and pass a small farm, which has goats, chickens and cows. The beach is beautiful, but I feel an underlying terror there. It is as if time is standing still. I walk towards the sea and bend down to touch the water. There are black shimmering rocks underneath. It feels warm and deceptively inviting.

As I look ahead, I can see my parents there. I had struggled when I first read that article on refugees escaping by boat and landing on beaches in East Kenya. But I don't have any difficulty in picturing them anymore.

I can see them on the boat, younger than I have ever known them. The water moving them up and down. They are cramped in with so many other desperate bodies. The boat capsizes as they come closer to the shore. I see my mum struggling and my dad reaching out for her. I can see them trying to swim to shore, their drenched clothes sticking to them. I can see their dark brown skin, bright against the sun. I can see the agony on their faces. I can see them weak but determined as they drag themselves onto the shore. I can see them coming towards me. I step away from the water.

I can see the Kenyan police waiting for them on the beach. I can see the people from the boat being separated into groups of men and women. I can feel my mother's fear and confusion; it is the first time she has been in a country where she doesn't speak the language.

I stand on that beach thinking of my parents' ordeal, but knowing that they were the lucky ones. How many had died trying to get here?

I walk down the beach and find shipwrecked and abandoned boats, embedded deep into the sand. When are they from – from the 1990s, from our refugee crisis?

There is a gentle breeze. I walk ahead and see teenage boys who are getting ready to go fishing. I see a farmer feeding his chickens. It is quiet enough for me to hear my own breathing. It is a stark contrast to the beach I was on yesterday, which was filled with so much life, music and joy.

I wonder if personal and political disasters leave marks on places. Did the natural world know what had taken place, did it honour it, preserve it for people like me to come back and bear witness to it?

I ask to leave after being there for less than an hour. Abu Bakr looks surprised. I feel like a failure, but I don't have the endurance to stay for much longer.

When I get back to the hotel, I thank Abu Bakr profusely. I send the videos from the beach to my mum and dad. 'It hasn't changed,' Baba tells me.

I stay on my bed for hours afterwards, looking up at my ceiling fan that goes round and round in circles. I get up to look up an oft-used quote by William Faulkner in his work *Requiem for a Nun*: 'The past is never dead. It's not even past.' People often stop there, but I think what he goes on to say is even more interesting: 'All of us labour in webs spun long before we were born, webs of heredity and environment, of desire and consequence, of history and eternity.'

I walk onto my balcony and watch a group of children playing excitedly in the pool, their mothers looking on. How much of who I am, standing in this moment in time, has been determined by those first few steps my parents took on that beach?

I look at my emails and see that the communication officer from UNHCR has contacted me. My trip to Kakuma has been approved: she has sent me instructions on how to book a flight to the camp for the next few days.

I used to think that our naturalization process would bring an end to our journey, but have I not spent the past few years seeing another generation of refugees get on the same boats, make the same frenzied journey to safety? I want to bring my parents' memories to life, but what have they suffered that I don't report on now, that we don't see, hear and read about every day over the past decade?

What ending can I write when refugees still die in their hundreds in the Mediterranean? How can I write about the past being the past, when so little has changed for refugees in the present?

There is no moving on: just a terrible cycle repeating time and time again – unless the world finds a way to confront it, to break free. The children's squeals of laughter wake me out of the trance I am in. The time is now.

12
WELCOME BACK TO K-TOWN

I didn't expect to be able to return to Kakuma refugee camp. In the autumn of 2021, when I first got in contact with UNHCR, the refugee agency of the United Nations, to ask about a visit, I was told the camp was currently closed to all but emergency humanitarian personnel. I was given the same answer when I asked again just before I departed for Kenya. I came to accept that it wouldn't happen.

When I tell my parents I am going, my dad congratulates me, but my mum is annoyed. 'Why are you going back?' I laugh off her question, but she then tells me that it isn't safe, and that she doesn't want me to go.

I tell her I have to; that it is important to me. She sighs. 'After all we did to get out?' I don't know how to answer that question. She asks me to stay safe. I promise her I will.

I fly back from Malindi to Nairobi and spend another night in the city before flying to Kakuma on a UNHCR flight with aid agency workers. I will be staying in the camp for four days.

When I see the camp from the plane, I am taken back by just how large it is. I take a deep breath when we land at 12.30 p.m. All the logistics that have yet to be organised buzz around me; how will I get to the hotel from the airport? Could I just walk into the camp and interview people at random? I feel small on that runway and question why I have come. What am I hoping to achieve?

Stepping out of the aeroplane, I see young children and several women looking at us through barbed wire fences. An aid worker besides me tells me many in the camp love to see the plane land and leave.

I stand awkwardly on the runway track as minivans from different organisations come to collect their workers. I ask if there is a cab company I can call, but I am told there isn't. The hotel I am staying in is a thirty-minute walk away. Someone suggests I get a motorcycle taxi, and I consider it, but am unsure how I would fit my suitcase on the back, when a man from UNHCR spots me and offers to give me a lift to the hotel, which he says is opposite the UNHCR compound.

I check into the hotel, which is a few minutes' walk from the camp. It was built by a former Somali refugee who had resettled in Canada and become quite successful. The hotel is staffed exclusively by refugees from the camp.

It is at the hotel's restaurant where I meet with Pauline, UNHCR's on-site communication specialist. She wears a white t-shirt with leggings and has a beautiful smile. We instantly strike up a friendship. We are soon joined by Yannick, a photojournalist and filmmaker, who agrees to be my fixer in the camp. He is twenty-eight and a refugee himself, from the Democratic Republic of Congo. 'Welcome back to K-Town,' he says, after I introduce myself.

We talk about the weather and how lucky I am that it is so cloudy. Whenever my mum and I spoke about Kakuma, she always complained about the heat. After we have lunch, we walk towards the camp. We cross the barrier. What had gone through my mum's mind when she first entered the camp? She had been in her early twenties, younger than I am now.

We walk to an Ethiopian cafe, which sells the best coffee in Kakuma, I am told, and then to the Somali market, which is a maze of shops selling clothes, books, suitcases, fresh fruit and even mattresses. It is like the maze from my dreams.

'How does it feel to be back?' Pauline asks me as we walk through the camp.

I am honest. 'I'm not sure yet.'

I stop to speak to one Somali female shopkeeper, Faduma, who I am told has lived in Kakuma since 1992. The time period she has called this place home spans my entire life. She doesn't recognise me as Somali.

'What is your mother's name?' she asks. I tell her but there is no light of recognition on her face.

Faduma tells me her eldest child is studying in Canada at a university. They had won a scholarship, she says, proudly.

'It is incredibly rare for camp residents to get a scholarship to a Western country. Only around one in a thousand students manage it,' Pauline tells me. I wonder how difficult it is for students, born or raised in Kakuma, to choose between taking the incredible opportunity to study abroad and start a new life, but leave loved ones behind, or stay and be stuck too.

Another shopkeeper, who is also a Somali woman, joins our conversation. 'What tribe are you?' It is one of a handful times in my life when I am directly asked this question. I tell them I don't know.

We walk on and I am introduced to a community champion who represents her local block in the camp. The camp elects a local council where residents' voices are heard. This woman has been in Kakuma for twenty-two years. It is such an extraordinary stretch of time to live in a place like this. I don't say this to her.

The community champion tells me of the struggles of being a woman representative: elected men won't pass on crucial information to her and often speak over her or other women during meetings.

'To do the role well, you have to be able to argue with men,' she tells me.

'Do you like arguing?' I ask.

She responds with a sly smile: 'Sometimes I enjoy it. When I know they're in the wrong, I do.'

We decide to call it a day and walk out of the camp, but as we do I hear people singing. I walk back towards the sound and I see it is a church choir practising. They sit in a circle and follow the instructions of the leader of the group, a short man with a guitar who stands in the middle. They invite me in and let me sit as they rehearse. 'You are most welcome here,' the leader says. I smile as they sing several songs for us.

Pauline and I then go to the local restaurant and bar situated just outside the camp. It caters to refugees, local residents and humanitarians.

I excuse myself to use the toilet. 'It might be better to wait until you return to your hotel. These toilets are like the ones at the camp,' Pauline says with a grimace.

'Oh I remember the camp toilets. I've used them before and can do so again,' I tell her and walk to the toilet. I smile when I am confronted with the hole in the floor that terrified me as a child.

I return and we watch the sunset, a yellow-orange blaze that slowly turns into black. It is beautiful. Did I enjoy watching sunsets here as a child too? New memories did not come flooding back as I walked through the camp. Instead, I feel I can finally claim the memories I already have as my own. Until now, it had felt as though my childhood in Kakuma happened to someone else. But I could finally see them in Technicolor: the brown of the mud, the bright pastel colours of the market.

I think of my mum, I think of my friend Fatima and her family. I think of the people we shared our living encampment with. I can't see their faces, just wrap myself in the way they once made me feel. I think of Shayshay, of Amina.

Kakuma is crucial to everything else that came after it. It is the foundation of who I am.

I was here then and am here now. There is great power in telling myself that. It centres me.

I sleep for a really long time that night. It is only after I have woken up that I realise how on edge I was the day before.

I see a text from Pauline telling me she won't have time to accompany me today, and passing on Yannick's number instead. I call and message Yannick while having breakfast. He soon joins me, and we come up with a game plan for what and who I'd like to see in the camp. We get on a motorcycle taxi and head towards the oldest kindergarten in the camp, which was set up long before I arrived as a child. He thinks it is the place most likely to be the nursery school I went to.

'Do you remember this place?' Yannick asks when we get there. I shake my head.

I don't allow myself to say with any certainty if the school we tour is the one I attended. But it feels comforting to stand in the courtyard. I think back to my memory of my first day at school, of how hot that morning was.

Could this truly be the place Fatima and I came to school? I turn all the way round and drink everything in. The school is closed and quiet.

The headteacher, a short middle-aged woman, spots us and comes out of her office. She asks what we are doing and when I explain she invites us into her office. Her name is Meracare. She lets me interview her.

I look around her small office and see a board of the number of students in each year group. The students are divided by their ethnicity – there are South Sudanese, Congolese, Ethiopians, Burundians and Somalis. There are 568 students in the nursery school, all between the ages of four and five years old.

'Due to the new curriculum, the school doesn't take on anyone older than six years old, but in the olden times, seven-year-old children would have also attended the school,' Meracare says as I sit down. She sits behind her desk.

'Children older than six are placed in the camp's primary schools. They go on to graduate to attend the secondary schools in the camp.'

The largest group currently are the Sudanese students, who dominate the young population in the camp. 'There were many Somali students, but the numbers have gone down over the years,' Meracare.

'Why are you in Kakuma?' I ask.

'I am a refugee who left Sudan. I was a teacher in Sudan and started teaching in the camp after I arrived in 1998. I was first a class teacher, but moved up to become a headteacher.'

Meracare tells me the previous headteacher, who recently passed away, was called Consetta. 'Maybe you met her?' she asks. Consetta joined the school in 1996, when the surrounding area was less developed, but the name doesn't ring any bells for me.

The school originally catered to children from the Ethiopian community, but they now attend the Orthodox Christian church for their learning. 'The leaders of the community decided that a school must be built for them,' Meracare says.

The school had gone through a number of refurbishments and changes to the curriculum since it was first built. It now teaches language, mathematics, environment and psychomotor activities, or physical education. 'The classrooms are an okay size.' Meracare says, 'It accommodates around seventy young learners.'

'Do many of the students here go to university?' I ask.

Meracare says many do. 'You feel so proud about these learners once they go for further learning. And then they come and introduce themselves to you. And then they tell you, "I was once a learner here."'

I am not the first young person who had been taught in this camp to return to it. A few have come back to thank her for taking the time to teach them. She tells me of a teacher in the school, known as Will, who had trained in Nairobi. When she first met him after he was hired, she didn't recognise him. She smiles recollecting her surprise when he'd introduced himself as one of her students, and told her that he returned to the camp to teach.

While she loves her students, Meracare speaks of frustration with the teachers' pay and working conditions. She tells me they had a strike recently for better pay. They stayed home for a week: the schools in the area effectively shut down. The strike was partially successful as their pay did go up, but not by enough.

'It doesn't fulfil our needs. We wanted more. We had a visitor in Dadaab who told us the teachers there are paid more than us. We tried to ask the officers here and they said Dadaab is very different from Kakuma, the insecurity there is very high,' Meracare says. Simply put, teachers in Dadaab are paid more as it's a more dangerous posting.

There are other notable differences between Kakuma and Dadaab. The latter is inhabited almost exclusively by Somali refugees and is the largest refugee camp in the world. It is a lot less diverse and multicultural than Kakuma, where refugees have fled from a number of different countries.

The camps are almost 1200 km apart. I wonder how different I would have been if I was raised in the other.

Meracare now has ten teachers, three of whom are women. One of them is a young Somali woman who is in charge of supporting children with disabilities. These children are taught in the same classroom as their peers because of the recent drive for inclusive education.

'Previously, we used to have their classes separate, but now when inclusion came in then we put them together. No matter which kind of disability, they are deserving and they have to stand together,' Meracare says. There are also ten support staff, caretakers, two cooks and security.

'How do schools work in London?' Meracare asks me. I tell her the model is not too dissimilar to the one in the camp.

The change of curriculum in Kakuma also meant that every child went to the next level of learning, 'so that no child was a failure,' Meracare explains. I tell her that it is the same in England.

Most of Meracare's students are born in the camp. 'The school is free for all learners. It is run by UNHCR,' Meracare says. 'Education remains free for the students until they reach secondary school. Then they have to pay 1,000 Kenyan shillings per term.'

'How was the school impacted by the Coronavirus pandemic?' I ask.

'The schools were immediately shut down in the camp. While the caretakers were still instructed to come and clean the school, the learners stayed at home,' Meracare says.

Back home in London, I had seen my brothers struggle with online learning, but they at least had access to strong Wi-Fi and their own laptops. How did the children in Kakuma manage?

The teachers were initially worried, but found a solution in something less high-tech, but perhaps more durable. 'We gave radios to different sections of the camp. We would call community leaders in the morning and tell them to gather the learners in the area. They then listened to the radio and made notes. The children learned from the radio for a year before they were finally able to return to their classrooms,' Meracare says.

We talk about the Covid-19 death rate, and how devastating it was for global cities like London. Things were nowhere near as dire in Kakuma, though people did die from the disease.

'Were people's bodies burnt in London?' Meracare asks me. I am taken aback by the morbidity of the question.

'People dwell on it so much over the radio, they say they don't want to burn [the deceased] because burning is not our culture. This is a Western culture, but in Africa, when you bury someone, even your grandchildren will come and say this is our grandmother or grandfather who passed away a long time ago. So they still see,' Meracare explains.

I sign her visitor book before I leave. 'Try to come back when the school opens. It would be nice for you to talk to the children,' Meracare says.

Yannick then takes me to one of the oldest settlements in Kakuma, an area the refugees dub 'Hong Kong'. There are lots of different rumours about why it is called Hong Kong – one refugee I speak to says it's because of how innovative the area is. Was this the area my mum and I had lived in?

We walk through Hong Kong and head towards a youth community centre. As we do, a young man called Michael introduces himself to us. He knows Yannick well and describes himself as a rapper. He perks up when he learns that I once lived in the camp and that I have returned.

'Welcome back to K-Town!' he shouts. I will hear this greeting often.

Michael does an impromptu rap about being from Hong Kong: I can tell that he is either drunk or high. The atmosphere shifts. He leaves, briefly, when we tell him we are going to the youth centre.

There is a class on sexual and gender-based violence going on at the centre. I walk in and the students all turn to look at me. I apologise and walk straight out. A soft-spoken young woman named Rebecca, who is leading the class, follows me out. She explains what is happening and welcomes me to the camp.

'The youth centre runs a number of different classes from learning English to career guidance. It is an important source of information and community for the young people in the camp,' Rebecca tells me. 'I'm sorry, I have to get back, but it is truly lovely to meet you.'

She gives me her number and tells me to reach out to her before returning to her class.

I watch by the door as she continues running the lesson. I can't help but smile that such a young person – probably only in her early twenties – has already become a community leader and role model to the teenagers in the class.

Rebecca shows what she has been taught in training run by NGOs. This happens a lot in Kakuma: most courses run by humanitarian organisations have a cap on the number of people who can attend. So those who go often go on to run those classes for the other residents who couldn't attend, making sure the skills and information they've learnt is passed down. It is a striking instance of community in action.

Yannick tells me the best example of this is among the photographers and journalists in the camp. He takes me to a media studio called Dream Magical Studio, which was first set up in 2017. It is one of many media hubs to have sprung up in the camp. We are welcomed by two young male photographers and filmmakers: twenty-one-year-old Akuok and twenty-six-year-old Atem. They are both South Sudanese refugees.

There is a Mac laptop and several cameras in the shack. It is dark and a lot cooler than the outside. In the back, there are a bundle of wires, wrapped around each other, and a few older laptops that don't look used.

The NGO FilmAid has for the past few years been running workshops and training for young residents in the camp interested in film and photography. These workshops are fiercely popular, and slots on the courses are capped. So, as with Rebecca's teaching, whenever a refugee got a spot, they then run those same workshops, to the best of their ability, to anyone younger who is also interested. They also share the cameras they have; some of these are donated, while others save up to buy their own.

Akuok and Atem are in the middle of editing photos when I walk in. They form a series of portraits of residents in the camp. There is a whole album of them.

'It was common for young people in the camp, particularly the women, to reach out and ask for pictures to be taken of themselves,' Yannick tells me. 'They wear the best outfit they have for these pictures.'

The photos are incredible. I love seeing everyone's unique style; they are often a mixture of traditional clothes from their own culture and other ideas they see in the camp and across the world.

'People did these photoshoots as a way to express their identity,' Yannick told me. 'It is like a fashion show here sometimes.'

Each and every one of the subjects must have spent years of their life being reduced to a number: the numbers at a specific border, the numbers that died or survived during a particularly dangerous crossing, the numbers still living in camps. These pictures are a declaration of their humanity: they have not just survived but are living.

As well as taking people's portraits, Akuok and Atem are often hired to photograph weddings, graduations and other important events. They do this without pay. Some photographers connected to the studio have had paid commissions from NGOs and news organisations to create short films or take pictures, but this is exceedingly rare.

The two young men are hungry to be able to do more and to tell their own stories. Atem, the older of the two boys, first came to Kakuma in 2007. 'I love to take photos and tell stories using photography,' he tells me. There were a lot of stories told about Kakuma from people on the outside, he explains, and these can be both positive and negative. 'But as refugees, we have our own stories. We are the ones to tell our stories to the world. We wouldn't want others to come out and tell our story.'

'What's it like being a photographer in the camp?' I ask Atem.

'Here in Kakuma, we have different nationalities from different countries. We cover their events to create memories for them. So let's say they are in Kakuma, but are then resettled. Those memories, they would carry them with them wherever they are and be able to show other people,' he tells me. Photography is a way of keeping the camp with them long after they have gone.

Atem tells me he likes photographing and filming weddings because it tests his technical ability. The space to work in is often cramped and getting the right shot is a challenge, but he prides himself on always finding a way. Atem wants more challenging work. He believes media companies should hire refugee photographers and filmmakers when covering the camp because they are intimately aware of the area. 'We are connected with the people within so it would be easier for us to find the target of your story, or the person who will tell your story best. It would be easier for us to communicate with them than them coming here.'

Akuok is more nervous to talk to me, but eventually comes out of his shell. He came to Kakuma in 2001, when he was just a baby, and the camp is all he has ever really known. He was first trained as a photographer by his friends and, when he became committed to photography, he got the opportunity to do the training at FilmAid.

'The good thing with photography is it comes with a lot of adventure. It's an easy way of expressing your feelings, of speaking your mind. Most of the time, the world right now, people get more interaction with things that they see and things that they hear. My story will be a little bit easier to tell through photos and maybe videos,' Akuok says.

'Why do you want to tell your story?' I ask Akuok.

'I like to tell my story because I'm the one that knows my story, what I have gone through, and I would be able to portray it in the way that I feel personally. If another person came here to tell it, they might omit information or add some information that's not good for the story.'

"Do you want to be a journalist?" I ask Akuok.

'Given the chance, I'd like to become one because within refugee communities, there are a lot of stories that need to be done and be uncovered. Given the chance, I'd love to uncover it,' he tells me.

I think of his use of the phrase 'given the chance', and the extraordinary role that chance plays in Kakuma: in who gets resettled, who is given the resources they need to thrive and who is left behind. It feels criminal that young refugees like Akuok and Atem are sitting in their studio waiting for the opportunity to showcase their talent. They aren't the only ones. There are young refugees across the camp, bursting with energy and talent, just waiting for their chance. Some are able to pass the time with training and workshops that help develop their skill, but others succumb to worse.

When we leave the studio, we bump into the young rapper Michael. His speech is slurred. When we try to say goodbye to the rapper, he refuses to let us go. 'I ain't going nowhere,' he says. I look at Yannick, who doesn't look worried, and, speaking Swahili, he manages to convince the rapper to let us be on our way.

Yannick tells me that Michael is high and has become an addict in recent years. He used to be heavily involved with the media hubs that sprang up, focusing on the music side of things, but had been filled with despair about how stuck his life was. He was born in the camp and now didn't believe that he would ever leave it. 'It's really sad,' Yannick says. 'A lot of young people turn to drugs and alcohol.'

It makes me think of the Somali word 'buufis', which literally means 'to inflate or blow'. It was initially used to describe a longing to leave the country and go abroad by Somalis living in Somalia. I had first come across the term while looking at studies on refugee mental health while studying for my masters. Buufis had taken on a new meaning following the outbreak of war. Somali refugees in camps in Kenya began to use the word to describe their hopes and dreams of resettlement. It now refers to a deep-seeded desire to leave the camp, make a permanent settlement elsewhere, preferably in the West, and finally stop being a refugee. The term buufis spread rapidly across the Somali diaspora in Africa. It was later used by Somalis and researchers to describe mental health problems.

Buufis sufferers differ, but a common denominator is a feeling of disconnect from reality, and severe distress at not being resettled.

Does Michael suffer from buufis? Did he want to stay with me as a means of escape? I'm not sure what exactly I can help him escape from. Did he want me to physically take him out of the camp or did he want to escape from his life through talking and hanging out with me? I stop myself. Why on earth would I be of any importance to him?

Yannick notices my silence. He asks if I want to take a break and have lunch. Once we sit down, I ask if he is up for telling me his story.

He had been living in Kakuma since 2011. 'When I arrived, I didn't even imagine I'd spend more than five years here,' he says.

'Why did you want to become a photographer and video journalist?'

He sighs and pauses before answering. He was passionate about journalism even as a child, he tells me. He remembers telling his dad as much. At the time, his dad asked him if he liked politics, and he said he didn't. His dad then told him that since he didn't like politics, there was no way he could be a journalist. He let go of the dream.

Then the war broke out and he fled to Kakuma. He doesn't tell me what happened to his father or other members of his family and I don't ask. Yannick had initially lived with his cousin in Kakuma, who was then resettled in the US. His cousin's resettlement forced him to find a way to financially support himself. 'Life then became a bit harder,' he says.

Yannick came across an advert for a media class which focused on TV, production and film. He applied and got a spot. When he started the class, he had hoped it would be a good way to pass the time and hopefully learn something new. But it had instead reignited his childhood passion for storytelling.

'Why is it important to have refugee journalists?' I ask.

'I think it's a good thing to have refugee journalists to tell our stories. Here in the camp we have journalists from the outside come to tell stories about refugees,' Yannick says.

He stumbles a little as he tries to express the problems with these foreign journalists and the perception of refugees that often colours their reportage. 'We are just vulnerable,' he finally manages to say. 'But we know the life we live here. We know everything we go through so it's easier for us to express ourselves, to tell the world who we are. We are real people.'

Yannick is frustrated with the restrictions he has to work under. Much of his work with NGOs is rigorously scripted and they are forbidden to tell certain stories. 'They choose the story that we are supposed to tell,' he explains. Good stories about the camp or the impact the aid is having from a specific NGO are fine to tell, but more nuanced stories about difficulties within communities and the challenges international organisations create are discouraged.

'What do you feel when you're taking pictures?' I ask.

'When I am behind the camera, I feel like I am in my safe space,' Yannick says.

Our conversation moves on to the coverage of the war in Ukraine. Many in the camp are disturbed at how the media portrays the refugees – with one contributor on BBC News describing his agony at seeing 'Europeans with blue eyes and blonde hair' fleeing war.

For Yannick, the coverage made him realise the prevalence of the Western perception that Africans such as himself are built to withstand pain, as if 'we are used to suffering; that it is our nature'. This sits heavily with me.

He tells me of his dream of exploring the world. 'I want to discover the hidden stories. Sometimes I will tell you a story which people are seeing with their eyes, but there are hidden stories, which maybe people are afraid to take out and tell the world people are going through this. So my passion is to go around the world, because not only Africans are suffering. There are people outside of Africa who are suffering, and we need to tell their stories.'

Yannick shows more empathy for the rest of the world than it has ever shown to him. I want to tell him that, but I'm afraid it'll embarrass him. I decide against it. We say goodbye after lunch and I thank him for his help. We plan to see each other again tomorrow.

I spend the rest of the afternoon alone in my hotel room. I don't have any more interviews or anyone to hang out with. I leave my room later that evening due to a blackout. I sit in the restaurant and wait for the power to come back on. After a few hours, it becomes quite clear the power won't be returning any time soon. I don't have access to the internet and my phone, as well as my Kindle, will die soon.

I feel alone and vulnerable in the darkness. I miss my family and my friends. I miss London. I miss the relative ease and comfort of my life over the past twenty years, and the innocence that I had carried with me years into adulthood.

I order a tea and white chocolate cake: it is too hot to have any substantial dinner. The cake is unbearably sweet and filling. Somehow, I manage to eat it all.

The days at Kakuma quickly blend into each other. I meet Yannick in the morning and we walk to an interview he helps set up, talking about our likes and dislikes along the way. He asks me often whether I am remembering my time in the camp any more clearly, but I politely say no. I just have to believe it was me who once lived here, and not some other child.

My favourite day with Yannick is the one where I am shown the music of the camp. He tells me there are many musical artists in Kakuma. I listen as he talks about the rappers, Afrobeat artists and singers that have emerged from the camp in the past ten years. They intermix familiar beats from their own cultures with what they hear in the camp and abroad.

We visit the record label Exile Key. It is meticulously designed, with a strict blue and white colour scheme. There is a well-kept garden in between two buildings. One is a recording studio, the second a place for creatives to relax and hang out. It is their oasis.

We sit outside with the co-owners of the media house, who ask me to explain why I want to talk to them. They visibly relax as I tell my story. We speak for several hours.

They are especially passionate about building their capacity and empowering other refugees. 'What good would it do if one person in a community had a skill and it died with him?' one man asks. The question stays with me.

Yannick then takes me to watch the making of a music video for an upcoming young rapper. Yannick had given his camera to a mentee of his who is the director. 'I like giving what I can to the young people I have trained and seeing them do something positive with what they have learnt. I like seeing them do something they are passionate about,' he says.

There are people in charge of audio, lighting and other camera equipment, backup dancers and background extras waving flags. They all look to be in their late teens, some even younger.

There is a Canadian flag in the mix. 'Why is that there?' I ask Yannick.

Yannick shrugs. 'It might be to do with the fact that a lot of people from the camp have resettled in Canada.' I laugh.

I laugh a lot that day, especially when a group of teenage girls arrive, wearing full faces of makeup. 'They are the video vixens,' one backup dancer tells me. The girls are playing at being adults, like any group of teenagers back in London.

I find myself sitting beside a thirty-year-old man called Rey, who is wearing a crisp white shirt, camel-coloured slacks and black dinner shoes. Yannick introduces him as the best director in the camp. Rey is quick to add that he is also an award-winning actor, playwright and dancer. 'I was invited to a film festival in Zambia to screen a short film I directed and starred in, but I couldn't go,' Rey says.

'Why?'

'I needed special permission to travel to the film festival. I applied but I just kept waiting, waiting, waiting,' Rey slaps his hands together, still frustrated.

'It didn't arrive in time?' I ask, and he shakes his head.

I watch them shoot the first few scenes of the music video. It reminds me of the grime videos that were recorded around my council estate in East London. I smile to myself when I remember how I tried to meticulously remember the rap verses as a teenager in a doomed effort to bump up my 'Black British credentials' in my school. Would I have done the same in Kakuma, or would I have felt comfortably Black, surrounded almost exclusively by refugees?

We walk to another location. One of the dancers sits beside me during a break in filming. He is twenty-one years old and has lived his entire life in the camp. We joke around with each other for much of the afternoon, but just before I leave, he asks me if he has much chance of being resettled like I was. His family fled Uganda, but he has no interest in going back. He wants a new place to call home. I stay quiet for a lot longer than I want to, trying to grasp at the right words to tell him.

'I don't know,' I say, and feel pathetic for doing so. Another beat passes between us. 'Do you pray?' I ask him. I want there to be something bigger than any of us for him to be able to turn to.

'I don't go to church anymore,' he says with a smile. 'Do you dance?'

'Not as well as I want to.'

He laughs and says: 'It is the easiest thing in the world to move your body in place.' He leaves before I get his name.

The exchange reminds me of how often I danced in the camp as a child: of my mother's story about me dancing to our neighbour's tune, back when I was Shayshay. I think about how freeing the simple act of dancing is, particularly when so many doors seem so tightly shut.

During my final lunch with Yannick, I ask if he knows of any young people from the camp who turn to people smugglers to try and get to Europe.

'Many left to take their chances on the boats in 2014 and 2015,' Yannick tells me.

'Do you know what happened to them?' I ask.

'No, I haven't heard back from any of them. I don't know whether they made it or not,' says Yannick. 'I think many of them died.'

'Have you ever been tempted to take this risk?'

He shakes his head: 'No, never.' He would rather make a living and a life for himself in Kakuma. He would rather wait and see.

We say goodbye after that meal. I tell him I'd keep an eye on his work and he says he will look out for my book. I watch him walk away back into the camp before turning to go to my room.

It is Mother's Day and my thoughts turn to my mum – not as I know her now, but the mother she was to me in Kakuma. She faced the same impossible decision. She was just twenty-four years old then. If she had waited for resettlement, I could still be here. I would have lived my life having only known the camp. Our leaving meant that we risked imprisonment or death. What would I have done in her position? And why, decades later, are people being forced to make the same choice in the same camp?

I get some internet data and send a message to my mum. I have so much I want to say, but I don't know how to put it into words. I tell her I love her and that I miss her. For now, that will have to be enough.

On my final night at the camp, there is another blackout, and the generator is turned on. I sit quietly as it buzzes away, thinking about how I will be turning thirty in a few weeks.

People in the camp often asked me if I had new memories come back to me while I've been here and I'm disappointed that the answer is no. The memories I do have feel less rootless and more my own. I can place them here, and myself. But I didn't find new ones.

In Somalia, it was easy to think of who Amina would have been if the war hadn't happened and I had stayed. It's difficult to admit that my second mission, of reconnecting with Amina the child, has been a failure. I haven't found my childhood self here. Amina remained as elusive to me as ever before. I have come to accept that that girl is gone. I wasn't getting Amina back, no matter how much I wanted her or how hard I tried.

I was around fifteen when my mum passed the UK citizenship test. When she passed, something dramatic quietly happened to me: I stopped being a stateless person. I was born stateless and for half of my life I was not considered a national or citizen of any country. And then, while working through my GCSEs, I got paperwork that told me that I belonged to a country. I have always felt grateful for my British citizenship, but it's not until this night that I start to come to terms with the magnitude of what it meant to no longer be stateless, to have a country I could call home.

I realise that night that I am at a midway point, looking at a life split in two: half lived as a refugee, a stateless person, and half as a citizen of one of the richest countries in the world. Every moment after this coming birthday – every day, every hour, every minute that follows – will mean I have lived longer as Aamna, the British citizen, than anything else. The distance between me and the refugee I was, and those in the camp today, will grow wider and wider.

I am glad that I have come back. I don't want to walk into the coming chapters of my life completely untethered from the past. I don't want to forget what happened to me and my family, and I don't want to turn a blind eye on the refugees that live today.

I feel strained that night, like the versions of myself I contain are threatening to collapse in on me. I sit with all that I was and all that I am. In Somalia, I experienced a homecoming to my Somali identity. Here, tonight, in Kakuma, I experienced the homecoming of a refugee. And now, at the end of the trip, I am experiencing another homecoming – to myself.

PART THREE

13
GIRLHOOD ON TWO FRONTS

I returned to the UK days before my thirtieth birthday. My husband and I went for a meal and then to watch the adaptation of Andrea Levy's novel *Small Island* at the National Theatre: I was given press tickets as I had written an essay for the play's programme. I had been asked to write a companion piece to an edited version of an essay Levy wrote about what it was like to grow up in the UK as the daughter of the 'Windrush generation'.

I squealed when I first got the request. I first read *Small Island* as a teenager during my A-levels, and it remains one of my favourite novels. It is a story about four characters: Hortense and Gilbert, who migrate from Jamaica to London, and Queenie and Bernard, an English couple residing in London. Through their lives, Levy weaves a much bigger tale about the relationship between the UK and the Caribbean.

When we got to the theatre, I saw my name on a small poster advertising the programme. The small stand, which stood proudly on the main ticket desk, noted that as well as Levy's essay, the programme included a piece by Aamna Mohdin: 'On being Black British and finding a sense of belonging'. There I was.

I thought back to that A-level English class, when those copies of the book were first handed out. I had not heard of Levy before. We discussed the immigrant experience in class and I didn't find myself shrinking. It was the first time I had seen it expressed so beautifully.

I couldn't stop thinking about how extraordinary it was that I was asked to write about Black Britishness by such an important British institution. I had spent so much of my life wondering if I was British, what it means to be Black on this island and whether I belonged. That anyone cared about my thoughts on the subject floored me. I had waited my entire life for someone to expose me as some fraud. When the theatre went dark and the play began, I let out a deep breath.

Throughout the play, I kept thinking of the years I lived in the UK, first as an asylum seeker and then as a refugee with leave to remain. I thought of how I navigated this strange island. I had been so desperate as a child to fit in and be liked. But I also wanted to be noticed.

As we headed home, I realised that I needed to also explore all of the awkward, painful and important moments in my childhood in Britain that led me to that theatre. I want to reclaim other parts of my identity: who I am as a Somali and a refugee.

The journey away made me a lot more contemplative about the story of my life in Britain. Before I left, I used to think that everything worth telling began with the war, and ended once I came to the UK. The trip to Somalia and the refugee camp in Kenya had been about two returns, but now I was home it was clear that the story I was telling wouldn't end there. Those two returns made me realise there was also something to say about how I became Aamna, a Black Briton.

So my third return was a temporal one, not a geographical one: to my girlhood.

It is not a particularly remarkable story. It does not involve dodging bullets or passing days in a refugee encampment. But it is mine, and after returning from the trip, I found myself needing to tell it.

I didn't permanently settle in a British school until I was eight or nine years old. I had moved around too much in the first year or so after I arrived in the UK. I learned many lessons once my family and I settled down.

The first was to keep weird supernatural occurrences within my family to myself: when the teacher asks you to do a five-minute presentation to the class, use that time to introduce yourself to your new schoolmates. Don't get up and tell everyone about each time your mum and other family members were possessed by jinn.

In Islam, jinn are invisible spirits that live among us. They are very different to the genies that were popularised by *Aladdin*. My mum told me they were malignant creatures that had the power to possess and cause other physical and mental harm. I was terrified of them as a child.

I had started my new primary school in Year Five with another new pupil called Amanda. The primary school was a large Victorian building built in 1897; it had three floors and I remember excitedly climbing the dark, cavernous staircase. On our first day, the teacher asked me and Amanda to prepare something to read out to the class for the end of the week. We were told it should be about five minutes and that we could talk about whatever we wanted. I walked home eager to make a lasting impression on my new classmates.

I wrote between four to five pages of notes in my workbook. My parents were impressed. They didn't read what I had written, but wished me good luck.

I didn't feel nervous when the teacher called me up first. I took my notebook with me and began telling the class about jinn. I told them about the time they had possessed my mum during a birthday party. She was pregnant at the time and her stomach had moved in a weird way. She had collapsed to the ground and her sisters began praying over her. She then spoke in a deep scary voice, and her eyes had rolled to the back of her head.

'She groaned—' I said, and stopped to look up from my notebook at the rest of the class. It has been twenty years since that moment, but I can still remember their disturbed faces. Perhaps this wasn't what the teacher had meant when she asked me to get up and talk about something; perhaps I hadn't realised until now that my family were as far from normal as you could get.

I had a choice to make: I could either stop or carry on. I saw that I still had a couple of pages left of my story. I took a deep breath and pushed on. I told them about the parties we had where there were multiple possessions by jinn, where it seemed like the spirit jumped from one adult to another. I spoke with less confidence by then as I snuck looks at the rest of the class. The tension in the room was by then unbearable. They looked at me aghast, and I was met with a stunned silence when I finished. I rushed to my seat and avoided eye contact with anyone.

'Right, well thank you so much for sharing that,' my teacher said. The teacher looked uncertain when she asked Amanda to get up and do her speech. She breathed a sigh of relief when Amanda said, 'Hi everyone, I thought I'd use my time to properly introduce myself and tell you five interesting facts about me.'

She told us how many siblings she had and what her favourite colour was. She was quick to make the class laugh. I desperately wanted to be her at that moment. I struck up a friendship with her and a few other students who lived near me. I would watch their mannerisms and copy them. I liked the TV shows that they liked, and listened to the bands they told me about. If they asked me if I knew about a singer or an actress, I always said yes, even if I didn't. I wanted, more than anything else, to pass as a British girl.

I learned more about myself, something that's easier to do when not dodging border guards or fighting for life's most basic necessities. I learnt how much I love to read. Shortly after my disastrous jinn presentation, the teacher read out an excerpt from a book about a boy wizard. I don't think that anyone had ever read fiction to me before that class. I was entranced as she read the first chapter. I was both sitting in that classroom, yet also somewhere else in my mind, somewhere far away and exciting.

Like many children of the nineties, I developed Harry Potter fever. The teacher told us we could borrow the book from the school library, but all the copies were checked out by the time I got there. I didn't know when there would be another copy I could take out, so I asked my parents if they would buy me the book and they agreed. My dad would go to the local bookshop and get a copy for me.

I was barely seeing my dad at the time. He was working night shifts as a security guard. I would get up when he returned from work at the crack of dawn, eagerly awaiting my first book that was mine and mine alone. But he turned up empty-handed for the first few weeks. He would tell me he forgot: at one moment I was brought close to tears when he opened the door and I saw he didn't have a book on him. He eventually told me he didn't know what book to get because he kept forgetting the title. He asked if I could get the teacher to write the title on a piece of paper. Many years later, he confessed he had been unable to pronounce certain words like 'philosopher' to the bookseller.

I marched back to school and told my teacher the problem. She smiled and wrote it down on a piece of paper. I ran back home, desperate to give my dad the paper before he went to work. The next morning, I stood waiting in the hallway as he unlocked the door. He laughed when he saw me and gave me the book. I kissed him and told him he was the most wonderful man in the world, which made him laugh more. 'Tell your mum that when she wakes up,' he told me.

I read the book in one weekend, and told my dad there were three other books in the series. We got into a routine then: I'd get the teacher to write down the book title, and my dad would buy it on his way home from work.

My dad joked that I'd end up bankrupting the family at the pace I was reading these books. He changed tack and took me to my local library the following weekend and got me a membership. We fell into another routine: every Saturday we would go to the library and he would patiently wait as I agonised about which books to take out and which to come back for. On the walk back, we would talk about the books I had read and what I thought of them.

Books opened up a new world of understanding Britishness. I wasn't reading socio-political books, just children's fiction, but they taught me what I wanted to know about being a child in this country. These showed me which values I should hold dear, what British people dressed and spoke like, what children's rooms looked like, what hobbies they had, what they got up to during the weekends and school holidays.

The books showed me that we weren't just considered financially impoverished – which I thought was ludicrous, as the flat we lived in was the biggest place I had ever called home – but culturally poor as well. My family's own cultural loves and pursuits were not reflected in what I read, so I began to see them as backward, while my continued religious education, which involved memorising the Quran and learning about the philosophies and pillars of Islam during the weekend at dugsi (Islamic school), felt out of step with what the other students in my class were learning in their spare time.

I was also taking, for the first time, consistent lessons in maths, English and science. This final year of primary school was crucial: it was the year we would be sitting our SATs. This kind of testing was completely alien to me, and the importance of the tests was drummed into us from the first day of the year.

I went home and told my parents about the upcoming tests. My mum had asked if I would repeat a year if I failed and I told her no. She then told me not to worry and that I would do fine.

'When I was your age, I remember the end of year tests I had to do with my sister Mama Sacidiya. She was scared she would fail, but I was confident I'd be the best. I remember how I strutted to that exam with such conviction only to later see that I had failed, but Mama Sacidiya had passed,' Mama told me, and we both laughed.

Still, I was competitive in school and wanted to be one of the best. My dad fuelled my drive, saving up what little money we had to find me a tutor in maths and English in the holidays. He would also offer me money, ranging from £10 to £50, for good grades.

My dad always told me that education was key to achieving success in this lifetime, while learning the Quran and praying was vital for succeeding in the afterlife. One of my earliest political memories was watching Tony Blair make a speech about the importance of education on TV with my dad. This was why, my dad told me, they had come to the UK.

At the time, SATs were graded between levels 1 and 6, with each level having its own letter to mark whether it was a high level 4 (4A) or a low level 4 (4C). I was told that students were expected to reach a level 4: the exceptional students would be aiming for level 5.

On the day of our results, our teacher took each student aside to tell them what they got and speak privately with them. My teacher saw the disappointment on my face when I failed to get a level 4 and instead achieved around 3As across the board. 'You should be proud of yourself,' he told me and squeezed my shoulder. My dad told me the same when I got home, but I still felt miserable for the next few days.

I found it easy to absorb the official and unofficial rules of being British. I was a young, malleable child eager to look like my classmates. My parents, who were more established in their language and culture, struggled. So as I learnt the way of this new world we had been thrown into, I was also teaching it to my parents. I grew up explaining the education system to my parents as I went through it. I would explain what SATs, GCSEs and A-levels are and what grades I needed to get. It wasn't until years later, when I was talking to one of my brothers, that I realised we had vastly different parents growing up.

When my brothers were being taught to swim, my mum would pack all their essentials in a bag for them. They didn't have to return from swimming practice telling mum that they needed to bring their own towels, shower products and moisturisers as well as spare underwear. When my brothers went on a school trip, my mum packed a special lunch for them. They didn't have to return from a school trip telling my mum that though we qualified for free school meals, it was embarrassing to not have your own packed lunch for these days out of school. During parents' evening, my brothers didn't have to translate what the teacher was saying: my parents had picked up the language by the time they were in school, or I went in their stead.

I don't write this embittered or angry at my parents. They did the best they could and were learning as I was. Nor do I think my experiences were particularly unique. Many refugee and migrant children occupy two spaces as they learn to integrate: in one, they're digging their own roots into the country; in the other, they're ensuring that their parents have what they need. These children are not just explaining and translating the goings on of the outside world, but are often their parents' passports to accessing vital services.

I'm not sure when the shift happened or if it was subtle, but by the time I was a pre-teen, I went from just a child to something more. I was my family's go-to translator, the person who filled in benefit and immigration forms and a co-parent for my brothers. I learned at twenty-nine, while researching for this book, that there is a name for this: 'the parentified child'.

Researchers describe 'parentification' as when a child performs the role of a parent in the family system. This child could be expected to act like a parent to their siblings or to their own parents, or both. Some of this research explores the pathological toll of parentification on the child; other experts point to positives.

I dug into this research once I returned from Somalia and Kenya. As I did so, I found myself shrugging off studies that pointed to the negative aspects of being parentified and over-identifying with those that pointed to the positives – I am an independent, loyal, ambitious and fiercely determined individual. I didn't see myself as an anxious adult who was bad at setting boundaries.

There is a simple and obvious reason why: I don't want to criticise my parents, even when they are deserving of criticism. Our circumstances meant I had to grow up very quickly and couldn't remain a child for long. I don't think that's right, but I also don't blame them.

It's a difficult conundrum. I do sometimes feel frustrated at how often I have been the first port of call when my mum needs support, or my brothers want me to help them. But I cannot conceive of a world where I wouldn't.

I felt a frenzied excitement at the prospect of getting my first period. I would stare, hard, at my knickers whenever I used the toilet, to look for any signs of it. I was eleven and just about to finish primary school when a girl in my class, Naomi, told me she had got hers. We crowded around her during break.

'I was out shopping with my mum when I suddenly felt something weird down there,' she told us and we all giggled. 'I thought I had peed myself and my mum hurried me to the toilets. And then we realised what happened.'

We bombarded her with questions: did she have to throw away her knickers? Was there a lot of blood? One teacher had told us of a white sticky substance that can come before, did that happen to her? She nodded. We revelled in the grotesqueness of it all and shooed away the boys who would normally hang out with us that day. Naomi basked in the questions. She had transformed before our very eyes.

I would check for my period religiously, but still nothing came. Whenever I was bored, I'd run out of the toilet and tell my mum I had started my period and she'd roll her eyes when I started laughing. She seemed far less excited about the changes that I wanted to run headfirst into.

It must have been a strange time for my mum. She was seeing me grow in a way her mother never had. She never got to talk to her mother about her first period and so many other firsts.

I was an immensely curious child and for the most part, my parents encouraged me, even if it was embarrassing for them. One day, students were talking about sex: what it is and that it was needed to make babies. The myth of the stork hadn't reached the concrete of the East London playground.

My dad would pick me up every day and we'd get two buses back home. On a packed bus home, I asked him: 'Have you ever had sex with mama?' He looked startled and I added: 'Someone in school has been saying that you need to have sex to have babies.' He took a moment to consider before responding: 'Yes, we did have sex. Your friend is right.'

I didn't say anything for a while. Just before we got off the bus, I turned to him and said: 'You and Mama are bad Muslims.'

But I often found myself hitting my parents' limits. My mum tried to keep me close, but I found many of her rules bizarre and restricting. I wasn't just growing up, but changing in an environment that was foreign to her. When I was first invited to my first slumber party, she told me I couldn't go.

'Why would I let you sleep at someone else's house when you have a perfectly fine bed here?' Mama said. This was her logic for most things. When I asked to go trick or treating during Hallowe'en, she initially forbade me. 'Why would I let you go out begging for sweets from our neighbours? So people think I don't feed you?'

She did eventually let me go trick or treating, but only to the neighbours on our block, wearing her black abaya and a witch mask I got from the local pound shop. We often negotiated compromises like this, bringing my father in whenever there was a deadlock.

The traditional passage of girlhood into womanhood – where a girl is made and then destroyed, and a woman steps into her place – happened in two places at once for me: at home, where I learnt to become a woman as a refugee, and in the outside world, as a British citizen to be.

I often thought of the afterlife, and whether one went to heaven or hell. These weren't concepts, but real destinations in my house. My mum had not only memorised the entire Quran, like many other women, but also understood it, and could cite the relevant scripture for any given moment. And she did. As I grew up, so did the expectations to practise modesty and what Muslims call the hijab. While most think the hijab is just about covering a woman's hair, it's also about covering up most of your body and wearing loose-fitting clothes and about behaviour like lowering one's gaze.

At the awkward age of thirteen, I held a fashion show for my parents and their friends to show off the clothes I bought. Some of the outfits were too small, but I still strutted out in them. I realised I did something wrong when I saw the stern look on my dad's face.

I ran off and my mum followed. The both of us sat in her room as she explained that I was growing up and needed to dress modestly from now on. I just nodded, not telling her that while I was probably too big for my clothes, I didn't feel big enough to be anything but a girl. I didn't like the idea of womanhood she painted: it made me feel trapped and invisible.

When my mum asked me if I would wear the headscarf, I resisted, and then agreed to do so only if I could wear it like a bandana. While I didn't really want to wear the headscarf, I also didn't want to go to hell or, worse, disappoint my parents.

I had befriended many boys on my local estate and at my school while at primary school. I would often have them round to my house so we could listen to the rap CDs I had stolen from my older cousins, and so that I could impress them with how many of the lyrics I had memorised. While I'm thankful my fantasies of becoming a rapper began and ended in the summer between primary and secondary school, so did many of my male friendships. I turned to focus exclusively on my friendship with girls. I used to think this was of my own choosing, but now, as an adult, I can see the disapproving looks from my mum when I brought the boys to our house.

When I finally did get my period, they were long and heavy, and sometimes I had them multiple times a month. I complained often about feeling tired and fainted a few times. A quick blood test confirmed I was anaemic, and I was given iron tablets. Though I was still young, I wasn't scared of what the doctor told me. I again felt almost comically proud.

I remember when my parents' friends came to visit excitedly telling a man in his early twenties all about my anaemia. I rushed to the kitchen to grab my tablets to show him. He just nodded. Later, my mum told me not to talk to men about my periods. I was learning a lesson that applied both to the world of my parents' home and the world outside it.

When I left primary school, my name stopped being spelt 'Amina'. On my first day of secondary school, it had been changed by my parents on all the school documents to 'Aamna'.

I don't know if I ever got an explanation for why it had anglicised. I think, deep down, I liked the break the name offered me. Amina had a chaotic and disrupted childhood. She was always playing catch up. Aamna fitted in comfortably with the rest of her classmates. She auditioned for the school musical, successfully won her election to become head girl and danced with her friends at the end of year parties.

Aamna was on her way to becoming a Black Briton.

I grew increasingly uncomfortable with my name once I started interviewing my parents in 2020. As I found out more about our story, I started to wonder if the change from Amina to Aamna was less of a transformation and more of a loss.

I kept thinking about my own by-line at the *Guardian* and the name I'd publish this book under. Should it be Amina or should it stay as Aamna? I initially tried to ignore this question. I was put off by the administrative hurdles I'd have to jump over to get my name professionally and legally changed. I also didn't want to cause a fuss, as most of the people in my life knew me as Aamna. Why cause trouble now?

But I couldn't simply make the yearning to confront this question go away. While in Kenya and Somalia, I was Amina.

I asked my close friends to start calling me Amina on a trial basis. They agreed, swiftly changing my name on their phones. It wasn't an immediate change and my friends often apologised for falling back on Aamna, but I love how supportive they were. I didn't tell my parents I was doing this. I wanted to come to a decision before I told them.

And, for a few days, it felt good. I felt like I was reclaiming a piece of myself. The good feeling soon turned sour, however. I began to cringe whenever someone called me Amina. It felt wrong and performative.

I realised that the change wasn't something I necessarily *wanted* to do. It felt like something I *had* to do, and that I was betraying my past if I didn't.

After a few months, I told my friends that I was bringing the experiment to an end and would stick to Aamna. My name on their contact lists changed again. I felt disappointed at first, like I was letting myself down, but a good friend of mine told me that it is still possible to honour my past, and acknowledge the girl Amina, without taking away from my present.

I thought that by reverting back to my old name, I would ease the discomfort I sometimes feel about my identity. But that didn't happen. I would feel that discomfort whether I am Amina or Aamna. I needed to learn to live with it. This discomfort is a lingering, residual effect of displacement. There is no solving that or overcoming it.

14
BLACK AND BRITISH

I was desperate to get a bank account when I started secondary school. I am not sure why. I didn't have an allowance and my mum just gave me money as and when I asked for it. But suddenly that was no longer enough.

'I need my own bank account.' I told my mum in the evening during the school week.

'Why?' Mama asked.

'I just need one. Mama,' I told her, aggravated. 'I just want my own one.'

'Fine, we can go open one over the weekend,' Mama said, turning back to the show she was watching on TV.

My mum took me to our local NatWest branch. I remember smiling at the woman on the reception desk as I said: 'I'm here to open my first bank account.' I beamed at my mum.

The cashier nodded. 'You need documents to prove your identity and evidence for proof of address.'

As I was a child, it was fine for mum to provide a proof of address for us, but the cashier then asked for my British passport or birth certificate.

'I'm sorry, I don't have either. I just have these Home Office travel documents,' I said. They were the only identity documents I owned.

The woman looked at them and shook her head: 'Sorry, but we need a passport or birth certificate to open an account for you.' She looked truly apologetic when she said it, but I was embarrassed and angry. I knew no one was at fault and tried to think about the situation logically, but I couldn't. I hadn't really thought about whether I had a birth certificate until that moment or what the lack of one would mean. I existed but I couldn't prove it.

I was quiet on the walk home as my mum tried to make me feel better.

'Don't worry Coco, I'll take care of your money for you. Haven't I always given you what you want? And inshallah, we will get our British passports soon.'

When I got home I looked at my younger brothers and felt a gulf between us. They had birth certificates and booklets detailing their development and education. I didn't even know what vaccinations I had had.

When trying to make me feel better didn't work, Mama told me off. 'Why do you even need a bank account anyway?'

I don't remember exactly when we got a positive decision on our asylum claim. I only have one specific memory about our immigration status: some kind of official meeting I attended as a six- or seven-year-old child. My mum and I were in a room surrounded by white adults. I was given a piece of paper and crayons to draw on. My mum had a translator. I felt safe and happy beside her. I'm not sure what country I am in in this memory.

Things moved very quickly once we had our leave to remain in the UK. My mum was soon invited to apply for British citizenship. To get it for herself and her children, she needed to pass the 'Life in the UK' test, a policy brought in in 2002 by the Labour government. As well as passing the test, aspiring Britons have to take a citizenship oath and make a pledge at a civic ceremony.

The test was no small feat. My mother had stopped formal education in her early teens. While her English speaking and listening skills were developing, she struggled to read. And with my baby brothers requiring her attention, she didn't have any time to sign up for English classes. I wasn't sure whether she would pass the first time, but I shouldn't have doubted her. She was determined to succeed.

I was fourteen or fifteen then. I found online study guides and practice tests. We also bought the recommended textbook. We would go through chapters together, with me translating what I could from the textbook and then quizzing her. We sat side by side in front of the computer every night for several months.

Whenever she got answers correct, I fed her ego. 'You'll do amazingly, Mama,' I said. If she failed, or got below the pass mark, I told her not to worry and that we still had plenty of time before the test. 'You are an amazing teacher and my best friend,' she told me one evening. I hugged her. I felt so close to her then, so loved.

She was seven months pregnant when she sat the test. If she failed, it would not just mean that she couldn't get a British passport, but that her children would not qualify for one either. She had her test in the morning, and ran into my room as soon as she got home. I was the first person she told that she had passed.

'The guy running the test was staring at me. Everyone who entered that exam that day had failed. Only me, I passed! The man was looking at me like this. He told me to go downstairs. I asked him why, I thought the people who were sent upstairs had passed and I was the only one to fail. When I got downstairs, he said, "You know something, you passed and only made one mistake." I was surprised. I was praying, saying oh Allah! I got all the questions right except one. He was shocked. I told him I had memorised it like the Quran,' Mama tells me when I call and ask what she remembers about the test. She laughs and I giggle alongside her. The test was on a computer and she wore headphones and listened carefully to the male voice that read the instructions and questions.

I had been happy on the day she passed, but I hadn't fully realised its significance. My mother left the house as an asylum seeker with leave to remain, and she returned as a soon-to-be British citizen. We celebrated with pizza and episodes of our favourite reality TV shows: *Big Brother* and *America's Next Top Model*.

My dad also passed. 'Why am I always an afterthought?' he bellows, on one of the days I am at home interviewing my mum.

My mum laughs. Less a laugh, more of a cackle. 'Don't be jealous of our relationship.'

'You are important, Baba, I promise,' I tell him.

He nods, unconvinced. 'You would think in a book of our lives...' He doesn't finish as mum starts shouting back. We all sit down to eat after she has the final word.

My mum put on her best scarf and dress on the evening of her citizenship ceremony. My dad took her, but I stayed behind to look after my brothers. 'I was too happy. I finally felt that I belonged to a country,' she tells me. 'And I now had a passport that was respected by other countries.' Mama continues, 'I could go wherever I wanted in the world. I feel free. I could go anywhere. No one would say, "You are a refugee," or something like that. I could go to any office and say, "I am a British citizen." I have an ID that wherever I go they would accept. And my children could also have British passports.'

There is a picture of my mum at her citizenship ceremony. The man beside her is in lush red robes and holding a golden stick. 'I am so happy in the picture. A woman gave me the certificate and said, "Congratulations, you are expecting your new baby." I said, "Thank you." Everyone was so happy. We were a lot of people that had come from so many different countries. It was really emotional. I was very happy because this country had given me so many different things. And that's it,' she finishes.

Soon after our British passports arrived, we went back to the same branch of NatWest, and I opened my first account.

I often forgot my Oyster card as a teenager and would be forced to walk back from school. When this happened, my friends would try to get me to sneak onto the bus, but I didn't have the stomach for it. 'I'll just see you tomorrow,' I'd shout once the bus arrived, and would then walk towards Barking town centre.

On one of those days, there was a demonstration by the English Defence League (EDL) in the town centre: around a hundred white men waving England flags outside the main station. There was a significant police presence. The men looked so angry, and I didn't understand why. I watched them for a long time and was startled when a few stared at me and began shouting at me. I decided to walk the long way home. I was ashamed then; of being an immigrant, of being Somali, of being Muslim. It was our presence that was drawing them here.

Though the vast majority of EDL protesters would come to Barking from other areas, their protests there were quickly becoming a regular occurrence. These protests never remained peaceful: residents in the area would share stories in mosques of Muslims being randomly attacked, with one so badly injured he needed surgery on his face.

In September 2004, when I was twelve and had just started Year Eight, the British National Party (BNP) had won their first council seat in London since 1993.[1] The party was overtly racist: the BNP candidate, Daniel Kelley, gained the seat from the Labour party with a 470 majority, in what was described by the *Guardian* as a 'landslide victory'.

Kelley's election followed a worrying documentary on the EDL that many of us had watched. A BBC undercover reporter infiltrated the BNP in Bradford.[2] He found men within the party who bragged about posting dog faeces through the letterboxes of British Pakistani homes and fantasised about firing at mosques with bazooka guns.

My family and friends told me incessantly not to go anywhere near the pub by the station. I would roll my eyes, wondering what business I would have there anyway. One of my schoolmates took particular care to warn me not to be near the station alone at night. I knew what she was getting at, but I didn't like talking about the BNP or EDL then. I felt that by talking about them, I was being reminded of my differences from my classmates.

I hated that once I was on the path to becoming a British citizen, I was being met with violent resistance by those who hated me.

The BNP would continue to make significant gains in my area. In the 2006 local elections, when I was fourteen and had begun my GCSEs, Labour, the governing national party, had control of the council with 38 seats. The Conservatives, who were the second biggest party nationally, had only won one seat. The BNP won twelve seats.[3] They were now the second biggest party in the local council and became the official opposition.

The roots of the problem lay in Barking's history. Due to overcrowded and dangerous inner-city slum housing in inner London, David Lloyd George's government first started moving tens of thousands of working-class families out of the city into new council homes in outer London boroughs like Barking and Dagenham throughout the twenties and thirties. These new homes boasted indoor plumbing and private gardens.

The borough thus became the site of a successful social experiment – one that would be used as a shining example of the modern welfare state.

Many families were relocated to Becontree Estate, which, when built, was declared the largest housing estate in the world by the local authority. The estate had 26,000 new homes housing 120,000 people.[4] In 2021, on the hundredth anniversary of Becontree Estate being built, I walked around it. It is a short bus ride from my parents' house. The council had a range of events to celebrate the anniversary, including exhibitions of models of the estate in its previous incarnations.

Becontree was built to create healthier homes for its working-class residents. The local planners reserved specific sites on the estate for doctors' surgeries and other medical clinics. Voluntary organisations, such as the Dagenham Tuberculosis Care Association, operated on the estate and helped with the prevention and treatment of infectious diseases. These organisations also supported families by providing better nutrition, transport to hospitals and clothing. There were regular health reports that assessed overcrowding, unfit properties and disease outbreaks.

It was depressing, then, that on its centenary, the area was a Covid-19 hotspot. Becontree had changed so much from what I was seeing in the archives that I wondered if I was in the right place. I didn't stay for long or talk to anyone as the area had the highest case rate of Covid-19 in the whole country.

I reached out to the council for some data to better understand how Barking went from one of the crown jewels of social housing to the impoverished, debilitated place it was today. I learned that at the turn of the millennium, when I had just arrived in Barking, just 5 per cent of households in the borough rented privately; now that proportion is around 25 per cent. Average private rents on those very properties have increased by 50 per cent since 2011.

Many now also live in overcrowded homes. In 2021, there were around 5,000 households on the council's social housing register who needed to be re-housed. The rate of homeownership in the borough had dropped from 58 per cent to 49 per cent since 2006. In 2021, the average house price was more than ten times the earnings of an average local person.

It wasn't just the quality of housing that declined: jobs too had gone. Ford Motors had opened a large plant in Dagenham in 1931, making use of the huge new pool of labour brought by the estate. At its peak in the 1950s, Ford employed more than 50,000 people there.[5] The workers there would go down in Britain's working-class history when a strike by its female staff led to the passing of the Equal Pay Act. Other employers included the power station and May & Baker's, a chemical plant.

But by the mid-1970s, these factories were shells of their former glory. All but a small part of the Ford factory had closed by 2002, and by 2017 Ford Dagenham employed fewer than 4,000 people.

These downturns coincided with significant changes in the population, partly driven by immigration. From 2001 to 2011, Barking and Dagenham's population increased by 13 per cent, according to the data sent to me. It grew again in the following decade, increasing by 17.7 per cent, from around 185,900 in 2011 to 218,900 in 2021. The borough's population growth outpaced the national average: population grew by 6.6 per cent in England.

I didn't notice much of this change when I was at school in the area. I loved the diversity of my school and I don't remember experiencing or seeing racial abuse by the other students and teachers.

So I was horrified when a BNP councillor was elected in my ward in 2006. I would walk home and wonder which of my neighbours had voted them in. Did they do so because of us? Would they attack our houses next? The far right was an unbearable but inescapable presence in the area. Migrant communities were warned against so called no-go zones, which were a stronghold for BNP and EDL supporters, such as certain pubs, and not to go to the station late at night.

I no longer felt safe – and I also felt angry. It was a political anger I hadn't felt before. I was angry because of the BNP's commitment to destroy the joy and peace my family had been able to cultivate. My life in the UK had felt like an oasis until the meteoric political rise of the far right.

I was once embarrassed about who I was, and where my family had come from. But my embarrassment changed to fury when my mum came back home one day and told me that a fascist had hurled racist abuse at her. She brushed off my questions of whether she was hurt or okay.

'Tell people that I always fought back,' Mama says when I tell her I'm going to write about the far right in Barking.

And she certainly did. When another driver told her, 'Fuck off to your country,' she got out of her car and threw her shoe at them. 'I don't know English that well, but I know how to defend myself,' she told me. She looked me in the eye. 'You shouldn't be afraid of them.'

My mum wasn't just brave, she was hilariously antagonistic. When the radiators downstairs had broken and the council hadn't responded to our repair request, she asked me to email our local councillors. One was from the BNP. I refused initially and was scared of what would happen to her if we got in touch or if she went to his surgery.

'What will happen to me?' She laughed. 'BNP? I don't care if he is ATP, LNP or whatever. His job is to serve his constituents, I am his constituent.' We can't remember if she ever met the councillor in person. We do remember that our heating was quickly repaired soon after.

My mum and I became eligible to vote in our first national election at the same time. It was 2010 and the election was a month after I had turned eighteen. The excitement I felt was dampened by the fact that the BNP's leader, Nick Griffin, was personally running against our MP, Margaret Hodge. The national media focused intensely on the race and those nearby, which quickly turned ugly. Bob Bailey, an East

London BNP councillor in nearby Romford and the party's London coordinator, was filmed in a physical brawl with local Asian teenagers.[6]

In the run up to the election, Griffin told reports that in power his party would allocate billions of pounds as a means of 'encouraging' those of 'foreign descent' to return to their home countries.[7]

The Labour party said it would firmly oppose the BNP, but it was hard to have much faith in them. I remember feeling my stomach sinking in 2007 when Hodge proposed that local British-born families should get priority for social housing over newly arrived immigrants. I had just turned fifteen. Hodge suggested there would be an exception for 'genuine refugees'.[8]

I wondered then, as I do now, how a local resident could tell who was genuinely in need of accommodation and support and who was exploiting the system. I wondered then, as I do now, where these immigrant exploiters were. I had not come across them on the estate I grew up in.

The far right's presence did not go unchallenged. Around a thousand anti-fascist activists worked hard to denounce the racism of the BNP. With Labour party activists, they delivered 150,000 letters and leaflets, knocked on 22,000 doors, made around 9,000 contacts, delivered 20,000 questionnaires.[9] They held large political meetings at town halls and community centres to emphasise that we were stronger united than divided. I was able to find strength amid these political activities to not only assert that I belonged, but to tell the far right to fuck off.

Still, I was nervous on election day in 2010. I went with my mum to the community centre that had been turned into a polling station for the day. It was a short walk from our house, but it's hard to quantify or describe the distance we had put between the undocumented refugees we were to the citizens that we had become that day, exercising the right to vote.

The exit polls showed that although the Conservatives had won the most votes, no party had won enough for an outright majority in parliament. Locally, things had gone well: I woke up to a text from my friend: 'What does a bus have that the BNP doesn't? Seats!' I burst out laughing. Not only had Griffin been thrashed in the parliamentary election, but the party had lost all their local council seats. The party never recovered from their loss in Barking and Dagenham and would become non-existent in ten years' time.

When people used to ask me where I was from, I'd say I grew up in London, but my parents came from Somalia and I had ties to Yemen. I rarely said British, and never called myself English.

I don't think there's ever been an exact moment when I truly felt British. I thought it would come when I was allowed to live in the UK permanently, when I was able to vote, or when I got my first adult British passport and was able to move more easily through borders knowing that I could always return. It never did.

I enjoy all the benefits that citizenship gives me, but they don't make me feel British. When I was growing up, Britishness was synonymous with whiteness. There were white British people and then there were us, the people they tolerated, and at times didn't.

I do remember when I slowly began to feel Black British, though.

I couldn't call this country my own until I embedded myself into Black British history, culture and community. The descriptor Black before the nationality British was a duality that spoke deeply to me. I was drawn to the Black British's community dynamism, that it carved itself into the very fabric of British society and had the confidence to see itself in the country's future. I laugh at the racist chant 'there ain't no black in the Union Jack' because I can't conceive of my Britishness outside of my Blackness. They go hand in hand.

When I was in school, I learned about Blackness from the US. I consumed African American culture, listening to the music and watching the TV shows and movies that were exported to the UK. I would switch the channel from BBC period dramas with all-white casts to American sitcoms like *Moesha* and *One on One*, and feel the warmth of seeing someone who looks like me on screen.

But there was still a disconnect. Black American culture didn't reflect the slang I heard in school or the jokes we made on my estate.

For me, this started to change during the early 2000s, when I started secondary school, with the advent of grime. The unrelenting sound with a 140bpm backbone, which was born from reggae, dancehall and garage, felt like the UK's response to hip hop. Suddenly, I found myself being able to turn to the UK when looking for an answer to the question of what it means to be a young Black person.

I found myself sneaking out of home to go to house parties and drown myself in sound-system culture (I'm sorry Mama and Baba, but I wasn't always going to the library or watching films with friends). I read novels by Zadie Smith and Andrea Levy, and screamed myself hoarse cheering on Mo Farah at the 2012 Olympics.

It was electrifying to discover while at university that the presence of Black people in Britain stretched back centuries, and that this included Somali people. I felt interwoven into the country's history. Before then, I knew very little Black British history outside of the North Atlantic Slave Trade, and even then we didn't spend that many lessons on it.

What little Black history I was taught was US history. While I was being taught about the monumental Montgomery bus boycott in 1955, I was clueless about the Bristol bus boycott in 1963, one of Britain's first Black-led campaigns against legal racial discrimination.

Soon, Black British was no longer just a box I ticked on survey forms. It became who I am. This feeling only solidified as I covered the Black Lives Matter movement in the UK.

While I felt comfortable calling myself Black British, it wasn't until a few years ago that I felt as proud to proclaim myself Somali. I wasn't able to combine the two identities, and feel proud to call myself British-Somali, until I returned from Somalia.

Now, when someone asks where I'm from, I tell them I'm British-Somali. I was able to reach this far less convoluted answer once I began researching the history of Somali writers in the English literary canon while in Mogadishu. I sat in my hotel room and smiled as I read about writers I didn't know, like Ibrahim Ismaa'il, as well as those I knew, Nuruddin Farah, and those I adore, like Nadifa Mohamed. I was smiling because I was finding, in real time, something I desperately wanted to be part of.

I came back from the trip and began excitedly thinking of what my contribution would be to this canon: as a Somali refugee, as a Black Briton, as a British-Somali.

15
THE TRAUMA THAT BINDS US

I wasn't there when my mum had her first panic attack over a decade ago. She woke up one morning and found she couldn't move her legs. She was gripped with an overwhelming sense of panic and lay there crying. The weight on her legs eventually passed and she found herself able to move again. She didn't know what was happening to her.

'Before it comes, I find that my mood is off. Suddenly, I don't want to do anything and I don't want to talk to anyone. I just want to be alone and asleep,' my mum tells me.

I went round for lunch soon after returning from Mogadishu to ask whether she would feel comfortable with me writing about our mental health struggles. I wanted the world to know how strong, funny and dynamic a woman my mum is, but soon became worried that I was feeding into a stereotype: the 'Strong Black Superwoman', resilient and stoic.

'I don't want to paint over the years when you struggled, when we both did. I want to be honest about our struggles,' I tell her.

'Of course I struggled, do you think someone could go through a war and not have struggles?' Mama quips.

'So can I write about it?' I ask.

'Yes, I trust you.'

My mum's attacks are always triggered by some minor stress in her life – the type of things that she has previously always been able to cope with. An argument with her sister sparked a bad one in the kitchen; one of my brothers caused another one when they got into an fight while watching TV. The panic attacks kept coming. When they first started, she didn't know what they were or why they were happening.

I didn't find out my mum was experiencing panic attacks until I saw her have one. We were sat beside each other in our living room one evening. I noticed that she grew increasingly breathless and suddenly gripped her chest. She whispered that she was struggling to breathe. I thought she was having a heart attack.

I don't remember why we didn't call 999. I just remember walking beside her, as she gripped her chest, to the nearby walk-in clinic. We walked for around ten minutes, but it felt like we were endlessly wading through water. It was dark and cold. I was so scared, but I pushed my fear down. I'm not sure how old I was – I just remember thinking I was too young for this to be happening. I was too young to lose my mum. A terrible voice in my head whispered: 'Did your mum not lose her mum as a small child?'

I also felt angry at my mum. I was angry that she was in pain, angry that we had to go to the clinic, angry that it had to be me with her, angry that I couldn't run away from it, angry that I couldn't be weak.

We were seen immediately at the walk-in clinic. Some of the other patients who had waited longer than us in the reception room stared daggers at us. I didn't care. My mum's breathing got more ragged as a nurse took us to another room. The nurse measured my mum's heart rate and gave her some breathing exercises to do. I wanted to scream that she needed emergency care, but I kept my mouth shut.

It took me a while to realise that what the nurse was doing had worked. My mum was calmer and breathing more easily. The nurse took off her white gloves and told us that my mum was experiencing a panic attack. My mother looked at me, confused, and though I had been translating for her for many years, I couldn't find the right words in Arabic or Somali.

The nurse gave us a leaflet on mental health and tried to talk to my mum about therapy or taking medication. My mum shook her head vigorously at both options. When she left, I took the leaflet with me. I told the nurse I would explain once we got home. I don't remember the walk back.

I'd never felt more distant from my mum than I did that night at the clinic. She looked visibly shaken and I couldn't understand why this irrepressible figure in my life was suddenly so small and vulnerable.

My mum told her GP what was happening. She was given antidepressants and told to do a type of therapy called cognitive behavioural therapy (CBT). She didn't want to take the medication and didn't know what CBT was. She was given a worksheet and told to go through it before a therapist called her on the phone.

The entire exercise felt futile to me, but I was desperate for it to work. My mum didn't understand many of the words used on the worksheet and the person calling her only spoke English. I went round to the house the day before her call with the therapist and went through the sheet with her. She balked when I asked if she had any suicidal thoughts. Suicide is deeply forbidden in Islam.

'A'oodhu billah [I seek refuge in Allah from the devil], Coco, why would you ask me that?' she yelled.

When her panic attacks persisted, my mum was invited to go to a group therapy session. She went after some encouragement from me. She wanted to leave as soon as she walked into the group session.

'It was a bunch of white people sitting in a circle talking about stressful things in their lives,' Mama said. 'I stood out badly with my hijab and left the moment I could.'

She stopped engaging with therapeutic services after that.

I used to think my mum was reliving the worst memories from the war, like the soldiers suffering from PTSD that I saw in movies. I thought that was driving her panic attacks. I was wrong.

'I used to have bad dreams about what happened in the war a long time ago, when we were in Kakuma,' my mum told me when I asked what she thinks her trigger is. 'But that was only for a short time. I don't have pain from that time.'

I was surprised, but I shouldn't have been. My parents have dealt remarkably well with the initial trauma of the war. And though their exposure to the war was significant – they lived through bombardment, saw people die, almost starved and were constantly running for their lives – it wasn't debilitating. It didn't stop them from living their lives, from moving forward.

My mum's experience with the NHS drove me to do my undergraduate dissertation on Somali mental health in 2014, focusing on the struggle our community has in accessing support. In that year, my mother slowly opened up to me about what happened to her: how thirsty and hungry she had felt, how her loved ones died, how she went to sleep to the sounds of shelling and bullets.

She often laughed as she told me these harrowing stories. Her jokes were her armour. It was through our shared laughter that she told me the most important thing about her experience: 'I am not this poor victim that people should feel sorry for. I don't want people to feel sorry for me. I am Faatma and the war is just one thing that happened to me, there's so many other things to know about me.'

Through my research, I learnt that there was no direct translation for the word 'depression' in the Somali language. This wasn't something that I had come across before, as I spoke to my mum in Arabic and English, and my dad solely in English. I thought back to the jokes they made whenever I was a moody teenager, telling me I was 'depressed'. I hadn't realised then that they had adopted that word into their vocabulary. Had my mum simply not appreciated the clinical implications of that word, that it didn't just mean being sad?

For some Somalis, mental health is seen as more of a spiritual problem than a medical one, so they are more likely to turn to family members, prayer or traditional and religious healers for support. Some Somalis point to supernatural causes for mental ailments, including possession by spirits. I thought about my childhood and my presentation on jinn, and how often family members, including my mum, collapsed from these so called possessions. Were they a cry for help?

Kamaldeep Bhui, a psychiatry professor at the University of Oxford, notes that the mass migration and resettlement of Somalis across the Western world has led many to shift their cultural conceptions of mental health.[1] The words 'depression' and 'anxiety' were adopted into the vocabulary to varying degrees.

I visited a Somali mental health community group called the Hayaan Project, run by community organiser Abdi Gure, which supports the London Somali community with mental health issues. It was an eye-opening experience. Abdi told me that mental health is seen as a binary issue among the Somali community: someone is either sane or insane. There was very little in between. I found this difficult to come to terms with, particularly as our community has been so significantly traumatised by war and forced migration.

While I tried to encourage my mum to turn to therapy and medication, she instead reached for the Quran and her prayer mat. Her faith deepened during this time of crisis. Religion plays a critical role in the healing process within the Somali community: the two cannot be separated. The mental health professionals my mum interacted with failed to appreciate just how intertwined the two were. So did I.

I saw how my mum's experience wasn't unique. In one study, a Somali woman said that dodging bullets and bombs was less stressful than dealing with hostile letters from the government, living in poor housing conditions under the constant threat of eviction, learning English and trying to understand what was happening with her child in the new school system.[2] When I told my mum this, she laughed and agreed.

The interviewed woman's perspective was echoed by the research of psychologists Ken Miller and Andrew Rasmussen,[3] who advocate for a new model of understanding refugees' mental health issues. I spoke to Miller and he described how he and Rasmussen have developed their proposal examining the psychological impact of displacement – from social isolation in a new country to inadequate housing, poverty, discrimination and uncertainty regarding the immigration process.

Their research suggests that these factors can be even more debilitating for refugees than the events that took place during the war; issues such as poverty are likely to be constant. With time, these challenges deplete a refugee's ability to cope. 'The salience of trauma and loss in refugees' war stories led the field to overlook the stressful nature of life in exile,' Miller and Rasmussen write. This resonated deeply with me.

I also spent an afternoon with leading clinicians at Nafsiyat, an organisation based in North London that provides intercultural therapy. I did this because the help my mother needed wasn't there for her. I was scared that if I didn't find some way to get her feeling better, then I'd lose her.

I learned that, like my mum, many Somalis spoke of somatic problems, such as headaches, back pain and insomnia, rather than specifically of emotional distress.

I made a conscious decision to start listening to the physical problems my mum spoke to me about, and threw out the CBT worksheets that asked her to note down specific emotions or feelings.

Something that came up time and time again over the course of my research was the difference between what Somali refugees thought life would be like in London and the reality they were forced to operate in. Many were unprepared for the social hierarchy in the UK, which placed them at the bottom due to their race, religion, gender and refugee status.

'I was told the UK is a fair and equal country for everybody, but there is a lot of racism and hatred of Muslims. It is not good and I was shocked by it. But it is still better than the racism in some Arab countries. I can be a citizen here and so can my children, but that was never the case in Saudi,' Mama tells me.

My mum was particularly unprepared for how othering it would be to wear a hijab and religious outfits like the abaya in the UK. For just over half her life, she easily blended in, but since coming to the UK she has stood out, or, worse, found herself a target of harassment or abuse.

I ask her what stresses her out the most about living in the UK. 'That's easy,' Mama tells me. 'Not speaking the language. Even now, it is not my language, not the one I can express myself best in.' My mum isn't alone in this regard. The Health of Londoners Project cited language barriers as refugees' biggest single obstacle to accessing healthcare.[4] She struggled to explain what was going on and to advocate for herself, and at times still does. 'I'm not sure what I would do without you,' my mum once said to me.

My mum comes alive when she speaks Arabic or Somali, but often she feels small speaking English. Research shows that we can most effectively express emotional distress in our first language.[5] The severity of a person's mental health issues can be accentuated or minimised depending on the language that is used during consultation and therapy.[6]

I initially tried to find my mum an affordable therapist nearby who could speak Arabic or Somali. I couldn't find this kind of service on the NHS so I looked for a private one, but had no luck there either. The therapists either weren't taking any new patients or we simply couldn't afford them. I then considered whether to get an English-speaking therapist who would allow me to come with her and translate. My mum said she would be comfortable with me being in the room with her, but I didn't go ahead with it. I knew my presence in the room could colour what she did and didn't say. I didn't want to be the reason she was limiting herself.

I was thrilled when I finally found an Arabic-speaking therapist who said she could see my mum for free, and that I could join their sessions every now and then. I called her excitedly.

'Mama, I found an Arabic-speaking therapist in North London,' I said.

'North London?' she exclaimed. 'How far away is she?'

'She is based in Finsbury Park, Mama, but it's only an hour on the Overground from Barking,'

'Thank you for looking, Coco, but no, that's too far. I can't go,' she said.

I knew I couldn't force her to go, but I felt like shaking her. Did she not realise that she needed this? Did she not know how difficult it had been to find the right therapist? Didn't she know how scared I was for her?

She didn't, because I hadn't said any of this to her. Until now.

She did what I expected her to do. She sighed, and though I couldn't see her I knew she was rolling her eyes, and laughed. 'You are always too much, wallahi,' my mum said to me. 'Stop being so white.'

I turn back to my dissertation's conclusion. In my summarising statement, I brought my findings together: mental health practitioners need to find a healthy symbiosis between Western psychiatry and a patient's local knowledge and values. Services that are culturally relevant are far more likely to be successful. Family and community are an essential part of recovery. And environmental and political factors cannot be overlooked: good mental health relies on secure access to things like decent housing and benefits, as well as social and clinical opportunities to talk about the past and trauma.

My mum's mental health struggles haven't had the same kind of academic conclusion, but she is doing better. Her panic attacks and low moods have subsided significantly, though she does get flare-ups. Whenever that happens, she knows what to do, and if she needs support from her family, she can ask for it. She no longer suffers in silence.

'We did all of that together,' my Mum says, and I laugh that I didn't see that then. My mum has signed up for the gym and regularly goes to women-only classes, as well as to the sauna. She has found her own way to cope.

Despite our fighting, I have been able to give her what she needed, and later, she would do the same for me.

The first time I went to therapy, I was let go after a few weeks. I went to my university counselling service because I suddenly found myself irritable, randomly crying throughout the day, struggling to sleep at night. The latter was the most difficult part. Sleep has always come easily to me: my friends have always laughed at how I'll be chatting away one moment and out cold the second my head touches the pillow. If I was tired enough, I could sleep through anything. I could sleep on couches, a plane or a car. So I hated finding myself getting up in the middle of the night, my mind racing.

At the time, I was in the middle of a prolonged argument with my parents. I had moved out of home to be closer to university. I was less than forty-five minutes away, but they disapproved and were upset with me. A lot of my anxiety and frustration was down to this.

My therapist, who was white, suggested that I focus on myself and cut ties with my family if I felt like I couldn't live the life I wanted with them. I ended up doing the opposite. I went back to my parents and, through distraught tears, told them just how much I needed them in my life. I apologised for how I had left the house and told them I wanted to return. They sat on either side of me and held me as I sobbed.

I then threw myself at my university work. Sleep had come back to me once I caught up. I returned to the therapist, telling her I was feeling a lot better. She let me go after my third or fourth session, telling me I didn't seem to have any problems any more and didn't need the full six sessions.

I graduated from university, won a scholarship to study for my Masters and, once I graduated, started my career in science journalism. I worked for a year, writing about everything from medicine to environmental science. In the background, I could see Europe's refugee crisis unfold. I ignored it until I couldn't anymore. I felt drawn to it. I wanted to help to humanise the crisis.

The second time I went to therapy was a couple of years after my first reporting trip to Calais, the one described at the start of this book. The nightmares had returned, but this time I was finding myself lost and trapped in the so-called Jungle, desperate to get home. My insomnia returned, and some nights I would be kept awake by a sharp pain in my stomach.

I began panicking that I had misquoted people in my articles. It became debilitating and obsessive. After an article of mine was published, I'd re-read it and worry the quotes I used didn't match the transcript. I would then pull up the transcript and relisten to the relevant section in the interview to see if the published quote matched. It always did. I would feel momentary relief and try to get on with the rest of the day – but the panic would slowly return and build up until I was sitting down, opening the same transcript and checking again. The feeling was worse if the story was read by many people: I was constantly terrified that I would somehow be exposed as a fraud.

I knew this wasn't normal, so I reached out to the NHS to try and get talking therapy. The service hadn't been of great help for my mum, but I told myself I was different and understood mental health better than her.

I was referred to CBT therapy and given twelve sessions with a young white woman. We never talked about where these anxieties and compulsions had come from, only that they were 'bad thoughts'. We went through exercises to break the cycle. I was inundated with worksheets and leaflets at the end of every session and I struggled to get through them before the next session. There was too much information and I felt like I was left alone to wade through complex exercises. I felt a whole new empathy for my mum. If I struggled at this, what chance would someone who didn't speak English well have?

I panicked when the therapist once again told me I was doing really well and suggested we end our sessions earlier than prescribed. I refused and told her I didn't feel like I had really scratched the surface of what was causing my anxiety and obsessive behaviour. She didn't seem interested at all in exploring my past as a refugee, which I was slowly coming to grips with.

I don't want to disparage CBT. At the time, it did help me put a lid on my anxiety and I know it's been hugely helpful for many people. It is cost-effective, accessible and easily disseminable. But for me, and for my mum, it felt like putting a plaster on a bullet wound. I felt like the focus was to put me back together so I could function just well enough to work. On that front, it did work: I learnt to do my job despite the anxiety I felt. The exercises I was taught helped whenever I felt paralysed by fear that something terrible was about to happen to me.

I patched myself together and was determined to push myself as much as possible. That year – 2018 – I got my dream job at the *Guardian*. My friend invited me to spend a week with her in New York. Just before I left, I sent her an email. I often did when I was feeling confused and alone. It feels weird now to reread the email I sent five years ago.

'At work, I feel really dazed. Whenever my stories are held back or editors don't show much enthusiasm, I am overwhelmed with this horrible, crushing feeling. One thought rings in my head: I have failed, I am a failure. At night, I have bizarre dreams I can barely remember the next morning,' I wrote.

During this time in my life I was also travelling alone internationally for the very first time. I always felt hot and clammy, whatever the weather. I was scared I would be sick at any moment as I went through passport control and security. At one point, before a work trip to Colombia, the anxiety was so severe I feared I would faint. I gritted my teeth and pushed through: I couldn't countenance not going on these trips.

Why put myself through that? I turned back to my emails to my friend. 'I feel haunted by the people who didn't leave – the war, the refugee camp, or abject poverty. What right do I have to be sad or distraught when people died, went hungry, while I escaped, while I survived? I feel like I owed them – now just a blur of faces and sounds – to not just survive, but to thrive. If I don't become a success, break through barriers, and make something of my life, what right do I have to be here and not them?'

I returned to therapy for a third time, weeks after deciding to write this book, to deal with my survival guilt. This time, I chose a trauma-informed therapy. It felt different, and awkward, as I detailed earlier in this book. It was hard: the therapist forced me to confront some of my most difficult memories, from my mother's deportation to the time I almost died from malaria in Kakuma refugee camp. I'd often leave the therapist feeling drained, but I was making progress in a way I never had before.

I was able to confront a repressed memory from my time in Kakuma that I had felt too scared to share. I was in a tent, and deathly ill with malaria. My mum was sitting beside me, fear etched on her face. There were other children in that tent. Some had died.

'Do you remember that time?' I ask Mama now.

'Remember? I have never forgotten.'

'Do you remember when I would fake seizures to make you laugh?' I say, and start giggling.

'Yes,' Mama says, but I can hear her smile down the phone. 'You always think you're so funny.'

Therapy allowed me to go back to the tent as an adult and reckon with those children's deaths. I went back to the room in the German airport where my mum was asked to strip. I went back to my arrival in the UK, the time that passed waiting for my parents. My adult brain tried to reason and understand what my childhood self could not and often fell short.

I have tried to talk to my mum about these moments, but she finds it difficult. When I say, 'I had a bad childhood,' she is defensive: 'Don't say that, yes it was difficult in parts, but you didn't have a bad childhood.'

I tell her that there is a difference between saying that bad things happened in my childhood and that she was a bad mother. I need her to allow her to let me be in pain. I need her to allow me to be something other than brave.

I don't have many memories of allowing myself to lie in my mother's lap and let myself cry. But I have started to do so in recent years. She reads the Quran over me whenever I do.

My mum now sends me voice notes throughout the day telling me how much she loves me; to my joy, my dad now tells me he loves me when we hug goodbye. I wonder what conversation they had to bring that on.

We have begun to talk about the past often. We find a new way to talk to each other, one that acknowledges that we see each other differently now. We can look at one another's wounds and the tissue that has grown around them.

16
WE WERE GIRLS TOGETHER

It's funny how you can go so much of your life without remembering who you are and then, after one gentle push of a domino, the rest cascades into place.

I had gone some way to honour my childhood self, Amina, since 2020. I had diligently noted my parents' story, I had stopped running away from the past, I had remembered. Yet, deep down, there was still a restlessness inside me. Amina needed something more.

When I was alone, I would try to remember the face of the girl whose hand I held on that walk to school in Kakuma, but found I couldn't. Perhaps the restlessness would go away if I could hear her voice? I wondered if Amina would also find peace if she could talk to her first friend.

I asked my mum if we could find Fatima. My parents said the chances were low, but that they would try.

They began their search in real earnest in late summer of 2021, a year after I decided to embark on this project. My parents went back through their contacts and family members and asked about Fatima and her family. They didn't get anywhere for a year, then suddenly, on an overcast mid-September day in 2022, I got a call from my mum.

'We found her. We found Fatima,' Mama said, and squealed with laughter. I was lying in bed when I answered the phone. I started laughing alongside her and jumped out of bed.

'She is in Holland,' Mama said. 'When I called her, she didn't know who I was. She said sorry I don't remember you. We talked for a little bit and then I said, "Do you remember Shayshay?" and she said "Yes!"' My heart was pumping hard in my chest.

Fatima, my mum had learned, is safe and living in the Netherlands. She is a mum of four children. Three of her children, all under the age of twelve, were living in Kenya at the time that my mum made contact with her, while her youngest, a daughter, was born in the Netherlands and living with her there. My mum said that Fatima was trying to resettle her other children from Kenya to the Netherlands. She sent me and my mum a picture of her youngest daughter and we cooed over how cute she was. My mum then told me off for not yet having children. She never misses an opportunity to do so.

I couldn't stop looking at the picture of Fatima's daughter. She was around two years old. Fatima was fighting for a better life for her children and herself. In her lifetime, she walked in my shoes, as a child refugee, and now walks in my mother's, as a refugee mother.

My mum sent me Fatima's number after we got off our call, but I couldn't bring myself to call her yet. I didn't know what to say after all this time. The instincts that I would have had as a reporter weren't there.

There was so much to take in. She was so close – and had been for a few years. I kept repeating two things to myself that night: she is living in the Netherlands and she is safe.

I went round to my parents' house a few days later for lunch. My mum asked if I had called Fatima and I told her I hadn't yet. She then turned, in the middle of cooking, and reached for her phone. Before I realised what she was doing, she called Fatima and I panicked. 'I'm not ready,' I mouthed. I gasped when Fatima answered the phone and my mum rolled her eyes.

My mum went into the garden and started talking to her. I stood beside the door for a moment, then walked out to join her in the garden.

'Here's Shayshay, who wants to say hi,' Mama said. 'She doesn't know Somali, but you guys talk to each other in the way you know.' She passed the phone to me and I started giggling, nervous beyond words. The phone was on loudspeaker. The conversation took place in Somali.

Me: Salam Alakum...
Fatima: Wa'alakum Salam, how are you?
Me: I am fine, how are you?

My mum started laughing and I did too. It was surreal.

Mum: Say, 'How are your kids?'
Me: How are your kids?
Fatima: They're good, alhamdulillah. Do you have any children?
Mum (shouting): She doesn't have any children! Can you talk to her? She keeps saying she doesn't want children now.

I laughed louder, both embarrassed and amused.

Mum: She has been married for many years.
Fatima: Why not?
Mum: Exactly! She keeps saying she is too young and she has to work. She won't listen to me. You talk to her.
Fatima: I've already had four children.
Mum: That's what I always say to her! Mashallah, Fatima has four children.
Fatima: My eldest daughter is twelve years old.
Mum: Mashallah!
Fatima: It's better to have them young.
Mum: It's better to have children young, at least then the grandparents can help you. It's better when there isn't a big age difference between the children and parents.

I stood back and watched them talk. Fatima told my mum she was hoping to be reunited with her other children and her siblings soon enough. My mum told her she would be praying for her and the rest of her family. They promised they would now stay in touch. When my mum said goodbye, I shouted: 'Goodbye Fatima.'

My mum turned off the phone and faced me with a look that said: 'See, now that wasn't hard, was it?'

Fatima's mum called us later that afternoon. I listened and watched as my mum and her caught up. They were both laughing at the phone. 'She just spoke to Fatima right now,' Mama said.

She then passed me the phone and told me to say hello; I spoke, painfully aware of how bad my Somali is. 'That's how she speaks Somali now,' my mum said to the phone. 'She doesn't remember a word of the Somali that Shayshay once spoke.'

It felt strange to hear her say that. She named the gulf that existed between the child I had been and the woman I was now.

I went home and wondered if that would be enough. Would Amina be sated with that conversation? Would I be able to move on? I didn't: still I dreamt of that walk to school. I tried to focus on her face, but I couldn't. Still, I heard the yearning for that girl.

I thought I had done all the travelling I would need to for the book, but again, I was wrong. I had one more return to do before bringing this story to an end. I needed to see Fatima in person. I delayed doing it for a while. First I told myself I needed to go to Somalia and Kenya first. But when I came back, I stayed at home for a few months, before my mum nudged me about Fatima.

'Do you want me to call her? The three of us can talk together again, but maybe on FaceTime?' Mama asked.

I shook my head. 'I need to go see her myself.'

I asked my mum to go with me, but she refused. 'I can't be there with you, I'm sorry. This is something you have to do without me,' she told me. I couldn't stand the idea of being alone for this trip so decided to take my younger brother Ibrahim with me. He was desperate to leave the country after living through lockdown between the crucial ages of eighteen and twenty.

I booked our flights to the Netherlands. I didn't know what I'd tell Fatima when I saw her. I didn't know what questions I'd ask. I waited for the words to come but they didn't. I sat down with my notebook, my skin buzzing and my heart racing, but I couldn't write anything down. I didn't know where to begin.

The only time I got writer's block while working on this book was while trying to write about Fatima. I loved interviewing my parents for this book, and the words came easily to me while I was in Kenya and Somalia, but I hit a wall when trying to make sense of hearing Fatima's voice again. I have always been able to turn to books whenever I struggle to make sense of what is happening to me. I understood the need to see her, and the restlessness within, after reading Toni Morrison's *Sula*. The book had been on my to-read list for years, but I had never got around to it. I had found it, or it had found me, just when I needed it.

The novel follows the lives of four Black women living in Ohio in the 1920s. The book focuses on two families, the Peaces and the Wrights, and explores the racial and gender dynamics of this era through the tender friendship between the youngest girls in both families: Sula and Nel.

It wasn't until I reached the end, when Nel says, ' "We was girls together," ' that I knew what I wanted to say. Morrison writes that Nel yells the words, 'as though explaining something'. The passage settled between my bones and filled me. It speaks to the extraordinary impact early friendships between girls can have on the women we become.

Fatima and I might have been strangers on that call, but once, 'We was girls together.'

Ibrahim and I sit at the airport trying to remember the last time we flew together. It is ridiculously early and we are both nearly delirious from the lack of sleep.

'I think it was only once, when you were a baby. We went to Saudi Arabia because Jiddo was really ill,' I say to him as we eat our cold breakfast in the waiting lounge.

'I don't remember that,' he replies.

'You wouldn't, you were under one. We didn't even have passports, just refugee travel documents. It was a lifetime ago.'

The flight to Amsterdam is uneventful. I have a slight panic, like I normally do, when we reach border control. I checked to see if there are any Covid restrictions beforehand, and there weren't, but I am still afraid I have missed something. As I hand over my passport, I worry that, like in the US, I won't be allowed in now it shows that I have recently travelled to Somalia. The border guard spends seconds with me and my brother before we are allowed through.

We eat lunch as soon as we land and I laugh whenever my brother baffles the waiter by calling him 'boss man.' Our hotel is slightly outside the city centre and we have a nap as soon as we get in. When we get up, we go out for dinner and then grab some snacks for our hotel room. I am relieved when my brother tells me he wants to stay in and watch *Love Island* that night. I don't think I have it in me to go out. We plan to get up early the next morning and spend the entire day sightseeing.

We have so much fun over the next couple of days that I almost forget why we are in Amsterdam. On our last afternoon in the city, I take my brother to the Rijksmuseum. I want him to start feeling comfortable in those spaces a lot earlier than I did. While we are in the Renaissance section of the museum, my brother is drawn to Jan Mostaert's *Portrait of an African Man*. I tell him the artwork is considered to be the earliest portrait of a Black African in the history of European art. He asks me to take a picture of him beside it. 'An African man next to an African man,' he says and we both laugh.

It is also the day before Eid and we decide to fast. We talk about whether to do so for a while – it is not expected of a Muslim to fast while travelling, but my brother says he is keen to do it together.

When we finish sightseeing, we grab our bags from the hotel and head towards our great-aunt's, on my father's side of the family. I look up her house on Google Maps and see it is near The Hague. I didn't realise that The Hague is the English way of saying Den Haag, thinking it was an entirely different city. 'I'm an idiot,' I tell my brother and he shakes his head. 'You're the smartest person I know,' he replies.

Once we get to the city and change trains to go to my great-aunt's, I realise I am returning to another important time in my family's story. It isn't until this moment that it occurs to me that I am returning to the neighbourhood I was last in before I made that fateful journey to the UK; that it would be the first time returning since I crossed over. A bizarre sense of déjà vu takes over as we walk towards her house and knock on the door. 'I have been here before,' I tell my brother.

One of my cousin's children opens the door and our family swallows us. I haven't seen some of them in years. They embrace and fuss over us. My great-aunt tells us off for not calling her when we reached the train station, insisting that someone would have picked us up. I tell her not to worry. We feel exhausted by then, having fasted for over twelve hours, and decide to take a nap before maghrib prayer. We grow tired again as soon as we break our fast.

I look at pictures of my great-aunt's children as teenagers and it crystallises the image I have of them in my head. Her children are in their thirties now, with children of their own. They tell me off for waiting decades before coming to see them again.

I tell my cousins why I am there and the book I am writing. I tell them about Fatima and my great-aunt calls to get her address. We haven't spoken since that first time, but my mum has told her I am coming. She doesn't answer the call initially and I worry that I have overstepped the mark by being here. When she finally answers, she tells us to come the day after Eid for tea and biscuits.

Fatima sends over her address and I groan when I see she lives in the opposite end of the country, at the furthest northern point, and that we will have to drive back through Amsterdam to get to her.

My cousins insist they will drive me there. They tell me that asylum seekers and refugees are now being housed further and further away from urban, diverse areas like The Hague. The government is incredibly hostile to refugees. 'In comparison to refugees now, we had the red carpet rolled out for us. Now they put them in resettlement centres that look like prisons,' my cousin says.

Later in the evening, as we are catching up, she turns to me and asks: 'Do you remember that time when we went to Amsterdam—?' I cut her off before she finishes: 'And you burst into the toilet I was in!' We laugh. I get a weird thrill that she remembers that moment just as I do. She asks her mum how long we had stayed with them, but she can't remember. 'I just remember how hard it was for your mum,' she says. 'She got turned away so many times!'

Asma had been just a teenager then. 'Do you remember how we coached you before you got on the ferry?' she asks me and I shake my head. I find myself holding my breath and she goes on. 'We had to teach you a few Dutch words and sayings.'

I don't have any memory of this, but that isn't a surprise. I don't have any memories of the days leading up to my departure or the journey itself. I just remember being in a house in London, waiting for my aunt to pick me up. No matter how much I try to remember that goodbye with my parents, I just can't.

I put down the tea I am drinking and ask Asma the question I have been desperate to know the answer to: 'Was I scared?'

She laughs, shaking her head, and tells me I was the most self-assured child she'd ever met. 'You were like an actress getting ready for the performance of a lifetime.'

I sleep terribly the night before we drive to Fatima's house. I keep getting up in the middle of the night and, for the first time since going on the trip, I desperately want to be at home. I feel both physically and emotionally exhausted. Again, I ask myself, why am I doing this?

My cousins come to pick me up in the morning. They wait for me to have breakfast and can tell I am nervous. Ibrahim is relieved he doesn't have to come and can stay with our cousins, playing video games.

'If she doesn't speak English or Arabic, and you don't speak Somali very well, how have you been talking to each other?' one cousin asks me. I bite my lip when I say we haven't really. She raises her eyebrow and looks at her sister. I sink further into my chair and wonder, for the umpteenth time, if this trip to Fatima's house is a bad idea. Am I making my cousins go on a three-hour round trip just to intrude on a stranger's life?

'Lucky for you that we're here to translate!' my cousin says, cheerfully.

The drive takes about an hour and twenty minutes, out of the city and across the Dutch countryside. 'Wow, she really lives in a secluded rural area,' my cousin says as we look for a place to park. Fatima's house is on a cul-de-sac and some of her white neighbours stare at us. Many houses have the Dutch flag waving proudly on their front garden.

I walk up to the front door and knock. I can feel my heart in my throat at this point. A little girl comes to the living room window and peers through the curtains. I look back at my cousins and we laugh nervously. 'Does she know we are coming?' one cousin asks when there are several more beats of silence and I nod. 'Your mum and mine both talked to her,' I say.

A short woman with a headwrap then opens the living room curtains and looks at us. 'Who are you?' she asks.

I am taken back and say: 'Err, it's Amina Mohdin, Faatma John's daughter.' She stares at me in confusion. I whisper: 'It's Shayshay,' and her face brightens with recognition. She smiles briefly and closes the curtain. I turn to look at my cousins and let out a breath I didn't realise I was holding in.

Fatima opens the door and lets us in. We stand awkwardly beside each other before we hug, and give each other a kiss on each cheek. She takes us to her living room and sits us down, but it feels unbearably tense. We are definitely intruding. We speak briefly, but I notice she doesn't make much eye contact. She then rushes off to the kitchen and begins cooking. She moves with a frantic energy.

Fatima's daughter Sumayah runs into the living room and jumps on my lap. She looks even cuter than the photos, with a smile that takes up most of her face. I distract myself by trying to make her laugh.

Fatima comes in and gives us water, drinks and cookies. We thank her and tell her to sit down with us and she agrees for a moment, yelling at her other daughter to finish cutting the vegetables. I smile at her and she looks at me cautiously. My cousin asks her how long she has been in the Netherlands.

She moved there in 2020 with her husband. She had lived as a refugee in Kenya before then. She points at Sumayah and says she is her fourth and youngest child. She gave birth to her here. 'She will never know about the refugee struggle,' she jokes and we smile at her. I am not sure how true that is.

Fatima had been detained in a reception centre for a year and a half before being offered this house, she says. Though it was far north, and away from any Somali community, she accepted it.

'I didn't want to be stuck in the reception centre any longer than necessary,' Fatima says. 'Social housing out here is also a lot bigger than what we would get in places like Den Haag.'

It is really difficult to live somewhere remote. 'We have one bus that comes here, but it doesn't operate during the school holidays,' Fatima says. 'And the neighbours are all white and scary. I close the curtains and don't ever open the door when my husband is out.' He is at work, she adds.

Fatima had been separated from her three other children for several years, and still was when my mum first tracked her down, but her children had made it to the Netherlands a few months after we first spoke.

'You must have been so happy when you reunited with them,' I say in Somali. She finally looks straight at me. We smile at each other. Though there were others in the room, the moment feels intimate and ours.

'Ahh, Shahshay, Shahshay, Shahshay,' she then bursts out saying. 'Shahshay from Kakuma.' How strange it is to now be sat beside each other, decades later, on the other side of the world.

'Do you remember Kakuma?' my cousin asks. And Fatima shakes her head.

'I don't really remember anything from that time. It was a very long time ago,' she replies, curtly.

I drink some water and say: 'I don't remember much of that time, but I do remember you. I remember going to school together and my mum said you used to protect me whenever someone tried to pick on me.' She smiles, nods and rushes back into the kitchen. I don't push the subject further than that.

When we see just how much food she is cooking, we try to get her to stop. 'We don't want to put you out and we have a long drive home,' my cousin says. I can see Fatima stirring the lamb stew. It smells incredible. 'I won't hear it,' Fatima yells. 'You will not leave my house without having eaten. No way!'

I burst out laughing and feel a rush of familiarity. She is just as bossy as she was as a child.

My cousin gets up and goes into the kitchen to try and tell her we can't stay long. Fatima shakes her head and refuses. 'You will sit down and eat. I won't hear any different.' My cousin comes back, looks at her sister and me and whispers: 'I hope you are both hungry.'

We all sit on the table and watch Fatima and her eldest daughter bring out dish after dish. She has made roasted chicken, lamb stew, two different salads, rice and chapati, all served with a variety of hot sauce. I tell Fatima to sit with us, and put Sumayah on my lap.

'Why can't you spend a few days with us, Shayshay?' Fatima says. 'It is so unfair of you to come back after all this time only to leave after a few hours. Today especially is such an important day for us.' I ask why and she says: 'My six siblings are coming on a plane from Nairobi today. I was able to get them resettled here with me.'

We congratulate her and she beams back at us. She looks at her phone and says they should be landing in Amsterdam airport in the next few hours. I apologise for intruding, but she hushes me and tells me again that I should stay. 'Next time, inshallah walaashay,' I say to her and it feels right.

Other than the two of her siblings who are eighteen and nineteen, the rest are all children. She hopes the older ones will be able to get housing of their own soon.

As well as her children, she will be raising her siblings. Fatima doesn't see it as a burden. 'My sisters helped raise my children when I was here and they were in Kenya. They will be a great deal of help for me here. My eldest is really excited for them to come,' she tells me.

It is then that I notice her eldest daughter at the door. She is half hidden, somewhat afraid to come into the room. She looks at me with an intensity I don't yet understand. Her mum turns back to her and says: 'Amina, will you stop being so shy and come in. Come and say hi to your namesake.'

I don't know what to say as she walks timidly towards me. 'Go on and hug your namesake, Amina,' Fatima says, and Amina comes over. I hand over Sumayah to my cousin and turn to her. I hug Amina. She feels so small in my arms. I realise I must matter to Fatima, like she matters to me.

I realise then that though the Amina I was is gone, she was real. She was real to Fatima, just like the Fatima in Kakuma was real to me. Through her, through me, the girls we were together, live on.

After we eat, I help clear up the plates despite Fatima's protests that I sit down. Amina hovers around me and I ask her if she is in school. She knows a little English and nods. She tells me she really likes the Netherlands. I ask if she has friends in school and she nods again.

'We're praying she'll be as smart as you, Shayshay,' Fatima says as she walks into the kitchen. I laugh and say: 'I'm sure you'll be smarter, no?' I look at Amina and she smiles shyly and nods.

Just as we are gathering our things to leave, Amina runs upstairs and comes back down with a bag. It is full of bottles of perfume, scarves and some clothes. I am mortified that I came empty handed.

Fatima and I hug for a long time in her hallway when it is time for me to leave. She makes me promise that when I next come over, I will stay for several days. Before I reply, her phone rings. Her siblings have just arrived in Amsterdam airport. I hug her again and kiss her on both cheeks before I leave. I don't have the words to tell her how happy I am for the reunion to come. Are there words that can truly convey just how special this moment is?

Refugees often live their entire lives in stasis. Fatima has been trapped in exile for decades; her refugee status has been passed on to her children. I realise I am meeting them just at the point that they will be able to move forward with their lives. And, most importantly, they will do so together. I leave smiling.

I close Fatima's door behind me and walk into the cold. It is dark. I hadn't noticed the sun had gone down. All the same, the whole world feels brighter.

GLOSSARY

Allah yerhamo: 'May Allah have mercy on him'
Alhamidduluh: 'Praise be to God'
A'oodhu billah: 'I seek refuge in Allah from the devil'
Baati: a loose-fitting Somali dress often worn at home
Dhagaxtuur: Stone-throwing
Dirac: a dress-like Somali garment worn to special events
Haram: forbidden
Iskaa Wax u Qabso: volunteering
Inshallah: 'God willing'
Jalle: comrade
Khamis: a long robe often worn by Muslim men
La illaha illa Allah: 'There is no god but Allah'
Macawis: a traditional Somali sarong-like garment
Mashallah: 'God has willed it'
Somalia Hanoolaato: 'Long live Somalia'
Salam Alakum: 'Peace be unto you' (common Islamic greeting)
Wallahi: 'I swear to God'
Walaashay: sister
Xabad: bullet
Xafiiska Siyaadda: Political Office
Xafiiska Xiriirka Dadweynaha: Office of Public Relations

NOTES

Author's Note

1 https://www.kcl.ac.uk/suella-bravermans-talk-of-a-refugee-invasion-is-a-dangerous-political-gambit-gone-wrong
2 https://www.theguardian.com/media/2015/apr/20/katie-hopkins-sun-migrants-article-petition-nears-180000-mark
3 https://www.unhcr.org/global-trends
4 https://www.amnesty.org.uk/resources/truth-about-safe-and-legal-routes

1 A Fine Line

1 Gerlach, F. M., Timberlake, F., & Welander, M., 'Five Years On: An analysis of the past and present situation at the UK-France border, five years after the peak of the Calais "Jungle" Camp', *Refugee Rights Europe*, 2021. Available online: https://resourcecentre.savethechildren.net/document/five-years-on-an-analysis-2 (accessed 12 August 2023)
2 Mohdin, A., 'Inside the Jungle – the sprawling refugee encampment at the heart of Europe', *Quartz*, 5 November 2015. Available online: https://qz.com/523144/calais-refugees (accessed 12 August 2023)
3 Mohdin, A., 'Rio Olympics 2016: The refugee team proves that running is the world's fairest sport', *Quartz*, 15 August 2016. Available online: https://qz.com/755895/

the-olympic-refugee-team-proves-that-running-is-the-worlds-fairest-sport (accessed 12 August 2023)

4   Mohdin, A., 'Calais clamps down as asylum seekers say: "They just beat us"', *Guardian*, 18 September 2019. Available online: https://www.theguardian.com/world/2019/sep/18/migrants-in-calais-suffering-from-random-police-raids (accessed 12 August 2023)

5   Cawl, Faraax M. J., & Faarax Maxamed Jaamac, *Ignorance is the Enemy of Love*, trans. B. W. Andrzejewski, Zed Press, London, 1982

6   Andrzejewski, B. W., 'Review of Garbaduubkii Gumeysiga (The Shackles of Colonialism)', *Northeast African Studies*, 1, pp. 79–81. Available online: http://www.jstor.org/stable/43660352http://www.jstor.org/stable/43660352 (accessed 12 August 2023)

7   Mohdin, A., Swann, G., & Bannock, C., 'How George Floyd's death sparked a wave of UK anti-racism protests', *Guardian*, 29 July 2020. Available online: https://www.theguardian.com/uk-news/2020/jul/29/george-floyd-death-fuelled-anti-racism-protests-britain (accessed 12 August 2023)

8   Jama, Z. M., 'Silent Voices: The Role of Somali Women's Poetry in Social and Political Life', *Oral Tradition*, 9(1), 1994, pp. 185–202. Available online: https://journal.oraltradition.org/wp-content/uploads/files/articles/9i/8_jama.pdf (accessed 12 August 2023)

9   Ibid.

10 Andrzejewski, B. W., 'The literary culture of the Somali people', *Journal of African Cultural Studies*, 23(1), 2011, pp. 9–17, https://www.jstor.org/stable/41428137 (accessed 12 August 2023)

11 Cawl, Faraax, & Yoll, A., 'Against the enemy of love: Faarax Cawl, author of the first modern novel in Somali, talks to Andrew Graham Yooll', *Guardian*, 12 March 1982. Available online: https://www.proquest.com/historical-newspapers/against-enemy-love/docview/186346853/se-2 (accessed 12 August 2023)

12 Andrzejewski, B. W., 'Storyteller for Somalia', *Guardian*, 18 May 1991, https://www.proquest.com/historical-newspapers/story-teller-somalia/docview/187147213/se-2 (accessed 12 August 2023)

2 When Faatma Met Mohamed

1 Mbitiru, C., 'Refugees allowed ashore', *Associated Press*, 29 July 1992
2 'British Somaliland', The National Archives. Available online: https://www.nationalarchives.gov.uk/first-world-war/a-global-view/africa/british-somaliland (accessed 12 August 2023)
3 Galbraith, J. S., 'Italy, the British East Africa Company, and the Benadir Coas', *Journal of Modern History*, 42(4), December 1970, pp. 549–563. Available online: https://www.jstor.org/stable/1905828 (accessed 12 August 2023)
4 Samatar, A. I., *Africa's First Democrats: Somalia's Aden A. Osman and Abdirazak H. Hussen*, Indiana University Press, Bloomington and Indianapolis, 2016, pp. 19–26
5 Omar, M. O., 'The Road to Zero: Somalia's Self-destruction', HAAN Associates, London, 1992
6 Ibid, p. 20
7 Aidid, S., 'Haweenku Wa Garab (Women are a Force): Women and the Somali Nationalist Movement, 1943–1960', *Bildhaan: An International Journal of Somali Studies*, 10, 2011. Available online: https://digitalcommons.macalester.edu/bildhaan/vol10/iss1/10 (accessed 12 August 2023)
8 Omar, 'Road to Zero', pp. 20–23
9 Ibid., pp. 24–33
10 Ahmed, A. J, *Daybreak is Near: Literature, Clans, and the Nation-State in Somalia*, Red Sea Press, New Jersey, 1996, p. 36
11 Omar, 'Road to Zero', p. 25
12 Ibid., p. 29
13 Ibid., p. 42
14 Omar, 'Road to Zero', pp. 51–52
15 Ibid., pp. 46–50

NOTES

16 Williams, M., 'Somali Vote Won by Ruling Party; 69 of 123 Assembly Seats Go to Youth League', *New York Times*, 31 December 1964. Available online: https://www.nytimes.com/1964/04/05/archives/somali-vote-won-by-ruling-party-69-of-123-assembly-seats-go-to.html (accessed 12 August 2023)

17 Jama, H. A., *Who Cares about Somalia: Hassan's Ordeal; Reflections on a Nation's Future*, Schiler, Berlin, 2005, p. 131

18 Potholm, C. P., *Four African Political Systems*, Prentice-Hall, New Jersey, 1970, p. 228

19 Al-Maeena, K., 'Somalia must be saved from its "leaders"', *IslamiCity*, 6 August 1996. Available online: https://www.islamicity.org/90/somaila-must-be-saved-from-its-leaders/ (accessed 12 August 2023)

20 Ingiriis, M. H, *The Suicidal State in Somalia: The Rise and Fall of the Siad Barre Regime 1969–1991*, University Press of America, Lanham, Maryland, 2016, p. 28

21 Ibid., p. 70

22 Omar, 'Road to Zero', p. 72

23 Ibid., pp. 95–98

24 Sheik-Abdi, A., 'Ideology and Leadership in Somalia', *Journal of Modern African Studies*, 19(1), 1981, 163–172. Available online: http://www.jstor.org/stable/160610 (accessed 12 August 2023)

25 Omar, 'Road to Zero', p. 107

26 Ibid., p. 116

27 Ibid., p. 110

28 Ibid., p. 119

29 Ibid., p. 125

30 Barre, S., 'Selected Speeches of the SRSP Secretary General and the Somali Democratic Republic President, Jalle Mohamed Siad Barre', 1979, Marxists.org, https://www.marxists.org/archive/siad-barre/selected-speeches.pdf (accessed 12 August 2023)

31 Africa Watch Committee (Ed.), 'Somalia: A Government at War with Its Own People: Testimonies about the Killings and the Conflict in the North', 1990

32 Omar, 'Road to Zero', p. 132

NOTES

33 David, S., 'Realignment in the Horn: The Soviet Advantage', *International Security*, 4(2), 1979, pp. 69–90. Available online:https://doi.org/10.2307/2626744https://doi.org/10.2307/2626744 (accessed 12 August 2023)

34 Ostermann, C. F., & Welch, D., 'Transcript of Meeting between East German leader Erich Honecker and Cuban leader Fidel Castro, East Berlin (excerpts)', 1977, Wilson Center Digital Archive. Available online: https://digitalarchive.wilsoncenter.org/document/transcript-meeting-between-east-german-leader-erich-honecker-and-cuban-leader-fidel-castro (accessed 12 August 2023)

35 Africa Watch Committee, 'Evil Days: 30 Years of War and Famine in Ethiopia', 1991. Available online: https://www.hrw.org/reports/Ethiopia919.pdf (accessed 12 August 2023)

36 Omar, 'Road to Zero', p. 164

37 Ibid., p. 12

38 Grespin, W., & Marchese, M., 'Things Fall Apart: Soviet Assistance to the Somali Armed Forces, 1960–1977', *Journal of African Military History*, 2022. Available online: https://doi.org/10.1163/24680966-bja10013 (accessed 12 August 2023)

39 Lorde, A., *Collected Poems of Audre Lorde*, W.W. Norton, New York, 2000.

40 Mohamed, I. A., 'Somali Women and the Socialist State', *Journal of Georgetown University-Qatar Middle Eastern Studies Student Association*, 1 March 2015. Available online: http://dx.doi.org/10.5339/messa.2015.4 (accessed 12 August 2023)

41 Omar, 'Road to Zero', p. 182

3 The Great Escape

1 Ingiriis, M. H., 'The Making of the 1990 Manifesto: Somalia's Last Chance for State Survival', *Northeast African Studies*, 12(2), 2012, pp. 63–94. Available online: https://www.jstor.org/stable/41931314 (accessed 13 August 2023)

2 Omar, 'Road to Zero', p. 206
3 Kapteijns, L., *Clan Cleansing in Somalia: The Ruinous Legacy of 1991*, University of Pennsylvania Press, Philadelphia, 2012, p. 105
4 Ingiriis, 'The Making of the 1990 Manifesto'.
5 Omar, 'Road to Zero', p. 211
6 Biles, P., 'Victorious Somali rebels promise free elections', *Guardian*, 29 January 1991. Available online: https://www.proquest.com/historical-newspapers/victorious-somali-rebels-promise-free-elections/docview/187215363/se-2 (accessed 13 August 2023)
7 Biles, P., 'Refugees from Somali strife stranded off Kenyan coast', *Guardian*, 4 May 1991. Available online: https://www.proquest.com/historical-newspapers/refugees-somali-strife-stranded-off-kenyan-coast/docview/187169788/se-2 (accessed 13 August 2023)
8 Omaar, R. 'Somali rebels fight in streets of capital', *Guardian*, 31 December 1990. Available online: Available online: https://www.proquest.com/historical-newspapers/somali-rebels-fight-streets-capital/docview/187118814/se-2 (accessed 13 August 2023)
9 Michaelson, M., 'Somalia: The Painful Road to Reconciliation', *Africa Today*, 40(2), 1993, pp. 53–73. Available online: http://www.jstor.org/stable/4186905 (accessed 13 August 2023)
10 Africa Watch, 'No Mercy In Mogadishu: The Human Cost of the Conflict & The Struggle for Relief', 26 March 1992. Available online: https://www.hrw.org/reports/1992/somalia (accessed 13 August 2023)
11 Human Rights Watch (1992), 'Human Rights Watch World Report 1993 – Somalia', *Refworld*, 1 January 1992. Available online: https://www.refworld.org/docid/467fca601e.html (accessed 13 August 2023)
12 Biles, Peter, 'Aid trickles in as famine threatens Somali capital', *Guardian*, 24 April 1991. Available online: https://www.proquest.com/historical-newspapers/aid-trickles-as-famine-threatens-somali-capital/docview/187099883/se-2 (accessed 13 August 2023)

13 Taylor, Diane, 'UK and French coastguards "passed buck" as 27 people drowned in Channel', *Guardian*, 12 November 2022. Available online: https://www.theguardian.com/uk-news/2022/nov/12/uk-french-coastguards-passed-buck-people-drowned-channel (accessed 13 August 2023)
14 Mbitiru, C., 'Refugees allowed ashore', Associated Press, 29 July
15 International Organization for Migration, 'Mediterranean: Missing Migrants Project. Available online: https://missingmigrants.iom.int/region/mediterranean (accessed 13 August 2023)
16 Griggs, Haden, 'Every Step a Novel: Historical Circumstances and Somali American Identity,' *All Graduate Plan B and other Reports*, Utah State University, 2020. Available online: https://digitalcommons.usu.edu/cgi/viewcontent.cgi?article=2478&context=gradreports (accessed 13 August 2023)

4 The Making of a Refugee

1 Marozzi, Justin, 'The Somali love of '"rude" nicknames', BBC, 7 March 2014. Available online: https://www.bbc.co.uk/news/magazine-26354143 (accessed 14 August 2023)
2 Research Directorate, Immigration and Refugee Board, Canada, 'Kenya: Information on the screening of Somalis since 1990', Refworld, 1 October 1992. Available online: https://www.refworld.org/docid/3ae6ab0634.html (accessed 14 August 2023)
3 Knight-Ridder News Service, 'Somali refugees contend with Kenyan backlash: resentment rises as influx grows', *Washington Post*, 4 September 1992. Available online: https://www.baltimoresun.com/news/bs-xpm-1992-09-04-1992248039-story.html (accessed 14 August 2023)
4 Human Rights Watch, 'Human Rights Watch World Report 1993 – Somalia'

5 Perlez, Jane, 'Deaths in Somalia Outpace Delivery of Food', *New York Times*, 19 July 1992. Available online: https://www.nytimes.com/1992/07/19/world/deaths-in-somalia-outpace-delivery-of-food.html (accessed 14 August 2023)

6 Africa Watch, 'No Mercy In Mogadishu: The Human Cost of the Conflict & The Struggle for Relief', 26 March 1992. Available online: https://www.hrw.org/reports/1992/somalia (accessed 13 August 2023)

7 Perlez, Jane, 'Mission to Somalia; Somalia Famine No Different: Children Are the First to Die', *New York Times*, 8 December 1992. Available online: https://www.nytimes.com/1992/12/08/world/mission-to-somalia-somalia-famine-no-different-children-are-the-first-to-die.html (accessed 14 August 2023)

8 Richburg, Keith B., 'Legacy of Woe Awaits "Lost Generation" of Somalia', *Washington Post*, 13 September 1992. Available online: https://www.washingtonpost.com/archive/politics/1992/09/13/legacy-of-woe-awaits-lost-generation-of-somalia/afa6db85-c431-4f83-b93b-a5873b488605/ (accessed 14 August 2023)

9 Biles, Peter, 'A dictator's legacy cripples Somalia's hope of salvation: Mogadishu', *Guardian*, 17 February 1992. Available online: https://www.proquest.com/hnpguardianobserver/docview/477406724/B8A0B980446C4C9DPQ/1?accountid=133107 (accessed 14 August 2023)

10 Biles, Peter, 'What Will Happen to Siad's Children?', *BBC Focus on Africa*, February 1992, pp. 5–8

11 Human Rights Watch, 'Seeking Refuge, Finding Terror: The Widespread Rape of Somali Women Refugees in North Eastern Kenya', hrw.org, 1 October 1993. Available online: https://www.hrw.org/report/1993/10/01/seeking-refuge-finding-terror/widespread-rape-somali-women-refugees-north-eastern (accessed 14 August 2023)

12 Research Directorate, Immigration and Refugee Board, Canada, 'Kenya, Ethiopia, Djibouti, Yemen and Saudi Arabia: The Situation of Somali Refugees', *Refworld*, 1

August 1992. Available online: https://www.refworld.org/docid/3ae6a80ac.html (accessed 14 August 2023)

6 Finally in Europe

1. BBC, 'Somalia country profile', 26 April 2023. Available online: https://www.bbc.co.uk/news/world-africa-14094503 (accessed 14 August 2023)
2. Foreign, Commonwealth & Development Office, 'Somalia travel advice', gov.uk, 3 July 2023. Available online: https://www.gov.uk/foreign-travel-advice/somalia (accessed 14 August 2023)

7 A Journey Back in Time

1. Ahmed, Ali Jimale, *Daybreak is Near: Literature, Clans, and the Nation-state in Somalia*, Red Sea Press, New Jersey, 1996
2. Nguyen, Viet Thanh, *The Sympathizer*, Corsair, London, 2016

9 Lunch with the Youth of Mogadishu

1. BBC Staff, 'Mogadishu attack: Somali troops end deadly siege at Elite Hotel', 17 August 2020. Available online: https://www.bbc.co.uk/news/world-africa-53798834 (accessed 14 August 2023)
2. Mohdin, Aamna, 'The journey of learning, losing, and reclaiming your mother tongue or childhood language', *Quartz*, 18 December 2017, https://qz.com/1155289/even-if-youve-forgotten-the-language-you-spoke-as-a-child-it-still-stays-with-you (accessed 14 August 2023)
3. Palaiologou, Lydia, 'A Sociolinguistic Perspective on L1 Attrition in First-Generation Immigrant Children', *Journal of English Language Teaching and Applied Linguistics*, 3(10), 2021, pp. 41–44. Available online: https://doi.org/10.32996/jeltal.2021.3.10.5 (accessed 14 August 2023)

NOTES

10 The Permanence of Exile

1. James Baldwin, *Giovanni's Room*, Penguin, London, 2007

14 Black and British

1. Tempest, Matthew, 'BNP wins first London seat since 1993', *Guardian*, 17 September 2004. Available online: https://www.theguardian.com/politics/2004/sep/17/thefarright.uk (accessed 16 August 2023)
2. Wainwright, Martin, 'Five arrested for racist boasts in television exposé of BNP', *Guardian*, 20 July 2004, Available online: https://www.theguardian.com/uk/2004/jul/21/race.thefarright (accessed 16 August 2023)
3. Staff and agencies, 'BNP thanks Labour minister for publicity', *Guardian*, 5 May 2006. Available online: https://www.theguardian.com/politics/2006/may/05/localelections2006.uk (accessed 16 August 2023)
4. Gubacsi, Beata, 'Healthy Homes: Building Becontree', *The Polyphony*, 2 September 2020. Available online: https://thepolyphony.org/2020/09/02/healthy-homes-building-becontree (accessed 17 August)
5. Arnot, Chris, 'When the wheels came off the dream | Communities', *The Guardian*, 25 February 2009. Available online: https://www.theguardian.com/society/2009/feb/25/ford-dagenham (accessed 17 August 2023)
6. Jones, Sam, and Taylor, Matthew, 'Fight breaks out between BNP councillor and local teenagers', *Guardian*, 5 May 2010. Available online: https://www.theguardian.com/politics/2010/may/05/bnp-christianity-black-voters-dagenham (accessed 17 August 2023)
7. Siddique, Haroon, 'BNP would offer non-white Britons £50000 to leave UK, says Nick Griffin', *Guardian*, 29 April. Available online: https://www.theguardian.com/politics/2010/apr/29/bnp-non-white-britons-resettlement-grants (accessed 17 August 2023)

8 Revill, Jo, and Doward, Jamie, 'BNP backs Hodge in housing row', *Guardian*, 26 May 2007, https://www.theguardian.com/politics/2007/may/27/thefarright.communities (accessed 17 August 2023)
9 Muir, Hugh, 'Barking: where the BNP were humiliated and Labour learned a lesson', *Guardian*, 7 May 2010. Available online: https://www.theguardian.com/commentisfree/2010/may/07/barking-bnp-labour (accessed 17 August 2023)

15 The Trauma that Binds Us

1 Bhui, Kamaldeep (Ed.), *Racism and Mental Health: Prejudice and Suffering*, Jessica Kingsley Publishers, London, 2002
2 Scuglik, Deborah L., et al., 'When the Poetry No Longer Rhymes: Mental Health Issues among Somali Immigrants in the USA', *Transcultural Psychiatry*, 44(4), 2007. Available online: https://doi.org/10.1177/1363461507083899 (accessed 17 August 2023)
3 Miller, Ken, and Rasmussen, Andrew, 'The mental health of civilians displaced by armed conflict: an ecological model of refugee distress', *Epidemiol Psychiatr Sci*, 26(2), 2016, pp. 129–138, doi:10.1017/S2045796016000172 (accessed 17 August 2023)
4 Palmer, David, and Ward, Kim, '"Lost": listening to the voices and mental health needs of forced migrants in London'. *Medicine, Conflict and Survival*, 23(3), pp. 198–212, DOI: 10.1080/13623690701417345 (accessed 2 October 2023)
5 Westermeyer, Joseph, 'Cross-cultural psychiatric assessment', in A. Gaw, ed., *Culture, Ethnicity, and Mental Illness*, 1st edn, American Psychiatric Press, Washington, DC
6 Ibid.

BIBLIOGRAPHY

Africa Watch, 'Evil Days: 30 Years of War and Famine in Ethiopia', September 1991, hrw.org, Africa Watch Committee, https://www.hrw.org/reports/Ethiopia919.pdf

Africa Watch, 'No Mercy in Mogadishu: The Human Cost of the Conflict & The Struggle for Relief', 26 March 1992, hrw.org, https://www.hrw.org/reports/1992/somalia/

Africa Watch, 'Somalia: A Government at War with Its Own People: Testimonies about the Killings and the Conflict in the North', Africa Watch Committee, January 1990, https://cja.org/wp-content/uploads/2019/07/Africa-Watch-Somalia-A-Government-at-War-with-its-Own-People-Jan-1990.pdf

Ahmed, Ali Jimale, *Daybreak is Near: Literature, Clans, and the Nation-state in Somalia*, Red Sea Press, New Jersey, 1996

Aidid, Safia, 'Haweenku Wa Garab (Women are a Force): Women and the Somali Nationalist Movement, 1943–1960', *Bildhaan: An International Journal of Somali Studies*, 10, 2011

Al-Maeena, Khaled, 'Somalia must be saved from its "leaders"', *IslamiCity*, 6 August 1996, https://www.islamicity.org/90/somaila-must-be-saved-from-its-leaders

Andrzejewski, B. W., 'Storyteller for Somalia', *Guardian*, 18 May 1991, https://www.proquest.com/historical-newspapers/story-teller-somalia/docview/187147213/se-2

Andrzejewski, B.W., 'The literary culture of the Somali people', *Journal of African Cultural Studies*, 23(1), 2011, pp. 9–17, https://www.jstor.org/stable/41428137

Andrzejewski, B. W., 'Review of Garbaduubkii Gumeysiga [The Shackles of Colonialism]', *Northeast African Studies*, 1, 1979, pp. 79–81, http://www.jstor.org/stable/43660352

AP, 'Police Open Fire in Somali Stadium', *New York Times*, 11 July 1990, https://www.nytimes.com/1990/07/11/world/police-open-fire-in-somali-stadium.html

Arnot, Chris, 'When the wheels came off the dream', *Guardian*, 25 February 2009, https://www.theguardian.com/society/2009/feb/25/ford-dagenham

Baldwin, James, *Giovanni's Room*, Penguin, London, 2007

Barre, Siad, 'Selected Speeches of the SRSP Secretary General and the Somali Democratic Republic President, Jalle Mohamed Siad Barre', October 1979, Marxists.org, Ministry of Information and National Guidance Somali Democratic Republic, https://www.marxists.org/archive/siad-barre/selected-speeches.pdf

BBC, 'Mogadishu attack: Somali troops end deadly siege at Elite Hotel', 17 August 2020, https://www.bbc.co.uk/news/world-africa-53798834

BBC, 'Somalia country profile', 26 April 2023, https://www.bbc.co.uk/news/world-africa-14094503

Bhui, Kamaldeep, *Racism and Mental Health: Prejudice and Suffering*, Jessica Kingsley Publishers, London, 2002

Biles, Peter, 'Aid trickles in as famine threatens Somali capital', *Guardian*, 24 April 1991, https://www.proquest.com/historical-newspapers/aid-trickles-as-famine-threatens-somali-capital/docview/187099883/se-2

Biles, Peter, 'A dictator's legacy cripples Somalia's hope of salvation: Mogadishu', *Guardian*, 17 February 1992, https://www.proquest.com/hnpguardianobserver/docview/477406724/B8A0B980446C4C9DPQ/1?accountid=133107

Biles, Peter, 'Refugees from Somali strife stranded off the Kenyan coast', *Guardian*, 4 May 1991, https://www.proquest.com/historical-newspapers/refugees-somali-strife-stranded-off-kenyan-coast/docview/187169788/se-2

Biles, Peter, 'Victorious Somali rebels promise free elections', *Guardian*, 29 January 1991, https://www.proquest.com/

historical-newspapers/victorious-somali-rebels-prom ise-free-elections/docview/187215363/se-2

Biles, Peter, 'What Will Happen to Siad's Children?', *BBC Focus on Africa*, February 1991, pp. 5–8

'British Somaliland', National Archives, https://www.natio nalarchives.gov.uk/first-world-war/a-global-view/africa/ british-somaliland

Canada: Immigration and Refugee Board of Canada, 'Kenya: Information on the screening of Somalis since 1990', *Refworld*, 1 October 1992, https://www.refworld.org/ docid/3ae6ab0634.html

Cawl, Faarax M. J., *Ignorance is the Enemy of Love*, trans. B. W. Andrzejewski, Zed Press, London, 1982.

Cawl, Faarax M. J., and Andrew Yoll, 'Against the enemy of love: Faarax Cawl, author of the first modern novel in Somali, talks to Andrew Graham Yoll', *Guardian*, 12 March 1982, https://www.proquest.com/hnpguardianobserver/ docview/186346853/EC08F09DC9014238PQ/1?accoun tid=133107

David, Steven, 'Realignment in the Horn: The Soviet Advantage', *International Security*, 4(2), 1979, pp. 69–90, https://doi.org/10.2307/2626744

Foreign, Commonwealth & Development Office, 'Somalia travel advice', gov.uk, 3 July 2023, https://www.gov.uk/ foreign-travel-advice/somalia

Galbraith, John S, 'Italy, the British East Africa Company, and the Benadir Coast', *Journal of Modern History*, 42(4), 1970, pp. 549–563, https://www.jstor.org/stable/1905828

Gerlach, Fae Mira, et. al., 'Five Years On: An Analysis of the past and present situation at the UK-France border, five years after the peak of the Calais "Jungle" Camp', *Refugee Rights Europe*, 2021, https://resourcecentre.savethechild ren.net/document/five-years-on-an-analysis-2

Grespin, Whitney, and Matthew Marchese, 'Things Fall Apart: Soviet Assistance to the Somali Armed Forces, 1960–1977', *Journal of African Military History*, 2022, https:// doi.org/10.1163/24680966-bja10013

Griggs, Haden, 'Every Step a Novel: Historical Circumstances and Somali American Identity', *All Graduate Plan B and other Reports*, 2020, Utah State University

Gubacsi, Beata, 'Healthy Homes: Building Becontree', *The Polyphony*, 2 September 2020, https://thepolyphony.org/2020/09/02/healthy-homes-building-becontree

Human Rights Watch, 'Human Rights Watch World Report 1993 – Somalia', *Refworld*, 1 January 1993, https://www.refworld.org/docid/467fca601e.html

Human Rights Watch, 'Seeking Refuge, Finding Terror: The Widespread Rape of Somali Women Refugees in North Eastern Kenya', hrw.org, 1 October 1993, https://www.hrw.org/report/1993/10/01/seeking-refuge-finding-terror/widespread-rape-somali-women-refugees-north-eastern

Ingiriis, Mohamed Haji, 'The Making of the 1990 Manifesto: Somalia's Last Chance for State Survival', *Northeast African Studies*, 12(2), 2012, pp. 63–94, https://www.jstor.org/stable/41931314

Ingiriis, Mohamed Haji, *The Suicidal State in Somalia: The Rise and Fall of the Siad Barre Regime 1969–1991*, University Press of America, Lanham, Maryland, 2016

International Organization for Migration, 'Mediterranean: Missing Migrants Project', *Missing Migrants Project*, https://missingmigrants.iom.int/region/mediterranean

Jama, Hassan Ali, *Who Cares about Somalia: Hassan's Ordeal; Reflections on a Nation's Future*, Schiler, Berlin, 2005

Jama, Zainab Mohamed, 'Silent Voices: The Role of Somali Women's Poetry in Social and Political Life', *Oral Tradition*, 9(1), 1994, pp. 185–202, https://journal.oraltradition.org/wp-content/uploads/files/articles/9i/8_jama.pdf

Jones, Sam, and Taylor, Matthew, 'Fight breaks out between BNP councillor and local teenagers', *The Guardian*, 5 May 2010, https://www.theguardian.com/politics/2010/may/05/bnp-christianity-black-voters-dagenham

Kapteijns, Lidwien, *Clan Cleansing in Somalia: The Ruinous Legacy of 1991*, University of Pennsylvania Press, Philadelphia, 2012

Knight-Ridder News Service, 'Somali refugees contend with Kenyan backlash: resentment rises as influx grows', *Baltimore Sun*, 4 September 1992, https://www.baltimoresun.com/news/bs-xpm-1992-09-04-1992248039-story.html

Levy, Andrea, *Small Island*, Review, London, 2004

Lorde, Audre, *Collected Poems of Audre Lorde*, W. W. Norton, New York, 2000

Marozzi, Justin, 'The Somali love of "rude" nicknames', 7 March 2014, https://www.bbc.co.uk/news/magazine-26354143

Mbitiru, Chege, 'Refugees allowed ashore', *Associated Press*, 29 July 1992

Michaelson, Marc, 'Somalia: The Painful Road to Reconciliation", *Africa Today*, 40(2), 1993, pp. 53–73, http://www.jstor.org/stable/4186905

Miller, Ken, and Rasmussen, Andrew, 'The mental health of civilians displaced by armed conflict: an ecological model of refugee distress', *Epidemiol Psychiatr Sci*, 26(2), 2016, pp. 129–138, doi:10.1017/S2045796016000172

Mohamed, Iman Abdulkadir, 'Somali Women and the Socialist State', *Journal of Georgetown University-Qatar Middle Eastern Studies Student Association*, 2014, http://dx.doi.org/10.5339/messa.2015.4

Mohdin, Aamna, 'Calais clamps down as asylum seekers say: "They just beat us"', *Guardian*, 18 September 2019, https://www.theguardian.com/world/2019/sep/18/migrants-in-calais-suffering-from-random-police-raids

Mohdin, Aamna, 'Inside the Jungle – the sprawling refugee encampment at the heart of Europe', *Quartz*, 5 November 2015, https://qz.com/523144/calais-refugees

Mohdin, Aamna, 'The journey of learning, losing, and reclaiming your mother tongue or childhood language', *Quartz*, 18 December 2017, https://qz.com/1155289/even-if-youve-forgotten-the-language-you-spoke-as-a-child-it-still-stays-with-you

Mohdin, Aamna, 'Rio Olympics 2016: The refugee team proves that running is the world's fairest sport', *Quartz*,

15 August 2016, https://qz.com/755895/the-olympic-refugee-team-proves-that-running-is-the-worlds-fairest-sport

Mohdin, Aamna, Swann, G., & Bannock, C., 'How George Floyd's death sparked a wave of UK anti-racism protests', *Guardian*, 29 July 2020, https://www.theguardian.com/uk-news/2020/jul/29/george-floyd-death-fuelled-anti-racism-protests-britain

Muir, Hugh, 'Barking: where the BNP were humiliated and Labour learned a lesson', *Guardian*, 7 May 2010, https://www.theguardian.com/commentisfree/2010/may/07/barking-bnp-labour

Nguyen, Viet Thanh, *The Sympathizer*, Corsair, London, 2016

Omaar, Rakiya, 'Somali rebels fight in streets of capital', *Guardian*, 31 December 1990, https://www.proquest.com/historical-newspapers/somali-rebels-fight-streets-capital/docview/187118814/se-2

Omar, Mohamed Osman, *The Road to Zero: Somalia's Self-destruction*, HAAN Associates, 1992.

Ostermann, Christian F., and Welch, David, 'Transcript of Meeting between East German leader Erich Honecker and Cuban leader Fidel Castro, East Berlin (excerpts)', 1977, Wilson Center Digital Archive, https://digitalarchive.wilsoncenter.org/document/transcript-meeting-between-east-german-leader-erich-honecker-and-cuban-leader-fidel-castro

Palaiologou, Lydia, 'A Sociolinguistic Perspective on L1 Attrition in First-Generation Immigrant Children', *Journal of English Language Teaching and Applied Linguistics*, 3(10), 2021, pp. 41–44, https://doi.org/10.32996/jeltal.2021.3.10.5

Perlez, Jane, 'Deaths in Somalia Outpace Delivery of Food', *New York Times*, 19 July 1992, https://www.nytimes.com/1992/07/19/world/deaths-in-somalia-outpace-delivery-of-food.html

Perlez, Jane, 'Mission to Somalia; Somalia Famine No Different: Children Are the First to Die', *New York Times*, 8 December 1992, https://www.nytimes.com/1992/12/08/world/mission-to-somalia-somalia-famine-no-different-children-are-the-first-to-die.html

Potholm, Christian P., *Four African Political Systems*, Prentice-Hall, 1970

Research Directorate, Immigration and Refugee Board, Canada, 'Kenya, Ethiopia, Djibouti, Yemen and Saudi Arabia: The Situation of Somali Refugees', *Refworld*, 1 August 1992, https://www.refworld.org/docid/3ae6a80ac.html

Revill, Jo, and Doward, Jamie, 'BNP backs Hodge in housing row', *Guardian*, 26 May 2007, https://www.theguardian.com/politics/2007/may/27/thefarright.communities

Richburg, Keith B., 'Legacy of Woe Awaits "Lost Generation" of Somalia', *Washington Post*, 13 September 1992, https://www.washingtonpost.com/archive/politics/1992/09/13/legacy-of-woe-awaits-lost-generation-of-somalia/afa6db85-c431-4f83-b93b-a5873b488605

Samatar, Abdi Ismail, *Africa's First Democrats: Somalia's Aden A. Osman and Abdirazak H. Hussen*, Indiana University Press, Bloomington, 2016

Scuglik, Deborah L., et. Al., 'When the Poetry No Longer Rhymes: Mental Health Issues among Somali Immigrants in the USA', *Transcultural Psychiatry*, 44(4), 2007, https://doi.org/10.1177/1363461507083899

Sheik-Abdi, Abdi 'Ideology and Leadership in Somalia', *Journal of Modern African Studies*, 19(1), 1981, pp. 163–172, http://www.jstor.org/stable/160610

Siddique, Haroon, 'BNP would offer non-white Britons £50000 to leave UK, says Nick Griffin', *Guardian*, 29 April, https://www.theguardian.com/politics/2010/apr/29/bnp-non-white-britons-resettlement-grants

Staff and agencies, 'BNP thanks Labour minister for publicity', *Guardian*, 5 May, https://www.theguardian.com/politics/2006/may/05/localelections2006.uk

Taylor, Diane, 'UK and French coastguards "passed buck" as 27 people drowned in Channel', *Guardian*, 12 November 2022, https://www.theguardian.com/uk-news/2022/nov/12/uk-french-coastguards-passed-buck-people-drowned-channel

Tempest, Matthew, 'BNP wins first London seat since 1993', *Guardian*, 17 September 2004, https://www.theguardian.com/politics/2004/sep/17/thefarright.uk

Wainwright, Martin, 'Five arrested for racist boasts in television exposé of BNP', *Guardian*, 20 July 2004, https://www.theguardian.com/uk/2004/jul/21/race.thefarright

Williams, Matt, 'Somali Vote Won by Ruling Party; 69 of 123 Assembly Seats Go to Youth League', *New York Times*, 31 December 1964, https://www.nytimes.com/1964/04/05/archives/somali-vote-won-by-ruling-party-69-of-123-assembly-seats-go-to.html

ACKNOWLEDGEMENTS

It is impossible to thank everyone who has helped me over the past four years. So much has fed into this project, from passing conversations while having lunch in London or Mogadishu, to those who poured their hearts out to me (both loved ones and strangers). With that said, this book wouldn't have been possible without the following people:

My Mama and Baba, for opening up and trusting me with your story. I love you both so much.

My husband Chris (our Yusef) for your comradeship and love, and to our son Ismael who all this has been for.

My wonderful family: Ismahan, Umalquair, Amina, Sacidiya, Aaliyah, Ilham, Loula, Umal, and the boys: Aamir, Ibrahim, Hamid, Hussein and Ashraf, as well as my in-laws: Sue, Bill, Nicole, Sarah and Gill.

My agent Jane, who has guided me brilliantly over the past few years, my editor Allegra, who understood the vision for the book from the day we met, and the team at Bloomsbury, especially Lauren.

To my friends Jonas, Ellen, Yasmin, Max, Olivia, Rosamund, Yazz, Patrick, Eshe for all the drafts they read, for making me laugh and keeping me sane.

To those from Somalia's lost generation who spoke to me and took me into your homes, I continue to admire your resilience.

And my parents again, for everything.

A NOTE ON THE AUTHOR

Aamna Mohdin is the *Guardian*'s first community affairs correspondent, reporting on the social, political and economic experiences of the UK's diverse communities. She was previously a reporter at Quartz where she led the publication's coverage of the European refugee crisis. Mohdin's work has been awarded the British Journalism Award 2022 and shortlisted for the British Press Awards. She lives in London.

A NOTE ON THE TYPE

The text of this book is set in Bembo, which was first used in 1495 by the Venetian printer Aldus Manutius for Cardinal Bembo's *De Aetna*. The original types were cut for Manutius by Francesco Griffo. Bembo was one of the types used by Claude Garamond (1480–1561) as a model for his Romain de l'Université, and so it was a forerunner of what became the standard European type for the following two centuries. Its modern form follows the original types and was designed for Monotype in 1929.